Jennie About to Be

Books by Elisabeth Ogilvie

The Road to Nowhere
The Silent Ones
The Devil in Tartan
A Dancer in Yellow
An Answer in the Tide
The Dreaming Swimmer
Where the Lost Aprils Are
Image of a Lover
Strawberries in the Sea
Weep and Know Why
A Theme for Reason
The Face of Innocence
Bellwood

Waters on a Starry Night
The Seasons Hereafter
There May Be Heaven
Call Home the Heart
The Witch Door
High Tide at Noon
Storm Tide
The Ebbing Tide
Rowan Head
My World Is an Island
The Dawning of the Day
No Evil Angel

Books for Young People

The Pigeon Pair
Masquerade at Sea House
Ceiling of Amber
Turn Around Twice
Becky's Island
The Young Islanders

How Wide the Heart
Blueberry Summer
Whistle for a Wind
The Fabulous Year
Come Aboard and Bring Your Dory!

Jennie
About to Be

ELISABETH OGILVIE

McGraw-Hill Book Company

New York St. Louis San Francisco Bogotá Guatemala
Hamburg Lisbon Madrid Mexico Montreal Panama Paris
San Juan São Paulo Tokyo Toronto

First McGraw-Hill Paperback edition, 1985.

ISBN 0-07-047782-5

1 2 3 4 5 6 7 8 9 F G R F G R 8 7 6 5

LIBRARY OF CONGRESS CATALOGING IN PUBLICATION DATA

Ogilvie, Elisabeth, 1917–
Jennie about to be.
I. Title.
PS3529.G39J4 1984   813'.52   83-22204
ISBN 0-07-047782-5 (pbk)

Book design by Roberta Rezk.

Whether we be young or old,
Our destiny, our being's heart and home,
Is with infinitude, and only there;
With hope it is, hope that can never die,
Effort, and expectation, and desire,
And something evermore about to be.

William Wordsworth

One

E ARLY on a March morning, a blackbird was singing from one of Uncle Higham's chimney pots in Brunswick Square. Officially it was spring. Thousands had died in the usual London winter, like the victims of some ritual sacrifice to ensure the return of spring, if not of the sun. Tamsin had died, a thirteen-year-old slavey with no meat on her bones, too small to lug heavy coal scuttles upstairs or earthen slop jars down. If God had marked this particular sparrow's fall, He had done nothing either to stop it or to break it.

Jennie Hawthorne, who woke every morning thinking of Tamsin, did not rage against God for His refusal to take responsibility for His own acts. Her father had reared four daughters to believe that God had created the world but not the rules. Once the terrestrial globe was set spinning in space, as they could spin the globe in his study, it created the immutable laws of nature; once mankind began, it designed its own system by some quite dreadful trials, horrifying errors, and some happy surprises. The combination of natural and human laws would never reach perfection, Papa had stated, but it could certainly be improved upon. In the meantime he considered himself fortunate to be raising his daughters in the world of Pippin Grange and its surrounds, enclosed as safely by the gentle Kyloe Hills and the North Sea as the orchard was enclosed by its high wall of gold-lichened rosy brick. The fruit ripened sweetly here in spite of the sea winds blowing across the Fenwick Flats. So did the Hawthorne girls.

Carolus Hawthorne had expected that before he died they would all be women grown, safely established, armored by his somewhat cynical

1

philosophy against Life's more brutal shocks. He had almost succeeded by that late summer afternoon when his heart suddenly stopped and toppled him from his saddle in Ember Lane as he was riding home from Belford.

Sylvia was already married to her hunting parson; Ianthe had procured on her own a situation as companion and governess in the household of a wealthy young widow, who had come to Beal to recuperate in the sea air after her husband's death. But Jennie and Sophie were still at home. Sophie, fifteen, and in torrents of grief, had been kindly assimilated into the family of the distant cousin to whom the comfortable old Elizabethan house had passed by entail.

Jennie (Eugenia), twenty-one, had been taken off to London by her mother's sister. "We'll make you a good marriage," said Aunt Higham with steel in her voice and her eye. After years in London she was still a north country woman and always rose with a ferocious relish to the toughest challenge.

London had been endurable.

"The true gift of God," Papa had said, "is the courage to endure. He doesn't dispense the blessings and the blows. He plays no favorites. He gives us strength to deal with the worst that can be done to us."

"But I would die of grief if anything happened to you, Papa," Jennie had once passionately told him when she was about fourteen.

"That would be mere self-indulgence," he had replied, "if not the supreme vanity. You would be saying, in effect, that your suffering was so great that God couldn't give you enough fortitude to bear it. You would be saying you were greater than God."

Jennie sighed over the wreck of an enjoyably emotional and dramatic gesture. Papa laughed and reached up a long arm and picked an apple from over his head. It had gleamed among the thick dark leaves like a golden apple of the Hesperides; he gave it a polish on his blue sleeve and handed it to her.

"One of Eve's finer accomplishments was introducing us to the apple," he said. He took one for himself, and they walked slowly in the dense orchard grass, in the cidery heat of September.

That was one of her happiest memories in a collection of happy ones; in the London September seven years later, less than two weeks after the funeral—William's surplice blowing in the summer wind that sang in the churchyard yews—it had been a talisman, a touchstone. *Endure*, she said grimly to herself all during the first endless days and in the hours when she lay awake. *Otherwise you are guilty of self-indulgence and vanity.* "Oh, Papa!" she gulped, and wept. God didn't forbid tears, any more than He had ordained that she should have to suffer the agony of homesickness along with the pain of losing Papa. There was no one, nothing she could blame, and that was infuriating. No. *He* sat up there, armored in regal indifference, showering strength like rain, and you could take it or leave it. *He* didn't care. Weeping in rage, she took.

So the winter had been gotten through, and this was the morning of the day when Jennie Hawthorne was going to run away. She had chosen the fifteenth of March as appropriate. "Beware the Ides of March," she and her sisters used to croak at each other on the fourteenth. "Julius Caesar", done in sheets, with the most beautiful pieced coverlet from the cedarwood chest for Julius's imperial raiment, was their favorite drama. They could all quote from anywhere in it, and did at length with hardly any provocation, so often that Papa finally refused to attend another performance of the Pippin Grange Players unless they changed the play. "Romeo and Juliet" then became the favorite.

Remembering, Jennie found herself sliding backward into the sweet and enervating melancholy that could immobilize her. She bounded out of the bed in a room only marginally warmer than it had been all winter before Tamsin started the morning fires. At first Jennie had offered to do her own fire—she was used to it in Pippin Grange—but Uncle Higham had explosively cleared his throat, and Aunt Higham shook her head at her.

Today was the Ides of March, and she was going to run away, or make plans in that direction; she qualified it, being a realist. A fine sunrise would have been a good omen, but at least it wasn't raining.

Her nightgown of thin cambric muslin, with lace insertion threaded with ribbons, was part of the new wardrobe the Highams had provided for her. So was the wrapper of fine creamy wool. But she bundled herself into her old dressing gown, woven in a coarse brindle-colored wool from sheep on the home farm of Pippin Grange. It was roomy and warm, meant to be worn for comfort, not for style, in the old house at the edge of the North Sea, so when she wrapped herself in it, she was in one sense home. She slid her feet into the shapeless slippers Martyn, the shepherd, had sewn out of Ebony's hide, fleece side in, when the wether

died of old age. Ebony had been born and orphaned the same spring
when Jennie was born. He had been mothered by Sylvia and Ianthe,
and his baby cries had blended with Jennie's; when she crept on the
lawn, he was as playful and interested as the dogs. Six years later he had
officiously attended the baby Sophie, stamping a hoof imperiously at the
dogs.

Martyn had made slippers for both her and Sophie, and the girls
fondled them, blind with tears because the fleece should have been on
the broad back they'd scratched or the rump they'd slapped.

"Old lad'll warm thy toes for many a year yet," Martyn said. Ebony's
fleece had held off the winter drafts scudding along the tilted floors of
Pippin Grange, where lucky Sophie still wore hers. They and the robe
didn't belong in this London room with its delicate satinwood furniture
and hangings of pastel-flowered cotton. The contrast amused Jennie, and
if the maids were scandalized, they didn't show it, and her aunt didn't
know what lived by day in the depths of the wardrobe, behind those
panels painted with classical garlands.

Jennie took her little marquetry keepsake chest from on top of the
armoire. The key was in her workbox, and she rummaged through it,
compounding the usual tangles. As always, she thought her untidiness
had finally lost her the key, and panic brought out a fine sweat on her
body, but then, as always, she found it. This time it was in her needle
case.

She got back onto the narrow bed and, sitting cross-legged like an
Arab in a tent among the four slender posts and under the deep ruffle
of the flowered tester, opened her box. She handled the contents, one
article at a time. There were a seal from Papa's watch chain and her
share of her mother's few jewels; she'd gotten the topazes because of her
eyes. There were her father's copy of Milton from his student days, her
silver christening mug and porringer, and one of young Sophie's sketch-
books. Her head drooping, her long, tangled brown hair falling forward
past her ears and curtaining her face, she turned the pages. There was
Papa, talking to the dogs. Sylvia's Carolus Jerome on a blanket in the
orchard. (Papa's watch was being saved for him.) There was herself with
Nelson, the old pony. She sniffled and slapped the book shut.

Last was a little drawstring bag of claret velvet. She unknotted the
ties and poured out among the blanket folds thirty gold sovereigns. Each
of the girls had received, through William, such a gift from their father,

who had nothing else much that was tangible to leave them. There had been a note with each gift, every note different from the others, but the message was the same. The sovereigns were not to be frittered away on foolish luxuries, but were to be used for some great and urgent need of either the flesh or the spirit, and this need was to be soberly considered before money was spent on it.

Young Sophie's note had admonished her to wait until she was twenty-one, which gave her six years for turning over great and urgent needs and discarding them. Jennie had no idea what Sylvia would consider suitable; William was not badly off, or he'd never have been able to keep hunters. Whatever Ianthe did with her hoard, Jennie wasn't likely to know unless she used some of it to come home. She had gone to London with the repectable young widow, who then went mad over a great but immoral (and married) pianist, and now she had run off to Switzerland with him to bear his child. They had taken Ianthe and the other children along.

Sylvia had lamented, but William was pragmatic. "Ianthe, incorruptible herself, will exert a positive moral influence over those children, my dear. So she is necessary there, and besides, she'll be seeing a good bit of beautiful country. If anything should go very wrong, she now has money of her own; she won't be stranded in a penniless condition."

Neither will I be, Jennie thought now. *I am going to run away, and if that, dear Papa, isn't a great and urgent need, what is?*

She put the sovereigns back in the claret velvet bag, locked it in the keepsake chest, and put that away on top of the armoire. She tucked the key in the needle case and promised herself that whenever she arrived at her destination, she would untangle all the cottons and silks and keep her workbox incredibly neat for the rest of her life.

Then she went to her window and opened it to the damp, mild morning. The air was reasonably fresh because not too many fires had been lighted yet. She had to lean out a good way to see into the square; her room was on the side of a corner house, facing across a narrow street to a row of tall windows kept primly curtained at all times except when the maids did the rooms. All she knew of the people there was that the cook kept a cat. This large tabby now sat on the wall by the high gate that opened into the mews, and watched the sparrows that chattered and picked in the street. The blackbird went on singing overhead.

The square was empty in the misty sunrise until the baker's boy came to it as if to a stage that had been waiting for him; the blackbird provided the overture, and now the boy's whistle joined the bird's. Alone in the world as far as he was concerned, for this moment he was a free and happy soul.

Between him and the blackbird Jennie was jolted from composure, born of decision, into agony. Now she was frantic to escape; she suffered physically, her throat constricting, her lips parching. Her heart missed beats. She hadn't known that anything could be worse than her first homesickness last autumn and through the London winter, when the city seemed to crouch palpitating and helpless in an everlasting rank-smelling fog.

But to see that boy *free* out there, to hear the blackbird and know how the north looked on such a morning! It wouldn't be spring there yet; there could still be savage gales off the North Sea, and late snows, and the worry over the early lambs. But if it should be fair up there today, the sea would be cornflower blue to the horizon, the wet sands would be all a dazzle, and the sun laying a bloom of gold on the ancient bricks. You'd be looking for the first snowdrops in the orchard with old Nelson nudging you between the shoulder blades and trying to get his nose into your pockets. You'd be expecting the day when the swallows came and the hills first showed a green as transparently fine as silk gauze. The gulls sounded different these mornings, too. There was always at least one somewhere on the Grange rooftop.

That's where she was going when she found out where in London one took the stagecoach to the north. She and Aunt Higham had been delivered directly to Brunswick Square by the post chaise hired for the journey. Her ignorance about travel was the only obstacle. Once she knew where to go, she would have to decide how to get there and how to leave the house when everyone was otherwise engaged. She considered simply telling her aunt that she was going, and at the prospect a disturbance in her stomach compounded her other discomforts. She concentrated on the sight of Lindisfarne, the Holy Island, in the morning light; lying across the water like a part of Atlantis risen radiant from the sea, with the gulls crying welcome.

She wouldn't go to the Grange, of course, except later to visit, if she could bear that. William and Sylvia would welcome her. Her sovereigns would pay her way, and she could make herself useful to everyone until she could find a situation.

When it came to that, William might agree to helping her get to Switzerland, perhaps convoyed by some earnest young embryo clergyman escorting his mother to Geneva. Ianthe wrote that other musicians, poets, and artists occasionally came to stay, some with their wives and children, some with their mistresses and children. English or Scottish governesses were much desired, but they were inclined to depart without notice when improper approaches were made to them or—more commonly—their wages weren't paid for months. Ianthe's employer was conscientious about pay, her lover was faithful, and Ianthe was having the time of her life.

"If I could just be on the spot when one of those governesses left!" Jennie said. "Oh, Lord!"

Two

S HE COULDN'T fault her aunt and uncle; they were doing what they considered their duty. Her young cousins liked her, and to lessen her sense of dependency she was teaching them, by her father's methods. Between lessons, and sometimes during, she entertained them with exhilarating tales of her growing up, which both nourished and alleviated her homesickness.

On the surface there was no reason why this state of affairs couldn't remain in balance for a time, her aunt taking her about in society while the children profited from her tutoring. But the tacit understanding was that she would be married, or at least betrothed, as soon as possible. If the Highams were doing their duty, her duty was also clear. Charlotte, for whom this room had been especially furnished, had no doubt whatever that she'd be in it by her seventeenth birthday, though she was a gentle child and didn't complain about being kept in the nursery now.

"I owe it to Lottie to go away," said Jennie virtuously. She rose from her knees and shut the casement on both the boy's and the bird's whistling. "Uncle and Aunt Higham needn't reproach themselves with anything. They will have done their best. One cannot ask for more."

She put away the old robe and slippers and got back into bed. Her body strained so hard to be gone that her heart raced as if she were running. She picked up her volume of Mr. Wordsworth's poems and began to read his "Ode on Intimations of Immortality from Recollections of Early Childhood." The eloquently simple lines gave dignity to her sadness.

From Aunt Higham's viewpoint the scheme should have been working well by now. The girl was educated, a disadvantage which might have

8

been transcended if she'd had even a modest fortune, but she had only a pittance from her mother, just enough to keep her in hairpins and ribbons. However, she had good country manners, nothing artificial or simpering. She had fine, clean-cut features, she was naturally graceful without having attended deportment classes, and she liked to dance. She was thin but healthy. She had no monthly pains and vapors, a benefit which would cancel out the financial drawbacks if a man was looking for a strong young woman of good stock to give him heirs.

"You'll make a fine wife if you know enough when to hold your tongue," her aunt told her. "You'll get nowhere with that saucy way of yours! You frighten a man, asking him what he thinks of this poet or that philosopher. George Vinton stares as if he can't believe his ears: 'Does God exist?' I thought he'd strangle!"

"I asked him theological questions, suitable for a curate," said Jennie. "He must have studied Emmanuel Kant at Cambridge."

"Fiddlesticks!" said her aunt. "Anyone would think you were trying to drive him and the rest off. Save that bluestocking talk until you've married the man and the first one's on the way. Then he'll run from you only as far as Almack's or Newmarket, and he'll always come home again."

"What sort of curate would go to Almack's or Newmarket?" Jennie pondered aloud.

"George Vinton will have some money when his mother goes, and he has the reversion of a very fine living when his uncle dies. You'd be the mistress of a bigger rectory than William's, and close to a cathedral town, too, with great chances of preferment for George." It tasted good to Aunt Higham. "I will thank God if Charlotte has such a chance offered her."

"I think George would be willing to wait for her," Jennie suggested.

"Fustian!" her aunt snapped. "You're the one to be married off first. A woman like you could make George Vinton go far. He needs a strong hand. But you'll have to keep your heretical thoughts to yourself and not go questioning the existence of God in ecclesiastical circles."

"I was only trying to stir George up," Jennie explained. "He was sitting there looking quite torpid."

"More like a bird hypnotized by a snake," her aunt said dryly.

"Anyway, I don't question God's existence. Only His motives."

"Oh, Lord!" Her aunt rolled her eyes toward the plaster wreaths on the ceiling. She shook her head. But her mouth twitched at one corner.

"You're a good lass, Jennie, and you were always my favorite, for you look the most like my sister. You're an Everden far more than any of my children are. You have her way of holding yourself, the long neck and the tilt of the head. And of laughing. When I see you dancing, if it weren't for the difference in fashion I'd think it was Isabel."

It was an astonishing speech to come from Aunt Higham, and she stood up quickly, as if she repented instantly this gush of emotion. Jennie stood, too, and her aunt gave her a hard pat on the shoulder. "There's more than George, you know, my girl, and the choice has to be yours. But don't be like the poor soul who went all the way through the woods looking for the right stick and had to pick up a crooked one at last."

"And remember to keep my tongue behind my teeth."

"Aye, remember that," her aunt said. "*I* had to."

Keeping one's mouth shut was not a Hawthorne trait. Free speech had been one of the few luxuries possible for the Hawthorne girls. Raising his daughters in an old house entailed on him without any money to go with it, their widowed and scholarly father had decided that about all he could do for his girls was to give them the best education possible and allow them to run what some called wild.

The elderly, unorthodox scholar had also found it cheap and practical to let them ride, roam the sands and marshes, and climb the hills in nankeen pantaloons, short jackets, and boys' boots until they were thirteen or so, saving their frocks and slippers for special occasions.

Thus they had had exceptional freedom. It was his gift to those whom society would cage soon enough. He thought it was a dreadful world which penalized a human being for being born a female, and his girls' condition as adults would not be bettered by their having been reared in ignorance and trained to a false and hobbling docility.

Therefore, Jenny had not the best training for being a demurely marriageable lass in her aunt's house. To her there was something degrading in being beautifully dressed and having one's hair done by a maid so that one could be paraded like a mare or a heifer at an auction.

Besides, she hadn't seen anyone yet with whom she could bear to think of sharing the marriage bed.

"It's rather wonderful with someone you love," Sylvia had told her after a month of William. "It makes you understand John Donne better, too. But I'd abhor doing it with someone I *didn't* love." She shuddered.

"One might just as well be a light woman, except that she'd be paid for it, and a wife isn't."

The parson adored Sylvia, and she was complacent in her own right. If you made a man fall in love with you, the advantage wasn't all to him. William said he had resented God's taking away his first wife but forgave Him when He sent Sylvia to him. Jennie forbore telling him that God had nothing to do with it; Sylvia had had her eye on him since she was fifteen, and even now Jennie couldn't be sure that when Sylvia had knelt beside her bed, looking as devout as Desdemona before Othello fell upon her with that pillow, she hadn't been praying for the parson's wife to be painlessly removed by the time Sylvia was old enough to marry him.

In spite of Papa's theories, Sylvia believed stubbornly in a gruff but benign Personage, someone like Papa, only more glorious, who inclined His ear unto her and heard her cry. This was a useful attribute for a parson's wife.

But if Sylvia knew what Jennie now knew, she would be hard put to make excuses for her God.

She knew now, for instance, that outside the pleasant crescents and squares, the parks where the Quality rode, the theaters and ballrooms, there lay the filthy warrens of a destitution and vice she hadn't believed could exist; she wouldn't have known now except for the little girl who used to light the fires and black the grates.

She'd hopelessly and helplessly wept at her chore one morning, blinded with the tears that wouldn't stop flowing from her swollen eyes, not able to keep her nose from running. Jennie caught her at it, dried the child's eyes, made her blow her nose on one of the new handkerchiefs, and heard in broad Cockney, made almost unintelligible by the hiccuping sobs, the story of the mother dying in childbirth after the father had beaten her, and of his attempts to violate his own daughter. Now she was terrified for fear she wouldn't give satisfaction here and would be sent back; one of the maids had spoken sharply to her this morning.

Jennie was sickened and appalled by the child's terror. She learned then what put girls on the streets or in the river. At home, when one heard of any sort of abuse, there was something to do at once; she could have gone to her father or to Sylvia's parson or to one of the eccentric old ladies who were part of the country's flora and fauna. *Someone* would have said, and enforced it, "That child shall never go back to that man again."

Even if there were no way of punishing the man, the girl would have grown up safe belowstairs in some country house, the father or uncle or brother forbidden the premises.

Jennie's homesickness was now compounded by bitter frustration. She didn't know Aunt and Uncle Higham well enough; they could very well put the girl out after hearing her story, as if she were a plague carrier. As for the London variety of eccentric old ladies, any of the bejeweled and beplumed specimens Jennie had met didn't look as if kindness toward the lower orders extended past being sure that the horses weren't chilled. The rector of the church which the Highams attended was so grand in the pulpit on Sundays and such a *bon vivant* on weekdays that one couldn't imagine approaching him. George Vinton was so green, for all his dandified airs, that he'd have strangled with horrified embarrassment if he hadn't burned to death with his blushes.

When she wasn't being homesick that winter in London, she was suffering for Tamsin and murderous toward the father. Tamsin never overflowed to her again; she was afraid of being caught at it. The fear of losing her place was contagious; it was a constant pain gnawing at Jennie's stomach. She lived a double life, as a grateful niece trying to live up to her obligations and as a prisoner of her passions. She could not even write it all out to Sylvia, who could have done nothing to help.

Tamsin died as quietly and humbly as she had lived, of a fever which was survived by the stronger, better-nourished girls. She died in a clean bed in her garret room at Brunswick Square, tended by the girls and women of whom she had been so unnecessarily afraid. She died unravished by her father, and she would never have to go on the streets, where she would have died a far different death after long miseries.

Uncle Higham had seen that she was decently buried. There was no more need to be anxious for her now, so one reason for the pain in Jennie's stomach was gone. But for the rest of her life she would remember Tamsin with the depressing ache of an old injury.

William and Sylvia were snug in the rectory, thinking God had made a gift of each to the other. They were good people; they acted swiftly when they saw distress. But she condescended wearily to their innocence. When she reached the north again, she would tell them what London was really like.

With thirty gold sovereigns, she thought on this morning of the duet by the blackbird and the baker's boy, *I could even go to America, if I knew how to get started.* She put down her book and lay watching the light brightening on the ceiling, and let herself go in a fantasy about taking a ship for America. With the addition of an inexpensive wedding ring, she could call herself a widow, because a widow could move about more freely than an unmarried girl. She'd say she was going to relatives there, traveling alone because at the last moment her maid had become ill, or had refused to go across three thousand miles of ocean, or had eloped with the coachman.

Jennie passed lightly over the possibilities of storms or shipwreck. She smiled with gracious sadness on the officers and other passengers. There were some who would have courted her if they had not respected her grief. The delightful fantasy ended when the ship docked because she could imagine neither what she would see nor what she could do there.

No. Home to the north first, and then, if nothing presented itself by summer, on to Switzerland. It was a pity she couldn't simply say to her aunt, "I would like to go home. Not to Pippin Grange, of course, but William and Sylvia will have me until I situate myself."

If only her aunt and uncle would give in gracefully. (This was the purest fantasy.) She could depart with their blessings, and George Vinton would still come calling, she thought dreamily. He might be saved for Charlotte after all, though Jennie was sure her young cousin's romantic ideal was something rather different.

"*George Vinton!*" Jennie said it aloud, and shot up like a jack-in-the-box. "*He's* the way!"

She needed only to know where to go to take a northbound coach, and how to get there, and if she couldn't find this out from George Vinton without arousing his suspicions, she was a fool and deserved to be caught out.

There was a tap at the door, and Tamsin's successor, a brawny, good-natured girl, brought in her hot water.

Three

"**Y**OU MUST HAVE more porridge, Jennie," said Aunt Higham. "You're very thin. Be lavish with the cream. A pleasing slenderness is one thing, but there's nothing worse than being scrawny."

"I'm eating an extra roll, Aunt," Jennie said with an affectionate smile. She was even fonder than usual of Aunt Higham this morning, because she was leaving her.

"Then use more butter. There's no need to scrimp here. Lottie, pass her the honey."

"*Monstrous!*" Uncle Higham barked. Jennie knew it was neither the honey nor herself that was monstrous, but the state of the nation.

So the day that was to turn her life around—if she could manage it—began as all other days had begun here. As usual, while she sat at breakfast with her aunt and uncle and cousin, she thought her own thoughts while Uncle Higham delivered his morning pronunciamentos on the idiotic behavior of Parliament, the lunacy of the King, the depravity of the Prince of Wales, the infamy of the Orders in Council which had caused the Americans to lay down their embargo; the colonies, as he persisted in calling the United States, were not to be forgiven their retaliation. The embargo was just as evil as Napoleon's blockade. They were strangling British trade to the death; if all the Highams ended up in the workhouse, it would be on the heads of the Americans and the French, and, of course, the criminal imbeciles responsible for the Orders in Council, he added, trying to be fair and turning purple in the attempt.

Since Sir John Moore had fallen at Corunna in January, Uncle Higham had been extremely gloomy, and he was not cheered now by reading in his morning paper that Arthur Wellesley had asked for, and been given, leave to lead an expeditionary force to defend Portugal.

"Of *course* Bonaparte can't be allowed to go on gulping down one country after another like a plate of oysters. Of *course* he must be crushed!" He crushed him with a huge meaty fist beside his coffee cup, which leaped off the saucer and fell back again. "But I don't trust this Wellesley. Something peculiar about that family! Flashy, unpredictable. Look at this woman! Disgraceful! Man should resign from the Army!"

"The woman's not a Wellesley, Roger," his wife said briskly. "She's his sister-in-law. The Wellesleys are well rid of her, but God help the Pagets." Lady Caroline Wellesley had just left her husband and young children to elope with Lord Paget. "Went off in a hackney coach!" Something about that made Aunt Higham want to laugh, but the impulse was bound and gagged.

Charlotte's larkspur eyes were vacant; these days she was reading *The Mysteries of Udolpho* on the sly in Jennie's room, and her thoughts moved in gloomy Gothic circles, searching for a demon lover.

"It's Paget who should resign," said Aunt Higham, "not Arthur Wellesley."

Her husband glared at her. "He's the best cavalry officer in the Army. Nation needs him. War, war," Uncle Higham growled at his plate. "I'm sick of it. Country's sick of it. The whole world's dying of a plague of stupidity."

He was a large man, red of face and hair, with reddish brown eyes, and with a thick prow of a nose projecting between fleshy cheeks, and jowls folding over his cravat. The broad curve of his middle made a fine display of his figured waistcoat, chain, and seals. He still had good muscular calves for silk stockings, which may have been one reason he held forth about the immorality of the pantaloons that were replacing honest, manly knee breeches.

He had never gone out of his way to make Jennie welcome, and at first she had felt humiliated and angry in his presence. But in time she realized that he had never gone out of his way to make her feel *unwel-come. He treated her as a member of the family—that is, he favored her with a comment or barked out a question when he felt like it, and otherwise ignored her.

After her father's charm and humor, Uncle Higham's manner was a shock, but it was the salutary shock of cold water dashed into the face to stop a faint or to startle a child into letting go its breath. It was instant notice that home was gone forever and the family broken up. Her aunt was not demonstrative, so Jennie was flung in to sink or swim. She had floundered, choked, thought she was going down for good, and had shot to the surface again, gasping but surviving.

She had survived to the point where Carolus Hawthorne's daughter was thinking very vigorously for herself while her amber eyes, seemingly as innocent and transparent as a young hound's, were fixed earnestly on first her uncle's face and then her aunt's. George Vinton would be here this afternoon or evening, if not this morning; the bird was unable to stay away from the cobra. If she suggested a walk in the garden, Aunt Higham would be pleased to keep the children away.

If he came this morning, there was even a chance that she might be away before nightfall. The thought of the ecstasy of heading north from London made her almost dizzy; she wanted to shut her eyes and swing with the sensation.

There was a stir in the room like the change in the tide. Breakfast was over, and Uncle Higham was about to be seen off to business. Charlotte returned reluctantly from Gothic grottoes. The two girls walked behind the senior Highams out into the marble-floored foyer. From the head of the stairs there were rustlings and whisperings as the younger children gathered. Mavis, the tall parlormaid, appeared suddenly and soundlessly, like an apparition; Jennie suspected her of lying in wait in the library. Uncle Higham scowled at his greatcoat, and it was whisked away. His hat and gloves were presented, and he turned to select his stick from the collection in the tall Chinese urn; he always walked when the weather was fine.

Charlotte, while looking respectful, was dreaming again. Aunt Higham waited, her hands folded across her middle, also respectful but hardly browbeaten. There was a sense of held breath at the head of the stairs while Uncle Higham's hand hovered over the collection of sticks. Suddenly it pounced. When he lifted out the chosen one, he looked up at the bronze hanging lamp as if he were listening.

"Good-bye, Papa!" The chorus came. Derwent's voice was the loudest because this wasn't one of his jail days; he could never be sure, until he saw the stick come out, if Papa was about to announce that it was time that Derwent spent some time on the business premises of Higham Brothers, Ltd.

Now Papa waved his hat at them, admonished them to be good, and was swept out the door on a wave of fervent promises. Mavis closed the door behind him with reverent ceremony, and instantly the house came to the boil. Mavis disappeared as magically as she had appeared. Aunt Higham went to the kitchen to give the day's orders; she was not one of those women who feared to step into Cook's territory. The children rushed down the stairs, and Charlotte floated into the drawing room to practice her music on the new Broadwood pianoforte.

Jennie was surrounded by the children's giggling, stamping, hooting version of a Red Indian dance. Ann and Marjorie were six and nine; Derwent was ten, and his dream was to run away to North America and be adopted into a tribe of Red Indians. He wanted to go before he could be sent to public school, which gave the shape and substance to his chronic nightmares. Some Higham cousins had gladly given him the dreadful details. Only Jennie and Charlotte knew this; Jennie would have liked to go directly to the parents but, as with Tamsin, she didn't dare. Charlotte hoped his tendency to heavy colds would keep him home.

Jennie, trailed by noise like a comet by fire, went into the drawing room. She silenced the children with a finger to her lips and opened music for Charlotte to sight-read. The children ranged about the long room, staring at its riches. They spent so little time in this splendid place it was a treasure cave to them. There was the fascination of the circular convex mirror in its gilt frame over the mantel, in which they could see the whole room; the matching sofas with entire tapestry pictures set in their backs; the marquetry cabinets; the gold-framed paintings against the hand-painted wallpaper; the carpet that was a flower garden in itself; the fire screens painted with fantastic, fairy scenes; the crystal girandoles hanging from the wall sconces, flashing every color as the sun struck them. There were the Egyptian chairs with great paws for feet, and the Holy of Holies, the glass cabinet holding curios from wherever in the world their father's family had done business. They whispered covetously before it, breathing mist onto the glass, their fingers itching to hold miniature ship or elephant or man.

Charlotte's music tinkled through the tenuous morning light. She was silvery blond, and like Jennie she was very slender while the little girls were still round with baby fat. There was something so innocent and helpless about the nape of her neck as she bent her pale head toward the music that Jennie, thinking this could be the last morning she would stand behind the child like this, was suddenly stabbed with something worse than melancholy.

Charlotte in her own way touched her as much as Tamsin had. To be young was to be a victim in one way or another. Look at Derwent. At ten he should be completely carefree, bursting with happy expectations about life, but he was already terrified of it.

When I get away from here, she thought, *I shall write Aunt and Uncle Higham a letter and tell them they must not send Derwent away to public school. They'll burn it at once, of course, but they'll read it first.*

"Very good, Lottie," she said aloud, lightly pressing the girl's thin shoulders. "Now here's what I'd like you to do." She set her an hour's work and took the others upstairs, where they began an extremely active and noisy geography lesson. Tamsin's successor sat by the cradle watching the baby while Mrs. Coombes went downstairs for a restorative cup of tea in the kitchen as soon as Aunt Higham had left it. She was not young, and the children woke early these mornings.

The youngster by the cradle enjoyed the lessons and was taking in everything like a sponge. Jennie hoped the next governess would appreciate that. *The next governess . . .* Leaving the children made her feel like a criminal. *But they'd have had someone else if I hadn't come,* she thought, *and it's not as if I shan't be seeing them again. After all, I'm not eloping into utter disgrace like Lady Caroline Wellesley and her cavalry officer. I'm simply going home.*

After morning lessons the children went to play in the garden, and Jennie went to her room and took off the full holland apron guarding her violet-sprigged muslin morning gown from the wear and tear of governess life. She tucked up the hair that had come loose from the knot while they were dramatizing the Crusades, and washed her hands and face. Then she went down to the morning room, where Aunt Higham was entertaining early callers. She would rather have gone out and played rounders or Indians in the garden, which was a sooty and pathetic substitute for the moors and the seashore of home but was better than the absurd ritual of the morning room. Charlotte was allowed to join now, and she always entered the room in the poignant, ardent belief that something wonderful was going to happen.

Certainly nothing wonderful happened this morning. No males called, not even George Vinton. The girls had to sit erect, ankles genteelly crossed and hands gracefully folded while the ladies talked twaddle in the accent that sounded ridiculously affected to Jennie; she could hardly believe that Aunt Higham really cared about this nonsense. Charlotte was disappointed and trying so hard to keep still that she grew quite flushed and her eyes became watery as if she were feverish. Aunt Higham could not abide a fidget and said men couldn't either. A fidget was as bad as a rattle anytime.

Mavis appeared to announce that the carriage had come for Lady Clarke, and the last caller arose to go. "Adieu until three then," she cried. She was a bedizened old rack of bones who had talked on and on in a high, honking voice until even Aunt Higham became restive.

She was quickly on her feet now, agreeing, "Until three." They touched cheeks. Lady Clarke didn't keep a carriage; she could barely keep herself. Out of duty or pity, friends dropped her here and there, collecting her later.

When she had left the room, honking amiably away at Mavis, no one moved until the sound of her voice was shut off by the closing front door. "We will drive in the park this afternoon," Aunt Higham announced. "It's very warm and fine. Mademoiselle can give the children their French in the garden. Charlotte, you'll come with us today. Wear your rose pelerine and the bonnet to match; it puts color in your face."

"Oh, Mama!" Clearly the horrid session in the morning was worth it now.

"Jennie, you will wear your lilac."

"Yes, Aunt." Well, she'd paid for the clothes; she could give the orders. There'd be no meeting with George Vinton this afternoon, and the hope of today's escape had gone a-glimmering. But George would surely come tonight.

At a quarter of three, the girls met their commanding officer in the foyer and were inspected while Mavis stood by, professionally impassive.

"You look very well," Aunt Higham said. "I see you haven't forgotten your gloves and your reticules." Charlotte had reminded Jennie of these necessities. She had no clean handkerchief in her reticule, but her aunt needn't know *that*, she thought with invigorating defiance.

"You look very handsome yourself, Aunt," she said.

"Oh, Mama, you do!" Charlotte breathed.

"Perhaps," her mother admitted sternly. She wore a plum-colored mantle, and matching plumes dipped softly from the crown of her straw hat; like Jennie's, its brim was turned up roguishly on one side, but

Jennie's hat was trimmed with silk lilacs. "Put your gloves on before you go out," she commanded. She nodded to Mavis, the door was opened, and they went out into the spring afternoon.

The barouche waited; the coachman in maroon livery was as impassive as Mavis, but with a nuance of contempt. The two black horses were satiny in the sun. One did not greet the Higham horses by kissing their noses and asking how they did; one did not visit them in the mews with gifts of apples and sugar lumps. A few hundred miles away Nelson, still in his thick winter coat, would be browsing in the orchard. *Right now*, Jennie thought with a griping pain in her stomach, *my real life is going on back there. What am I doing here?*

"Well, Jennie?" her aunt said tartly. She was already seated, and Charlotte sat opposite her, back to the horses. She smiled at Jennie; the rosy silk lining of her bonnet reflected on her narrow face, and she was hoping there might be soldiers riding in the park.

In a shabby crescent they stopped for Lady Clarke, wearing brown kerseymere and crepe and a velvet turban with a veil. Their discreetness was shattered by her obvious rouge and such a powerful scent that even Aunt Higham's nostrils flared involuntarily. *Between that and riding backward I shall be sick*, Jennie thought hopefully. *I shall have to be taken at once back to Brunswick Square before I disgrace myself.* She imagined a geyser of undigested dinner shooting into Lady Clarke's lap.

The picture was so entertaining that it diverted the incipient nausea. After such an incident Aunt Higham might consider it a blessing, rather than an insult, that the bird had flown.

The first really warm and sunny day had brought crowds out to stroll or drive under the new leaves, but it was still damp enough to keep the dust down. Charlotte's head turned constantly; she was a kitten watching a swarm of bright butterflies. She was entranced by the occupants of the other equipages; the young men in their glossy curricles and phaetons behind matched pairs were all Phoebus to her, each driving his own chariot of the sun. Their lady friends dazzled in rainbows of pelisses, mantles, cloaks, Lavinia hats, jockey bonnets.

As for the riders of horses, Charlotte's eyes enameled them all with beauty; Jennie was sure that the girl saw not one portly or ungainly figure among them. They were all gods or heroes, and every horse kin to Bucephalus. The women in a splendid variety of riding habits and hats, feathered or buckled, or trailing vivid scarves, rode with stately yet graceful confidence, simultaneously managing reins, crops, and conversation.

Lady Clarke's brown velvet turban nodded in all directions, her quizzing glasses were at the ready, her other gloved hand kept raising and waggling the fingers; she might have been royalty. Aunt Higham was more restrained, but her broad face wore a tight smile of either pleasure or determination—it was hard to tell—and her bows were frequent.

A big bay dashed by them, and Charlotte seized Jennie's arm. "That was the Prince of Wales, I'm sure!"

Lady Clarke gazed severely through her quizzing glasses after the rider and honked, "Nonsense, child! The Prince is very stout."

Mortified, Charlotte whispered, "He *looked* like a prince."

"He may be a duke or an earl." Jennie comforted her.

A young man alone in a phaeton behind two grays came abreast of them and lifted his high-crowned hat. "Good afternoon, Lady Clarke! Madam! Young ladies!" A radiant smile for the girls, and the phaeton sped on. Both girls instantly twisted around to watch and were tapped smartly on the knees by Aunt Higham.

"Behave yourselves!"

Are we out to see or to be seen? Jennie asked silently, but she knew the answer. To be seen. Marketable goods.

"But who *is* he, Mama?" Charlotte said.

"No one either of you should know," said her mother. "A coxcomb, nothing more. He played ducks and drakes with his inheritance and now is owned by every moneylender in London."

Charlotte sighed. Jennie said to her, "All the really beautiful ones are flawed." She thought of George Vinton, and sighed herself. If he was the best she could attract, she was a sorry lot. Not that she wanted any of these either; their horses were the best part of them. And if this wasn't the last drive she endured in Uncle Higham's maroon barouche, she was an everlasting disgrace to the name and memory of Carolus Hawthorne.

A lady bowed graciously as her carriage rolled by; it was an elegant vehicle, with a footman on the box beside the coachman, and both in bottle green. Aunt Higham and Lady Clarke bowed in return, smiles stiff as grimaces, and then they turned to each other, both speaking at once.

"How she *dares!* I shouldn't have responded, but she took me by surprise! I feel quite *soiled!* They *say*—" Lady Clarke honked discreetly behind her hand, Aunt Higham bent avidly toward her. Charlotte's eyes ranged desperately over the traffic following and passing the barouche, as if she wondered which was permissible for her attention.

Jennie's head was hot in the small, tight straw, and its ribbons were scratching under her chin. Her hands burned in the gloves, and she was sweating inside the snugly buttoned pelerine. She wanted to rip off her gloves, she longed to unbutton at least partway before she suffocated or was steamed to mush like a haddock, but of course, that was unthinkable.

This could be one version of hell, riding backward through eternity in a crowd of the other Damned, boiling in your stays and forbidden to move. She turned her head to the side where the traffic was least, in an attempt to isolate herself in a secret world away from the noise and the uncaring, unknowing faces. *Mind over matter*, she commanded herself. She tried to think of tranquilizing poetry, but even Mr. Wordsworth deserted her, and if she finished the drive with a blinding headache and had to go to bed, she'd lose her chance to get George Vinton alone tonight.

Four

CHARLOTTE stiffened abruptly beside her, and a sharp little elbow knocked against her side. Was Charlotte also feeling ill? Then they could go home. With relief she looked around and saw the other three heads all turned like sunflowers toward the vision just coming abreast of the barouche.

There was a strong whiff of warm horse and leather, a musical jingling as the big chestnut tossed his head against restraint, breathing impatiently, his eyes rolling; there was a high jackboot black and lustrous, a magnificent thigh in tight buff doeskin. All eyes rose devoutly past the deep-cuffed white gauntlet, up the blue sleeve past the thick gold epaulet, to the face that shown upon them. The rider removed the big black cocked hat with its red and white plumes and held it against his breast. His head was fair.

If the others had been Phoebus, this was the Sun.

"Nigel, my love!" Lady Clarke's raddled old face contorted grotesquely with joy. She announced him as if it were the Second Coming. "My grandnephew, Captain Gilchrist of the Royal Horse Guards!" Her eyes were wetly shining. "Mrs. Roger Higham."

"Dear Auntie!" he replied in a pleasant baritone voice. "Your servant, ma'am." He addressed Aunt Higham.

"How do you do, Captain Gilchrist?" There was something new about Aunt Higham, or rather something past: the ghost of the blooming country girl she'd been. Who knew but herself what other ghost this completely glorious young man had conjured up? She'd settled for Roger Higham, but in this moment Jennie saw the lost girl in her aunt's solid flesh, and loved her as she never had before.

23

The Sun shone impartially upon them all with a flash of beautiful teeth, an irresistible creasing of his fresh-colored cheeks. He had also a romantic cleft in his chin, which Charlotte would have seen at once; her arm trembled against Jennie's. Jennie told herself *she* was moved only by the masculine beauty of both horse and man, because they were products of nature, like breaking surf or the full moon.

"Miss Hawthorne." Lady Clarke named her, but forbiddingly. There was an implicit warning to Jennie not to get ideas. Captain Gilchrist was clearly marked for something better than the Highams' poor relation.

"Miss Hawthorne!" A courtly inclination of the golden head.

She inclined her own head, trying for a remote, but possibly amused, dignity. Aunt Higham said, "My dear niece Eugenia is—"

Lady Clarke rode over her like a Roman legion. "And Miss Higham."

"Miss Higham!"

Charlotte was as rose-red as her pelerine; her lips moved without sound; she kept blinking, her fingers dug into Jennie's arm.

"And how does your mother do?" his great-aunt asked him. He answered something, controlling the impatient horse with negligent one-handed ease. Jennie recovered her pride and refused to stare, though she wanted to. She observed her aunt and guessed that she had hoped for something like this when she had invited Lady Clarke to join them. She was watching the captain with a religious attention, no doubt trying to decide whether her duty was to her niece or to the hope that Captain Gilchrist would still be eligible in about three years. That hope was also naked in Charlotte's eyes, as wide with wistful hunger as if she were ten and coveting a marzipan soldier in a shopwindow.

He would make a rather lovely one, Jennie thought with deliberate contempt, breathing slowly to calm herself. Of course he was handsome, but take away the great horse and the splendors of gold braid, jackboots, red sash, and plumed hat, and what would he be?

"What-what is the horse's name?" Charlotte suddenly blurted.

"Victor," he said with a smile.

Charlotte sank back, embarrassed by her daring but proud of it.

"Do you ride, Miss Higham?" he asked her.

"Not yet," she answered in mortification.

"Do *you*, Miss Hawthorne?"

"Yes," she answered crisply. "But not here. At home."

"And where is home?" He sat at ease and spoke to her as if there were no one else present.

Before she could answer, her aunt said, "It's in London now. Brunswick Square."

"Ah, but I detect a touch of the north."

"She'll lose that soon enough," said her aunt, as if promising.

"That would be a pity," he said.

"You would not believe how sought-after my grandnephew is." Lady Clarke honked in arrogant warning. *It really sounds better from a goose,* Jennie thought. "He has hardly a moment to himself. It is quite dreadful sometimes, how he is pursued."

"Come now, Auntie!" He grinned. "I don't see myself as a victim." He turned to Jennie. "Could you not ride here if you chose?"

"She may ride," Aunt Higham said rapidly. "It is only that Mr. Higham does not keep saddle horses."

"I know a fine little mare she might go on, Victor's sister. Victor would like her company through the park, wouldn't you, my boy?" The horse tossed his head and snorted.

Lady Clarke had a violent coughing spell. She became purple, and her eyes spilled water over her cheeks, making streaks through their vivid color. Aunt Higham was frightened. Charlotte stared in horror; the captain looking down like the sun at noon seemed merely interested and possibly amused. Finally the whooping gasps grew less, and Lady Clarke flapped a hand at Victor.

"Take the great beast away," she panted. "He brought it on . . . I can never be this close to a horse for long without having a choking fit . . . even as a child. Go *away*, Nigel, do! This instant, or you'll have my death on your head."

"Really, Auntie? That's devilish int'r'sting, you know. Never heard of such a thing before in all these years I've known you. . . . Your servant, ladies!" He put on his hat and cantered away. Jennie tried to read Aunt Higham's face and saw recognition replacing alarm, but so cannily that Lady Clarke could not suspect.

"It was always cats with me," she said comfortably. "I loved them, but oh, dear, what wicked colds they gave me."

Charlotte floated home through the first of those iridescent dreams from which all Gothic lovers would henceforth be forever exiled. Jennie retired to her room in a confusion of heat and chills, attacked by powerful physical sensations of desire and longing such as she had never known before. They couldn't be reasoned away by the argument that the superb creature on horseback was probably no more than that marzipan soldier.

She saw the girl of the morning, wrapped in the old robe and wearing the shapeless fleece-lined slippers, counting her gold sovereigns and aching to be gone, determined to be gone. She stared at this girl as one might stare at a specter, not frightened but incredulous. There was a slow tightening around her temples, and she put her hands to them to loosen the invisible band.

How could it *be*? How could she have become something utterly different in the space of a few hours, most of them extremely uncomfortable, from the creature who for six months had been one huge throb of longing for home?

Free of her clothes, she sponge-bathed in cool water and, shivering, told herself she had merely been charmed by the display, as she had been charmed by so much in London. But she knew she was lying.

It wasn't the blue coat and the boots, the mastery of the animal, the bared blond head against the spring sky. It was the way he had looked straight at her, as if he had seen Jennie Hawthorne—her own Jennie Hawthorne—beneath the straw brim and the silk lilacs. Not just any miss being shown in the auction ring, but Jennie Hawthorne of Pippin Grange, Northumberland, England, the World, the Universe.

He saw her and knew her.

She was at once despairing and exhilarated. She dressed for the evening as if he were to be there, though she knew he would not be. Charlotte looked feverish and was sent to bed early. Jennie thought wryly that if anyone should be sent to bed with the megrims, it was herself. She recognized her chaos, ridiculed it, and was powerless against it.

George Vinton came in that evening, along with other guests; Uncle Higham and his particular friends played whist in the library, and in the drawing room Jennie played backgammon with George. He must have been surprised by her gaiety, though she'd always been good-natured with George. Tonight she was like someone who was slightly drunk and immensely entertained by the fact, while recognizing the underlying desperation. Could she bear it if she never saw Captain Gilchrist again?

George's large, round, wondering dark eyes reminded her of Nelson's, except that with Nelson that expression sometimes meant that he was about to bite. There was no such doubt with George. He would always be predictable. Aunt Higham could run on about his prospects, but not even money from his mother, mixing with cathedral society, and having an uncle who called the Archbishop of Canterbury by his first name, were going to make him anything more than what he was. But surely there was someone waiting to love George Vinton and to make his rectory a happy one. Jennie felt very tender toward George tonight.

Passing among the game tables, Aunt Higham patted her shoulder, an unusual caress. She had been absentminded since they'd come home, but alone with Jenny for a moment just before the first callers came, she had suddenly said, "We didn't fit you for a riding habit. It didn't occur to me because your uncle doesn't think riding necessary for our girls. But I can see that it may be. We will see Mrs. Meacham tomorrow about yours."

George won the second game in a row and laughed like a conqueror. Euphoric with victory, he said, "I say, Miss Hawthorne, how about a turn in the garden? The moon's coming up. Let me get your shawl."

At dawn she had hoped to be riding north by moonrise. How long ago had she heard the blackbird and the baker's boy and thought: *If I can get George Vinton alone* —

"What I'd like better than that, Mr. Vinton, is to hear you sing."

Flattery assuaged his disappointment. "If you'll play for me."

"Of course!"

There was a pleasant stir of anticipation through the drawing room as they went to the pianoforte, where candles at either end of the keyboard burned in slender chimneys. In spite of his occasional incoherence of speech and his gobbling laughter, George sang in a sweet lyric tenor, every word exquisitely clear, as if the music allowed a different George to escape on wings of song. Tonight he sang the tender Elizabethan "Song to Celia," beginning "Drink to me only with thine eyes," and the poignant "Passing By."

Tonight his singing had for Jennie an almost intolerable pathos, as if he meant his songs for her, or for the way he had been willing to love her, as if he were already gazing into the time when she would be in his past.

She wanted to assure him that she wasn't worth it, while George's voice floated in the room like a seagull's perfect glide to the sea.

> *"But change the earth or change the sky,*
> *Yet shall I love her till I die."*

It was a great relief when tea came in.

Captain Gilchrist called the next afternoon, without his great-aunt. He called on the day after that, and on the evening after that. It became known that Auntie had suddenly felt unwell and had gone to Bath for the waters. Her grandnephew strolled like a tawny lion through the drawing room or, to be more earthy about it, a large golden tomcat in a town of tabbies. His laughter made the teacups rattle and the wine-glasses ring. In or out of uniform, he moved in an incandescent aura. George Vinton became invisible, and even Uncle Higham suffered partial eclipse, unthinkable in his own house, but he didn't seem ill-tempered about it.

Though the Captain was responsible for Jennie's recognition of this facet of her passionate nature, she never had the temerity to see him as a husband. Not hers, anyway, if ever anyone's. He surely had a sweetheart or a mistress who moved in circles the Highams never touched. His period of effulgence at Brunswick Square would soon end like a natural phenomenon when he tired of it.

In the meantime it was joyful torment to play the piano while he sang Jacobite songs in his virile baritone, or to stand up with him in the impromptu quadrilles and polkas he organized when he discovered that one of Uncle's whist partners could play for dancing. This was something neither of the Highams had known about the man, but somehow Captain Gilchrist found out and had him at the Broadwood and enjoying it.

One night the Captain came in full-dress uniform because he had to go on to a ball afterward. "Confounded nuisance, you know, but the Colonel's giving it for his daughter's birthday." *Does he intend you for her?* Jennie thought with a savage jealousy that shocked her. Then he said, "Let's have a polka! Where is that genius of the keyboard? Let's have him away from his infernal whist, what?"

During the dance he whirled her away from the others, out into the foyer across the marble floor, and she saw them in the glass that hung there, he huge in blue and gold with the red sash around his lean middle, she looking as frail as an early jonquil in her yellow silk muslin. Now that she knew his arm, his scent, the essence of *him*, there were times when she thought she could not bear it. The longer he amused himself at Brunswick Square, the worse the end would be, and in the meantime she was hard put to keep herself out of her eyes when she looked at him; she felt as vulnerable as Charlotte, as fragile as the jonquil that would die in a late snowfall.

To escape from him, if not from his arms, she looked everywhere and saw the children crouched on the landing, watching through the railings. She pointed them out, and he bounded up the stairs four at a time and gave each little girl a spin around the landing, leaving them all dazed but luminous. He saved Charlotte for the last.

"Thank you, Miss Higham," he said formally at the end of her turn, and kissed her hand. "You should be downstairs. You will be, soon."

She couldn't speak but looked past his arm at Jennie with such happiness and gratitude that tears came into Jennie's eyes.

Then he rumpled Derwent's head and said, "And *you* practice your dancing with your sisters, old man. You'll need it before you know it."

"Even if I'm going to be a soldier?" It was his new ambition ever since the Captain had been coming to the house.

"*Especially* if you're going to be a soldier. Dev'lish important. Colonel gives balls, you have to attend. Orders, you know."

"I'd rather catch Napoleon," Derwent said pugnaciously.

"Who wouldn't?" He laughed, took Jennie's hand, ran her down the stairs, and danced her back into the drawing room.

One moment she thought that if the sun were removed, she would die, and in the next she would concede that one couldn't die at will. But having lost all that had mattered to her in her life so far, she would be tougher, far less timid about taking risks. What worse could happen to her? Now she wouldn't scheme to run away; she'd simply tell the Highams that grateful as she was for all they had done for her, she was leaving London for good, and if it meant being a spinster all her life, so be it.

He rode beside the barouche again; he began appearing at affairs which she attended with her aunt and uncle, danced the two dances allowed an unengaged couple, sat out others with her, brought supper to her. She was nearly suffocated with embarrassment, knowing how they were watched and discussed behind fans. She hated Aunt Higham's tightly guarded but avid satisfaction, wanting to say, "Can't you *see* he's just amusing himself with the poor little country girl? Condescending to her so she'll have this shiny memory to keep?"

Jealousy scalded her throat and twisted in her belly when she saw the familiarity of other women with him, the moving lips and significant smiles of his partners while she sat beside her aunt with her gloved hands folded in her lap. Which one had been, or still was, his lover? She brooded over his beauty, so maliciously paraded within her grasp yet not for her, as if it were all a vast, complicated, and vicious practical joke played on her and her ambitious aunt.

That some women flirted with all their partners meant nothing to her; she saw only how they behaved with Captain Gilchrist. For her to dance with anyone else, even the most gallant and obviously admiring youth, was merely to go through a set of motions to music which jangled out of tune in her head. She resented the girls of her own age more than the married women; these London girls were years ahead of her in sophistication. Bitterly she admired their ease with him and wondered which was the heiress who would get him. How could Aunt Higham be so naïve as to believe he was serious about her niece?

The new riding habit was finished: bronze kerseymere almost the color of her eyes, with a velvet collar and three rows of small gilt buttons crossed with bronze silk cord. The narrow-brimmed white beaver hat with its short white feather was especially admired by all the children; even Derwent wanted to try it on.

The shoemaker had sewn boots of russet Spanish leather for her, and her gloves matched.

"Oh Jennie, you're so *elegant*," Charlotte said. Yes, she *was* elegant, at least in the cheval glass in Aunt Higham's room. And she knew that on a horse she would be as much at ease as any of those girls she admired and envied. But would he remember his offer of the fine little mare?

He remembered.

Five

I T WAS the first time they'd ever been really alone, though it was in a flow of riders and drivers. They walked their horses along the edge of the stream and talked; he asked her many questions about herself and seemed enthralled by life at Pippin Grange. He said he wished he could have known her father, but someday perhaps he would know her sisters. She asked about him; he was Scottish, but his father had died when he was small, and his much older half brother had become master of the estate. His mother later married an Englishman, so he had been brought up as an English boy in the Hampshire countryside. His stepfather was dead now, and his mother lived in London, in a house overlooking Hyde Park.

"Great old girl. Bless my soul!" Transparent astonishment. "We're almost there! Shall we go and make her give us some coffee?"

"We'll scent her drawing room with horse."

"The Mater won't turn a hair. Attar of roses to her. Before she was thrown by a horse and broke her hip, she was never off 'em. Augustus his name was. Great brute of a hunter. She never blamed him. First thing she said was 'Is he all right?'"

"And was he?"

"He was, and is. But he put an end to her riding days. That's why she goes into the country only over Easter and Christmas. I've a younger half brother now, who's the baronet. Only nineteen, but he's dashed good at it. Takes his responsibilities seriously." He laughed as if at a tremendous joke.

"My older half brother is master of estates in Scotland, my younger half brother is squire of a good part of Hampshire, and here *I* am. Enough to turn a fella's hair gray before its time, ain't it?"

He's about to tell me he's betrothed to an heiress, Jennie thought. Instead he said, "Here's the Mater's front door." His blue eyes were as innocent as the children's.

The ever-present urchin popped up as if he'd been lying in ambush in the areaway, called Nigel Capting, and said he would mind the horses for a penny.

"Right, old chap," said Nigel, helping Jennie down.

" 'Oo's the lidy?"

For an instant Jennie thought he meant her, but he was stroking the mare's nose as she dipped a willing head down to him.

"Juno," Nigel answered seriously, as if to an equal. "She belongs to the Major."

"Pretty little fing. Clever, too."

"She's a poppet," Nigel agreed.

As they went up the steps, Jennie murmured, "Friends?"

"Old friends. His brother was here first, with Dickon tottering behind him, just out of the cradle."

"Where is the brother now?"

"Transported to a better world," said Nigel solemnly. Jennie took a quick breath, and he said in a hurry, "Oh, not dead!" Reassuringly, he cupped her elbow in his big hand and pressed it. "The Major took him into his stables. Thinks he has possibilities as a jockey. So Dickon hopes for higher things."

"Shall you—"

He shook his head. "I have no stables. I'm the landless one, remember. But Dickon will survive, if he lives to grow up. His sort will likely own half of London one day. They think they do already."

As he lifted the horse-head knocker and let it fall, he added, "He has a meal each day in the kitchen. The Mater's orders. She has a number of friends, and she'll place the imp with one of them."

She'd suspected that Nigel never read a book if he could help it; at least such a hint never came into his conversation; how often did it get into anyone's conversation around here, with Aunt Higham forever warning her not to sound like a bluestocking? But this practical kindness and concern, especially after the winter tragedy of Tamsin, were an affirmation that depths existed and that there were more to be discovered and explored, if she should be lucky enough to have the chance. She doubted it.

"Oh, Captain Gilchrist!" The elderly parlormaid demonstrated the usual feminine reaction to Nigel's appearance.

"Good morning, Gertrude, my love. Is my mother at home?"

She took his hat and gloves as if receiving the crown jewels. "Lady Geoffrey is reading in the library, sir."

That sounded encouraging, but Jennie reminded herself that the Mater might merely be reading the Stud Book. She was not reading at all when they entered the library but was standing before the fireplace, awaiting them. She was a tall, stout woman, tightly stayed, wearing a dark blue gown with a high frill at her strong throat and a lace cap over her still-bright hair.

Nigel got his golden fleece, his blue eyes, and his fine color from her. She stood erect and didn't lean perceptibly on her ivory-headed stick. She must have been as magnificent on her big hunter as Nigel was on Victor.

"Well, Nigel," she said resonantly.

"I've brought her to meet you, Mama. Miss Eugenia Hawthorne." Jennie was propelled gently forward and for a blinding moment suffered a brief return of the prize-heifer illusion. Lady Geoffrey held out her hand.

"I'm so happy to meet you, child. How cold your fingers are! Come and sit by the fire. Nigel, ring for Gertrude."

"No need, she's hovering so as not to miss a word. Aren't you, Gertrude?" he called. There was an agitated rustling from the foyer.

"Madeira and chocolate, Gertrude," said his mother with equanimity. "This lass needs to be warmed up." There was a trace of Scots here, just enough to leaven the southern accent which had always sounded so affected to Jennie.

"I'm not cold, really," she protested. "It's mild out, but—"

"She's terrified of you, Mama," said Nigel. He led Jennie to a tapestried fauteuil and put her in it. His mother lowered herself into the opposite one.

"I don't see why she should be. I'm not terrified of *her*, and I must admit *entre nous*, child, I *have* been terrified by some of my son's presentations." Laughter boomed up from that impressive bosom. "My dear, it's not an inspection. You're not being trotted back and forth like a filly to show me your gait and conformation."

"I felt more like a heifer," said Jennie, which set Lady Geoffrey off again, and she struck her cane on the floor.

"You're not so demure as I thought. Spirit, Nigel! She has spirit, I can see it in the set of her jaw and the light in her eye, and she'll need it! What do they call you, child? Not Eugenia, I hope."

"Jennie." She could hardly credit this conversation. It *was* an inspection, no matter what they said, and she didn't know whether she was overjoyed or humiliated or would end up as she'd expected, the victim of someone else's entertainment.

The scene was overlooked from above the mantel by the portrait of a man in a peer's robes. He was aloof without being offensively superior about it.

"Take off that ridiculous chapeau so I can see your hair," said Lady Geoffrey.

Jennie stared back, tempted to disobey, but Nigel, who stood between them with his back to the fire, suddenly chuckled, and the whole scene turned comic. She removed the white beaver hat, looked at it with distaste, and Nigel took it from her.

"Ah, that's better!" said his mother. "What a lovely bay color. Does it curl of its own or do you frizz it?"

"It's my own curl," said Jennie.

"*Good!* Men hate the sight of curl papers, or should." She touched the thick chignon at the back of her head below her cap. "Staight as a stick mine always was, to my mother's and my nurse's despair, and I endured the torture because I was helpless. But I can assure you I didn't endure *silently*." She was laughing again. "As soon as I was engaged, I said, no more of this idiocy, my husband must take me as God made me. If he wanted to marry curls, he should have taken that little nincompoop Sarah Flowers. But we were both Scots and sensible, so it worked out well, curls or no."

The decanter and the chocolate pot were brought in, and the tray was placed on a taboret by her chair. Eyes downcast but managing to take in a good deal, Gertrude left as silently and swiftly as if on wheels. Nigel poured wine for his mother and himself, and Lady Geoffrey poured steaming chocolate into flowered French porcelain for Jennie.

"I know something about you, Miss Hawthorne," she said composedly. "I have my sources of information, as your aunt and uncle must have theirs."

It was rather a relief not to worry any more about what one should *feel*; the swift gush of anger had taken care of it. She would not make a scene, but she would see that both Nigel and his mother knew exactly how she felt. She looked up at Nigel, intending that her long, deliberate gaze should tell him of her pride.

He winked at her. Did he mean that she should simply humor an eccentric parent? Be secretly amused, and they'd laugh together as they rode back through the park? She accepted the chocolate and quickly took a sip which nearly scalded her into muteness.

"Nigel," said his mother, "has always done exactly as he pleased. If he brought you here because I asked him to, it's a mere formality, the surface observance of an ancient ritual. Whether I approve or disapprove of you, it makes no difference to Nigel."

Nigel, looking whimsically unconcerned, sipped his wine under his stepfather's portrait, while the late baronet stared over the blond head into great distances, as if trying to discern his wife taking fences on Augustus.

"And it makes no difference to *me*"—Nigel's mother went tranquilly on—"if Nigel chooses to marry a nobody from Northumberland with no connections to speak of, and no money. Let it be on his own head."

Jennie found herself on her feet. "I should like to leave now, if you please," she said to Nigel.

"Put the cup down first," he advised, not moving away from the mantel. She set it on the tray beside the pot, keeping her face turned away from both him and his mother.

"Good day, Lady Geoffrey," she said with frigid courtesy. "Good day, Captain Gilchrist. You will find the mare in my uncle's stable."

She turned to walk out. If perfect love cast out fear, so did perfect rage.

"*Jennie.*" He had never called her that before. His big hands clasped her shoulders and turned her around. She gazed stolidly at his chest, waiting to be released.

"May I call you Jennie, too?" his mother asked winningly. "Bring her back, Nigel, so I can apologize properly."

"I need no apologies," Jennie said. "I need nothing at all from either of you. I would like to make it clear that I never did expect anything. All I desire now is my absence from here as quickly as possible."

Nigel, keeping an arm about her shoulders, walked her back to the hearth, but she stood like a wooden doll and hoped she looked like one; they should not guess how deeply they had wounded her.

"Jennie, I went too far perhaps"—Lady Geoffrey went on in that winning voice—"but you're out in the great world now, not in the safe arms of Pippin Grange. Yes, I know about your home, and I know what it is to be thrust out of it. It happened to me. The old castle where I grew up was wretchedly cold and wet ten months of the year, but why do I always remember it in sunshine? Because it was there that I knew the pure happiness of a blessed childhood." She wasn't smiling now, and the Scots accent was strong. "No one ever told me how it would end. That it *had* to end. My one brother died while he was fishing in the loch, and my father died with most of his Highland regiment at Quebec. My mother and my sisters and I were driven out of our home. Oh, very nicely, you understand. We weren't chased away like tinkers or gypsies, with the keepers threatening to set the dogs on us. My father, by dying in battle, had brought honor to his family, so the hero's widow was offered a house. Far from the castle, I may add," she said dryly. "Far enough from the western Highlands so my sisters and I couldn't ride our ponies on the ancestral lands."

Jennie swallowed. "I am so sorry," she said.

"Well, it was a long time ago, and if we hadn't been driven away from there, I'd never have met Ian Gilchrist and had this bonny son." She looked up at Nigel with a teasing yet proud smile, and he returned it. "Mind you, I was no great catch if a man was looking for money. Ian had already succeeded to Linnmore, so I became mistress of a big house, as big houses go in the Highlands. He had already a son from his first marriage, and an infernally healthy son Archie was, so I knew that my boy's chances of becoming the Laird of Linnmore were very slight. It didn't matter. Ian and I made each other happy." She became reflective, gazing past Nigel's legs into the fire. "Yes, we were happy. But I was dispossessed again when Ian died. Archie was fair enough, we always got on well, and I could have stayed mistress at Linnmore House until he married. But an uncle who'd been left his guardian, and who had named me as the Nobody"—she gave Jennie a mischievous grin—"decided he should move in to take better charge of Archie's affairs. Won't you sit down now, Jennie, and drink your chocolate? I'll add some hot to it."

Jennie sat down. Nigel poured more wine. "I carried my little son to London, to an aunt—"

"Lady Clarke?" Jennie asked, and both mother and son laughed.

"Dear Lord in heaven, Cecilia was too busy being the queen bee of her own swarm to want to give houseroom to a young widow. No, I went to one of my mother's other sisters, and when my mourning was over, I was introduced to Society as your aunt has introduced you. I met a man who didn't give a snap of his fingers for what Society thought. He was a good father to Nigel, and he gave me another bonny son as well. He has been dead for three years, and I think I shall mourn him the rest of my life." Her blue eyes glistened, but there was no self-pity about her. "Two men like that in a woman's lifetime, Jennie. Think on it. I've been doubly blessed."

Nigel lifted his glass to the portrait. He said, "Four times blessed when you count those bonny sons, Mama."

"Perhaps. I'll know better when you're forty, my dear. Jennie, whatever these sons do—unless the baronet installs a harem at Warrington, which would be absolutely ruinous to the house—is their own affair. By the way, if Nigel hasn't told you yet about his prospects, besides rising in the Army, which I don't count because I don't like seeing my son a soldier, he has an adequate income from his father and stepfather, if he isn't foolish about it. As for Linnmore, Archie married late, Christabel is long in the tooth, and if she produces an heir, I should be dumbfounded, and so will he. *There*." She poured more wine for herself, sank back in the armchair, and smiled beatifically at Jennie.

"But Nigel—I mean, Captain Gilchrist," Jennie blurted out, "had never—I mean, *we've* never discussed—the word has never been uttered between us!" She was so hot she wanted to tear open the neck of her habit.

"Nigel's respect for ritual, remember. He must speak to your uncle. You're agitated, aren't you? Your cheeks are flaming. You aren't coolly laughing at this preposterous scene. That means that if the word had never been uttered, it has certainly been *thought*. Let me put it to you this way, and please give me the perfectly candid answer that I expect from Jennie Hawthorne of the honest north. If Nigel asked you tomorrow to run away to Gretna Green, would you go?"

"Dear Mater," said Nigel, "I'm beginning to think that if *you'd* elope to Gretna Green, my life would be considerably less complicated."

She ignored him. "Would you, Jennie Hawthorne?"

"Yes," said Jennie.

Lady Geoffrey waved at Nigel. "There you are, my love. You'd better run along now. Bamber Raleigh is expected, and we're driving out to Richmond Park, not to Gretna Green."

"A pity," said Nigel. He leaned over and kissed her. "I know now why certain evil persons threw their mamas into dungeons. It was the only way to stop them talking."

"Good day, Lady Geoffrey," Jennie said sedately.

"Don't forget that fantastic hat. . . . You have good color, and that means healthy blood. You're thin but not spindling. I like that. It's the lean horse that wins the race."

"So it was an inspection after all!"

"My dear, I wouldn't be a human mother if I didn't have some concern for the mother of my grandchildren. I'll be glad to see Nigel settled. London is full of sharks, all female, and Nigel can't resist them any more than they can resist him."

"Let us leave, Jennie," said Nigel, "before she produces a clergyman from a secret passage and marries us by force. I shan't see you tonight, Mama. I'll be on duty."

In the foyer Jennie stopped before a mirror to pin her hat. Nigel whistled "The White Cockade" and slapped his gloves against his thigh; Gertrude helped Jennie, smiling all the while, and Jennie was glad of the quick, capable fingers: her own felt all loose and unstrung.

When the front door closed behind them, Jennie said at once, "Your mother proposed for you!"

"That's the Mater," he agreed. "Always rushing her fences."

"But I accepted!" she said. From the roadway the horses and Dickon observed them with unblinking interest. "Nigel—Captain—it was done under duress so it doesn't count. You're quite free."

"But I don't want to be," he said imperturbably. "I had already told Mama that you are the girl I intend to marry."

She said in giddy bewilderment, "Am I dreaming this? What if my uncle forbids it?" Panic.

"He won't. I shall speak to him tonight."

"I thought you were on duty tonight."

"That is the duty," he replied. "Shall we ride now?"

When he escorted her into the foyer at Brunswick Square, Aunt Higham came out from the morning room all smiles, to ask if he would take a glass of wine; instead he asked her very formally if he might meet with Mr. Higham in the evening. She at once strangled her smile and became stately. She was sure that Mr. Higham would be happy to meet with Captain Gilchrist.

Halfway up the stairs, there were the children: Charlotte transfixed, her hand to her breast, a nymph in sprigged dimity; Marjorie and Ann giggling and shoving at each other, not understanding the scene but electrified by it. Derwent's small, pugnacious face was puzzled above the frill of his shirt. Mavis waited by the door to see Nigel out, so immobile she looked like a waxwork, but she could hardly wait to get down to the kitchen with the news.

Six

A UNT HIGHAM'S first step in the management of events was to take her niece out for the evening. They went to a soiree where a man read the exciting new poetic drama *Marmion* by Walter Scott, and a lady sang appropriate songs.

It would have all been endurable except that any place without Nigel was a place without sun. George Vinton was there, or rather a something whose cravat seemed to be choking him every time he looked at her; this object was called George Vinton but otherwise had no meaning for her. When they returned to Brunswick Square, she expected to go to bed in suspense and lie awake all night, but Mavis said, "Mr. Higham would like for both you and Miss Hawthorne to come to the library, ma'am."

"Has Captain Gilchrist been?"

"Yes, and gone, ma'am."

Was he smiling when you showed him out? Jennie burned to ask. She stood in frightened, dry-mouthed silence, twisting the strings of her evening reticule. Mavis turned from taking Aunt Higham's mantle to take hers, and she submitted meekly; usually she didn't want help.

"Be off to bed with you now," her aunt said to Mavis, who bobbed and was gone.

In the library Uncle Higham stood on the hearth with his back to the fender, his hands clasped behind him under his coattails. He was, for him, effusive, a state which would pass for mild approval in someone else.

"The boy is perfectly sound. Not that he didn't tell me anything I

40

didn't know already, but he told it to me straight, and that's a good sign. His stepfather did well by him, and he's next in line for a considerable property in Scotland. No titles involved, but what is a title compared to solid property? Oh, I believe there's an earldom somewhere, but there are so many people between it and him that it's not worth mentioning."

However, he had mentioned it, and Aunt Higham must have been torn again between duty to her ward and to her daughter.

"Scottish earldoms," her husband pontificated, "are worth nothing unless they sit upon coal mines, and this one doesn't. The property in hand belongs to an older brother, and it's unlikely"—he harrumphed hard enough to cause a vibration in his jar of pipes on the mantel behind him—"that there will be a son born. . . . Those Highland landlords are showing signs of intelligence, turning all that empty space over to sheep. There should be something very nice for young Gilchrist in time. Very nice indeed." Uncle Higham rocked onto his toes and back to his heels. "In the meanwhile he has a promising career in the Army. We'll meet again for the formalities, of course, but I think we can safely assume"— another shattering *harrumph*—"a successful conclusion to the business." He nodded at Jennie, who was then kissed on each cheek by her aunt and told to go to bed because she needed her strength.

"The wedding will be at Saint George's in Hanover Square, of course," Aunt Higham said to her husband as Jennie was leaving the room. "I shall commence my lists tonight. I won't be able to shut an eye until I've done *something*."

All at once weary, Jennie was brushing her hair before the mirror on her toilet stand, observing herself by candlelight with unusual detachment, when Charlotte crept in. "I've been lying awake waiting for you. I saw them when *he* left. They were shaking hands, and Papa called him 'My boy' and clapped him on the shoulder." She giggled. "He had to reach up to do it, And I knew it was all right, Papa has consented. Oh, Jennie, aren't you excited? How can you *bear* it?"

"I don't know," said Jennie. The two girls hugged. Charlotte quivered in her arms, a bundle of fine silver wires.

"You know Mama! She'll have the wedding all planned out by tomorrow morning! May I be your bridesmaid, Jennie? *Please?* Has he kissed you yet? What was it like?"

"Yes, you may be my bridesmaid," Jennie said. "No, he hasn't kissed me yet."

"Not even when he proposed?"

But he didn't propose to me, Lottie, love. His mother did. There were warning signs of a fit of giggles, and she was afraid it would completely take her over if she allowed it. She said solemnly, as if announcing a death, "The park was really too public."

"Oh," said Charlotte in disappointment. "I should like to be proposed to in a forest glade or in a garden; at night, with moonlight and a sweet smell of flowers, and a nightingale."

"Perhaps it will be so for you, my darling," said Jennie. "Now go to bed before your mother catches you, or Mrs. Coombes."

"Nanny is snoring," said Charlotte, "but you're right about Mama. She'll think I'm feverish and dose me again." They kissed good-night, and she went out like a ghost in her childish white wrapper.

Alone, Jennie sat on the edge of her bed, shivering but not from cold, because a fire burned in her grate. She felt as if she'd been snatched by the great third wave, whipped around, beaten, half-strangled, half-drowned, and then tossed up on a foreign shore: the great Eugenia Hawthorne, who'd sworn to take charge of her own life. The simple ecstasy of seeing Nigel come into a room, of hearing his voice, of being in his arms when they danced, or of riding with him mornings in the park—it was all gone, stolen greedily by their elders. They hadn't had one kiss—even little Lottie was astonished by that—and already their future had been taken out of their hands, as someone would remove a precious object from a baby's fingers.

And if I wanted anyone, she wept, *it wasn't a soldier any more than a curate!*

The Blues seemed safe enough, as part of the household cavalry, but how could you be sure of anything? She'd heard the talk, some of it from him, of young men pulling all possible strings to be transferred into a fighting regiment. "Keen as mustard, those chaps. All cock-a-hoop to go fight Boney under Wellesley, you know. Dev'lish fine soldier."

Why hadn't she the courage to ask him then if *he* was keen as mustard and all cock-a-hoop to go?

I'm engaged to a soldier, she thought, *engaged by his mother and my uncle. And he could be killed fighting Bonaparte, and they'll have made me a widow before I've been married a year. Everything will have been arranged for me, even that.*

She cried herself to sleep. Once she awoke and muttered drunkenly,

"I want none of it, not even Nigel." She fell asleep again, comforted by the knowledge of her gold sovereigns. She would need them when she was cast out for her ingratitude.

But when they had the garden to themselves the next morning, even though she knew the children were staring down from the nursery windows, the simple ecstasy came back; it wasn't soap-bubble fragile after all. They kissed in a dark, shady nook between sooty laurels and the wall. A far cry from Charlotte's moonlit glade with a nightingale, she told him, and they laughed against each other's lips, and kissed again. It was as if she had always known how; the difficulty was in making themselves stop. . . . And perhaps he did not want to go and fight; how could a man want to make love and war both at the same time? If England were attacked, that would be different, but this Wellesley didn't need Nigel to defend Portugal and drive the French out of Spain.

She didn't ask him; she only hoped. In the meantime they were given the leeway allowed an engaged couple, in between his duties and her visits to the dressmaker, milliner, mantua maker, and shoemaker.

"I have so many new clothes already," Jennie protested to Aunt Higham. "You've already outfitted me completely. I need only a wedding gown."

"Fiddlesticks. You'll be an officer's wife now, a matron, not a girl. You must be dressed for the position. Has he said where the wedding trip is to be?"

Could there conceivably be something they weren't managing? Rather than admit that the wedding trip hadn't been mentioned to her, she said, "He wants to surprise me."

Aunt Higham snorted. "There'll be surprises enough without that one."

She appreciated not having to prepare Jennie for the events of the marriage bed, though she pretended to be shocked when Jennie told her she knew. Then she dropped the pretense. "I dread telling my own girls," she admitted. "I don't know what Charlotte thinks marriage *is* and where she came from. You and I were lucky to be country lasses."

Privately Lady Geoffrey gave Jennie some of the jewelry given her by Nigel's father. Officially her gift to the couple was Jennie's portrait, to join the other Gilchrist brides in the gallery at Linnmore House. She wasn't up on the fashions in painters, she said, but Bamber Raleigh knew a friend who was anxious to secure commissions for his godson. Jennie and Nigel were not knowledgeable either, but they looked at the painter's work and liked it, so the portrait was begun.

Now fittings were interspersed with sittings. Nigel attended when he could; otherwise the children's French governess went with her to the studio. She wore the bronze-colored riding habit, but it was agreed that she could hold the hat in her hand.

"You have a good head," the artist told her, "and it's natural for you to have it uncovered, as if you are a free spirit which needs to have wild, clean spaces in which to exist. . . . That hat is the silliest bit of frippery I ever saw, by the way."

He was the first artist she had ever known, a fat, untidy young man who talked easily with her as he worked. He was both unpretentious and unselfconscious. He asked her where in the north she had grown up, and what she told him inspired the background for the figure.

Of her two chaperones she preferred Mademoiselle, who did fine needlework from which she never lifted her eyes, and seemed occupied by her own thoughts. Jennie and the painter rambled on as if she weren't there. When Nigel came, he ranged uneasily about the studio like a restless horse in a box stall, or else he sat and stared unnervingly first at the artist and then at Jennie. At these times the artist didn't talk but whistled all the time under his breath as he worked, and Jennie was so overwrought by Nigel's proximity that she was given to sudden nervous starts and changes of color and temperature.

When it was just herself, the artist, and the Frenchwoman, the studio sessions were the most restful hours of that febrile time of preparation. Nigel and his mother approved the finished work; she was pleased with it and even more pleased when the artist told her she was the best subject he'd had so far.

"I believe you've brought me luck," he said. "I hope I've done the same for you."

"I'll bring my children to you to paint," she promised, laughing. Who needed luck when they had Nigel? "But then you'll be painting Royalty and won't have time for us."

"Don't be too sure of that," he warned her. "Just remember your promise."

Ianthe sent her a lace veil from Switzerland. Sylvia couldn't make the long journey from the north because she was pregnant again, but

Sophie came in care of a London lady who was returning home after spending Easter at a house near Pippin Grange. Sophie's gift was a pair of shellwork pictures she'd made herself. She brought a silver bowl from the cousins, and William and Sylvia sent her her father's old set of English poets, all in new leather bindings.

The two young girls were to be Jennie's bridemaids, and the Hampshire baronet would stand up with Nigel. It would be a quiet wedding, with a breakfast afterward at Brunswick Square. The insignificant Earl without coal mines had been sent an invitation as a courtesy, and being in London he had accepted. It took more than that to confound the Highams, who were not impressed by titles, but Charlotte and Sophie were all of a flutter. A baronet and an earl, *too*?

"He's a harebrained old nincompoop," said Nigel. "No, I take that back. Any hare is a positive genius compared to my dissipated and decrepit cousin. Let us pray," he said piously, "that he passes up the wedding breakfast."

Except for Sophie and the Highams, Jennie would have no one of her own to see her married. She had a moment of feeling like a virgin being prepared for a sacrificial altar so that her blood would bring in good crops or a total victory over Napoleon.

In that case, she thought, *they will erect a monument to me, something tasteful in marble, with wreaths and urns and great classical maidens half-draped. The Prince of Wales will place a wreath on their huge feet.*

"What are you laughing at, Jennie?" Sophie asked. "I came to tell you that Nigel's here. Isn't he beautiful? I love William," she said loyally, "but Nigel's like Apollo."

"Don't tell him," said Jennie. "There are quite enough women now telling him such things. How he's going to cut himself down to one woman's adoration is beyond me."

She went along the passage to the stairs, Sophie pattering behind her; Charlotte caught up with them, and the two whispered and chuckled, they had become Best Friends overnight. Sophie was a dark, sturdy child, already developing a bust. Beside her Charlotte looked as evanescent as a snowdrop.

Nigel had just come from a review in Hyde Park, and he dominated the foyer in his blue, scarlet, and gold. Derwent had escaped Mrs. Coombes and was wearing the black cocked hat with its red and white plumes; he practically disappeared under it, and the gauntlets nearly reached his shoulders.

"Why don't they make boots like yours in *my* size?" demanded a fierce treble from inside the hat.

"Don't take offense at this, old man," said Nigel, "but you're still a bit short for the household cavalry." He looked up and saw the girls on the stairs.

"Ladies," he said hollowly, and laid his hand over his heart, "if I was a poetical sort of fella, I'd know exactly what was the thing to say about two bright stars and the moon goddess."

"I think you do very well as it is," said Jennie.

They sat alone in the morning room, drinking coffee on the sofa before the fire, and he told her that he was resigning his commission and going to Scotland to become his older half brother's factor.

"I was going to take you there anyway for the honeymoon. Spring in the Highlands, what? Jolly! If the weather is fine, that is. It can be deuced bleak in the rain." He looked worried, and she put her hand on his fresh-colored cheek.

"Rain or snow, that needn't bother *us*. But is this a sudden decision?"

"Sudden, sudden! Ten days ago. Today was my last review." He took her hand from his cheek and kissed it. "The Mater said I should tell you at once. But I'm a coward, my angel. What if you had your heart set on being a colonel's lady?"

"Oh, Nigel!" She pulled her hand away. "How *could* you? If that's what you think of me, perhaps we're marrying far too soon. We don't know each other at all."

He looked stunned, and she relented, but she was thinking she'd been at least half-right. "Tell me about it."

"The Mater wrote them about the wedding, thinking Christabel would leap at any excuse to come back to London, and in return *I* got this rather confused letter written in old Archie's inimitable style, just the way he talks, telling me there'd been a clash with the old factor and he'd left. Grant's not that old in years, mind you, but he's always been there. Took over from his father. Decent chaps, both of them."

"What was the clash about?" Jennie asked.

"I don't know. It was with Christabel, I swear, not Archie. She wanted to raise the rents, perhaps. She has the fortune, so things must go her way . . . I don't care!" He was jubilant. "There's a house for us, and the fishing and the stalking are superb. You'll have your own horse to ride. It will make up to you for Pippin Grange."

"Oh, love," she whispered. "I can't believe it. *Scotland!* I never wanted to be a colonel's lady, and I'm so happy!" They embraced and kissed. Each time it was harder to separate; now there were voices in the hall, and they parted reluctantly, still holding hands.

In an attempt to be cool she said, "But do you know how to be a factor?"

"I know enough to do what they want me to do."

"Are they coming to the wedding?"

"Archie says the stramash with Grant has put Christabel under the weather. Her delicate nerves, you know." He grinned. "She's healthy as a horse, though not as good-looking as the worst of 'em. If anything's upset her, it's this wedding. She knows she's past foaling, but I'd swear she was hoping I'd die a bachelor."

"She's not going to like me then," said Jennie. "But there's no law that says everyone has to love Eugenia Hawthorne."

"Old Archie will. He'll be bowled over. He likes pretty girls, and you'll ornament the ancient pile. By heaven, it's been grim at Linnmore! Christabel has the servants call her Madame instead of Mistress. She's English in everything. She brought her own staff because she won't have Gaelic spoken in the house, and she pays them the earth to suffer the isolation."

He slapped his thigh. "That reminds me. I'm losing my man along with the commission. There aren't many good ones who want to leave the splendors and the females of London for the Scottish wilderness. I'll pick out a chap there and train him. What about a maid for you?"

"I've never had my own maid, darling. Tell me more about Christabel. She sounds dreadful."

"Well, if old Archie drops into the Gaelic when he's talking with a groom or a tenant who doesn't speak English, she's on him as if he'd uttered an obscenity or blasphemed the Holy Ghost."

"I detest her already," said Jennie. "Do *you* speak Gaelic?"

"I remember a bit from my early childhood, and later I was taken there on some long holidays, to keep me in touch with my heritage, don't you know? But some of the people have a little English."

"How will you get on with them as factor?"

"Swimmingly! I always did."

She could believe it. "I want to learn Gaelic," she said ardently. "I want to be able to talk to the people in their own tongue."

"Just don't let Christabel know you're doing it," he said. "She'll have fits. She'd have changed the name of the place if she could, but it looks English enough to suit her. Only she will call it *Linn*more, not Linn*more*. I doubt Archie told her that it's the Gaelic *linn* for 'pool,' and *mor* for 'big.' You'll see where it comes from."

"*Linn*more," she repeated as if it were a mystical incantation. "The Gilchrists of Linn*more*. Will that be us?"

"Yes, and we'll start a new dynasty. How would you like to be a matriarch?"

"Please, Capting, I'd like to be married first, Your Worship."

Seven

S EVERAL TIMES Jennie wondered uneasily if she should contribute her
sovereigns toward the expense of the wedding. In her rare moments
alone she often read Papa's letter, hearing his voice speak the words:

"This is for you to have and to hold, to use as you will. I wish it
could be for some startling, inexplicable, wonderful, irregular cause, some
bold stroke for a woman to make. In any case, it is not to be fribbled
away on fashions, on trips to Bath and Brighton. But if ever you or yours
are in need, your father will have put out his hand to help you."

No. This was not the time to use the sovereigns. She hadn't asked
for anything more than for her and Nigel to be joined by a parson, and
a family breakfast afterward. But Aunt Higham was stage-managing the
affair, and she was enjoying herself, and Uncle Higham went around
these days in a mood of Olympian benevolence. Whether it was because
an awkward young girl would soon be off his hands or he was genuinely
touched by young love and spring weddings, one accepted without question the gifts of the gods.

Her sovereigns were safe then, and the small quarterly allowance
from her mother would also come into her own hands. The only question
was whether she should tell Nigel about her gold hoard.

First things first. Get married, get to Scotland and settled in her own
house, and then make up her mind.

She dismissed her conscience.

Uncle Higham said Nigel's decision to give up his commission was
very sound. "Sheep will be the salvation of Scotland. Wool's always in
demand. Like wine, coal, and cotton [a few of the interests which sup-

ported his family in comfort in Brunswick Square]. The confounded Americans have lifted the embargo, and there's a monstrous big market waiting."

Aunt Higham was briefly disappointed, having seen Jennie as a colonel's lady, and good at it if only she could remember to keep her mouth shut. But Nigel came of the landed gentry, and even if the land happened to be in Scotland, she conceded that there were some very fine estates north of the Borders, and Edinburgh was a grand city, she had always understood.

The children were more loudly disappointed, the girls because he would no longer wear a uniform and would not even be married in one. Derwent was furious and would hardly speak to him at first. Nigel won him with an invitation to come to Scotland and learn how to fish for a salmon. "I shall come and fetch you myself," Nigel promised. "Just as soon as your arms and legs grow a little longer."

At intervals after that, Derwent, thinking himself unobserved, could be seen getting very red in the face, squeezing his eyes shut and gritting his teeth, in an effort to *grow*.

One night when Sophie came in to kiss Jennie good-night, she burst into tears, and Jennie rocked her in her arms as if she were still five.

"Darling, it's not the end of the world!"

"But it's so far away!" Sophie wailed.

"No farther than Pippin Grange is from London. Well, not too much farther. You travel north instead of south, that's all."

"But it's so wild up there! The Highlands are nothing like the Borders; they still have wolves and bears. The people don't speak English, and they're savage. They rose against the King!" She braced back, dark eyes staring to impress Jennie with this ultimate horror.

"Some, not all, and it was sixty-three years ago this month," said Jennie, "and you'll recall that Papa told us the poor devils who thought they were fighting for the true King were so viciously slaughtered that even a good many Englishmen thought it was too much blood altogether."

"But they hate the English for it! You won't be safe."

"Nigel's brother's wife is English. So are her servants, and as far as I know, they're bored, not afraid. Darling, I'm going to have a lovely house, with a drawing room and a garden, and I will have my own horse to ride. And I shall have you up for long visits and marry you to a handsome Highland gentleman." She looked over at Charlotte, curled up in the opposite chair. "There'll be one for you too, Lottie, love."

Charlotte sighed. "Whoever I get, I hope he has yellow hair like Nigel. And if he can't be an officer in the Blues, I'd like him to be a naval officer."

"Like Bobby Shafto," said Sophie, and they sang the song together, breaking up in cascades of laughter.

Everything had to be packed early to go to Scotland with them; they would be leaving after the wedding breakfast for the long drive to the Tilbury docks, there to embark upon *Minerva* for the voyage to Banff. This was Uncle Higham's gift; he was a partner in the new vessel, built to bring coal down from Scotland. On her maiden voyage the Nigel Gilchrists would be occupying one of the owners' staterooms.

The portrait would be sent later, when the artist thought it was dry enough to be crated and shipped to what he considered a soggy and freezing wasteland.

There were two new trunks for Jennie's possessions; she had never had so many clothes in her life. She herself packed the small old trunk that had come with her from Pippin Grange, starting out with her keepsake box, her books, the old robe and the slippers from Ebony, and, with less enthusiasm, her workbox. Her aunt then banished her, telling her to go back to writing thank-yous.

"You'll never put things as they should be, distracted as you are," she said, "and your warm things must be where you can find them quickly. It will be chilly on the water, and spring in the Highlands can't be told from winter, I hear."

When she'd heard about Scotland, she had quickly ordered underwear of Spanish lamb's wool, flannel petticoats, warm spencers, and cotton stockings. These were to go on top of everything else, as soon as the wedding gown was laid away.

Sophie and Charlotte helped wrap and pack the smaller wedding gifts, constantly marveling aloud to each other. There were so many things, most of them from people Jennie didn't know, that she was embarrassed. Aunt Higham took a tight-lipped satisfaction in the loot, but the girls gloated over the monogrammed silver tea and coffeepots, the silver sauceboats and candlesticks, the Spode china, the variety of tea sets; an ivory tea caddy inlaid with ebony; vases, Chinese figurines, paintings. The younger children were allowed to watch but not to touch, and Derwent was nearly overcome by the chessmen carved from Indian ivory, the horses' heads were so perfect. His clenched fists trembled with desire, and Jennie saw, and told him to touch all he wanted to.

Aunt Higham's gifts were many and practical: linens, blankets, pillows, and two eiderdowns. Lady Geoffrey had described the factor's dwelling as a grim, high, stone house, and she gave rich-colored hangings and cushions and a gold-garnished mirror with candle branches hung with crystal drops to brighten a dark corner. The house had the bare necessities of furniture but was soon to be ornamented with such frills as painted fire screens and lamps, a carved and gilded clock by Daniel Quare, a mahogany wine table fitted with its own crystal goblets, and tall japanned screens to keep off the drafts.

The sudden acquisition of so many *things* was overwhelming to Jennie. So was the whole business of preparing for a wedding; Nigel was seen only in snatches that were more exasperating than joyous. The whole household spun in a cyclone of energy that made the younger children very naughty, and Jennie secretly hated the abrupt drop from courtship into controlled chaos. How could love possibly survive it?

Everyone else seemed happy enough with it. There were new clothes all around; even Uncle Higham had a new suit made in which to give her away, and was seen to smile complacently when some especially handsome gift arrived. Nigel was pounced upon by Sophie and Charlotte the instant he appeared and was taken to see the latest. He always said obligingly, "My word!" no matter what it was. Occasionally he threw in something like "Very *distingué*," or "*Très recherché*, what?"

Once when Jennie was alone with him for a moment, she hugged his arm with both her hands and said, "Oh, Nigel, we're two babes in the woods being showered with gifts instead of leaves by a crowd of very peculiar robins. I supposed I may be house-proud one day and wear a lace cap indoors and cherish these things, but right now I can't see what they have to do with you and me."

"I know, my sweet chuck." He kissed her. "Pity that we're expected to behave like settled householders, ain't it? But that's only while they're watching us. Wait till we get to Scotland. How do you fancy being chased through the heather like one of those nymphs, wearing only a bit of gauze, which will come off in the escape?"

She pressed her face into his now-civilian lapel to stifle laughter while Aunt Higham greeted callers in the foyer. It was going to be all right; better than all right.

On the day before the wedding, with most of the packing done, all the fittings over, the wedding cake in the pantry veiled like another bride in protective gauze, there was a sudden lull. Aunt Higham retired to her room to rest, and the children were all taken by Mademoiselle to the birthday celebration of a young Higham cousin. Jennie asked Nigel to go with her to Tamsin's grave.

They walked, at her request; she had not had a long walk for days. London, the day before her wedding, was dank and gray, the sun a phantom through layers of dirty, stinking smoke. They bought lilies of the valley from a street vendor and went looking for Tamsin's grave in the crowded burial ground of a sooty little church on the edge of a slum. The older stones, blackened and illegible, toppled toward each other in such confusion one would think the bodies they marked had been buried in like confusion. A gravedigger found Tamsin's grave for them; he had dug it. There had been no room to put her beside her mother, he said.

It wouldn't have mattered to Tamsin, who'd had no time to mourn; from the moment her dear mother had been carried away from the sordid room, the child had been engaged in a battle to survive.

Carolus Hawthorne had taught his daughters that the body was nothing once the soul had gone, that it was pagan to make an altar of a grave; he'd like to have been buried in a corner of the orchard with no marker, and he had forbidden them to wear mourning.

Tamsin was surely free of her terrified little body, but Jennie was almost overcome at the sight of the name Thomasina on the stone. She gripped the lilies of the valley tightly, and her face went cold and still, as pale as the flowers in her hands.

Nigel's arm came around her waist. "Tell me about this," he urged gently.

"When I was miserable, she was so much more miserable, and she had reason to be. The very sight of her made me ashamed of my own weakness."

"She was only thirteen," he said, reading the stone. "What could a child of that age be so miserable about?"

"Nigel, don't you *know*"—she flared at him—"even if you're too fastidious to *think* about it, that all children aren't *nicely* raised? Don't you know about the little ones being sold to chimney sweeps, and sent to the factories and mines? And the children sold on the street for criminal *abuse*?"

Nigel looked as alarmed as if he'd embraced a wildcat, taking it for a tame kitten. He'd never seen her in a rage before.

"You know Dickon," she hurried on. "He takes your eye because he's bright and cocky; no one has beaten the spirit out of him. Dickon lives like a prince compared to most of them. When a child weeps with terror for fear she'll have to leave off being a general slavey because it's the first time she can remember of being *safe*—"

She whipped away from his arm so she could face him. "Nigel, would you rape a child?"

He recoiled at the impact of the word coming from her. "Good God!" he protested. "I wouldn't rape anyone!"

"Well, that's what this child had to fear. From her father."

"Good God," Nigel said again. He took out his handkerchief and patted his forehead. "So that's what it is. And you had to hear it."

"I could endure to listen to it; she was the one who had to live through it. Somebody had to hear it. I don't know if the woman who placed her with the Highams knew about it, or the minister who buried her. She was so ashamed she only told me one day because she was so desperate. One of the maids had spoken sharply to her, and she was terrified of being sent away. When she was sick, Aunt Higham told me how she'd come there. A good woman who used to be the parlormaid before she married asked for a place in the scullery for a motherless child, because the father was a drunkard and never in work. I didn't tell my aunt what I knew about the father."

"Poor little devil," Nigel growled. "I'd like to horsewhip the brute."

"One thing I'm grateful for," Jennie said. "Tamsin didn't know she was dying, but she did know that the maids were being kind, and Cook made special broth and puddings for her. She had her heaven then. I hope her father lives forever in hell." She put the fragrant little nosegay at the foot of the stone. "His hell has to be of his own making, of course. I hope he makes a good job of it."

"I say, are you an atheist?" he asked interestedly.

"No, but I wish I were. I'd like to think that evil flourishes by chance and not because of divine indifference. But God doesn't dispense rewards and punishments. On the seventh day He said, 'Well, there's your earth, make the best of it,' and He rested. And kept on resting."

"Was that before or after He extracted Adam's rib?"

"Oh, Nigel." She laughed weakly and leaned against him. "Keep your arm around me, please. People will think we're married already and you're being the uxorious husband."

"A *what*? It sounds improper."

"It means a foolishly fond husband."

"I'm a foolishly fond fiancé." He ducked his head and kissed her under the rim of her bonnet. If the gravedigger, excavating another small pit, noticed, he paid no more attention than he did to the birds that sang through the dirty smoke.

Eight

THEY EXCHANGED their gifts to each other the night before the wedding. She had a gold watchguard for Nigel, and he gave her a small diamond pendant on a delicate silver chain and tiny diamond eardrops like spangles of dew in the sunlight. Then he and the baronet (who had given them the chessmen) went off to a bachelor dinner held by Nigel's friends in the Blues, and his mother and Lady Clarke came to dinner at Brunswick Square. Jennie took Lady Geoffrey for a stroll in the garden while her aunt and Lady Clarke played backgammon; Uncle Higham and his whist cronies were playing their evening rubber in the lbirary.

"You must give Nigel an heir as soon as you decently can," Lady Geoffrey said. "So as to insure the possession of Linnmore. Otherwise one of those dissolute zanies in the Earl's family just might outlive the lot of you. Alcohol seems to preserve some creatures indefinitely."

At least she didn't say I should foal at once, Jennie thought. "Does it matter," she asked politely, "if it's a son or a daughter?"

"Not at all; a daughter can inherit, and of course her husband would change his name to Gilchrist." She patted Jennie's arm. "You're a good girl, my dear, and I'm happy for Nigel. Don't let Christabel bully you. Stand up for yourself as you did with me."

"Shall you come and visit?"

"I'm afraid not, with this wretched hip. The journey's too long."

"I'm sorry," Jennie said. Nigel's mother looked at her in the light from the French windows.

"I believe you mean it." She sounded surprised.

"I do," Jennie answered.

Lady Geoffrey gave her hand a little squeeze. "Ah, but you'll be coming to London!" she said. "Travel means nothing but fun to you healthy young things."

Jennie had never owned anything as subtly elegant as her wedding gown. It was sewn from gossamer-weight white silk tissue, embroidered with silver thread in diagonal stripes, simply cut with a gently rounded neck, and fell straight from the high waistline. Her slip, stockings, and long white gloves were silk; her slippers, white satin. She wore Nigel's diamonds.

Aunt Higham's maid had arranged her hair in Grecian ringlets, and Ianthe's veil was pinned into place and crowned with a wreath of white silk rosebuds and green leaves. She endured the whole grooming progress as if it were happening to someone else; she felt feverish, she saw her flushed cheeks in Aunt Higham's cheval glass, her aunt and the maid smiling proudly behind her, and she wondered with resignation and near hope if she were going to fall ill on the way to the church and thus postpone the wedding indefinitely.

She did not fall ill on the way to Hanover Square. Attended by Sophie and Charlotte in pale pink muslin, she was given away by an almost genial uncle in a Spanish blue coat (which clashed with his rufous coloring) to a handsome stranger in a forest green one, and they were married by a bishop who was a cousin of the bridegroom's stepfather. It was all rather like something one might have imagined in one's bath. In no time at all it was over, the register signed, and they were back in Brunswick Square, drinking champagne (probably smuggled) given by one of her uncle's friends. She thought she couldn't eat a mouthful of food, but she did not want to set off drunk on her honeymoon, so she did her best.

George Vinton was there, in clerical black for once. It looked like mourning, especially when he got a little tipsy and teary. The Earl had insisted on attending the breakfast and became drunk quite early on and was taken away by his entourage of two, protesting that he hadn't kissed the bride.

The baronet, the nineteen-year-old country squire, was very popular with the bridesmaids. The small children saw the cake cut, were given theirs, and were swept away by Mrs. Coombes; they came to Jennie's room to say good-bye when she was ready to leave. The little girls hugged her, tearfully promising to remember everything she'd taught them and all the songs and stories. Derwent scowled the whole time, furious with the world, but when she kissed his cheek, he flung his arms around her neck, squeezed hard, and then bolted, red-faced, from the room.

Sophie and Charlotte wept but enjoyed it. They had make a pact to catch the bouquet together and had accomplished it with a little help from Jennie, who had been forewarned. Now they told her they meant to have a double wedding. Then they hurried back downstairs to the baronet. Aunt Higham had seen to the disposal of the wedding gown and the strapping of the last trunk to go down the back stairs. Now she and her husband waited for Jennie in the passage outside her room.

"God bless you and keep you, love," her aunt said, embracing her. "You're as sweet a bride as your mother was." She was wet-eyed. "Write to me," she commanded.

"I shall, dear Aunt Ruth." She gave her hand to her uncle.

"Thank you for all you have done for me, Uncle," she said. "I can never forget it."

He gave her a ponderously sober nod and didn't release her hand. "Eugenia, I shall tell you what I shall tell each of my daughters when the time comes. If anything goes amiss, you will always be welcomed back."

She was profoundly moved, but she knew better than to show it. She said solemnly, "Thank you, Uncle Higham."

Nigel came along the passage in his traveling clothes, and he and Jennie went down the back stairs to the kitchen to receive the congratulations of the servants. Nigel tipped them all handsomely, including Tamsin's successor. Then they went through to the foyer and were swept out on a tide of blessings and good wishes. Nigel's cavalry friends threw rice over them, and the younger children called from an upper window, "Good-bye, good-bye!"

About to step up into the maroon barouche, Jennie suddenly balked, freed her elbow from Nigel's hand, and walked around to the horses' heads. "Good-bye, David, good-bye, Jonathan," she said. She kissed each nose.

The coachman grinned. After seven months he had suddenly become a human being. "Good luck to you, Missis," he said, "and you too, Captain, sir."

Nine

I T WAS an idyllic sail down the Thames aboard *Minerva*, on immaculate decks under new canvas. Exhausted and at peace, Jennie and Nigel rested in the spring sunlight, wrapped in their traveling cloaks against the fresh breeze that filled the sails. There was an older couple aboard; the man was a Scottish associate of one of Uncle Higham's partners. They were on deck, too, to watch the green land slip by on either side and the other shipping large and small, but they left Nigel and Jennie to themselves.

Minerva entered the North Sea, and the idyll ended. Though Jennie had grown up at the edge of the North Sea and had often been soaked in its surf and its fogs, she had been on the water only in the finest summer weather, in their old rowboat whose leaks they could never stop so that someone had to keep bailing. Nigel was no more of a deep-water sailor than she was. They managed to eat dinner with the captain and the Sinclairs and to respond to the toasts that were drunk to them, but the sight of the lamps swinging in the gimbals was too much for Jennie. She retired with dignified thanks, trying not to clutch Nigel's arm too obviously. They reached their stateroom and collapsed on their berths, from which Jennie rose with a strangled cry to vomit into the chamber pot, with Nigel holding her head.

It was their first real intimacy. After that he bolted for the deck and lost his own dinner.

They spent most of the wedding trip being seasick. A stewardess had been engaged for this voyage to attend to Jennie and Mrs. Sinclair, but she'd overestimated her own capabilities and was of no use to them from the first night on. Mrs. Sinclair, a nimble little body whose stomach was apparently made of iron, moved briskly between the stewardess and the Gilchrists, dispensing brandy, broth, and advice.

"Yon lass below is far worse than you are," she told Jennie. "If she reaches Banff alive, she'll do well." She was helping Jennie brush her hair in a comparatively quiet interlude when Nigel had gone feebly out on deck.

"None of us will reach Banff alive," Jennie said weakly.

"It's not that bad! I've seen it much worse. Besides, while you can think of nothing but your stomach, you aren't worrying about French ships."

"I wasn't worrying about them in the first place," Jennie protested. "But I wouldn't care if they sank us right now."

Mrs. Sinclair laughed and said, "Ye'd drown that bonny lad of yours, too, just to ease yourself?"

"Believe me, Nigel wouldn't care either," Jennie assured her.

She and Nigel slept in separate berths, when they could sleep. In any case the berths were too narrow for two; Nigel was crowded when he was alone in one. The imminence of spasms of nausea if one moved too quickly precluded the mere thought of lovemaking. The only caresses were comradely gallantries like the fetching of a wet washcloth to cool a feverish face, tenderly removing a victim's shoes, and loosening the clothing after a tottery session on deck.

"We're passing your coast," Mrs. Sinclair told Jennie, but she didn't care.

The illness tapered off as wind and seas dropped and *Minerva* rode more easily. Appetites revived; they wanted more than beef broth and thin porridge. Very early one morning they were on deck to look at Scotland in the sunrise across pale blue water scattered with brilliants. Mrs. Sinclair pointed out Slains Castle on the cliffs among green fields, the old granite house honey-colored in the aureate light. A little farther on the surf played harmlessly in and out of the Bullers of Buchan, long chasms worn deep into the cliffs. They passed the ancient fishing town of Peterhead and moved on cautiously well off a long sandy shore studded with reefs and crags; the helmsman recited a distressing litany of lost ships' names.

They rounded Kinnairds Head outside Fraserburgh into clouds and showers, with just enough wind to carry them on to Banff. In the rain the royal burgh was a blurred huddle of grays, browns, and black between its white sands and the brilliant green of the surrounding land, and the harbor was full of shipping. The biting chill and damp didn't discourage Jennie; she had known such Mays in Northumberland, and she had the clothes for them, thanks to her aunt's insistence on the lambs' wool underwear and flannel petticoats. She felt better than well after the long sickness; she was in tearing spirits, like Nelson when he raced around that paddock as fast as he could go on a spring morning.

Alone for a few moments, watching Nigel as he stood talking with Mr. Sinclair, she remembered as if down a perspective of years how he had first appeared to her. Now again he shone new-minted for her, this time against the bleak, soaked background of the old town, and the sight of him thus was like the return of the sun; Bel fires were called for, to celebrate. *But in between we have seen each other at our worst,* she thought. *Demoralized with nausea, weakened beyond shame. And if he loved me as he tended me the way I loved him when I was struggling to get his boots off and not vomit all over him, then we have nothing to fear.*

They ate dinner with the captain and the Sinclairs that night, the first real meal since they'd begun the voyage. The captain, a Yorkshire man, joked about the way they'd spent their honeymoon. They slept well all night, and Jennie complained that it wasn't natural to have the floor flat and level underfoot. The stewardess brought them tea and hot water in the morning for the first time. She was very white, with dark violet circles under her eyes.

"How will you get home again?" Jennie asked, thinking she'd leave the ship as soon as she could.

"The same way I got here, ma'am," the girl answered with spirit. "If I had the money, I still wouldn't travel overland. Better the devil you know than the devil you don't."

"You mean you'd risk nearly dying of seasickness?" Nigel said.

"It might be I'd stand it better, sir. Besides, the cook has been good to me." Color stained her pallor, and Nigel teased her about it. He gave her a tip, which she refused at first, saying she'd been of no use to them, but he waved her out in the grand manner.

"Love goes where it's sent," he said, "even into a—forgive the barracks room talk, my love. You won't hear any more of it, I promise you."

"I've heard that old saw before, and I think it was around the barnyards before it ever reached the barracks. I'm glad to see that you can shave yourself. I thought you might have to have a valet do it for you, and our marriage would become a triangle."

"If anyone's going to cut my throat, I'd rather be the one."

"Oy, it's a rare treat to watch you, Capting, sir," she said. He grinned and nicked his chin.

"First blood to you."

"Oh, Nigel!" She was upset. "Is it deep?"

"No, it is not, but don't watch me. It's unnerving. I want so much to swoop down on you, my hand's trembling. I shall be slashed like a Heidelberg student."

They were seen off with a hearty breakfast and the good wishes of the captain and the first mate. Nigel had expected to hire a carriage to take them to Inverness, and a wagon to move their goods, but the Sinclairs were being met by their own chaise-and-four, and invited the Gilchrists to ride with them. Sinclair himself picked a man to transport the gear.

"He's a good man. He'll not take his own time or cheat you."

The showers had passed in the night, so when they drove out of Banff, the sun was burning through the thinning mists and turned slate roofs to polished silver, blindingly bright. Old stone took on the lustrous nap of fur or velvet. The broad Moray Firth opened out on their right, changing from pewter gray to marbled green and blue and white.

"It's lovely country where you're going," Mrs. Sinclair said, "but wild."

"Much wilder a hundred years ago," her husband said. "There's law and order in the hills now, except for the whisky-smuggling, but they consider that their God-given right," he added dryly. "If they've a safe place to hide a still, then it must be meant for them to have a still. And who's to begrudge them besides the excisemen? There's no doubt that Scotland has profited commercially from union with England, but the profit doesn't go very deep."

The combination of Jennie's greedy interest and his being on Scottish soil again loosened his tongue like wine.

"When you see the dispossessed, you will see it all. They're turning them out for sheep. Evicted off lands where their forefathers lived in time out of mind. Many times it's been fertilized with their ancestors' blood."

"Now, Roddie," said his wife, "it's a fine day, and these young folk—"

"There were abuses in the clan system, certainly," he said to Jennie. "A lunatic here and there, abusing his life-and-death powers, and his people with nowhere to turn. But a man nurtured with the knowledge of his responsibilities is a far different man from one who is simply a landlord."

She said quickly, "But it isn't that way at Linnmore, is it, Nigel?" The men sat opposite the women, riding backward, and he smiled across at her, a caress with his eyes.

"No, Mistress Gilchrist, it isn't."

Mrs. Sinclair laughed like a girl. The three of them were ready to keep a light mood; the firth was blue, the sun now shone with a rare unclouded splendor, the northern chill couldn't blight the exuberance of the new greens. Only Mr. Sinclair resisted.

"It's fine, the sheep," Mr. Sinclair said. "We need wool and mutton, too. But no need to throw helpless folk onto the roads or across the seas. There's room for all! It's a wicked thing when a glen where once hundreds of souls lived now belongs to six hundred sheep, two shepherds, and three dogs."

She wished she were sitting next to Nigel, so she could put her hand through his arm and draw from the contact the assurance that the Highlands were all she had dreamed them to be: wild, free, and uncorrupted. She was defensively angry with Mr. Sinclair; she wanted to tremble with indignation that he should so abuse her hopes.

Deliberately she turned to Mrs. Sinclair. "You must come to see us at Linnmore. I shall write you when the house is settled."

Mrs. Sinclair nodded comfortably.

"And the ministers are hand in glove with the lairds," said her husband. She leaned forward and gently touched his hands, folded over the head of his stick.

"There's nothing you can do about it, my lad."

"It's an ill thing to exchange men for sheep, and they've barely begun. Before they've done, the Highlands will be a wilderness ridden with ghosts." He sat back in the corner, his face turned to the window, his black shoulder cutting them off as if he were repenting his eloquence.

Mrs. Sinclair told them what they were passing, and insisted upon a stop at Elgin to stretch their legs and show Jennie the cathedral.

One felt that no human voice should be raised in the silence among the magnificent ruins. Battered, broken, given over to birds and little wild four-footed things, it rose in scarred grandeur toward heaven as its builders had intended. The successive destroyers, beginning with the Wolf of Badenoch in 1390 and ending with Cromwell's men, were dust now, but the cathedral still stood.

Nigel had been brought here once as a child. "There was an old man who could give you the whole story, chapter and verse, but all that stayed with me was the Bloody Vespers, when the Inneses and the Dunbars had an infernal row during a service. I always hated being dragged to church, and I thought it would be topping to have a battle instead of a sermon."

Mr. Sinclair, who had been gloomily poking around with his stick, said, "Aye, it would be an improvement on some of the sermons I've had to endure."

"They were great glovemakers in Elgin," Mrs. Sinclair said. "Saint Crispin is the patron saint of shoemakers and glovers. There he is, knocked about a bit, and here he is again."

Jennie hardly heard her. She was reading an epitaph on a tomb:

> THIS WORLD IS A CITE
> FULL OF STREETS &
> DEATH IS THE MERCAT
> THAT ALL MEN MEETS
> IF LYFE WERE A THING
> THAT MONIE COULD
> BUY. THE POOR COULD
> NOT LIVE & AND THE RICH
> WOULD NOT DIE.

Who had composed this cynical epitaph? The man who lay in the tomb? There was nothing pious, reverent, or hopeful about it. It appealed to her, yet it gave her a touch of the cold grue, and Nigel was too far from her, walking away down a long grassy aisle.

She went to him once, trying not to run.

Ten

T HEY DINED on fresh salmon at an inn in Elgin where Mr. Sinclair was well known. He announced that the Gilchrists were his guests.

"Oh, come, sir," Nigel protested. "It's too much. You're already carrying us in comfort to Inverness."

"Silence, lad." Sinclair lifted his glass toward Jennie. "Let us drink to the bride."

His wife winked at Jennie and said, "And may your husband never cease to astonish you even after thirty years."

Thirty years! It was more than her present lifetime. *We'll be grandparents then,* Jennie thought. She could not imagine it. Thirty years with Nigel. *Bliss.*

They drove on toward Inverness. The Sinclairs drowsed; Nigel and Jennie smiled at each other, looked away, were drawn back again, not able to touch except with their eyes and their low voices as they called each other's attention to some sight along the road or out on the firth.

There was more traffic on the way now. Sheep and cows accompanied by drovers and dogs. Riders on horses or garrons, the sturdy Highland ponies; carriages and carts, farm wagons. Walkers: those who looked as if they had errands, and the others who looked as if they lived on the roads. Were these the dispossessed? She didn't want to know, yet she *had* to know, to put her mind at rest, to convince herself that they were like tinkers, who chose that life.

Mr. Sinclair roused from his nap and talked about the Findhorn Sands off to the right, where Findhorn Bay opened to the firth. The sands were devouring everything; they had swallowed a house in one night, pouring themselves through doors and windows.

Jennie gazed out at a new party of walkers, and some of them looked up into the chaise without humbleness. This was a ragged group, possessing a few goats and some thin small black cattle. They carried bundles on their backs, and iron pots dangled atop the loads. There were some babies in arms or riding shoulders or hips. Several of the old people were lame and used crutch sticks, and the seams were dug deep in their faces. They were making such an effort that they had no use or concern for her, and she felt herself blushing with shame at her own comfort.

When the chaise had rolled on past them, the rested horses trotting happily toward their home stable in Inverness, she tried to forget what she had seen or at least to assure herself they had been people of the roads who would have fought any other way of life.

Mrs. Sinclair said, "This is Macbeth's country, you know. Duncan was murdered in the old castle of Inverness, and Cawdor still stands. Of course, Shakespeare was more than a wee bit astray, but then what can you expect from a Sassenach?" She laughed and patted Jennie's knee. "We don't hold that against you, lassie. But Macbeth was a *good* king, you know."

It wasn't until they were passing Culloden Moor that she fell silent, as if the influences here were too strong even for her, and her husband sank into deep gloom until they were well out of the area.

After that the first glimpse of the old gray town of Inverness roused them all up and sped the horses. Mr. Sinclair shed ten years and began telling Nigel about the Caledonian Canal that was to provide ships with a safe, smooth passage from the western seas through the Great Glen to the Moray Firth, saving them the often deadly voyage around Cape Wrath. For Jennie, Mrs. suggested dressmakers and milliners and praised the Northern Infirmary.

"Aye, the town's grown a bit since Old King Brude of the Picts had his fortress here and Saint Columba himself stood outside its wooden gates. We've had all the kings and the cutthroats. Cromwell, and Bonnie Prince Charlie (but all he did was blow up the castle), and then Butcher Cumberland came after Culloden, the monster that he was. How the poor old town suffered then."

"Everything looks serene and charming now," Jennie said.

"It's a grand town to live in," said Mrs. Sinclair. "Make your man show it all to you and take you out to Loch Ness. You might get a blink of the Monster, though it's no horror. It's never done a body harm; it just wants to be left in peace and quiet, poor beast."

Addresses were exchanged, and good wishes, and they were set down at the Caledonian Hotel in Inverness.

Jennie washed her hair and soaked herself in a tin bath before a glowing coal fire in the grate. It was her first hot bath since the morning of the wedding: huge sponge, rich lather of Pears' soap . . . She'd done the best she could aboard the ship, but nothing, absolutely nothing, could compare with the embrace of all the hot water you wanted and all the time in which to parboil yourself gently, then to rise like Venus from the foam to the embrace of thick towels in a warm room. She hoped Nigel in the next room was enjoying his bath as much.

They hadn't ordered a meal, only baths. The curtains were drawn against the sunset light, windows shut against street noises. The broad bed with lavender-scented linen: what would it be like, their nakedness together in those sheets? Sylvia had prepared her for some discomfort but said it would all be worth it and then had added with blunt northern honesty, "If you're lucky."

Jennie understood. She remembered the talk around the washhouse when Mary Ann's sister came to help with the washing. Jennie had been fifteen or so, and Mary Ann's daughter was newly married. She was not much older than Jennie. They had played together, picked daisies and currants for Mary Ann's winemaking, and then all at once Violet was "walking out"; was betrothed and unspeakably important about it; was *married*, and Jennie left back in childhood, while Violet was to be mistress of her own little household with the son of Martyn, the shepherd.

The morning after the wedding Jennie had gone out to help wash the blankets by treading on them in a wooden tub of sudsy rainwater. She'd heard Mary Ann's voice before the woman knew she was there, and the anguish in it had stopped her short.

"She's been used something cruel, good little lass that she is, and never one to be caught out under the hedges. Yon stallion was gentler with the mares than Jem's been with the child. Hardly able to move in the morning she was, and she crawled around to get his breakfast, and as soon as he was away to his work, she was away home across the fields, crying out about the hurt and the blood. Shouldn't wonder if he's damaged her."

Had Jem *beaten* her? Jennie wondered in horror. The sister groaned and sighed in sympathy, and Mary Ann said, "My Will was in a rare old rage, said he'd take him out and cut it off!"

Cut *what* off? . . . Then she'd been discovered, and Mary Ann had driven her away in a fury inexplicable at the time.

What was even more inexplicable was the fact that Violet had gone back to the man who'd used her something cruel and drawn blood. She'd tried to get her father to interfere, but he would not, and Ianthe told her to forget it; it was none of their business.

But when Violet was with child, and showing it, she was placid and smug, walking with her arm in Jem's to church or across the fields of an evening to call on her parents or his. When the baby was born, they both appeared stolidly pleased with it, and from the way Mary Ann and Will acted toward their son-in-law one could almost believe that outcry in the washhouse had never happened.

Jennie tightened now at the prospect of pain, but she had Sylvia's word that everyone didn't start off like Jem and Violet. She rose and stepped out of the bath onto the fleece put there for the purpose and dried herself. They had not yet seen each other without clothes; she hadn't even seen herself completely undressed ever since they sailed on *Minerva* and the seasickness had begun. Mrs. Sinclair had suggested she'd be more comfortable in a nightgown, but at times she'd been afraid they'd be wrecked and she'd be tottering to the lifeboat in only a bit of cambric. Taking off her shoes, her dress, and her stays was as far as she would go. Nigel shed his cravat and shirt at times, but he was always ready to make a sudden dash out on deck.

Oh, we were a pair all right, she thought. Orphans of the storm. The next long journey must certainly be overland.

She put on a fresh lawn nightdress and a matching peignoir with narrow lace frills at the throat and cuffs and tied with yellow satin ribbons. She rang for the maids to take away the bath, and while she waited, she walked about the room, brushing her damply curling hair. The Grecian ringlets had long gone; she hadn't liked them anyway, she'd hardly known herself with their dangling and tickling around her forehead and ears.

The girls bailed the bath and carried it away. She wondered if they guessed how newly married she was; a nightgown and a frilly peignoir before sundown, no supper ordered—they probably knew it all. She was not embarrassed. She could hardly understand their accents, but they had a solid country look that was familiar, and they were merry in their courtesy toward her, as if they were all equals.

They had lighted some candles, and she walked back and forth with her shadow for company. As the wedding had become unreal once it was all over, now the sea voyage had moved into the realm of things that had never happened.

Nigel came silently into the room behind her back, when she was standing before the mantel looking down at the fire.

"Jennie," he said in a low voice. She turned around and saw him outlined in the candlelight. So must some supernatural lover have appeared to a girl who cast ancient spells in her room at midnight. There was a story like that; the girl had been sorry forever after.

But Nigel in a blue dressing gown was no demon lover. He'd held her head while she was sick, and she'd held his, which was hardly the stuff of Gothic terrors. Now he came to her in unsmiling silence, picked her up, and carried her to the bed. He laid her down on it and began to untie the yellow satin ribbons. She didn't take her eyes off his face. It crossed her mind that he must be experienced about this; without watching his hands, she knew they weren't fumbling. The peignoir was laid open, and she was lifted, now helping slightly, so he could get the sleeves off her arms. Her nightgown was peeled off over her head, his hands firmly guiding and suggesting her own motions. She heard him catch his breath. Then he said crisply, "Turn over," and she did, so that he could take away the peignoir from under her.

She lay passively on her side, away from him, but if her skeleton lay quiet within her flesh, it was the only part of her that was. He knelt on the bed and kissed her shoulder, down her back, the rise of her hip. It was all she could do not to roll over, put her arms around his neck, and draw him down to her. The impulse startled her. *Am I a wanton?* But it was as if she had always known it was there.

"*Jennie,*" he whispered. He turned her on to her back. There was a glisten like tears in his eyes. Then he straightened up, took her peignoir away, and tossed it onto the chair. She stretched like a cat, delighting in her own nakedness and his viewing of it. Yes, she was a wanton, and who'd have guessed it?

He stood looking down at her. "You'll not need much coaxing."

"No." Her voice trembled but not with fear.

He began to undo his robe. "Shall I blow out the candles?"

"Not yet. I want you to keep looking at me. I want to look at *you.*"

"Are you sure?" His smile was endearingly doubtful.

"I'm sure."

He turned from her as he took off the robe and threw it over her clothes in the chair. The sweep of his back from shoulders to the narrow waist and small buttocks was beautiful; his legs were long, smooth-muscled, neither bandy nor spindle-shanked.

Then he came to her, and for an instant her breathing stopped altogether. How could there be enough room in her for *that*? But Sylvia had accommodated William and said it was good.

"What are you thinking, love?" Nigel said huskily. "I shan't hurt you. I'd die rather than hurt you."

"I'm not afraid," she said.

"I'll leave one candle. You're too beautiful to love in the dark."

"So are you." She held out her arms to him, wishing she could take him into her at once. She was unprepared for the sensuous shock of flesh against flesh and his hands stroking her body, and for the freedom to run her hands over his shoulders and sides, and over his chest, and down to the flat, hard middle where the soft yellow hair began to thicken. She floated on a summery sea of exquisite sensations that came rippling one after the other, and no end to them. Drunkenly she thanked those upon whose bodies he'd learned how to make love to his wife. But how had she learned to make love to him? There was no doubt that she was a born wanton, and nobody had ever guessed. She laughed against his mouth, and when she did, she felt his tongue slip in, feeling for hers. His hand went from her hip across her lower belly and between her legs. Her breast rose against his, she sighed against his lips, and her legs fell open to him.

It was a long night. She wished for it to be a week of night. Sometimes she opened her eyes and saw the unsteady light from the candle trembling over unfamiliar walls and ceiling, and had the impression that this room existed solely for them in a tower all alone at the top of the world. She rushed past pain, holding Nigel with arms and legs. She remembered him saying over and over in her ear, like a prayer, "Oh, my God, my God."

Afterward they lay still joined, him half on her, while their heartbeats slowed, and they sank into a near sleep, glued to each other by sweat and their embrace. When he roused up and cautiously withdrew himself, she felt a pang that was more than physical. Why could they not have slept together as one creature?

He blew out the guttering candle, then lay down and pulled her against him so that they slept spoon-fashion for the rest of the night.

They were awake at dawn; Nigel had ordered an early breakfast, and the hot water would arrive before that. Her nightgown had been left under her, sparing the sheets, and she bundled it deep into the bottom of her bag. She would wash it herself when they got home.

She might be tender in spots, but it had been worth a week of seasickness. If she was a wanton, she was proud of it; she could meet Nigel's speculative eye without a blush, and then they had a fit of laughter.

"Sylvia never said anything about fun," she remarked over the finnan haddock.

He raised an eyebrow. "Apropos of what?"

"I was thinking aloud. Do you really like marmalade on your roll with *fish*?"

"Have to have it. It's Scotland, so marmalade at breakfast. It's like the wine of the country. . . . Regarding last night, my love. The popular conception is that only a man's mistress should behave like that."

"Do you disapprove?"

"When I can have a wife and mistress in one body? And how does the body fare this morning?"

"I'm glad I needn't ride astride to Linnmore."

"No riding a cockhorse to Banbury Cross, what?" He laughed uproariously, throwing himself back in his chair, then jumped up and came around the table and took her face in his hands. "Oh, my sweet Jennie, you don't know how happy you make me. I knew the minute I laid eyes on you that day that I had to have you."

"I knew, too," she said. "I went home with my head spinning." She pressed his shoulders through the stuff of his shirt as if to be sure he was really there. "Nigel, it took so *long* from that day, but now it all seems like the twinkling of an eye."

Eleven

A WAGON from Linnmore was waiting at Inverness to carry their gear, and the Linnmore chaise took Nigel and Jennie and their necessary personal luggage, since the wagon would not reach the estate for several more days.

They were two days driving north, stopping frequently to rest the four horses. They rode through old stone towns and along empty roads where ruined castles watched with dead eyes from barren hilltops. Occasionally there was a living one, with the master's flag whipping in the wind from a tower showing above surrounding trees. There was not much woodland except around these great houses or in young plantations set out on otherwise bleak land by forward-looking proprietors. Occasional fishing villages huddled on the shores like clusters of winkle shells on kelp.

Nigel kept Jennie entertained by telling her everything he knew about the places through which they passed. In Strathpeffer there were chalybeate springs which the local people claimed could cure anything but death itself. In the Ferrindonald region the whisky smuggling had the excisemen half-mad with frustration. The chaise stopped to allow a funeral procession to pass them: dour, slow-pacing men carrying and following a coffin. Nigel, the coachman, and the lad riding postilion stood on the roadside with their hats held reverently against their breasts.

"That coffin's as likely to be as full of whisky as a corpse," Nigel said, keeping a long face.

"Aye," the coachman answered mournfully. "Did you see the minister with his white bands and all? If he's a clergyman, I'm John Knox himself."

His name was Iain Innes. He was only up to Nigel's shoulder, bandy-

72

legged, gray-headed; his brown face full of creases, but he had the eye and the step of a boy. He seemed to be enjoying the wedding journey as much as the bride and groom did. The postilion was his son, Dougal, a freckled redhead without much to say, but an incandescent grin. He sang or whistled while he rode.

Gorse blossoms captured the sunshine on open slopes; cattle grazed on rich pastures. Everything was lustrous with early May; even the showers sweeping down from the mountains were over in a quick gemmy sparkle.

Jennie was charmed with the Highland people so far, the easy voices and lilting accent, the good manners she met wherever they stopped to rest themselves and the horses. They spent the night in an ancient seacoast town dominated by a Celtic saint of whom she had never heard. They wanted to make love, after brushing arms and holding hands all day, but they felt crowded and public in the small inn. They could hear too plainly the voices of the two men in the next room, drunkenly arguing the long-dead Jacobite cause. One of them suggested that if Napoleon conquered England, he might return a Stuart to the throne. The other burst into tears about all the braw laddies away in yon papist country fighting English wars for a German Geordie.

"Someday," he prophesied between hiccups, "the Sassenachs will come crying for Hielan soldiers for another war, but there'll be none left. What has not been killed already will be emigrated and never come home again." He stopped, evidently struggling with his emotions; then words broke free. "It's not the 'Forty-five that's our doom; it's the sheep!"

At the first of the discussion Nigel and Jennie, lying in bed, had been stifling their laughter against each other's flesh, turning it into tormenting kisses. But at the end of it they lay still, raked by the man's harsh sobs. His friend didn't speak for a time, then he said with rough tenderness, "Och, Calum, the Hielans will never die as long as you and me is in it."

"And you and me," Jennie whispered against Nigel's throat.

In the afternoon of the next day they turned away from the sea and drove inland. In the clear white light the hills continually changed shape and position, waves of cobalt and indigo washing up against the wall of mountains. These were still capped with snow and streaked with the tangled white threads of waterfalls. Bright-edged clouds reared up behind them and slowly moved across the sky.

The travelers met no one else on this road, not even a solitary walker.

They drove through a landscape of bog, moor, and patches of water catching the sky like shards of mirror. Sometimes there was a thatched stone cottage half-hidden in a fold of land, with a few goats about it. Once two children stood staring at the chaise, and Jennie waved, but one couldn't be sure if they were really children or dwarfs, or even flesh and blood under their dingy wrappings. They were like small stone images. She turned to call Nigel's attention, but his head was tipped back, and he seemed to be peacefully drowsing. Up on the box Iain Innes was whistling a tune in time with his son and the horses' gait. She wished she were up there with him, asking him questions; he'd have likely put a surname to the odd little beings and turned them back into human waifs. His common observations would have changed this setting into something ordinary. But supposing it was not ordinary to him but a haunted place, and he was whistling for courage up there?

I am tired, she thought, *and when I am tired, I am full of dread signs and premonitions.* She was foolishly relieved to see signs of peat cutting off to her left, laughed silently at herself, and shut her eyes to rest them.

Iain and Dougal Innes went on whistling. She slipped into a half doze. The journey had reached the point where it seemed to exist for itself alone. The purported destination now seemed more remote than when she had left England. She knew the name, but nothing more except that she would live in a tall stone house. In her uneasy half dream she saw the house like a jail, standing alone in a harsh volcanic landscape. Oh, yes, somewhere there was a deep pool, a black tarn on which no birds rested, in which nothing reflected and nothing lived.

She was being whirled helplessly along like a leaf on the wind by a robber bridegroom; no, a demon bridegroom. She was almost afraid to look at him through her lashes, for fear the transformation had begun, or had already happened.

She struggled to wake herself, welcoming the niggling irritation of common things, like ribbons scratching under her chin, and had she really needed the wool underwear? Whoever had said it wouldn't itch under stays lied.

She untied the ribbons and pulled off the hat. *I hope I haven't conceived this soon,* she thought in panic. *Not yet, please God. Let me have a year first. Well, six months anyway.* Why was she asking God? *He* had nothing to do with it.

She started to unbutton her pelerine, wishing she could get out and walk. Nigel's voice said, "Keep on undressing. I love it."

She forgot premonitions and panics when he took her in his arms as if they'd been separated by at least one large ocean, if not the whole world.

"What have you been worrying about?" He kissed her throat. "I've been watching you."

"That was very dishonorable of you, Capting. And I haven't been worrying. I'm tired of traveling, that's all."

"It won't be long now." He cuddled her against his chest. The chaise climbed a rise and began the descent on the other side. Nigel said exultantly, "We're on Gilchrist land now, by God!"

She sat up to see. They crossed a packhorse bridge over a roaring brown current just as a quick, hard shower blew down on them; when they drove through the village of Linnmore, the few people caught out in the wet were running for cover and paid little attention to the chaise rattling along the one street. As they passed through the small market square, with its tall stone Celtic cross, a stoutish man walking away from a shop stopped and ceremoniously raised his hat; rain pelted his white head, and he and Nigel bowed to each other.

"The Reverend Doctor Fitzroy Macleod." Nigel sat back, and the chaise went on. "You won't catch *him* running. God sent the rain, so take it and be joyful. No matter if there's a month of it."

At the other end of the village, set apart from the rest of the houses, the manse had for Jennie a Calvinist gloom. The square tower of the church was almost hidden behind massive old yews black in the rain.

They left the basin that held the village, and the horses' pace picked up. The sun came out, and the earth gently steamed; they traveled into a land of forested hillsides and high ridges, where great old pines stood black against luminous mists. Flooded burns came hurling down in white cataracts over glittering boulders, throwing rainbows of spray. Silvery pale birches climbed slopes where last year's bracken lay bronze and gold in death. Trembling with suspense, almost oblivious of Nigel's arm around her and his breath warm on her ear and cheek as he too looked out, she watched buzzards drifting on the wind against a broken blue and white sky and the black flight of a pair of ravens. Small birds flew up from roadside puddles as the horses passed.

The chaise rolled over another stone bridge above a stream deep in a ravine which would be a jungle of green in a few weeks; only the ubiquitous gorse, yellow as butter, was blooming now. It seemed to Jennie that she could hear the thunder of that unseen water through the noise of the carriage wheels and the horses' hooves on the stone. She felt a sharp regret at leaving it so quickly behind her; then, as Nigel kissed her earlobe, she remembered that the stream was on Gilchrist land and she was Mrs. Gilchrist. When she had her own horse, she could come back to this place and stand on the bridge and look down to that mysterious flood.

The road began a gradual winding descent into a broad valley. The forest ended and pastures began, and plowed fields, divided by dry-stone dykes. The encircling wall of hills dwarfed the stone houses and barns of the farms which they sheltered. Cattle grazed ankle-deep in the thick grass. Three big shire horses saluted the carriage horses as they went by, and were answered in kind by one of the four.

"What crops will be growing there?" Jennie asked about the tilled fields.

"I'm no farmer, my love. I suppose it will be barley, rye, and oats, of course! I know *that* much! Where would a Scot be without his oats?" He grinned and gave her a squeeze. "I'll have to learn, won't I? But I can already tell a cow from a horse, though. And *those* are sheep." He pointed to a small flock scattered across a broad field and halfway up a hillside. "Cheviots. The Great Sheep that'll put an end to the scrawny Highland beasts forever. They're tough, they're hardy, and they can make a man a fortune in meat and wool."

"I know about sheep," said Jennie. "Don't forget where I grew up. I hope Mr. Gilchrist isn't counting on that small flock to make his fortune."

"Those are only the beginning," he said. "The farmer back there is from the Borders, and he brought these with him. Look at those lambs!" he exclaimed. "Sturdy little beggars."

A farm servant trudging along the road touched his cap, and Nigel returned the salute with negligent courtesy, as if to the manner born. The prospect of all this, starting at the village, belonging to Nigel and their children, caused an upheaval in her stomach.

She had nothing of her own, but her children would have. She saw the lambs through a mist of homesickness and envy. The tiredness and apprehension she had felt earlier came over her like the enervating forerunner of illness; she felt as if she had expended herself so lavishly for so long, beginning with the first shattering sight of Nigel, that now she had no reserves left with which to experience anything but a leaden melancholy.

She couldn't let Nigel know. She lay back in his arms, shutting her eyes. "I can hardly wait till we're there," she murmured. "Just to know we're at journey's end."

He was kissing her face all over, gentle little kisses like a bird drinking. Did some men know these things naturally? She must ask him when she had recovered from this awful feeling.

Twelve

H E STRAIGHTENED and made a gesture, and she sat up and looked out past him. A long L-shaped farmhouse, much like those at home, sat at right angles to the road, and the farm wife and a girl were in the angle, surrounded by assorted poultry and several dogs. A kitten rode the woman's thick shoulder. She had a broad, very red, smiling face. The girl curtsied, but the woman waved, and Jennie waved back.

In the pasture beyond the barn, two ponies watched them the way the shire horses had done. One of them threw up its head with a shrill whinny.

"What is that farm wife's name?" Jennie asked.

"Elliot, I think. Christy Elliot."

"I like her," said Jennie. "Now tell me where the moors are. You did promise me a moor, didn't you?"

"Up there." He waved toward the rising land to the west. "You'll see." They drove between more cultivated fields and crossed another stone bridge over a placid stream that flowed silently between marshy banks, a mirror for the sky and the cattle that drank from it. Then the road entered a long avenue of beeches. The leaves were still so young they made a translucent ceiling over the roadway.

"These were set out by my great-great-grandmother," Nigel said. He was sitting forward now with boyish anxiety, watching for something. Jennie preferred watching *him*. She wondered if she'd ever get tired of that, but she couldn't imagine it.

The horses slowed, and Nigel opened the door and was out on the road almost before the wheels had stopped turning. He handed her out, saying urgently, "Look back the way we came. Look *back*." She obeyed, amused and curious.

"I'll just drive along a wee bit," Iain Innes said from the box. "Not to spoil the view."

Jennie heard the horses walking away along the sharp bend. She looked among the beech trunks for bluebells. In the new silence, birdsong rang among the treetops, and she thought she saw a greenfinch.

"*Now*," said Nigel. He turned her around and walked her forward.

"Linn Mor," he said.

It was not the black tarn seen earlier in her nighmarish drowsing. Small winged insects danced above the sparkle and shimmer; three swallows came down on them and flew off again, swooping low over the twinkling yellow heads of the daffodils growing thickly on the far side. Beyond the flowers a long lawn rose to a red granite mansion of many windows, chimneys, gables, cornices, and bays. What softened it in Jennie's eyes, and even gave it a kind of ponderous grace, was the forested hill rising behind it in a cloudlike mass of fresh greenery, accented with dark firs.

Nothing moved about Linnmore House. No smoke trickled from any chimney that Jennie could see; no shadows shifted behind a tall window; no cat or dog sunned on the broad steps leading to the imposing front door. From here there was not the faintest hint that stables and other outbuildings existed.

"Look," said Nigel. "The water's smooth again. Quick!" All at once the house was reflected, but in its upside-down incarnation it was decked with daffodils. An improvement.

"I used to think there was a monster in the pool," Nigel was saying. "Someone must have told me that to keep me from going near it and drowning myself. It's very deep."

"And it's very silent. The house, I mean. Stately, but—" It seemed too forward to tell him she could not imagine herself ever at ease in that place. It was like some enormous mausoleum. "Are you sure they're at home?"

"Positive," said Nigel, "unless the butler has gone mad and done away with them. First the cook, then the maids, and then the master and mistress, and—"

"*Don't*, Nigel!" She pinched his arm. "Have you ever climbed that hill?"

"The last time was when I was twelvish. That's Meall na Gobhar Mor, the Hill of the Great Goat. Shonnie, the gardener's son, and I slept up there one summer night." He laughed. "We didn't sleep much. We thought every ghost and evil spirit we'd ever heard of was coming to get us, not to mention the Great Goat with eyes of fire."

"Tell me about *him*."

"He's lost in the mists of antiquity. He's probably meant to be some form of the Devil."

"I'm going up there. If there's no track left, I'll make one. But I want to see the moor first, and I shall see it this afternoon."

He squeezed her hand in the crook of his elbow. "My dearest love, you needn't do everything all in one day. You have a lifetime." He turned her in the direction of the chaise, which waited a little distance off in the shadow of the trees. Dougal stood at the horses' heads.

"But do you realize how long it's been since I've really *walked*, in pure air? I don't count London at all!"

At the western side of the pond a drive branched off to the right to circle back to Linnmore House. The chaise went by it along the narrow road through the woods, and at the end of fifteen minutes' ride they came to the factor's residence, Tigh nam Fuaran, the House of the Springs. It was the tall, plain stone house Lady Geoffrey had described, and it stood unobtrusively in deep afternoon shadow at the foot of a high ridge. The ridge took the eye before the house could; it bore a broken line of old Caledonian pines black against the sky. They were like aged soldiers, worn and twisted by the years; some had lost limbs, but they were still valiant.

The instant Jennie set foot on the ground she knew that this place, in contrast with Linnmore House, pulsed with life. The house was very plain, its windows small and few compared to the display of glass at the mansion, and its severely plain front door was reached by a steep staircase. But small birds fluttered and chirped in the ungroomed shrubbery, and there were wild flowers on the unmown lawn. The scent of peat smoke was tossed about on the wind. A blackbird sang on a gable as if he'd flown from London to welcome her here. If she'd been hungering for an omen, the blackbird was it.

Two maids erupted from the front door, leaving it wide open behind them, and ran down the steps. One girl was still pinning her cap.

"Slowly, slowly!" Nigel called to them. "Don't break your necks!"

They laughed as unaffectedly as the bird sang. The little red-haired one, fussing with her cap, was inarticulately beaming, bobbing up and down in curtsies like a wound-up toy, her freckles disappearing in her blushes. The taller girl was dark-haired and gray-eyed, with pink and rounded cheeks.

"Welcome, Mistress Gilchrist!" she was saying. "Welcome, Captain Gilchrist!" Her voice was light and sweet, speaking English charmingly accented with the Gaelic lilt and sibilance. "I am Morag. This is Aili."

"How do you do, Morag and Aili?" Jennie shook hands with each.

"Well, you look to be a pair of deuced fine girls," Nigel said. Morag accepted this with composure, and Aili ducked again, making a sound too tiny for a giggle.

"Where is that Fergus now?" Iain Innes asked. "We have work here."

"He's just coming!" Morag fluted, looking anxiously around. "Och, there he is!" Fergus came around the northern corner of the house with an awkward rolling walk. He was an almost dwarfish man or youth with a big, shaggy black head and heavy black brows making a bar across a lumpy, swarthy, expressionless face. He and Dougal began unstrapping the luggage, Dougal talking all the time in a rapid stream of Gaelic, Fergus not answering.

The girls took anything they could carry and ran up the steps ahead of the men. Nigel and Jennie waited arm in arm until the trunks were taken in. Then they followed, and at the head of the granite steps he swung her into his arms and carried her across the threshold. He didn't put her down at once but revolved slowly in the center of the hall. Fergus and Dougal were on the oak staircase with a trunk, Iain behind them either encouraging or teasing, Fergus silently bearing most of the weight. From upstairs the girls' voices fluttered like the birds in the shrubbery.

"Look around you at your new home, Mistress Gilchrist," Nigel commanded.

Most of the light came from the open front door. She had an impression of paneling that glinted like dark water, stone floors, a few pieces of massive Jacobean furniture. A bowl of daffodils had been set on a carved chest. A tall clock ticked like a metronome, its brass pendulum gleaming through thin shadow.

"What do you think, my love?" Nigel asked her. "Fairly rugged, what?"

"I adore it already!"

He kissed her temple and set her on her feet. Then they saw the woman standing in the shadow of the staircase. Nigel laughed in surprise. "Who's this?"

She came forward. "I am Mrs. MacIver, the cook," she said. She was a big but lean woman, with large hands folded over her apron at her waist. Her sandy hair was pinned so tightly back under her cap that the harsh lines of her long, pale face were unsparingly emphasized. Her eyes seemed as colorless as her lips. "Would you be liking some tea now, or a glass of wine, Madam? There is also whisky in the house."

"Mrs. or Mistress will do very well, Mrs. MacIver," Jennie said. "Not Madam. How do you do?" She went forward with her hand out, expecting a glacial grasp, but it was warm and firm. "I would like some tea, please. Could it be brought up to our room?"

"Certainly."

Nigel then shook hands with her. "You might put a decanter of whisky on the tray. Now that I've come home to Scotland I must be a thorough Scot, mustn't I? Did Mrs. Archie engage you?"

"No, Captain Gilchrist. Mr. Grant asked me to stay on and help the young lady."

"I appreciate that!" Jennie exclaimed.

Mrs. MacIver inclined her head and dismissed herself, leaving through a door at the back of the hall. A tang of burning peat escaped past her.

"I didn't think Christabel would have put Highland servants here," Nigel murmured. "Decent of old Grant, wasn't it?"

"I wish I could thank him."

"I wonder who distilled the whisky kept in the house. It's likely that our stately Mrs. MacIver's kin have a still hidden somewhere in the heather."

The Inneses came down the stairs, Dougal grinning and Fergus following like a silent rough-coated black dog.

"It's fine you're home, Captain," Iain said. "Sending for you was one of the best deeds Linnmore ever did. You'll remember how it was here when you were a wee lad and when you were growing the long legs on you. You called it Paradise. I heard you with these ears the day you caught your first trout." He touched his ears. "Hamish was rowing you; he'd been teaching you and telling you all the time it was quiet and patient you had to be. *Quiet!*" He laughed. "You could no more be quiet than a young cock in the morning, till that day. You came up in the rain from the loch, carrying your trout and the water running off your nose, and saying, 'It's Paradise!' "

He tapped Nigel on the chest. "And I'm telling them now in the stables, that lad won't be wanting to ruin Paradise." He gave Nigel a nod as one equal to another. "Good day, Mistress Gilchrist," he said to her.

"Thank you, Iain, for a pleasant journey. You, too, Dougal."

"It's twice welcome you are, Mistress," Iain said gallantly. Fergus followed them out.

"Thank *you* for helping, Fergus," Jennie called to him. There was the slightest nod of his big tousled head; then he left.

With their arms around each other Nigel and Jennie went up the stairs. They met Aili at the top; she gasped and backed off, Nigel smiled down on her, and she went scarlet, tucked her chin in her fichu, and descended the stairs so precipitately that Jennie held her breath, waiting to see if she arrived at the bottom on her feet or her head.

Morag was waiting to take them to their room, a big corner chamber, facing east and south. Jennie's open trunk stood in the middle of the floor; otherwise the room was dominated by an immense four-poster bed in the heavy Jacobean style. The hangings of the bed and at the windows had a dark, thick pattern, but they smelled clean, and the sun-bleached linens were scented with some herbal fragrance other than lavender.

Morag drew their attention to the crewelwork coverlet. "Mistress Grant did all that with her own hands. Och, it was lucky she finished it before she died, the poor lady. It has been waiting just there in the chest all these years."

"Very lucky," Jennie agreed. Something else was called for. "And it's very beautiful." Morag stroked it, tenderly.

More daffodils in a pottery jug glowed on one of the deep windowsills, and a small fire of birch logs burned in the grate. There were the usual nightstand and toilet table with basin and ewer, and a towel horse hung with fresh towels; a deep chest stood under a south window. Two tall wing-backed upholstered chairs faced each other across the hearth rug. The furniture was all on the massive side except for a little mahogany card table on slender legs, set between the armchairs, and a cherry dressing table, old and delicately shaped, with a matching chair.

"Those came from the attics of Linnmore House," Morag said proudly. "One of the maids there is a very nice woman, for all she is English, and she found them for me, and Dougal wheeled them all the way in a barrow."

Nigel, amused, began, "But my wife is—" Jennie laid her fingers across his mouth.

"Northumberland isn't quite the same, my love," she said. "Why don't you look around your dressing room and see if it suits? I think your trunk is in there."

He kissed her fingers, pleasing Morag as well as Jennie, and went into the small neighboring room.

"We thought you might be liking to sit here of an evening till your other things come. Downstairs seems very bleak and bare. There are plenty of candles, you see." She pointed to the row of candlesticks on the mantel. "It will be snug here. The wee table you could eat from, if you chose."

"It feels very nice and homelike, Morag," said Jennie.

"Thank you, Mistress." She had a dimple in one cheek. "Would you like to bathe after your tea?"

"No, first I'm going to take a long, long walk," Jennie said with vigor. "I'd like my walking shoes. I think they're in the carpetbag."

"Oh!" The girl's gray eyes widened. "Madam Gilchrist is expecting you to dine with them at Linnmore House, at six. She is sending the dogcart."

Jennie just managed not to groan *Oh no!* "In that case, I had better bathe. The Captain, too. Nigel, we're dining at Linnmore House!" she called in to him; it effectively stopped his whistling.

"What gown will you be wearing?" Morag asked.

"Oh, anything. Whatever isn't too crushed." She knelt on the chest under the window and tried to see up onto the ridge, but she was looking out into treetops. She knew her disappointment about dinner was childish, but that didn't make it less.

"Is this all right, Mistress?" Morag held up a lilac muslin. "I'll take it down to Aili to freshen. And I will bring your tea."

She left with the gown over her arm. Nigel came in from the dressing room; he had shed his coat and cravat, and his shirt was comfortably open at the throat. Immediately he tumbled Jennie on the bed and began to undress her. "We'll send word that we're sick."

"No, we won't. Mocking is catching."

"We have an hour. Let's pretend we're playing favvers and muvvers under a hedgerow." He ran a hand up her leg.

"What if Mrs. MacIver takes it into her head to bring up the tea?" She tickled him in the ribs until he fought her off and fell back, panting, on the pillows.

"Did you ever hear that great piece of epic verse beginning 'Come tickle me, love, in these lonesome ribs'?"

"Did you just compose it?" she asked.

There was a gentle cough outside. Jennie bounced off the bed, straightening her clothes. *"Get up!"* she whispered. Nigel groaned and obeyed. She opened the door for Morag, who was solemn but rather pink. She was carrying a heavy tray, and Nigel took it from her and set it on the table. Morag quickly left, eyes downcast. Jennie sensed that she was trying to keep a straight face.

Besides the tea and the whisky, there was a plate of warm sultana scones and one of shortbread. The pat of butter had a thistle pattern pressed into it.

"Our first meal in our own home," Jennie said. They toasted their future, she with tea and Nigel with whisky.

"Very smooth stuff," he said. "It would be crime against mankind to do away with the still that produced this."

"Is that what Iain meant when he spoke about ruining Paradise?"

"Iain is half poet, half scoundrel. Paradise has already been ruined. The lads I played with are all gone. Some have emigrated, some are dead on the Continent, and others soon will be. Two have become coal miners out on the coast, and that's living death. The gardener's son, who was my special friend, was hanged for the murder of an exciseman."

"Oh, Nigel!" she exclaimed in pity and horror. He shrugged and kept turning his glass around and around in his fingers.

"It *was* Paradise once, at least for children. I remember that first trout, how it rained that day and I didn't care. I never felt the chill. It was glorious. I remember everything about that night when Shonnie and I slept on Meall na Gobhar Mor and thought the Great Goat was coming for us. We were too frightened to move, and it turned out to be his old pony looking for him." He looked into the fire. "Well, other good chaps besides Shonnie have died, and honorably, though I've no doubt Shonnie felt his was an honorable death and he went bravely." He set the glass on the tray. There was moisture on his eyelashes, and he was blinking. "But we have to look ahead, not back. We're too young to live on memories, like Iain Innes."

"Yes, we are," she said. "And we have everything to look forward to." She had never seen him like this before, and he was enhanced even more for her, if that were possible, by the discovery that he was not always a child of the sun but could taste anguish for lost friends.

Thirteen

N IGEL WAS FORBIDDEN to assist Jennie with her bath because they needed to keep their wits about them and not forget the command from the manor. He splashed noisily and tunefully in his dressing room and presently came into where she was lathering up with her Pears' soap before the fire. He was wearing the forest green coat and white breeches of the wedding.

"Oh, I *say*!" He leaned over the bath, and she threatened to decorate his coat with lather. He backed off. "Oh, Lord, what a beastly bore this dinner will be. Well, I'm off to the stables to see if everything's right for our horses when they come. Iain tells me Fergus all but speaks their language. He jolly well doesn't speak ours."

"Is he mute or merely independent?"

"I don't know anything about him. He's one of Grant's pets, from some remote glen on the estate where I've never been. There are a few such spots. We used to think they were haunted; we were told enough stories by the old men to keep us out of there. Now I know why. Small boys are like dogs for nosing out what's best kept secret, like whisky stills."

"You've stopped believing in ghoulies and gheisties, I take it."

"Not to mention the phantom piper, the water horse, the Black Dog or the Black Wolf, whichever the loch is named for, and the Great Goat, and the woman who weeps for the baby she smothered at birth, and—"

"Enough, enough!" She menaced him with more suds. He went out, laughing, and ran downstairs.

Slowly she sponged herself, gazing up at the windows, wishing she could see the ridge from here. She looked into the tops of the beeches and sycamores, and saw the unfurling new leaves like infant fists, but it seemed that she could feel the presence of the ridge and, beyond it, the moor. Irritation at Christabel's summons intruded like a toothache trying to start. Why couldn't they have been left alone on their first day here? Even if the cook had no big meal prepared for them, bread and cheese under their own roof would have been all they needed.

Then she suppressed the resentment; the older Gilchrists were simply being courteous, welcoming them to Linnmore. She began to whistle a country dance tune from home. It was a saying that whistling girls and crowing hens always came to no good end, but Papa always retorted that whistling girls and a flock of sheep were the very best crop a farmer could keep.

She dried and powdered herself and sat down at the dressing table in her drawers and chemise to do up her hair. There was a tap at the door, and Morag came in. Aili was behind her, carrying the lilac muslin. Jennie watched her in the mirror as she laid the gown tenderly on the bed, then stood off and doted on it like a loving parent.

"Thank you, Aili, it looks lovely," Jennie said. Aili scampered out, round-eyed as a rabbit.

"She's shy," Morag said.

"Yes." Jennie stood up so Morag could help her with the long back-laced stays. "How I hate these things! I never wore them until I was sixteen; my father didn't approve of them, thank goodness. So don't try to lace too tightly, Morag."

"I will not," the girl promised. "Everyone is hungry to see you and the Captain, Mistress."

"Do you remember my husband at all? It's been a long time since he was last here."

"Och, yes! I remember him! We wee ones looked up at him as a prince, always such a laughing one, bringing us sweets in his pockets. The yellow hair on him, and the long legs, and the way he used to make everybody smile! So when Mr. Grant told us the Captain was coming, it was like a *miracle*." She went from rapture to awe. "We had thought he was away to the wars, you see, and with Mr. Grant going, we have all been so worried. It could have been some coldhearted stranger from Inverness or even from the *south*." That word came in a horrified whisper.

She held Jennie's petticoat for her. "Why *did* Mr. Grant leave?" Jennie asked through the silken folds.

"How could I know?" Morag was gently apologetic. She lifted the lilac muslin from the bed. "You have so many bonny things. It will be such a pleasure to take care of them. And the Captain's, too, if he has no man. Aili is very good with gentlemen's things." It came out "chentlemen"; the b's were p's, the s's very sibilant.

Jennie knew when a subject had been changed. Very well, she would find out at dinner. Morag deftly did up the hooks and eyes, while Jennie put on her mother's topaz eardrops and pendant, and Morag's murmurs of admiration purled along like a brook. When Jennie wrapped herself in a deep shawl of lilac and purple silk, Morag was enchanted.

"Och, you look just beautiful!" she exclaimed. It looked as if the Captain weren't to receive all the adulations of the household, Jennie thought. She remembered her reticule and gloves, as a sop to Aunt Higham, and walked down the oak staircase for the first time as mistress of her own household when the tall clock struck the quarter before six.

Nigel stood outside the open front door, talking over the parapet to someone below. Behind her Morag said, "You will have a fine dinner at Linnmore House. The chef comes from London."

"London!" Jennie tossed back. "Oh, Lord, I thought I'd left it a world behind me!"

Then the memory of Tamsin struck her like a mailed fist driven into her middle. She imagined the child alive with her here: growing round-cheeked and shiny-haired from the good food and pure air, wearing the pretty prints and muslins they would sew for her. She saw what she had never seen: Tamsin laughing.

They were driven to Linnmore House in an immaculate dogcart, drawn by a large white pony driven by Dougal, who merrily doffed his bonnet but spoke only to the garron. The road led out of the woods surrounding the factor's house and went by pastures on the left that reached northward to the forested slopes of the hills that surged along the sky. Several horses and cows were grazing in the early-evening sunshine, and she recognized Bruce, Wallace, David, and William. Beyond the pastures, woods began again, but soon the red granite of the mansion showed through the trees; the solitary hill behind it grew higher and higher as they approached.

They drove across a short stone bridge over a brook that seemed to come from the hill and run down to Linn Mor at the foot of the lawn. The fine gravel of the driveway now rattled under wheels and hooves. Rhododendrons were massed around the house, so it wasn't quite as barren as it had looked from across the pond, but she still could not warm to the place, and she dreaded the evening.

A tall man in evening dress stood out on the drive to greet them, waving very long arms.

"Nigel, my lad!" He embraced Nigel; his broad smile showed a great many very large and long teeth, stained, but undeniably his own. He wouldn't let Nigel help Jennie but lifted her down himself.

"Jennie, my dear! Aye, you're featherlight, and a wee thing about the middle! May I claim a brother's privilege?" He leaned down and kissed her cheek; he smelled of tobacco and wine. His pale blue eyes, slightly bloodshot, had a watery glisten in their hollows between prominent cheekbones and bristly, brindled eyebrows. He had a big hump-bridged nose, reddish, and a narrow, thrusting jaw accentuated by his high stock. His thick dark hair was going gray.

He walked them into the hall, holding Jennie by one arm and Nigel by the other, laughing and talking at the same time. The laughter was startling at first, a kind of explosive whinny, but he seemed so genuinely fond of Nigel and was so welcoming to her, without any pretense at urbanity, that she liked him at once.

The hall was dominated by a huge but cold fireplace, with a display of ancient weapons arranged above it. When Jennie looked away from this, she encountered the eyes of the dead stags whose antlered heads decorated the opposite wall. Dismayed by this, she turned once more and met the gelid gaze of an impassive butler and an equally blank parlormaid, who outdid Mavis at it. The maid led Jennie up the baronial staircase into a bedchamber that looked unused, decorated for display only. It was very depressing, and the place felt cold and unaired. She shivered when she left off her shawl.

She followed the maid downstairs again to the warmth of coal fires. If this was the woman Morag liked so much, she gave no sign of being likable now. The men stood at the foot of the stairs; Archie whinnied happily at her; Nigel's smile was as warm as an eiderdown or his embrace. She wanted to take his arm, but Archie seized possession of her and escorted her into the drawing room, crying, "Here they are, my dear!"

The drawing room was so crowded with furniture, statuary, vases large and small, cabinets, tables strewn with bibelots, paintings, mirrors, two cut-glass chandeliers above and an extremely busy carpet underfoot, that Christabel was hard to discover. But Archie guided them to the fireplace like a proud spaniel carrying a woodcock to its master. Christabel sat enthroned in a fauteuil below the elaborately carved mantel.

"Here's Nigel back among us, and dear little Jeannie!"

His wife gave him a look of asperity. "Her name is *Eugenia*. How do you do, Eugenia? Good evening, Nigel." She didn't rise. Her short plump hand was given languidly to each in turn, but there was nothing languid about the way she looked at Jennie. Dark eyes under thick lids and dark-tinted Grecian curls missed no detail of the girl's face and dress, while her small mouth asked conventionally amiable questions about the journey. The survey was so deliberate it was almost entertaining, and Jennie felt her spirits lifting. She was relieved, too, that she didn't have to exchange kisses with Christabel. At last Mrs. Archie's eyes came back to rest on the topaz pendant with a sort of remote contempt, while she fingered the blaze of stones on her high bosom. There were gems in her hair, in her ears, around her short neck, on her fingers and wrists.

I do believe she's put on everything just to impress me, Jennie thought. It was strange that a woman of Christabel's age and wealth should work so hard to impress a girl she considered a nobody; no doubt that was the reason, and Christabel wanted to rub her nose in it.

"Are you delicate?" Christabel asked suddenly. "You look it. And this is a brutal place for delicate women."

"No, I'm not delicate," said Jennie.

"She's no flower of the south, Christabel," Nigel said. "She's Northumbrian, from the edge of the North Sea."

"A farm, wasn't it?" said Christabel carelessly. "I heard something of the sort."

Jennie considered telling her in broad Northumbrian that she was really a dairymaid in disguise, but just then dinner was announced. It was excellent, flawlessly served by the waxwork butler and the maid, whose discreet rustle as she whisked around the dining room, pale as milk under the stiffly ruffled cap, depressingly spoke London. The two would come alive in the kitchen, Jennie knew, and what would they be saying? She wished she could be a mouse in the corner.

Except for Archie's accent, Scotland was held at bay outside the windows, and inside here was London at second hand without the salt and spice and refreshing vinegar of the Highams. Christabel wanted to talk about London, and Jennie considered she was doing well by mentioning the Drury Lane Theatre fire, the opera, the newest display at

Madame Tussaud's, and the rage for the Scottish poet Walter Scott. But Christabel soon dismissed her as useless; she hadn't moved in the proper circles, and how could she? Her people were in *trade*. Christabel turned to Nigel with a wintry smile and began asking him about people of whom Jennie had never heard.

Archie attended as voraciously to his food and wine as if he'd just been released from a prison diet of bread and water. Jennie was glad to concentrate on her own food, while Nigel rambled on about Society like some old beau who lived out his days among his clubs, dances, race meetings, Bath, and Brighton. Christabel devoured it as avidly as her husband ate his dinner.

Jennie drifted back and forth between dismay, when she looked longingly out at Scotland past the bolted windows, and fascination when she saw Archie forking food into his mouth like a cowherd forking hay into a manger; then amazement took over at Nigel's new incarnation. She was afraid that she might soar off into uncontrollable laughter at any moment. How could she ever survive this evening?

We needn't stay too long, she promised herself. *She thinks I'm delicate. If I say I have a headache, she'll be pleased that she was right, and she'll go to bed tonight believing I'm too frail to bear a living child.*

The awful tide of risibility subsided. Christabel was now saying fretfully, "I *know* he must be at the castle by now, and we're being deliberately ignored."

"He was still in London when we left it," said Nigel. "He was at the wedding."

"He *was*?" Christabel put down her knife and fork.

"Oh, yes, he wobbled in on the arms of his son and daughter-in-law and managed to receive almost more attention than the bride. Rank has its privileges." Nigel chuckled. "He left the wedding breakfast very drunk."

"How did *she* look?" Christabel asked jealously.

"Not in the family way, dear sister. But I know, and Archie knows, that there is absolutely no way short of wholesale murder to eliminate all those tiresome cousins between Archie and the earldom."

Archie haw-hawed. "Quite right! Diabolical plot, poison rings, hired assassins—" He exploded again and had to gulp down a glass of wine to stop the cough.

"And supposing it did work, Christabel," Nigel said. "Then I would have to eliminate Archie. I rather fancy myself a peer, and Jennie would make a deuced fine countess."

Archie turned his pale blue eyes on Jennie. "She would at that!" He gave her a horsy grin, and she expected she'd get used to all those yellow teeth.

The dessert was a rich trifle, and afterward the women went to the drawing room. Christabel came only a little higher than Jennie's shoulder, and she was overweight, but she compensated by walking as if she wore a peeress's velvet and ermine over her sage green crepe and had a small black boy to carry her train.

Jennie prayed that the men wouldn't be too long, but she knew there was estate business to discuss. She sat opposite her hostess in a brocaded fauteuil twin to Christabel's; the coal fire burned jet and ruby in the steel basket grate. Christabel worked at a tapestry on a frame, and Jennie tried to think of something to talk about. A hideous possibilty attacked her; Christabel might expect her to be at her beck and call as a companion.

Perhaps if she acted stupid as well as delicate, Christabel would give up that idea. But it was impossible to turn bland and insipid and keep it up; besides, Christabel might like it.

"This is a very elegant room," she remarked, not insincerely; with its proportions, its many windows, its linenfold paneling and beautifully decorated ceiling, it had been elegant before Christabel had stuffed it full like a shop.

"An oasis in the desert, it's been called," said Christabel complacently. "There is not one great house for miles around that displays the taste and refinement of this one. The nearest is Roseholm, and they live like paupers there, and savage ones at that. *I've* spared no expense, nor needed to."

And thinks it's cruel hard that she doesn't get a title for her money, Jennie thought. "Who is that over the mantel?"

"Linnmore's father." She called Archie by the name of his property, as was the local custom, but she Anglicized the pronunciation. "And Nigel's, too, of course," she added. Unwillingly, Jennie was sure.

The painter must have been a romantic, or else the earlier Linnmore had been strikingly handsome. He stood against a background of black hills and clouds purple with distant storms, but in the foreground sunlight illuminated the tall dark man. His eyes gleamed in the shadows of his bonnet; he looked austere but serene. He wore a kilt of green, blue, and black tartan, and a plaid of the same was wrapped around him and over his left shoulder and arm, leaving his right arm free. That hand rested on a deerhound's head, and another deerhound lay at his feet, chin on paws; both dogs gazed luminously out at the two women. The man wore diced hose and buckled black shoes, and he stood amid heather in its rosy-purple August bloom.

For Jennie, he was worth the whole evening so far, and she hated to look away from him. She said finally, "He looks every inch an earl, or what you think an earl should be, but very seldom is. Much more so than the present one."

"*He's* a disgusting old reprobate!" Christabel snapped. She too stared up at the portrait, and Jennie suddenly felt sorry for the dumpy, over-dressed woman. How she must resent the very existence of Nigel and Jennie. If ever, by the most farfetched chain of coincidences, this branch succeeded to the title, it would probably be so long from now that Nigel would be the earl, or his son would be. Jennie had no desire whatsoever to be a countess, but it would be tactless to say so and thus underline the truth that Christabel's greed for it was eating at her like a malignancy.

"That was a most delicious meal," she said. Christabel brightened.

"I pay my chef a good deal to stay in this barbarous country," she said. "And he has three days in Inverness every three months and a holiday in England every six months." She laughed affectedly. "I'm always surprised when he comes back. He knows he has me quite at his mercy. But one must expect to pay well for the best." She sighed. "Your woman is an adequate plain cook, I believe. You may be able to teach her more. They were all Grant's people, you know, and if you have any doubts about them, we shall find a way to replace them."

"He asked them to stay on to help me, and the least I can do is give them a fair trial. I like Morag already; her smile and that soft Highland voice are quite delicious."

"You will soon learn not to trust those smiles and voices. These people are peasants, my dear. Of the better sort, of course," she added. "They can be trained into passable servants if you can break them of being too familiar. They have some curious beliefs. They don't under-stand that gentlefolk are a race apart, for instance." She added with conscious magnanimity, "Some of the men make excellent soldiers, once they accept discipline."

"Why did Mr. Grant leave?" She hadn't intended to ask it.

"He wished to emigrate," said Christabel, plunging her needle into the tapestry hard enough to dispatch either the nymph or her tame unicorn.

"I must warn you about the climate here, Eugenia. It is very harsh for the complexion. You should go out in the wind only when it is absolutely necessary, and always shade your face from the sun. I have a very good mixture made up for me by an apothecary in Inverness, to soften and purify the skin." She looked appraisingly across at Jennie. "You have the sort that is all very well now, while you are still young, but soon it will begin to weather most unbecomingly."

You hope, Jennie thought. "I shall remember your advice, but I need to be outdoors. Whatever would I find to do indoors all the time? Before the children come," she added with a spark of malice.

"My dear girl, you have a household to run and servants to oversee, and yours need more than most. Every corner of your house should bear inspection at any time."

How boring, with the moor waiting just over the ridge.

"You must do fine needlework," Christabel continued. "There is nothing more womanly, nothing more appreciated by a homecoming husband, than a wife bent over her work in a spotless room."

Suddenly Archie neighed out in the hall, and Jennie heard beauty in the sound. At the first sight of Nigel in the doorway she wanted to throw herself at him and take him home to bed.

Nigel stayed behind to amuse Christabel while Archie took Jennie on a tour of the house, beginning with the library which adjoined the dining room. Buoyantly he referred often to her as future mistress of it all. It would be a pleasant house with more life in it and a few less inanimate objects, but she didn't want to be rushed into planning the future before she'd slept one night in her own house. Besides, her living here would mean he'd be dead; had he no misgivings about that? But if this was his way of making her feel accepted and welcome, she appreciated his kindness. She looked for things to admire, found them, spoke of them, and his pleasure was worth her effort. She began to find him rather endearing.

After a series of crowded yet lifeless chambers, the billiard room was a relief. It was *used*; it had a comfortable shabbiness. "I get Armitage up here to play with me now and then," he told her in a loud whisper.

"Shocks Christy, but she pretends it doesn't happen. A shark at billiards that man is. A shark in butler's clothing. I'll have a fair chance with Nigel."

"And with me, too," said Jennie. "My father taught us all."

"Capital, capital!" He clapped his hands. "Women *should* play. They hunt, play cards; why not billiards, too?"

The light was almost gone when they came into the long gallery of family portraits. He showed her where hers was to hang. "We'll have to tie Nigel down and have *him* done, to be opposite you. Perhaps he'll consent to it now. Elusive fella. Always wriggly as an eel, the dear laddie." They laughed in shared love for Nigel.

She wondered if she'd have the opportunity to spend some time here when the light was good, so she could really look at all the portraits of Nigel's and her children's ancestors. Would Christabel permit her to be as free in the house as Archie was promising? Leading her away from the gallery, patting the hand he'd drawn through his arm, he was offering her the unrestricted use of his father's library; he'd heard that she was a bookish miss. "Mind you, I don't hold that a disadvantage in a woman if she likes to dance," he told her earnestly. "You do like to dance, don't you?"

"I love it," she assured him.

When they returned to the drawing room, Nigel was standing on the hearthrug under his father's portrait, wearing an expression of strained geniality. When he saw Jennie, it changed to rejoicing. He came to her in two long strides, holding his arms out, and she went into them.

"Isn't that a lovely sight?" Archie cried. "Ah, to be young and in love, and in the month of May!" Christabel ignored the brief embrace as if they were committing an indecency. They kissed as chastely as brother and sister and separated.

"Now, Jeannie, my lass," said Archie, rubbing his hands, "let us hear some expert fingers on the pianoforte."

"Her name is *Eugenia*." His wife rebuked him again.

"She'll always be Jeannie to me. Come along, my dearie." A bony hand gripped her elbow, and she was escorted to the piano. She didn't mind. It was out of Christabel's frosty ambience and near a bay window where she could look out down the long slope of darkening lawn to the spectral glimmer of the daffodils through the twilight. The piano was slightly out of tune, but the little Scarlatti melody tinkled charmingly in the drawing room. Nigel stood behind her, his hands lightly on her shoulders. Christabel, as well as Jennie could see her through the crowd of objects, was frowning over her work. The butler (the billiards shark) had come in and was lighting the candles.

"Sing for your supper, Nigel," Jennie said.

"That's right, that's right!" Archie slapped him on the shoulder. "It's grand having this young life in the house, isn't it, Christy, my dear?"

"Please don't call me Christy. The woman at the home farm is called Christy."

"And Christabel's such a musical name," said Jennie at her most winsome. Her sisters would have found it a bit too much. "Nigel?"

She played the opening bars of one of Robert Burns's songs, "Sweet Afton," and Nigel obliged, with no false modesty. Burns was a favorite of his, and he sang several songs. They finished with "Green Grow the Rashes, O," which had Archie capering around the piano in a dance of his own and clapping his hands. Over by the fireplace Christabel, apparently deaf as a post, placed one careful stitch after another. Tea was brought in, and the parlormaid was sent to break up the musicale, but Archie wasn't ready yet.

"One more, one more!" he insisted. For mischief Jennie struck up "The De'il's awa' wi' the Exciseman," and Archie laughed till he had to pull out his handkerchief and dry his eyes. Jennie then stood up, took Nigel's arm, and walked back to the fireplace.

Christabel, lifting the teapot, said composedly, "I do not care to hear that man's doggerel in my drawing room. He was nothing but a womanizer and a drunkard."

Nigel looked amused but not apologetic. Jennie said nothing. Archie exclaimed, "Och, but to quote the bard himself, 'a man's a man for a' that'!" Christabel gave him the look of a tyrannical nanny who sees her charge getting above himself and is about to whisk him off to bed without supper.

She handed Jennie her cup and said, "Eugenia, my dear, you must devise a different name for the factor's house. At present it has a quite unintelligible pagan one."

"But I like it," Jennie protested.

Archie spoke the name with a sliding, almost whispering intonation, quite different from his ordinary one.

Christabel's cheeks darkened under the powder. "It's a barbaric tongue," she said, "and those who cling to it are barbarians."

"Nigel told me that the name means 'House of the Springs' because there are so many near, and even one under the house," Jennie said mildly. "But when you said it was pagan, I was hoping it really meant 'House of the Witches' or 'Here dwells Asmodeus, King of Devils.' "

"And you'd be the one who'd be trying to raise him," said Nigel.

"And she'd be the one who could turn him into an angel!" said Archie. Christabel's cheeks were purplish now. Jennie could endure no more of her tonight. She set her cup back on the tea table and arose.

"I beg you will excuse us. We have been traveling many days, and I am tired."

"Of course you are!" cried Archie. "We must keep the roses in those cheeks and the sparkle in those eyes, mustn't we? After all, we'll have many such happy hours together, eh?" He rang for the butler and ordered the dogcart brought around. "We must have a dance! Clear *this* out of the way"—he waved at the precious clutter as if it were so much brushwood—"take up those carpets, have some musicians in for the waltzes and polkas, and a piper for the reels—you know Murdo Gilchrist, Nigel. Good company, good music! It'll be a grand way to introduce you to the countryside."

"We shall see." Christabel was glacial, but the cold couldn't numb Archie. After they had given their thanks and good-nights and were dismissed from the Presence, Archie waved away the servants in the hall and held Jennie's shawl for her, managing to give her shoulders a little squeeze. He came outdoors with them, still talking about his dance and how his wind was as good as it ever was.

They had to wait a few minutes for the dogcart, and Archie said, indulgently, "Sheena will be hard to put between the shafts. She thinks her day's work is done."

"And so it should be," said Jennie. "We could go on foot if I had my shoes." She longed to be walking away with Nigel into the silent twilight, disappearing from Archie and Christabel's world and emerging into their own as if into a new universe, which existed out there where the red afterglow still burned in the western sky.

Fourteen

M ORAG AND AILI waited in the candlelit hall; they were bidden good-night and waved off to their beds. Up in the master bedroom a small fire burned, cozy as a purring cat. Nigel and Jennie undressed each other with trembling hands, silently hilarious, drunker than any amount of wine could have made them, and tumbled naked into the herb-scented sheets.

Afterward they lay entwined and talked in a luxurious intimacy. This was one of the pleasures of marriage that Sylvia hadn't mentioned.

"Christabel seems to hate it here," Jennie said. "What does she do all year?"

"Waits for an invitation to the castle." Nigel's amusement vibrated in his chest under Jennie's ear. She was fascinated by this phenomenon.

"Do they have people often? Archie spoke of a dance."

"Archie loves dancing. He's a maniac in a Highland reel, and then Christabel pretends she's never met the man. So they don't have many dances, but some of their English friends come up for the fishing and the birds, and hoping to get a stag. The wives make good company for Christabel while the men are out all day, and they play cards at night and lower the tide in Archie's wine cellar."

He yawned, then felt with his lips past her cheekbone to her mouth. She met him avidly; one could never grow tired of kissing. After this pleasurably greedy interlude she said, "She's starved for London. Why can't they spend the winters there?"

"She must keep old Archie in line. A winter of dancing, drinking, and gambling, and he'd be more of a living skeleton than the Earl is."

"Poor Archie," she said, and meaning it. "He seems a very good-hearted man, and he wants so much to have a merry life. But I suppose he loves her, so that makes up for a great deal."

"She is also rich, and that makes up for everything."

"Poor Nigel then, with no rich wife." She ran her hand over his chest. "Tell me the truth: do they approve of your marrying a penniless girl?"

"Christabel doesn't, but she'll never tell me to my face. Archie can no more resist a pretty girl than he can a dram. If he had any doubts, they were forgotten when he lifted you down tonight."

"He told me he wished he could have been at the wedding. He sounded wistful."

"I think they'd have come, if only for a fortnight," Nigel said, "to get a look at you and your connections. But it's a long way to travel from home when you can't trust your factor."

"What was the trouble with him? Christabel said he wanted to emigrate, but I know it's not that simple." She didn't tell him she'd tried to find out from Morag. He hugged her and muffled her mouth against his chest.

"Whatever it was, it's over and done with. I'm the factor now, so forget Grant."

She got her head free. "I can't! He asked the servants to stay on for my sake. That was a great kindness. I gather that if he'd said the word they'd have vanished like some of your Highland fairies. I would like to thank him."

"He is a good distance off, waiting for a ship, if he hasn't already gone to America. Now will you be quiet and let me make love to you?"

"*Again*? Why, Capting!"

When she first woke in the morning, there was the blackbird again, her familiar. A cuckoo's call followed when the blackbird stopped for a moment; the sound was muted and hollow as if it had come from far away, but she knew the bird could be very close. There was a mélange of other bird voices, and to hear this as she had heard it at Pippin Grange was almost as enchanting as to wake up curled against Nigel's back. She kissed his neck, and when that didn't work, she leaned over him and flicked her tongue along the rim of his ear.

At once he looked up at her with one blue eye and said, "Who is this woman in my bed? Dear God in heaven, I am compromised for life!"

It was a gray morning, and the dining room was dim with the trees and shrubs growing so close to the windows. It was frustrating to know that the ridge was up there but she could not see it. Never mind, she was going out as soon as she had eaten; she had come downstairs dressed for it in a geranium red nankeen walking dress and wearing her half boots.

Morag served a large Scottish breakfast, assisted by a hard-breathing Aili. Speechless and blushing as usual, she went well out around Nigel like a kitten around a mastiff that could devour it in one bite. Jennie finally caught her glance and smiled at her, and Aili responded by rolling her eyes upward and blowing her red fringe up from her damp forehead. Morag was at ease; in the dark-paneled room she had the bloom of the apple blossoms at Pippin Grange, those whose petals were stained with rose.

"When will you be wanting to go through the house, Mistress?" she asked Jennie when they were finishing their coffee.

"Later this morning. Now I'm very anxious to be out of doors. Will you tell Mrs. MacIver that the breakfast was delicious?"

The girls curtsied and left. Aili's departure was an escape.

"If there's any sorrow in me at this moment," Jennie said, "it's for Tamsin."

"You're too young to keep grieving for what might have been," said Nigel, sounding fifty-eight instead of twenty-six. He pushed back from the table and picked up her shawl and gypsy straw. "Come along, we'll have our walk. I won't stop for a pipe now."

She took the straw bonnet out of his hand and scaled it across the room. "I've decided I'm not wearing *that*. We're not going for a walk in Kensington Gardens; we're home."

"That we are," he agreed. He left his own hat behind. With his fair hair and ruddy complexion he was the idealized version of the country gentleman. None of the authentic country gentlemen she'd known at home had looked in the least like this one. It was impossible that he would ever grow stout, bald, or florid in the cheek and purple about the nose, that a gouty foot could slow those legs, or that jowls could ever be a difficulty to arrange over a cravat.

They went along a passage between the dining room and the combined study and office, and went out a door on the northern end of the house. The cool, still air was scented with green growth and water. There to the west was the ridge like a high rampart built from north to south for a barrier between two worlds. Some crows were flapping and calling around the heads of the old pines, whose motionless silhouettes had a misshapen grandeur. They imposed themselves against the pearly sky as if for centuries they had been holding it back from crashing down on the house below.

In comparison to the noisy activity up above, the silence and emptiness around the clustering outbuildings at the base of the ridge were extreme. A glimpse of Fergus would have helped, but there was not even an open stable door.

They halted their stroll at the paddock gate, and Nigel said, "The horses will be here today. I haven't seen them, but I trust Archie's choice."

From the house there was an outbreak of laughter. They looked around and saw the two girls filling a basket with peats from the stack just outside the back door. Something was amusing them very much.

"Us, do you suppose?" said Nigel.

"I don't know, but I love to hear them," Jennie said. "And, Nigel, we must have cats and dogs here. I know now that's what I missed at Linnmore House last night."

"There's probably a cat or two around the stables; there always were. Archie doesn't care for dogs, but our father had deerhounds."

"They're in the painting. They look wonderful."

"Those two were Monty and Rob," said Nigel. "I never knew them, of course, but the men told me about them. One of them bit Archie badly once, and our father refused to have the dog put down. He swore Archie had done something to make Monty turn on him."

"Had he, do you know?"

He shrugged. "They swore so to me. They said he was jealous of the dogs because they didn't have to be sent off to school."

"No, they could stay home with his father, when he was exiled. Poor Archie," Jennie said. "How awful for him, his father preferring a dog to him. He must hate that portrait facing him every day of his life."

"Wouldn't do to shut the Old Laird away in the gallery. This way Christabel can exhibit a handsome father-in-law, if not a titled one."

He pulled her arm through his. "Come along now, I have a meeting later this morning. You can have a puppy or two if you want. There's always a litter at one of the farms. Spaniels, terriers . . . we might get a deerhound from Roseholm if you like. I'll find out if the Roses still keep them."

"How about a spaniel, a terrier, *and* a deerhound?"

"Anything!" he said exuberantly. He bent his head and kissed her. They walked beside the paddock out to a well-traveled track at its northern end. This ran east to join the drive from Tigh nam Fuaran to Linnmore House, and west the short distance to the foot of the ridge, where the ascent began in a coppice of birch and hazel. Beside the path there was a little fern-ringed pool dimpling constantly with the motion from the springs that filled it. Primroses spilled gold and ivory down its banks.

They climbed above the coppice along a diagonal track among thistles and wild rose tangles, blackberry canes, heather just coming to life, new bracken rising in green fountains from its flattened dead, and bristling dark thickets of gorse starred with blooms like tiny yellow roses. Water sometimes ran across the track and trickled over exposed rock faces; small birds were surprised bathing under miniature falls. There were streamlets following narrow courses whose mossy banks were jeweled with tiny plants. When Jennie stopped to look down at the house, she could hear the water like the voices of countless Undines.

The sun broke through the layers of pearl and gave a pigeon-breast luster to the roofs of Tigh nam Fuaran. The girls ran out from the house, Morag lithe as a deer, to spread towels on the drying green. Heat struck through Jennie's shawl, and she dropped it off her shoulders; a moist, aromatic warmth rose from the earth around her.

Nigel reached down a hand and pulled her up to the crest. The crows exploded from the pines with shouts of alarm or derision and went sailing out into space on wings turned iridescent by the sun.

A dead pine lying where it had crashed long ago showed that the pines were not immortal. But old enough, she thought. Nigel sat down on the fallen hero.

"Cheeky black devils," he said fondly, watching the crows. "Well, here you are, my darling. And there's the loch where I covered myself with glory."

The loch was all she saw at first, as if the treeless moor and the outer encircling rim of mountains existed merely to form the basin which held it: a sheet of white water suddenly filigreed with silver where a breeze touched it, turning milky blue when the nacreous cloud layers thinned.

The breeze that spangled the loch left it dulled again and reached the ridge. It was cold on Jennie's face, lifting the loose tendrils around her forehead and ears. The pine boughs stirred and sighed. Two buzzards came drifting over, mewing and whistling to each other.

Jennie now saw details that had been lost to her at first. Across the loch a flash of windows reflected one of those sudden appearances of the sun; when the flare died out, by shading her eyes she could distinguish the shape of a solitary cottage there in a crease of the land. Down on the loch a man stood up in a small boat, casting, and she could have sworn he hadn't been there a few minutes ago. Another cool puff of breeze brought her the bite of peat smoke and the bleat of a goat.

It came from below her, on this side of the loch. How could she have missed the spatter of thatched cottages, the grazing goats, the few little black cows and undersized sheep? It was as if the loch had mesmerized her like a great mirror.

"Look down there!" she exclaimed, but if Nigel answered, she didn't know it. The place was swarming with life. Several men were digging in the long strips of garden that must have been made with great labor out of the tough moorland. Two kids played King of the Mountain on a stack of peats. A group of women were just approaching the hamlet from the south, carrying creels on their backs, and children frisked around them like puppies.

"What are they carrying in those creels?" she asked.

"What? Oh, peats." He sounded preoccupied. "You can see the peat bed there on the slope at the southern end of the loch. That's one thing the men'll work hard at, cutting their peats. Have to keep warm and cook their grub, you know. But the women always bring the dried peats home on their backs, like ponies."

"It's too bad they don't have some ponies." She kept seeing something more. A man limped over uneven ground toward one of the garden strips, using two sticks to help him along. A woman with a baby in her arms walked to meet the peat carriers. Voices, both human and animal, were lifted and carried on the wind like the smoke from the holes in the thatched roofs.

"What do you call that?" she asked.

"Loch na Mada Dubh," Nigel said. "Didn't I tell you? The Loch of the Black Wolf. Or Dog. You can take your choice."

"No, I mean that little settlement down there."

He rose and stood beside her, his arm around her. "Oh, I believe they have some name for it among themselves," he said indifferently. "There are more of these anthills scattered over the estate. Look over there, my darling, above the peat. Can you make out the road? It begins at the back of the farms, follows a pass through this ridge, and travels west across the moor."

She looked obediently where he pointed, but she could hardly bear to look away from the scene below, as if it would vanish while her eyes were off it. She could see the line of the road cutting across the slant of the land among humps of rock like strange beasts sleeping in the heather.

"Yes, where does it lead?" she asked dutifully.

"It's the best way to reach the far western parts of the estate. At least you have a decent road for part of the way before you must take to the old tracks over the moor and in and out of the glens. But it ends properly at Roseholm. In my father's time there was a good deal of coming and going between there and Linnmore."

"But not now?"

He laughed and squeezed her. "If the Roses are the way they used to be, Christabel would find them devilish rough. Dogs underfoot, a piper parading the courtyard while they eat, and the last I heard they were still drinking toasts to the King over the Water."

"They sound entrancing. At least I'd know I was in Scotland. At Linnmore House one might as well be in England."

"We'll drive there one day, I promise you. I haven't forgotten the deerhound puppy." He held her tightly to him and put his lips against her temple.

A rooster's crow came up to them, small, shrill, but perfectly clear. She could even see him, standing on the peat stack where the kids had played.

"Oh, Nigel, let's go down there! I'd love to see the children and the kids."

"You'll not find it so charming at close range, sweetest. Now look over to the north; there's another way out through the hills, but it's hardly more than a pony track."

"To another part of the estate?"

"Yes, and those are superb hills for deer stalking. There will likely be a big house party then. They'll come for the sport, if not for Christabel's *beaux yeux.*"

She hoped she wouldn't be expected to admire newly dead stags; the mounted heads were bad enough. "As factor you have something to do with these cottages, do you not?"

"I have everything to do with them, you might say."

"Then tell me about the people. Who are they, and what do they do? You can hardly call it farming; they have so little garden space and so few animals."

"They exist," he said dryly. "And their reason for existing is that their ancestors lived there. Many of them are named Gilchrist."

"They're clansmen then."

He said with amusement, "I see you haven't forgotten what Sinclair said. But remember what else he had to say: those days are gone forever, and no great loss, what?" His hands urged her back toward the way they had come. "Shall we go and see if the horses have arrived?"

"Oh, yes!" But she kept looking around. A movement out on the loch caught her eye, and she exclaimed, "I think he's caught something! I wish we had a telescope. Is he one of the people from the cottages?"

"No, he's a different sort of tenant. He lives in that fairly decent place across the loch; he has special privileges." Nigel was offhand about it; he was anxious to see the horses. She went with him, but she was not done asking questions.

"But may they fish the loch, too?"

"No. Any trout they take from the loch would be at night, with a lookout posted to warn of the gamekeeper or one of his men . . . watch your footing there."

"But supposing a poacher was caught, would he be put in prison? Even *transported*?"

He laughed. "*Archie* do anything like that? Christabel would have the law on the poor devil at once"—he snapped his fingers—"and mourn because poachers can no longer be hanged. But not Archie."

"Then you wouldn't do it either." She stopped on the path and turned to face him.

"Send a man to prison or Australia because he took a fish or a bird? Good God! My, what big eyes you have, little grandmother." He kissed her, and she responded eagerly, with an amused recollection of those first hungry kisses behind the sooty laurels in a London garden. Here they were in each other's arms on a breakneck path, still behaving as if they couldn't stop but knowing they needn't.

The crows returned victoriously to the pines and shattered the poetry of the moment. "What was it about horses?" Nigel muttered in her neck. "I'd rather go to bed."

"So would I, but think of the servants. They'd be so shocked, except for Morag. She has a twinkling eye."

"That she has," Nigel agreed. A horse nickered from down below. "They're here!" he said happily. He went ahead so that if she slipped where the path was damp he'd break her fall.

"Nigel, have you found out what your other duties are, besides admonishing poachers? Can't Archie accept the rents from his own people? Papa always made quite an occasion of it; everybody took a dram."

"It's not difficult to deal with the farmers or the folk in the village," he said. "It's those out there on the moor."

She stopped and looked indignantly at his back. "You mean they pay rent to live on those miles and miles of empty land? *Clan* land?"

"My sweeting," he said with humorous resignation, turning back to her, "forget the word *clan* and all its romantic associations. Archie is the landlord here, and one day I shall be." He took her hand to draw her on. "And they are tenants."

"But what can they do to earn the money to pay? They must scarcely see a coin from one year's end to the other."

"The making and smuggling of whisky pay a good many rents in the Highlands. In the far reaches of the estate there's many a secret still, and perhaps even nearer to Linnmore House than you'd believe. My father knew, and pretended he didn't, but he always had whisky in the house in a time when it was not a gentlemen's tipple. And Grant took care not to know a thing."

"But suppose someone isn't in the smuggling? How do they pay their rents? What can they do, with most of the hale young men gone far away? It must be difficult or impossible for them to be always sending money home, if they have it to spare."

"My love, you needn't worry. They're here, aren't they? They have obviously survived for generations." He put his hands on either side of her waist and squeezed. "Bonnie wee thing," he said in Archie's accent.

"But *how?*" she persisted.

He sighed loudly. "The women weave cloth for the clothes, the men make all the brogues, and they have a little extra to sell in the town on market days. They all sell goats and kids too, a few eggs, turnips and cabbages in season. The men work on our roads or reforesting, and they can earn a few extra shillings when the sporting parties are here. If they don't owe rent, they can take their pay in meal if they choose; the estate has its own gristmill. It's for me to get them to work; Grant was more than a bit soft with them."

She gave him a great smacking, trollopy kiss on the mouth. "Ah, Capting, but you're the 'andsome one, and no mistake. So you're going to be the grand tyrant! You'll go for them and their few pence with savage dogs and a horsewhip, is that it?"

They heard the horses again. "Come along, my girl," said Nigel. "On your own two feet, or I'll toss you over my shoulder like a prize of war and carry you off to have my wicked way with you."

"I can hardly wait," said Jennie.

At the spring-fed pool she made him stop and lean over it with her, to see their faces framed by the curling fronds of fern and fragmented by the action of the water. "Pyramus and Thisbe," she said dreamily.

"Nip and Tuck," suggested Nigel.

"Supposing you're no more successful than Mr. Grant was," she said to the broken reflections.

"You're not a girl; you're a terrier digging out a rabbit."

"If I'm to be Mistress of Linnmore one day, I have to know all, don't I?"

"The terrier has such melting eyes. Very well. Grant wasn't Archie's heir, but I am. So I must be successful, and you're part of the reason, as you have just told me. There's more to it than rents with that lot and the others out there. Archie has great plans for their welfare, but they're stubborn and ignorant, and Grant humored them in it."

Holding hands, they walked through the birch and hazel coppice. "They could have better gardens, better beasts. They could have decent cottages with separate byres, but they don't want to give up the old ways of taking animals in under the same roof with them. They'd have proper fireplaces instead of a peat fire in the middle of the room, with the smoke supposed to go out a hole in the roof but kippering the inmates instead. It's no wonder some of them have coughs that sound as if their lungs were exploding out of their chests. I know whereof I speak. I was in and out of those hovels enough as a lad, drinking goat's milk from a sooty bowl and eating bannock cooked over a smoky fire."

She'd seen him as an officer of the Royal Horse Guards; she'd seen him dancing, singing, joking; she'd seen him giving Christabel his wicked caricature of a London buck; she'd known him as her lover. But here spoke a man with a social conscience and heavy sense of responsibility. If she had wished before that her father could know him, she prayed for it now. *Oh, Papa, if only it's true that you do know all. William says so, but I never could understand how it could be. Now I wish I believed it beyond a doubt, the way I believe in Nigel.*

"And besides drinking the milk and eating the bannock," she said, "you knew about taking trout in the night, with someone watching for the gamekeeper."

"Ah, those were the sweetest trout I ever ate! We'd go up to Old Lachy's to fry them in oatmeal. He lived away from the rest, so nobody could be fluttering and fretting about what we'd done. And if a keeper should walk in on us, how could he prove that Young Master Gilchrist hadn't provided some perfectly honest God- and Laird-fearing fish for his ill-chosen friends?"

Her mouth watered for the sweetness of the stolen trout in its crisp coating, eaten around a peat fire with the boys and Old Lachy, whoever he was.

"Is Archie a great fisherman?" she asked.

"He always was, but he seems to have gone off it lately."

"Isn't there plenty for everyone, not just that very special tenant out there all by himself?"

"Archie, good-hearted as he is, is a great upholder of tradition. He reserves his position as the Laird, and so he should. The landlord who forgets his authority is inviting anarchy. In any case," he added with a grin, "they're not dying of desire to fish the loch at night. I told you about the water horse. It was safe enough for the lads with me; they thought I had a charm against evil."

"Did you?"

"I let them think so. But there were times when the heart threatened to leap out of my breast when something *big* broke water out there, and I was convinced it was swimming straight for us. I was more afraid of the Black Wolf than anything else. You see, as long as you didn't *touch* the water horse, you were safe."

"Wouldn't it be wonderful if such monsters did exist? Awful, but wonderful."

Fifteen

ADAM WAS a big young gray with a calm eye. "Well, he's certainly not elegant," Nigel said, "but I believe he has a sense of humor." Adam gave his shoulder a sociable nudge. Dora, the mare, was a slender chestnut beauty, skittish, but responsive to Fergus's stroking and crooning.

"What are you saying to her, Fergus?" Jennie asked.

He stared at her with dead-black eyes under the thick, low brows, and after a moment he said something guttural and unintelligible. Then he steadied the mare's head between his hands and made the same sounds again.

"She was bought for Christabel," Nigel said, "but Christabel doesn't care to ride here. No Hyde Park."

"And she must watch her complexion," said Jennie. "I'm turning to boot leather before your eyes, you poor man." At this moment four men came riding around from the front of the house, one on horseback and three on garrons. They stopped at the paddock gate.

Nigel went at once to meet them. "Good morning, Patrick! Come here, Jennie, will you?"

Patrick MacSween was the head keeper, a square-set, ruddy man, black-haired, roughly handsome. He had a very soft voice. He held his bonnet in his hand while he talked with her. "And how are you liking your new home, Mistress Gilchrist?"

"I love it already. There is so much to see and do, but I want everything at once."

"Och, it will be even more interesting by and by, when the—"

"We must get to our business, my dear," said Nigel like a middle-
aged merchant of a husband.

She smiled and nodded at the other three men, who civilly touched
their bonnets. "Will you be wanting a dram?" she asked Nigel, in character as the merchant's wife.

"Don't hurry in; I'll speak to Morag," he answered.

The visitors' horse and ponies watched over the gate while she tried
to make friends with Dora. She thought she'd do better without Fergus;
the mare seemed to have eyes only for him, and the way he observed
everything, as unblinking as a cat, made Jennie self-conscious. But she
didn't like to ask him to go away. She put him out of mind and held
the halter with one hand, stroked the mare's face with her other hand,
murmured love words of her own, and persevered until she felt the change
come.

When she let go, the mare stayed instead of tossing up her head and
wheeling around to run. She made small sounds in her throat, and Jennie
kissed her between the eyes.

"Well, Fergus!" she couldn't resist saying smugly, and surprised what
might have been a rudimentary smile.

"I'll bring you something next time," she promised Dora. Adam
nudged her. "You, too. You're a pair of poppets."

Nigel and the men were talking in the office-study. So Nigel was
actually at work as his brother's factor, the man of business. Serious
matters were being discussed; she found herself tiptoeing reverently past
the closed door and laughed at herself.

The tour of the house started in the kitchen and pantry. They were
immaculate. The flagged floor was scrubbed, and the wooden work surfaces were scoured nearly white. The stoves were well blacked, and a
peat fire burned in a clean grate. The blue and white delftware in a
hutch cabinet reminded Jennie of home.

"Mr. Grant left if for you," said Mrs. MacIver. "It was a wedding
present to him and Mistress Grant from the Old Laird. You will be
wanting your wedding china kept in the dining room."

"I would rather eat from the delft. It suits the house."

"Oh, but you'll have lovely china surely," Morag coaxed, "to use
when you have guests! Will that wagon never come? Och, that Coinneach
has stopped too many times altogether." Aili was bouncing up and down
like a fat little water bird in anticipation of the wagon's treasures.

Mrs. MacIver took Jennie down to a clean, light cellar where the food was kept cold in a whitewashed buttery. A boy from the home farm fetched fresh milk and cream daily; cheese, butter, and eggs were brought as they were needed. All meats and vegetables came from the farms; game and fish were taken on the estate. They sent to Inverness for fruits, nuts, sugar and treacle, white flour, coffee, tea, and chocolate, and any other delicacies available.

Archie had laid down a selection of wines for a wedding gift. "A very fine start for your cellar," Mrs. MacIver said, and Jennie nodded as if she knew all about wines.

"Mrs. MacIver, I would like you to choose the meals for the time being," she said. "I'm most anxious to try everything Scottish. I have a good appetite, and so has the Captain, so you needn't be worrying about having food sent back from the table."

Mrs. MacIver nodded austerely. Feeling more and more like the lady of the manor, Jennie visited the rest of the house, attended by the maids. The drawing room had only a few heavy oak pieces and a dismal painting, of a snowbound moor and mountains, over the fireplace.

"Your things will be making it so beautiful!" Morag promised.

There were three other rooms on the next floor, sparsely furnished. There was a bed in only one of them, a majestic construction. "That looks old enough for Mary, Queen of Scots, to have slept in," Jennie remarked.

Morag giggled and then said reproachfully, "Och, the poor lady. Mistress Grant told me all about her."

The servants' rooms were upstairs under the roof. Respecting the occupants' privacy, Jennie merely glanced in and saw that the rooms were neat, made personal by a few little possessions, and were reassuringly airy. For summer weather, windows could be opened throughout. Mrs. MacIver's room was the largest, as befitted her position; Jennie saw a Bible beside the candlestick on the night table.

When the inspection was over, Jennie was ready to drop the lady-of-the-manor role. She was frantic to get out again. She would thankfully eat anything Mrs. MacIver chose to prepare; she didn't care if the girls kept their rooms tidy or not, as long as they themselves were tidy. She wanted only to be outside again under Scottish skies, hearing her blackbird and a Scottish skylark. She was going to climb the ridge again, sit on the fallen tree, and contemplate the moor again, the loch, and the hive of vitality below the crest.

The study door stood open, and the men were all gone, Nigel with them. She went to the kitchen to get a sugar lump for the mare, but before she could deliver it, the wagon had arrived.

Fergus was called to help the two men; the girls carried everything they could, and Mrs. MacIver appeared without being asked. Jennie would have gladly left everything heaped in the drawing room for the time being, but she found herself in the center of a cyclone; not a very fast cyclone, as nobody seemed to hurry, but a subtle, relentless one, accompanied by compliments and assurances in English and a great deal of Gaelic conversation spangled with laughter. Once she saw Mrs. MacIver smile.

Coinneach of the wagon, he who had stopped too many times altogether and gave off the fumes of it, was a tall man, and Mrs. MacIver had him standing on a kitchen chair to put up curtains and hang the mirrors and pictures. The carpets went down next. Then the Wedgwood and the tea sets were arranged on the dining-room shelves by Aili. She rubbed up the pieces of plate with a flannel before she set them out on the sideboard.

The drawing room blossomed, and the two girls flitted through it, humming with the ecstatic industry of bees in a rose garden. Everything left over was taken upstairs to one of the empty bedrooms; Jennie asserted herself about this. "I shall see to those things *later*," she said.

She told Mrs. MacIver to give the men a good dram each, and she and the girls were to sit down to a good cup of tea. Jennie would have tea herself.

"In the drawing room, Mistress?" Aili said hopefully.

She'd have liked to have it brought outside the front door, but the girls would have been devastated, they were so anxious to have her in the drawing room. She let them settle her there with the tea tray and then told them to go and have theirs and take their time. She poured a cup of tea and took it and a piece of shortbread out to the parapet and hoisted herself up onto it. The worst was over, and she was glad of it. She swung her feet, ate and drank, and was happy except for wondering how she could tip the men. She wished that somewhere along the way she'd been able to change one of her sovereigns.

Luckily Nigel came riding home while she was still sitting on the parapet with her second cup of tea, and he went back to the kitchen to tip and thank them. "Give Fergus something, too!" she called after him.

She had known exquisite intervals as a child and even more intense moments as an adolescent. But after her father's death and the breaking up of the family and the loss of Pippin Grange, she had believed she was no longer capable of those spontaneous skylark flights toward the zenith. Those were symptoms of youth, like the flower texture of a baby's skin, a new chick's down, a puppy's soft fur. For her to experience them now, as a married woman, first astonished her, and then they were reverently accepted.

"Surprised by joy," Wordsworth had begun a sonnet, and he knew whereof he spoke.

That first week she and Nigel covered much of the estate that lay east of the ridge. They rode on bridle paths through the woods from one section to another. Sometimes Archie joined them when he wanted Jennie to see a particular view, and he would display it as if he'd created it. At these times they'd be expected to stop at Linnmore House on the way home for a glass of wine, and Christabel always behaved as if she'd been dragged away from some great work of mercy or philosophical research. Aunt Higham had had a second habit made for Jennie when she realized how much she would be riding; it was dark blue kerseymere, very slim-fitting, with blue velvet collar and cuffs and a small blue velvet hat. The first time Christabel saw this she looked at it sidewise, as if Jennie were out in gossamer muslin with no underwear, and then said that they all smelled so strongly of horse it make her feel faint.

At night Jennie and Nigel played chess or cribbage before the fire in their room, or she read aloud to him, now that she had her books. He was always agreeable, no matter who the author was. He either fell asleep or pretended to, then suddenly rose up, removed the book, blew out the candle, and took her into his arms. She wondered if their child had begun yet. Surely when this miracle occurred in her body, she'd know it; she wished she'd asked Sylvia about this.

One afternoon they rode through the woods south of Tigh nam Fuaran along a rising trail to the mill. It was built astride the stream which, lower down, flowed so placidly through the pastures. Up here it furnished the power to grind all the meal used on the estate and most of the flour, except for the fine white stuff Christabel ordered from Inverness.

The miller spoke of that with subtle sarcasm. "They're saying the scent of yon bread fairly makes your teeths water. But you'll be knowing that already, Captain and Mistress Gilchrist. You're fresh from London, where all the grand things are."

"There could be nothing grander than the porridge here," Jennie told him. "Did you grind the oats for that?"

"Aye, Mistress." He tried to look grimly modest, but he couldn't help a sparkle which suggested that when he used to be thin and nimble and young, he'd been quite a lad.

From the mill they climbed diagonally up the forest ridge and reached the carriage road that led west across the moors. The hills and the mountains were preternaturally clear in the bright easterly atmosphere. All blurring moisture and haze had been sucked up to return as rain, but one should be willing to pay for such a day as this.

Only an osprey fished the loch today, hovering on beating wings high above the broad reflecting glass. Then suddenly it shot downward and hit the water like a cannonball. It rose with a fish in its talons and headed off to the north.

Jennie applauded. "Poacher," said Nigel, and laughed.

"Let's ride out on the moor," she coaxed. "It's too beautiful to turn back. It may rain for a week after this." She had seen the women loading their creels with peats, and she wanted to speak to them.

"We'll go a little way," Nigel said. "But at five I am having a meeting with Archie."

"About the new cottages? I won't let you be late for that."

Birds flew up from the heather on either side of the road, and one sang loud defiance from a dwarf shrub. As they approached the women and children loading peats, close enough to hear their voices, Jennie slowed Dora, but Nigel speeded Adam to a trot.

"I want to stop!" she protested. "I want to meet them!"

"We haven't the time today, love. And we shouldn't be interrupting their work. The midges must be driving them mad."

"There's not a midge out—"

"Not up where we are, but down there, close to the ground. Believe me, I *know*." He put a hand over hers and gently shook it. "It'll be no kindness to stop them. They want to be loaded and out of there."

"They're *looking*," she whispered. "They expect us to stop. Nigel, they might be mothers or sisters or wives of your old friends."

"I will see them later, Jennie dear." He saluted with his crop as he rode by. Jennie held Dora back and made a point of waving, so they wouldn't think the Captain's wife had not wanted to acknowledge them.

When she caught up with Nigel, she said, "You could have called out to them instead of going by like Wellesley reviewing the troops and disapproving of them."

He grinned. "If I was a bit stuffy, I'll make up for it later. I don't want to talk to any of them until we're ready to begin the improvements and I can tell them everything at once. Now they're bound to ask questions, and I don't want to give them time to discuss it. There's always one among them—I don't mean just among those women, but the lot— who'll convince the rest that the Laird has evil schemes in mind."

His reasoning satisfied her. "I may be able to help when the time comes," she said. "Talking to the women, you know. Morag can help with the language. I'm sure *they'd* like everything new for once in their lives."

"If anyone can convince them, you can, my darling."

Beyond the loch, the road ran in a pale stripe up a wave of land and disappeared over the top. To their right a track went off among the crags and wild growth; it dipped out of sight, but beyond it she saw, half-hidden by a rounded shoulder of gray rock, the gable and chimney of the cottage that stood alone over here.

"What does the very special tenant do besides fish in the loch?" she asked.

"Devil if I know. Perhaps he's like the lilies of the field; he neither toils nor spins. We'd better go back now."

"What's over the hills and far away, as the song goes? More lochs? More cottages? How far is it to Roseholm from here?"

"Many miles to Roseholm, through the hills." They turned the horses homeward. "But just along the road here, not too far, there's the Pict's House. We could bring out a bottle of wine and a cold bird and have a picnic. There's a jolly little stream where we can cool the wine and water the horses and dabble our bare feet like a couple of happy infants. Would you like that?"

"I'd adore it. Will the Pict be at home?"

He laughed. "It's always been called the Pict's House, but the minister and some other learned bodies think it's a monk's cell. They say there was a monastery four hundred years ago where Linnmore House is now."

"Wouldn't it be marvelous if Linnmore House were haunted by a hooded monk? But I suppose Christabel wouldn't allow it."

"Not if he couldn't tell her what's all the go in London."

"Just the same, I shall ask Archie about it. It will be a change of conversation next time we're there."

"There may be something in the library about it," Nigel said. "Archie never reads if he can help it, but over the years the family's acquired quite a respectable collection of books."

When they came into the house, Morag told them she and Aili had been putting new candles in the sconces and in the branches of the girandole mirror. "Would you be pleased to look? Everything is ready now."

Dutifully Nigel and Jennie went into the drawing room and admired enough to satisfy the girls, who then left them alone.

"I have a dreadful thought," said Jennie.

"What is it?" He looked worried.

"We have no excuse now for not entertaining Archie and Christabel. And Morag is aching for us to show off all this. Christabel, of course, will look down her nose at it. Besides, I've told Mrs. MacIver I want everything Scottish, and you know how Christabel is about *that*."

"I shouldn't worry, my duck. We have some leeway because this is still our honeymoon."

With a grateful passion she embraced him under a painting of Venus in a heavenly chariot drawn by doves.

Sixteen

T HE NEXT DAY began with showers before daylight that continued into late morning, and Jennie had no excuse not to write letters to her aunt and her sisters. She wrote to Lady Geoffrey also, and bullied Nigel into adding a page. The postbag went out on Sundays when the family drove to church in the village.

In the afternoon the showers let up, and a drying northwest wind blew across from the mountains. Nigel and Archie had business in the village, and Jennie was in suspense expecting a summons from Christabel to come and keep her company.

But no note came, and she could kiss Nigel good-bye with an enthusiasm not wholly due to his charms. He rode off to meet Archie by Linn Mor and go on from there. Jennie got quickly out of the house in case Christabel was belatedly seized by a deadly impulse and sent for her. She took a lump of sugar to Dora on her way to freedom; she had promised Nigel she wouldn't ride anywhere without him until she and the mare were thoroughly acquainted. "We *are* acquainted," she argued. "I know I can trust and handle Dora anywhere."

He shook his head. "Please, Jennie." So she gave in. It was nice to be so treasured.

She walked along the outside paddock wall, and the mare cantered along inside. Raindrops flashed on every twig, and Jennie's shoes were already damp, and so was the hem of her dress. She wore no bonnet and had wrapped herself in a russet merino shawl.

At the far end of the paddock she reached for Dora's head. "Good-bye for now, love. We'll have splendid rides together."

118

But the mare had seen something. She threw up her head to free it and stared past Jennie, her ears attentively pricked. Jennie turned around.

A solitary figure stood motionless on the road, so all at once *there* that it could have simply materialized from the stuff of bad dreams: dark bonnet pulled low, dark clothing, and the dark face just guessed at, so the eyes under the bonnet were unseen, but seeing, and they were watching her.

It was the first time outside Linnmore House that she felt unwelcome here; the resentment, or worse, came in all but palpable waves through the light airs of spring. She gazed steadily, unwilling to turn her back on she knew not what. At last she lifted her hand and called, "Good afternoon!"

But the words faded on an expiring breath as he went on without another look toward the ridge. He disappeared into the coppice, and in a few moments he reappeared on the track above it, small at this distance and moving fast. She gave him time to go over the ridge and vanish before she followed, and when she reached the crest, there was no sign of him. Her bad reaction seemed only silly now; he must have been one of the men from the cottages, wondering whether he should speak to her or not. Perhaps he worked in the stables or on the grounds of the mansion and had a free hour or two.

She had not been up here long enough to get over the impression of seeing into another world, and she doubted if she ever would. The moor kept changing colors as the day brightened and darkened. The loch was choppy today and looked cold under the clouds, summery-warm in the sun. The hills were plum-purple one moment, pale mauve the next.

With a sigh of pleasure she sat down on the fallen tree. The sounds of life around the cottages came to her now clearly, now muted, depending on the wind, and sometimes she heard the whistles of the raptors riding the upper air. She felt she could sit here for hours and never be bored.

There was a hiss of caught breath behind her, and she jumped and looked around. Morag had just come up over the crest. She was bareheaded, her black curls loose around her forehead and ears; she wore a tartan shawl over her blue dress and white apron, and carried a small basket.

"I was not expecting to see anyone," she said, the red rising up her throat and into her round cheeks. "My work is done for a little while. Mrs. MacIver said I might go for an hour."

"Well, so you may," said Jennie. "But why and where?"

"My father has not been well. I was taking him a wee sup of wine. It's Mrs. MacIver's own," she added quickly. "She made it last summer, from brambles."

"That can be very helpful for certain things," said Jennie gravely. "Do you live down there?"

"Where the little cow is pulling at the thatch. Och, she is a stubborn one," Morag said fondly. "New green to eat, but she will pull at the old thatch. She was always set on her own way, from the moment she came out of her mother and first got to her feet."

"I've known cows like that," said Jennie. "Does Aili live down there, too?"

"Yes, she is my cousin."

"May I walk down with you, Morag?" Jennie hadn't planned it, but there it was.

"The path is just this way." Morag hurried ahead; the back of her neck was pink and vulnerable under the loose wisps of hair. Hidden by the thickening spring growth, the path crossed the hillside, always going down until it dropped into a narrow transverse valley that hadn't shown up from the crest. It was deep enough so Jennie, looking back, could see the tops of the pines, but not where she had been sitting. They forded by stepping-stones a rushing brook cutting deep into the slope, then followed the track among erratic boulders on gradually flattening ground. The suggestion of peat smoke was now an acrid fact.

Morag stopped and looked back. "It's not very tidy," she said, not ashamed but warning.

"I don't care about that," Jennie said. "You don't go home at night, do you? You may, if you'd like to."

"The cottage is crowded. It gives them more room if I stay away, and I have a room of my own at Tigh nam Fuaran."

A few children playing a mysterious game among the random boulders saw Jennie and Morag first. They took one look at Jennie, ignored Morag's greeting, and scampered off to the cottages, shouting. This set a dog barking, which brought in a chorus of sheep and goats. The cow left off twitching at the thatch and bellowed with astonishing volume for the size of her, and the other cows joined in.

"They will be ready for us!" Morag said. "How can they not be?" She led the way between two cottages, with hens scurrying before them clucking hysterically. The children's warnings brought out everyone who hadn't seen the girls already, hushing children and dogs impartially.

Most of them smiled and spoke as their names, delivered in Morag's nervous English, came too fast for Jennie to repeat. She shook hands with everyone; the men took off their bonnets; the women bobbed. There were no young men except one, very pale and gaunt with flaming red hair, who walked with two sticks; she remembered seeing him from the ridge. Most of the other men were graying or already white, leather-tanned, but with young eyes. There were two pregnant women. One was young and blooming in comparison with the other, who looked sallow and worn-out with childbearing; four children pressed against her skirts like chicks around a hen, and one rode her hip.

There must have been about fifteen children altogether, of all builds and coloring. The oldest was a wiry boy who might have been an undersized fourteen. All were barefoot; all gazed at Jennie with the same sober curiosity the animals showed, but she got one delightful answering smile from the baby on its mother's hip.

Morag saved her mother and father for the last. The woman with her sleeves rolled upon reddened arms, taking Jennie's hand without hesitation, was unmistakably Morag twenty years older, years which had not defeated the gray eyes. Her hair was still as black as Morag's, twisted back from her broad face but showing curly wisps. She had missing teeth, but no cramped grimace of a smile to try to hide the fact. She shook Jennie's hand hard, and she didn't bob.

"Och, the lad chose a bonny one!" she exclaimed.

I don't want Morag to look like that in twenty years, Jennie thought, *but if she can be that merry and courageous, the rest won't matter.*

The father was cadaverously thin, grayish about the mouth, but with a sparkle in his deep-set pale blue eyes. "I was ghillie to the Old Laird," he said. "I mind the morning he poured me a dram and said, 'Drink up, Hamish. Drink to my new son!' God willing, I'll drink to *his* son before I die. To many sons."

"Many lads and lasses *both*," said his wife, winking at Jennie.

"You're Hamish?" she exclaimed. "You taught him to fish!"

"That I did," he said. He was pleased.

"I'm so glad to meet you all," Jennie said. "I'm so glad to be at Linnmore." She took care to place the accent right.

"When will he be coming to see us?" the young red-haired man asked.

"Soon! He has not been able yet to come down, his brother is keeping him so busy, but he told me about the times when he was a boy here."

Another man stepped forward. He was short and broad, with red cheeks and a crest of white hair. "Will you tell him, if you please, that we are ready to work on the roads, or indeed anywhere? Except on the enclosing." He shook his head at her. "Never on that." There was gentle shushing all around.

She asked quickly, "What do you mean by 'the enclosing'?"

"It is nothing to concern you, Mistress Gilchrist," the red-haired man said. "We are wishing to work, to pay our rent. We are not lazy. It is only that all work stopped when Mr. Grant went away."

"I will tell the Captain tonight," Jennie said.

Approval and hope ran through the group like wind through a wheat field. The pregnant young woman cried out, "Tell him my husband was a soldier, too!" She put her hand on the forearm of the gaunt red-headed man with the two sticks, and he nodded awkwardly at Jennie. She tried to think of something to say that wouldn't sound silly or patronizing.

She was saved by Morag, who said, "My cousin Alasdair Gilchrist. He is Aili's brother. He was wounded at a place I don't know how to say."

"Corunna," the soldier said hoarsely.

"But he lived," said the red-cheeked man. "I was a soldier, too, and I lived. Four others from these cottages have died in foreign lands. There are three there now. Alive or dead, we have no way of knowing. . . . And many more altogether from the estate."

"The General, they say, is a great man," a cool new voice interposed. "A rising man. But it seems he needs too many Highlanders to climb on. Sometimes I think he must drink their blood."

It was the man she had seen on the road; he hadn't been in the group when Morag introduced them, but now he sat on his heels against a wall. Morag's mother spoke to him in Gaelic, and he answered in English, smoothly sardonic.

"I have nothing but good wishes for the Captain and his lady. What does he have for us?"

There were murmured objections to his rudeness and reassuring glances at her. An old woman patted her arm, as if soothing a child. She lifted her chin, and said loftily, "He has at heart the best interests of all the people of Linnmore."

The man smiled. It was a humiliating smile; it ridiculed her. After all the cordiality she'd been made to feel inept and frivolous, a little girl playing at Lady of the Manor.

"I must go back now, Mistress Gilchrist," Morag said.

"Yes, we'll go." Jennie caressed the fair head of the baby on its mother's hip and got that marvelously uncomplicated grin. It comforted her, and she ducked her head to kiss the baby's crown.

"Beautiful," she said to the mother. "All the children are beautiful." They were not, but she knew they were so to their mothers. "Good-bye, everyone!"

They returned it in both English and Gaelic; the slight dark man against the wall neither moved nor spoke. The children, released from the iron grip of shyness, ran and leaped about them, and the dogs ran with the children. One of the boys came up to Jennie carrying a small black kid. She took it from him and hugged it, put her face in the soft fur of its baby neck, fondled a miniature hoof. Then she returned it, saying, "He is very handsome."

Morag translated it. The child gave her a blazing smile. He let the kid go, and it ran crying to its bleating mother.

The escort went as far as the brook, with the smallest children hoisted on the backs of the older ones. Jennie and Morag crossed by the stepping-stones, and the children boldly shouted their good-byes, very brave now that the lady was leaving. Morag gave them obvious admonitions, making shooing gestures, and they turned and started back over the rocky ground, talking among themselves. Those unencumbered with younger ones climbed up on the biggest boulders, jumped off with shouts, and raced for the next.

"The brook is forbidden for them to cross," Morag explained. "Or to play near. It is very deep in some places, and it is always fast. Long ago two children drowned in it."

"Who was that man?" Jennie asked. "The one who just came?"

"Alick Gilchrist. He lives over the loch. A Dia, he shamed me with his bad manners!"

"Gilchrist, did you say?"

"Many are named Gilchrist at Linnmore. My name is Gilchrist."

Jennie stopped in delighted astonishment. "Then you are all clanspeople."

"The old people still call it that. It makes it all the harder for them when—" She stopped and, as if to avoid Jennie's eyes, swooped down and snapped off a piece of uncurling fern.

"When what?" Jennie asked. "And what was meant by 'the enclosing'? Enclosing of what?"

"It doesn't matter, Mistress." Morag straightened up. A radiant confidence had replaced her embarrassment. "It doesn't matter at all, when the Captain is factor. For isn't he one of us?"

He was, indeed, and in the face of Morag's luminous certainty Jennie could now dismiss the man's cool insolence and the way he had smiled.

"The children have no school, have they, Morag?"

"No, Mistress."

"What about yourself?"

"Mistress Grant taught me to write and read. I went up to Tigh nam Fuaran as a very young girl."

"And Aili—can she read and write?"

"I try to teach her. She is a wee bit slow." She shook her head, laughing at herself. "It's not that fine a teacher I am."

"I would like to start a school here," Jennie said. "I know I can't reach all the children on the estate, but I can teach these, and you could help me. You could translate for me, and you could be teaching me Gaelic at the same time, so I could speak it to them."

It was nothing she had planned. The seed had germinated all at once when the children surrounded her. "I can teach out of doors when it's fair, up here on the ridge or on the drying green behind the house. Indoors when it's bad. We could use one of the empty bedrooms for a schoolroom."

"I will do anything you ask," Morag was promising, tearful with joy. "*Anything!*"

Papa would approve of her using some of her sovereigns for slates and everything else she needed.

"Would the parents let the children come, do you think?"

"They will be so grateful," Morag assured her. "They will make them come."

"We'll make it happy for them, Morag, with singing and stories. And *cakes.*"

"White bread and butter they'd like, Mistress." Morag spoke from experience. "When I first came here, it was better than any cakes to me."

"Then they shall have it," said Jennie. "Now I must think how to get slates and things. Are there any shops in the village?"

Morag looked distressed. "A few, but I am afraid—but perhaps in Dornoch or Kirkton—"

"Don't worry." Jennie laid a hand on the girl's arm. "They can be got somewhere, I know." She went ahead down the return track and stopped at the fern-fringed pool. Some long-stemmed purple violets had opened up and languished over their trembling reflections. The sight of them crowned the day for Jennie; the first violets had always been her personal good omen.

Seventeen

J ENNIE SPENT the rest of the afternoon wandering through the woods around Tigh nam Fuaran, absentmindedly looking for bluebells and more violets. She didn't want to pick them and take them home, any more than she wanted to imprison any of the birds she watched and heard, when she could put her mind on them. She was preoccupied with her school plans. She had never dreamed that she could contribute so much to the welfare of the estate, and she could hardly believe that she was involved in it so soon.

When she heard hooves on the road, she went out to meet Nigel. "Who's this bedraggled gypsy urchin?" he called.

"You have no idea how comfortable wet feet can be after a while," she said. "But wet hems drag a bit. Trousers are better. Kilts would be best. Nigel, why don't you and Archie wear kilts? Your father looks superb in his."

"And he wore the kilt when it was proscribed by law, too, which makes him all the more superb." Nigel dismounted and took her into his arms, and they kissed. Adam nudged impartially and emphatically until they separated, laughing. "He wants his supper, the tyrant," said Nigel.

"So no lallygagging. Go along, the two of you."

"Is he master or am I?" Nigel looped the reins over one arm and put the other around her, and they walked.

"Was your meeting productive?" Jennie asked.

"Oh, yes. . . . What have you been doing all afternoon?"

"I went down to the cottages." She had to stop to talk. "Oh, Nigel, you must visit them soon! They speak of you with such fondness, they're so happy you're here and so anxious to see you. Oh, and I met Hamish! Fancy, he's Morag's father. Did you know that?"

"Morag's father, is he?" Nigel looked bemused.

"And he was your father's ghillie."

"I shall have to get down to have a talk with Hamish."

"The men want to talk with *you*. They want to work; they're worried about their rents." Adam was tossing his head about and snorting in exasperation, so they walked on. "I like them, Nigel," she said fervently. "They are so warm and friendly and not servile. I'd *hate* that. They wish us many lads and lasses."

"I'm sure they do, but you mustn't make free of the place down there."

"I don't intend to intrude on them, but at home I went wherever I pleased."

"This isn't home. At least, not that home." He seemed as frustrated as Adam. "Oh, hang it, girl, you know what I mean!"

"No, I don't," she said mildly. "I thought this was our home, forever and ever, world without end."

"Of course it'll be ours when the time comes, but now it's Archie's by law and Christabel's by money, so we—oh, Lord!" He scowled at her. "Can't you see?" Adam lowered his head and gave Nigel's shoulder a hard shove. "And *you* keep out of this!" Nigel said to him, and Jennie began to laugh.

"Come along. Any moment now he could turn carnivorous. . . . I know Christabel calls the tune, my darling man. The first ten minutes with her told me all I needed to know. But, Nigel, I don't intend to be an elegant automaton that sits in a chair with its feet on a footstool and does fine needlework. I want to be occupied when I'm not with you, and I want to be useful. But I promise I won't go out of my way to offend her."

He looked relieved. "I love your spirit, Jennie, darling, but I don't want to jeopardize our life here. It can be very good."

"It's very good already," she protested. "It's almost perfect. But it can be even better. You and Archie are determined to improve things for the tenants—I refuse to say 'peasants,' that's her word—and I want to have a part of it. So, Nigel, my angel, I am going to have a school. At first it will be for the children close by, but with time—"

"Good God!"

"You're staring at me as if you'd just found out I've married three times before or that I'm going to elope with a groom. In a hackney coach," she added. "Like Lady Caroline Wellesley. Nigel, you can't be that horrified! Please tell me you aren't." Her stomach was roiling. "How could Christabel possibly object? It won't cost the estate anything; it will be nothing out of her pocket." She hugged Nigel's arm. "The way to make the parents accept change is through the children. You'll see, they'll be more than willing to have new cottages and learn modern ways. Morag says they'll be happy to have me teach the children, and then *you'll* be able to do anything with them; they're so relieved you're here, and not an Englishman or a Lowlander, who'd be even worse, Morag says. He'd be just as foreign."

"*Morag says*"! he repeated. "Why are you gossiping with the servants? And this school idea—"

"How can one possibly disapprove when children are taught to read and write and figure, girls as well as boys? In time I'll add needlework for the girls, starting with good plain sewing, and the boys could be taught joinery, and other trades, and then they needn't always go for soldiers. It's dreadful to think they should be born and reared only for cannon fodder."

"Oh, my girl, you're a romantic dreamer." Nigel wrapped her in his arms and rocked her against his chest.

"No, I'm not." She burrowed her head under his chin. "I know it can't happen all at once. *Petit à petit l'oiseau fait son nid.* That's the first proverb I learned in French. And I promise you I'll discuss the school with Archie. After all, he is the master here, and I shall respect him as such." She tilted her head back so she could look into Nigel's face. "With any luck I'll have his consent and his blessing before Christabel can get a whiff of it."

"You'll manage it if anyone can."

Adam snorted and sprayed them, which effectively broke them up.

"Never, never discuss a serious or romantic issue with a hungry horse as the third party," said Jennie.

Fergus came at a shambling trot to take Adam, who practically dragged him to the stables, while Dora called over the paddock wall.

"And now, my love," Nigel said to Jennie, "you'd better bathe at once. Hair and all. Sometimes they are verminous." He grinned at her expression. "A fact of life, my dear."

"Then you shouldn't have hugged me," she retorted, "because you may have caught a few facts of life from *me.*"

Eighteen

S HE TOLD THE SERVANTS they might go home Saturday night to keep the Highland Sabbath with their families. Mrs. MacIver was pleased without being effusive. It was a long walk to the village, but she was used to it, and sundown came later every day. The girls were ebullient at the chance of talking over with their families all the new and happy circumstances.

Only Fergus would not be going away, even on Sunday morning after he had done his chores. It was either his choice or because he had no home but his little room in the stables. "You'll not get a blink of him," Mrs. MacIver had told Jennie. "I'll see that he has food for the day."

"This isn't done, you know," Nigel observed. "Church is one thing, but twenty-four hours?"

"You mean it's not done by Christabel, who doesn't have Highland servants in the house."

"They'll take advantage."

"No, they *won't*," she said.

She could prepare breakfast, and she wanted to. Dinner would be at Linnmore House after church. This looked like being a set Sunday ritual, and she would gracefully accept it as the inevitable dark side of her new life. Besides, she might be able to lure Archie outside to show her around the premises, and then she'd get his permission to start the school.

That night Jennie and Nigel were alone in a house together for the first time in their lives. Candidly enjoying their own bodies and each other's, they made love in the long twilight, lying on the pillows and coverlets they'd spread on the floor beside the fire in their room.

Jennie raised a long naked leg and pointed her toe at the plaster rose on the ceiling. "It's heaven to feel so wicked and know we aren't."

"Wouldn't it be even more heavenly to feel wicked and *be?*"

"Is that why men go with light women, and supposedly respectable women take lovers?"

"How should I know?" he asked. "When do we have supper?"

"Are you changing the subject?"

"Only because making love makes me hungry." He got up and walked about the room, looking about seven feet tall. Firelight danced over his body and caught in his yellow hair. "I need to be restored so we can commence all over again."

"Oh, in that case—" She reached for her wrapper.

They went down to the kitchen and collected the cold supper and wine Mrs. MacIver had set out on a tray for them. They ate and drank sitting on the floor by their fire; afterward they made love again and fell asleep where they were, naked and uncovered. They roused up when the fire had been dead long enough for the room to chill and hurried into bed, snuggling their cold bodies together until they were warm and sleepy again.

Jennie woke with the dawn chorus echoing among the treetops outside the windows. She slid from under the covers without arousing Nigel, shivering, pulled her nightgown on over her head, and went into Nigel's dressing room, where she had tucked away in his armoire the carpetbag she'd forbidden Morag to unpack, saying she'd do it herself. The old wool dressing gown was there, and the fleece-lined slippers. She dressed in them, taking an affectionate joy in the reunion; then she brought out from the bottom the nightgown from that night in Inverness.

She took the gown downstairs and washed it in rainwater in a kitchen basin, scrubbing as best she could where it needed extra attention. Then she took it out and spread it on the drying green. The sun wasn't up yet, but the sky showed a fragile blue at the zenith. Even the knowledge that Fergus was in the stables with the horses and Nigel was asleep in the house couldn't take away the illusion that she was alone in the world, except for the birds who piercingly proclaimed their territorial integrity. She felt a regard for them as equals.

Mrs. MacIver had left a banked coal fire in one of the stoves, and Jennie expertly revived it; she'd learned from Mary Ann at home. The porridge was ready, after slowly cooking on the back of the stove all night. The eggs and rashers were in the pantry. She set the table with the delft and went up to wake Nigel and dress. She had included her big holland apron in that private carpetbag, and she wore it over her dress while she served breakfast.

"If we're ever reduced to living in a cottage without even one servant," she told him, "I'd do very well, you see. We could even keep a cow; I can milk; at least I've had a go at it, and the cow didn't seem to mind."

He gave her a slap on the bottom and pulled her into his lap. "And I can't do this with the maids, no matter how bewitching they are."

Archie and Christabel called for them in a shining midnight blue barouche, with ornate gilt G's painted on the side panels. The horses were Bruce and Wallace, and Iain Innes was on the box. His hat was as glossy as his boots; his breeches looked new; his coat matched the barouche. The whole turnout was undeniably smart, and Iain was as stolid amidst the elegance as any London coachman. She spoke to him by name, and he touched a finger to his hatbrim and seemed to look through her.

Christabel wore buff crepe trimmed with apricot velvet, a feathered hat with a scarf of veiling floating from it, and carried a parasol. Jennie, in her dress and pelerine of willow-green cambric, felt dressed like a schoolgirl, and the little white straw hat trimmed with lilies of the valley completed the illusion.

"Ah, Jeannie!" Archie fairly leaped from the barouche to hand her in. "What a flower you are this morning!"

"Thank you," she said demurely. She smiled at Christabel. It was going to be a long ride, a long service, a probably uncomfortable pew, a long drive back again, and a long dinner at Linnmore House while the day blazed mockingly outside those sealed windows. She'd be a fool if she didn't reward herself for all the suffering by getting Archie alone.

"Will there be a Gaelic service?" she asked.

"Ours will be in English," said Christabel. "It is the law now because so many people speak it. There's one for the Gaels, following."

"Not too well attended these days, Macleod tells me," Archie said. "I don't like it. If they start losing their respect for the Sabbath, God knows where they'll end up."

"Then if He knows, why should you worry?" Jennie asked. Archie haw-hawed and slapped his thigh.

Christabel was not amused. "A loss of respect for the clergy leads to anarchy."

"Anarchy sounds so violent," said Jennie, "and the people I've met so far seem far from violent." Nigel signaled her with a warning wink.

"Macleod will have to make some pastoral visits," he said lazily, "and round up his flock. Crack the whip. Threaten them with hellfire; they always used to be desperately afraid of that, as I remember."

Archie was pinching his lower lip and pulling at it. "It's not the same anymore. In the old days—well, only last summer—you'd see them on the roads on the way to the kirk. Never missed. In the winter it took a blizzard to keep them home. From all over the estate they'd come. They'd have to start at daybreak, some of them." He looked mournful. "I can't understand a bit of it."

"It's Grant!" snapped Christabel. "He undermined our authority in his sly way, and now we have Alick Gilchrist telling them the ministers are hand in glove with the landlords."

There was a silence. Archie cleared his throat, and Christabel fussed with a fold of her skirt.

"That's a handsome crop of oats," Nigel said.

"Aye, it is!" Archie agreed too vehemently for the subject.

A wagon waited in the road by the dwelling at the home farm, and the family and servants were getting themselves settled. Christabel nodded remotely; Archie and Nigel lifted their hats. Jennie sang out, "Good morning!"

A little while later Bruce and Wallace caught up with the wagon from the other farm; there were more greetings, and some candid stares as the farm people tried to get a good look at the Captain and his wife. Jennie gave them one of her best smiles.

"Oh, what a lovely baby!" she exclaimed of a large infant who looked like Henry the Eighth without a beard.

Archie at once leaned forward with a great grinful of teeth and said, "Aye, that's a very lovely baby!" Then he settled back and nodded at Jennie.

Looking overheated, his wife said in a thick, half-suffocated voice, "We don't as a rule call out from the carriage, especially to the servants."

"Och, what's the harm?" asked Archie, sounding very Highland.

It was while they were driving over the stone bridge above the deep ravine, where the air should have been fragrant with verdant new life, that they began to smell the smoke.

It hung heavy and rank, it made Jennie's nostrils prickle, and it stung her eyes. A thin haze soiled air that should have been crystalline, and the queer thing was that no one remarked on it. Christobel was holding a scented handkerchief to her nose, and her eyes were watery, but her face was empty. The men sitting opposite them ran out of conversation about the farms, the fishing, and the deer stalking. Archie played compulsively with the seals on his watch chain, while Nigel sat motionless, looking out as if he'd never before seen the country they were passing through and couldn't take his eyes off it.

The carriage rounded a curve of the sheltering hills, and she heard the church bell; at the same time she saw the dirty brown pall of smoke lying off to the northeast beyond a border of forest and low hills.

"Look at that!" she cried out. "There must be a terrible fire somewhere!"

Iain Innes turned his head at her outcry and looked back at her. "There was that, Mistress. A terrible burning and a sinful one."

Christabel took a sharp, quick breath, but before she could speak to him, he'd turned back, and it was as if he had never moved at all. *"Archie!"* Christabel said. "Did you hear that insolence?"

"What was that, my dearie? No. My mind was wandering." It was a poor lie. Jennie had sensed, if not seen, his flinching movement when Iain spoke, as if a thorn had suddenly pierced his hand. Nigel was fingering his cravat.

"They start easily," he said. "Someone knocks over a candle and—" He lifted his hands. "Or an enemy fires the thatch. Pehaps that was what Iain meant by 'sinful.' Let's hope that no one died in it." He sat forward and patted Jennie's knee.

The village stank with smoke, and the people who stood outside the front door of the church were either obviously disturbed by it or obviously trying to ignore it. As the smoke moved past the sun, the yews became black and funereal.

Iain drove the barouche away. Archie spoke loudly and toothily, neighed, shook hands, clapped shoulders; Christabel dispensed pinched nods and small, tight smiles. Nigel was handsomely at ease, bowing with the negligent grace that Royalty never seemed to achieve. There wasn't time to introduce Jennie to his old acquaintances because they went directly into the church to a pew under the pulpit, and the service began at once.

The minister was the white-haired man who'd taken his hat off to the chaise in the rain a week ago. His features were heavy, and his bad color wasn't improved by the black gown and the white Geneva bands.

His mouth turned relentlessly down at the corners, and his eyes were either weirdly enlarged behind thick spectacles or disappearing completely when the lenses caught and reflected light.

Jennie expected that he would speak of the fire, certainly in his prayer and possibly in his sermon. He did neither. He prayed with tremendous eloquence for the blind to see the Light and the deaf to hear the Word, and after the first ten minutes Jennie stopped listening. Was he approachable about her school? Did he even care about the poor? Not enough to go near them apparently. But perhaps he was a sick man; did Presbyterian ministers have curates? They should have.

Dr. Mcleod prayed for victory over the French and asked for holy leadership for the gallant generals. No mention of the gallant troopers and foot soldiers. She waited for a word about the young men from Linnmore. It didn't come.

The stench of the smoke seeped into the church. Throats were cleared, and noses discreetly blown. Dr. Macleod coughed and drank water, but he didn't mention the fire. Still, even if no one had died, surely there were people homeless; wouldn't it be as proper to pray for them as for the gallant generals? . . . Ask *this* man about her school? *Hah!* Jennie thought scornfully, and was homesick for dear William.

The sermon was concerned with one of the minor prophets, Habakkuk. Dr. Macleod had given Habakkuk a good deal of time and attention. One advantage of being pregnant, she thought hopefully, was that she could feel especially delicate on Sundays and unable to make the long drive here and back. Keeping her eyes uplifted and fixed on the black and white figure in the pulpit, she felt herself swooping toward sleep in giddy spirals.

Archie coughed resoundingly, and she jumped. Christabel's mortified annoyance was as palpable as the reek. Nigel's arm pressed hard against Jennie's, and they exchanged little grins with the pleased guilt of schoolchildren communicating under the master's nose.

Archie's cough set off a fusillade through the congregation, and Dr. Macleod raised his voice over it. Habakkuk conquered. She had never been so tired of a name in her life. She wondered how many of the congregation were actually entranced by Habakkuk and how many had learned to gaze glassily at the minister while their minds departed to other places. She was sure that Nigel, as relaxed as a well-fed lion on his native turf, hadn't heard a word after the opening sentence.

Finally the service was over, the benediction pronounced, and they

could go out, not into the sweetness of May but to the stinging haze.
Nigel introduced Jennie and the minister in the doorway. Dr. Macleod's
out-of-the-pulpit voice was moderated to an agreeable pitch, and grave
courtliness softened his massive features. His eyes did not look so strange,
an odd but pleasant greenish hazel.

"I hope you will be very happy here at Linnmore," he said. "It is a
beautiful part of the Highlands."

"I've loved it from the start," she said. "But I don't intend simply
to exist here. I'd like to start a—"

"*Jennie,*" Nigel said, "did you know there are some remarkable Pictish
stones in the churchyard? The carving's quite fantastic, wouldn't you say
so, sir?"

"Nigel, my boy!" Archie called from out on the walk. "Here's an
old friend of yours!"

"Perhaps Dr. Macleod will show me the Pictish stones and explain
them to me," Jennie said demurely.

"I shall be happy to, Mrs. Gilchrist." They walked away from Nigel,
down the shallow steps and around the corner into the churchyard. At
one side a family group all in black were visiting a recent grave; the
women wept silently. The yews and some tall old stones fenced off the
decorous sociability in front of the church and muted the sounds of
carriages coming up. She followed the tall robed figure across grass where
violets and wild strawberry blossoms grew.

He showed her the intricately chiseled Pictish stones and told her a
little about their origin. "I have so much to learn about my new country,"
she said humbly. "But I have something to give too. Dr. Macleod, I
want to start a school for the children in the moorland cottages. It seems
very wrong for them to be allowed to grow up illiterate."

It was abrupt, but she didn't know how long she'd have before she
was caught; she'd always been sorry for the fox, and now she felt like
one. He listened to her with his arms up the sleeves of his robe as if he
were cold. His eyes swam vaguely behind his spectacles, his mouth was
turned down at the corners again. What was he like when he was young?
she wondered. Did he ever laugh and sing and dance?

"My father told me," she said, "that the Presbyterians respect education almost as much as they do God."

It was brazen, but it worked. He shook his head as if a stinging fly
were goading him. "But surely you—" He stopped.

"Yes?" she prompted him. "Did you mean that surely I've discussed it with my brother-in-law? I plan to do that today, but I've been waiting until I could mention a little help from the manse." She smiled at him. "What possible objection could he have to my teaching the children for a few hours each day?"

"There should be none. But I had thought—I'd supposed—" He broke off, shaking his head again. Perhaps she'd been right about his health, and he was exhausted from the service, even light-headed.

"It takes time to start a school," she said, "especially when the childen speak very little English, or none. I need simple Gaelic texts, if there are such things. I thought you'd know, Dr. Macleod. Once they learn to read their own language, we can begin English."

He still didn't speak but seemed lost in a study of her. She said kindly, "Perhaps you will think about it when you are rested?"

Nigel appeared around the yews, his hat under his arm and his bare head almost silver against their darkness.

"Mrs. Gilchrist, I will do anything within my power to help you," the minister said suddenly. "I shall compose the texts myself, and make lists of words with their phonetic pronunciation to help you learn the language."

"I'm very grateful!" She put out her hand, and when he took it, he smiled for the first time.

"It will be a pleasure as well as my duty. . . . Nigel, you have a rare gem here, a wife not only of charm but of intelligence."

"Seems almost too good to be true, doesn't it? Hard to keep on eye on her, though. Disappears while you're looking at her. Don't dare let her go near the Fairy Hill for fear she'll vanish completely."

"Where's the Fairy Hill?" she demanded.

"You have a choice, Mrs. Gilchrist," said the minister. "There's many a fairy hill and glen, I'm sorry to say. If you ask the right folk, or perhaps I should say the wrong folk, they can always point out some enchanted or haunted spot."

"I know about the water horse, the each-uisge"—she pronounced it proudly—"and the osprey is the iolair-uisge. And uisge is water but also whisky."

"The water of life, my dear," said Nigel.

"You see, I already know some Gaelic. Dr. Macleod is going to help me, Nigel."

They had come around the line of yews. Only a few people remained from the first service, while the Gaelic speakers were straggling toward the open door. The barouche waited on the road; Christabel and parasol were already in place, and Archie stood talking with two men. The smoke shaded the day into a near twilight, one half expected cinders and bits of burning thatch to fall from the sky. Archie was attacked by another shattering cough.

"Where was the fire?" Jennie asked the minister. "Is it out yet? Was anyone hurt?"

"No one was hurt that I know of, Mrs. Gilchrist. It was one of those unfortunate things, all too common."

"I feel so for anyone who loses a home and possessions. Are they in your parish?"

"No, it's not part of the Linnmore estate," he said quickly.

"Too many cottages went," Iain Innes said from the box.

"Goodness, I hope we never have anything like that here!" said Jennie.

Nineteen

OR MOST OF THE RIDE home Christabel was in a fine old sulk, what
they'd called a flink at Pippin Grange. Archie endeavored to make
up for it. Jennie, euphoric about her school, helped him by showing an
ardent interest in everything he had to say, and the attention intoxicated
him. Christabel sat turned away from them; she must have been uncomfortable, but she maintained this aloof position all the way. By the time
they were rolling up the beech avenue, and Linnmore House's granite
was a roseate reflection in Linn Mor, Jennie wished for the courage to
refuse to dine. If only she could invent a queasy stomach and turn pale
at will, then Christobel would worry all afternoon for fear she was pregnant.

She retired with Christabel to the boudoir, to lay aside their wraps
and tidy up. At once Christabel asked her what she and Dr. Macleod
had been talking about for so long.

"The Pictish stones," Jennie said. "The carving is so eloquent."

"You were out of sight for so long, I wondered that Nigel didn't
object. Of course he was engaged in conversation with Miss Lamont of
Rowanlea." Christabel was so blandly nonchalant that it was comic. "A
handsome girl and quite well-to-do. It's a pity you were too busy to meet
her. They are staying at the manse, by the way. Her mother is Macleod's
cousin. He is likely to find this very confining. Some of these Scottish
clergymen are just too pious to be true. I'm not *au courant* of the village
gossip, but I'm sure the servants at the manse have a good deal more to
talk about than prayers before breakfast."

"Wouldn't that be the case in any household, even one that didn't

139

have prayers before breakfast?" Jenny wished she could have laid off her stays along with the other things. "If we have servants, we are bound to be greedily observed and commented upon, down to the smallest idiosyncrasy."

"Not by *my* staff," Christobel said complacently to herself in the mirror. The maid moved soundlessly around the room. "Of course, all of your and Nigel's doings will be common talk in the cottages. The sooner you replace those people with trained servants, the better off you'll be. You have a position to maintain, my dear girl. You're no longer a child, you have serious responsibilities."

Jennie met the eyes in the mirror and thought; *What nasty little glass beads. How could Archie have ever—* "I like the girls and Mrs. MacIver," she said.

Christabel sighed and sprayed herself with scent. The atmosphere of the overdecorated and closed room became even more stifling. "Don't tell me," continued Christobel, "that you and that man were discussing antiquities for *all* that time."

"We also talked about the poet Mr. Wordsworth," Jennie lied recklessly, "and I ventured a quotation." She lifted her eyes reverently to the ceiling and recited:

> " 'O joy! that in our embers
> Is something that doth live,
> That nature yet remembers
> What was so fugitive!'

"Dr. Macleod was *so* delighted because I knew Mr. Wordsworth's lines."

"I have never," said Christabel, "heard of Mr. Wordsworth."

Which disposes of Mr. Wordsworth, Jennie thought. *I wonder if he knows that Christabel has just extinguished him.* "I'm sure you *will* hear of him," she said. "He's very revolutionary. He expresses the beauty of the commonplace."

"Stop that!" Christabel snapped at the maid who was endeavoring to catch up a ringlet displaced by the removal of the hat.

"We were just moving on to the verse of James Hogg, the Ettrick Shepherd," Jennie continued, "when Nigel came."

"Eugenia, aren't you afraid you'll be lonely here without another bluestocking for companionship?"

"Oh, no! I have my books with me to keep me company when Nigel can't, and I shall send for others. And I love to be out. I adore nature! I should like to live under the open sky like a gypsy. I'm a great moor walker and hill climber," she prattled on; it was blatant, a little sickening, but she was borne by an irresistible current, and Christabel's frustration was worth it.

"The winters here are long and dark," Christabel said feebly.

"So are they in Northumberland. I'll be like those hardy souls Archie mentioned; only a blizzard will keep me in!"

"We might as well go down," said Christobel in resignation, as one who says, "I might as well proceed to the block and the headsman's ax; there's nothing left for me here."

Jennie felt a wicked and reviving little jolt of joy. Christabel did not like her at all, so she wasn't likely to be summoned often to be a companion.

"Such a distinguished old house!" she said cheerily on the double staircase, and had Archie rubbing his hands and flashing his teeth in an ecstasy of pride.

"It's a very great comfort to me to know you'll be mistress here one day!" he exclaimed.

Christabel said aridly, "The sauce will be quite ruined."

It was not. The meal was perfect, except for being too ample. Archie talked on and on about Linnmore House as if extolling it to prospective purchasers. Nigel was suave and bright, Christabel was ominously silent. After the dessert she made to take Jennie off, but Archie rose at once, carrying his wineglass in one hand and the decanter in the other, and said, "Now we shall have some music."

When was she going to get him outside, alone? Still, from the way he shone continuously on her like a tropical sun, she doubted that she'd have any difficulty when the hour arrived. Perhaps it would be better to have her plans all laid out on paper first.

It was late afternoon when they left. *Not again until next Sunday*, she was blissfully thinking as she accepted Archie's kiss on her forehead. But Christabel was not to let the field mouse escape.

"I should like you to come on Tuesday afternoon. Mrs. and Miss Lamont will be calling. I intended to introduce you to them this morning, but you escaped to the churchyard."

"Damned if I wouldn't find the churchyard a vast improvement over

Mrs. Lamont," said Archie, carried away by music, wine and Jennie's proximity. He and Nigel laughed immoderately.

Christabel said, "You might bring your needlework. If you have any."

They left on foot. Nigel was as desperate to stretch his legs and breathe deeply as his wife was. It had become warm and still, and she carried her hat in her hand, with Nigel taking her pelerine over his arm. They strode along at a good rate, their locked hands swinging between them. They were young and in love, and they sang loudly as they walked through the woods to Tigh nam Fuaran.

"Nigel, come for a walk with me over the moors," she said when they reached the house. "The way I feel I could tramp to the Pict's House with no effort whatever."

"I've work to do for Archie," he said. "Two letters to write. Archie's butler is off to Inverness tomorrow for his spring holiday, and he will take them. They're to be personally delivered, that's why they couldn't be trusted to the postbag."

"Oh, love, come for a walk with me!" she coaxed. "Write your letters in the morning."

"You know I'm never bobbish in the morning, except to throw a leg over a horse. *Or you.*" He grinned. "Besides, I'm not a genius at letter writing, though I have a passable fist when it comes to holding a pen."

"Why can't Archie write his own letters?"

"Because I'm his man of business. It's my duty to write the business letters, not his."

"I hope that when you're the Laird of Linnmore, you won't think you'll need a buffer between you and the rest of the world, including that one out on the moors. How long has it been, I wonder, since Archie's been up on the ridge, let alone visited the cottages, those and the ones farther away? Your father knew everyone on the estate and made christening gifts to the children. Morag told me. Even though he had a factor, when he wanted men to work he rode around himself to talk to them."

Nigel said angrily, "My father was a Laird in the old way. He was a simple man and lived in a simple fashion, but that way of life is not possible now. It has to change if these estates are to survive. And that leads me to remind *you*, my dear, that if Archie hadn't decided he needed a factor, we wouldn't be here. You'd be languishing in London instead of stravaiging over the moors like a gypsy."

"I think I'm in for a lecture about stravaiging when Christabel has me captive in her drawing room next Tuesday."

"Will you be a lady, at whatever cost? Christabel can't help what she is any more than you can help what you are."

"I think I shall tell her that, forgivingly, if she begins to bully me."

He took her by the shoulders. "You'll tell her *nothing* if you want to stay here. We can be sent away and never see this place again until Archie dies. Bear that in mind, and keep your sweet mouth shut and curved in a gentle smile."

"Oh, Nigel!" She laughed, and he kissed her open mouth. Then he put her away from him.

"Later," he said huskily. "Go change and take your walk. I must get these letters out."

Twenty

S HE TOOK SUGAR to the horses, and they watched her go away from them and then watched the place where she disappeared into the coppice. She went rapidly up to the crest of the ridge, giving the pines the affectionate respect due the beloved elders they had become for her. She sat down on the fallen tree and dropped her shawl back from her shoulders. The almost constant breeze played capriciously around her bare head; it was scented with unknown, unseen flowerets. The stench of the fire seemed to have existed on another continent, and she had thought once that she could never get it out of her nostrils.

The loch reflected azure back to the zenith. A Sabbath quiet lay over the cottages, and the animals grazed or lay peacefully in the sun. Why didn't Archie go down there himself if he was so worried about anarchy? That was a ridiculous word to be used in this place, but she'd heard it twice within a week. If anyone was undermining the Laird's and the minister's authority, why did Archie hide himself in Linnmore House while Christabel called his tenants either barbarians or stupid peasants? Perhaps the reason Archie hadn't been fishing the loch was that it was too close to one set of cottages, and he might hear something he didn't like or couldn't answer.

No wonder they were overjoyed to have as factor another son of the Old Laird, when this son had no wish or ability to deal with them.

"Good afternoon, Mrs. Gilchrist," a man's voice said softly.

He must have come up the steep track behind her, but she had heard nothing. Alick Gilchrist leaned against the nearest pine, and a shaggy brown pony grazed a little way off. The man's expression was politely equivocal, and he hadn't taken off his bonnet. If he was looking for signs of distaste or snobbery, she thought, he was about to be cheated of an excuse for resentment.

"Good afternoon, Mr. Gilchrist!" she said with a smile.

"It is a handsome prospect, is it not?" He waved his hand at the moor.

"Oh, yes! I'm sure this will always be my favorite view."

"How long do you think it will remain as handsome?"

"That's an odd question. Why shouldn't it remain so always? Oh, the seasons change it, but in winter there'll be smoke from the cottages to show life. There'll always be the loch like the sky's looking glass, and the mountains in and out of the clouds, changing their colors."

He took off his bonnet and sat down on the fallen tree at a courteous distance from her. His hair was not black, as she had thought, but a very dark brown.

"The cottages, then, you think will always be there."

"Yes, but improved. New ones, with proper fireplaces and chimneys. More windows. Separate stabling for the animals. But cottages always, and peat to burn."

"So the cottages are to be improved," he said musingly.

"Surely you don't disapprove!"

"Och, not at all. Anything that is done for the tenants of Linnmore I approve." With his elbow on his knee, and his chin in his hand, he studied her, and she tried to stare him down. His eyes were a darker gray than Morag's and narrowed with amusement, or possibly contempt. She should leave this place at once before he said something insolent; she picked up her shawl.

"Mrs. Gilchrist," he said in that soft voice, "were you ever hearing of *Bliadhna nan Corach*, the Year of the Sheep?"

She was caught, as always, by the Gaelic. "No, but tell me."

"I can see it would not be talked about in your presence. It was the year seventeen hundred and ninety-two, when the first Cheviots were brought to Scotland."

"I know the Cheviots," she said, glad to assert herself in something.

"It is said that they are a much better animal than the black-faced Lintons, the sheep of the Highlands. It is beginning to be said that they are a much better animal than the Highlander." Without raising his voice he said, "Do you know what is the most dreadful sentence for a Highlander to hear?"

"I should think for anyone it would be the sentence of death. When he knows he is dying, or that his wife and child are—"

"Those are very terrible moments. But the worst sentence is *Cuiridh mi as an fhearann thu.* It means 'I shall evict you.' "

She wrapped her shawl tightly around cold arms; she had gotten chilled very quickly. "Have they been afraid of that *here?* Because Mr. Grant went away and the Laird didn't come himself to talk with them?"

"Yes, they think it was discussed, and Davie Grant bitterly opposed it, so he had to go."

"They *think!*" she exclaimed. "What facts had they to go on?"

"It has happened, it *is* happening in other places." The Gaelic *s*'s hissed about her ears. "They could not find out what Linnmore intended. *I* could not find out, and I have no fear of walking into Linnmore House and asking questions, in spite of the lady. I have been there just now."

"And what did Ar—Linnmore say?"

"He was asleep, the man told me. And Madam would not have me come into her drawing room, and she would not come to me."

"Well, I can promise you," she said indignantly, "that my husband has *assured* me that improvements, *not evictions*, are planned, and I hope if you have any influence, you'll convince the tenants it's not the Devil's work that builds new cottages and makes the gardens better and the animals healthier."

He inclined his head. "Whatever is best for them I will help. I have heard about your school. Do you have Linnmore's leave for it?"

"Not yet," she said quickly, "but I expect to have it very soon, as soon as I show him my completed plans. Dr. Macleod is going to help me collect the materials."

One of his eyebrows went up. "Indeed! A day of wonders!" For the first time he really smiled. It stung her. *He* was probably the one who was terrifying the others with rumors of eviction, and Christabel was right about him.

"Do you approve of my school?" she asked boldly.

"Who am I to approve or disapprove?"

"I thought you were someone who cared about the children."

"A school is fine, if it does not try to turn them into little Sassenachs. Our pride is all that is left to us."

"I know what pride is. A man is nothing without it, and neither is a woman." She sensed his liking for that, or at least respect. "Mr.

Gilchrist, is there a fairy hill at Linnmore? I am not going to laugh about it or write amusing things to my relatives. I am quite serious."

"Some say the way into the Fairy Hill is through the Pict's House."

"Is that where it is then?" She was delighted. "Nigel and I are going to picnic there. Take a strupach," she explained, to show off her few Gaelic words.

"It will disappoint you," he said dryly. "It is not high; it is hardly a hill."

"Did you ever go looking for the way in when you were a child?"

"Och, we knew we could never find it. Only the Fair Folk can open it, from their side. But we never went under the lintel of the Pict's House, for fear we would never come out again. It was once believed that if someone disappeared, he had been stolen by the fairies. The poor soul would have been drowned or collapsed in some mountain pass in a blizzard."

"Were they believed to be happy with the fairies, or should they have been in a Christian heaven?"

"No one," he said, "has ever returned from either place to give an account of the amenities."

She laughed. "Tell me about the Pict's House."

"It is only the remains of a stone hut built into the slope. Some say a Pictish monk lived there in the old days, when Christianity was young in Scotland. Myself, I believe that. But when we were lads, it was different. We dared each other to pass under the lintel, but no one ever took the dare."

She saw him as a small dark boy, bare-legged in tattered breeches or a ragged kilt like the boys she had seen at the cottages. He'd have been impish and quicksilver, jeering at someone else's cowardice while trying to conquer his own.

"Did anyone ever hear music from inside the hill?" she asked. "I've read about that and wished I could hear it. Magic fiddling that nobody could resist."

He shook his head. "No, but we swore we did. To each other, not to our elders."

"There were things my sister and I never told either. . . . Was Nigel one of the boys?"

"No, he is younger than me." He stood up and put on his bonnet. "This has been very pleasant, Mrs. Gilchrist." The pony came to him, nodding its head. He mounted and turned the pony toward the track leading down to the cottages.

"Yes, it has been very pleasant," she agreed. "Good afternoon, Mr. Gilchrist." He touched a finger to his bonnet and rode away. He disappeared partway down, in the transverse valley she remembered, then reappeared farther along. The pony ambled toward the cottages, the rider drooping in the saddle as if he were half-asleep. A man came out of the shadow of a wall, and his red hair seemed to flame up suddenly in the sun; it was the lame man who walked with two sticks. Goats bleated. There was a stir of awakening around the cottages as the Sabbath moved to its end. If they hadn't gone to church for their own reasons, they had still kept the Day.

When she got back to the house, Nigel was just seeing off Patrick MacSween and one of his men. She went into the kitchen to get their light supper; a teakettle with a spirit lamp had been one of their more practical wedding gifts, and she made tea. Nigel came into the pantry, smelling of pipe smoke and whisky, and hugged her from behind while she was slicing bread. She leaned back contendedly against his chest.

"What would Dr. Macleod say about business meetings on the Sabbath?" She teased him. "Desecration!"

"I'd charm him out of his wrath. Besides, I didn't expect Patrick today, so I can't be blamed, can I? And I had to live up to the obligations of Highland hospitality. And I didn't get my letters written. What have you been doing?" He took the knife away from her and began whacking off thick wedges of crusty bread. "That's the way I like it. Ungentlemanly, what?"

"It's lovely. You might cut some ham and some cheese, too." She took out knives and forks. "I had a conversation with Alick Gilchrist up on the ridge."

"The devil you did!" He seemed more amused than annoyed. "What did you talk about?"

"He approves of my school," she said.

"Is that *all* he said?"

"Well, no. I asked him about a Fairy Hill, and he said the Pict's House was supposed to hide the entrance to it. When are we going to picnic there? Tomorrow, if it's fine?"

"My dear girl, it's back to business as usual on Mondays."

"What about business not as usual on Sundays? What did the keeper and his henchman need to talk about so urgently that it couldn't wait? Has he discovered a still? Does he wish to hang a poacher?"

Nigel picked a sliver of cheese off the knife and ate it. "Are you sure Alick hasn't been preaching revolution at you?"

"Not a hint of it," she said blandly. "Nigel, what is the reason for his special position around here?"

"I'll tell you while we're eating." They carried the food out to the table set with delftware. Nigel drank a cup of tea and ate two slabs of bread and butter with ham while she attempted to possess her soul in patience. Finally he said abruptly, "We share the same grandfather. His father was a half brother to ours, a by-blow, fruit of our grandfather's hot youth. He was born to a maid in Linnmore House. Our grandfather built that cottage for her and her heirs and made sure that it could never be disturbed. So—mustard, please—Alick is a fixture here, no matter how much his existence goads Christabel."

"So he's your first cousin," she said.

"Yes, not that any of us cherish the connection," he said dryly. "Sandy was the oldest son, by-blow or not, and it must have roweled him all his life, knowing our father was the legal heir. And Alick's presence reminds Archie that his father wasn't the firstborn. Thorn in the side, what?"

"Thorn in *your* side?"

"No, and he never has been." He picked up a slice of ham in his fingers and ate it in two bites. "He's a part of the place, like the pines up there. He wouldn't become a soldier; he won't emigrate; he's never had a mind to seek his fortune over the hills and far away. Like the song, eh?" He grinned at her. "We shall see more of him when he finds he can't go to Archie over my head with his complaints. Archie doesn't wish to hear them; that's why I'm here."

"What sorts of complaints?"

He shrugged. "Alick can always think of something. I expect we'll have more and more trouble with him." He didn't seem concerned.

"What about his family, his father? Sandy?"

"He enlisted and died in America during the war with the colonies, so I don't remember him, or his wife either. They had an allowance from my grandfather, and it's been passed on to Alick. Not much, but he can afford new boots when he needs them. More tea?" He held out his cup.

Jennie had read Nigel to sleep and was reading to herself when she became conscious of a stir in the house. It was nothing clearly audible, but rather like knowing that the tide has turned; the servants must be back. She got up and went out into the hall, quietly opened the door to the back stairs and listened. The door at the foot muffled the voices in the kitchen, but she heard an exclamation quickly stifled, an outbreak of sobbing, followed by murmurs of consolation. She went back to the bedroom; Nigel slept on while she put on a peignoir and her padded silk slippers. She went down the front stairs and through the hall to the kitchen door and knocked. All sounds ceased within. She called, "May I come in?"

Morag opened the door to her, unsmiling, ducking in a curtsy. In the candlelit room she saw Fergus just going out the back way, moving fast. Mrs. MacIver stood regally by the hearth. She looked extremely tall in black, and she was still wearing her bonnet, which was also black. Aili was red-faced, and her eyes were swollen as if she'd been crying for hours. When she curtsied to Jennie, her eyes overflowed. She scurried for the back stairs, bumping into things on the way.

"May I go to my room, Mistress Gilchrist?" Mrs. MacIver asked distantly.

"Yes, of course." Jennie nearly stammered in her bewilderment. What had she done? Had she offended, merely by coming to her own kitchen?

Mrs. MacIver lighted her candle from one on the table and took her stately departure. Jennie turned to Morag. The lovely color was lacking, and her eyes were like a doll's glass ones.

"Morag, whatever happened today? Is anyone hurt or ill? Is it"—she had to moisten her throat—"bad news from the war?" The thud of her heartbeat was sickening.

"No, Mistress," Morag said stolidly, her eyes fixed on a point beyond Jennie's ear.

"If it's something very private, I don't wish to pry. But if there's any way I can help, please tell me, Morag, I beg of you! Mrs. MacIver is plainly upset, Aili is wretched, and so are you. You don't hide it well, Morag."

"It's the burning!" the girl cried passionately. "Yesterday eight townships were put to the torch, and the people turned out with what they could carry in their hands and on their backs! Surely you knew, Mistress!"

"Surely I did *not*!" The scent was thick again in Jennie's nostrils, and Iain Innes spoke from the box. *A terrible burning, and a sinful one.* "But I know now that I smelled it. It's monstrous! It can't be true, Morag. Who told you this?"

"Alick Gilchrist, but—"

The troublemaker, thinking himself cheated of his heritage. "And how did he know?" she asked coldly.

"A man rode in to see him last night; he'd just come from it. He said they are clearing for sheep at Kilallan. Alick didn't come to tell us then; it was so late to upset everyone. He went before daybreak this morning to see for himself." Her eyes filled with tears. "Och, the poor souls! Over two hundred of them in all! Some had not gone away yet; they waited by the embers. One old couple had sat all day and all night by their dead cow. They said they don't know where to go. The young men are mostly away to war, and this is how they are paid, their wives and babies and their parents robbed and driven away like beggars or gypsies."

Her color had poured back, and she was beautiful in her rage. "Oh, Morag," Jennie whispered. She sat down because she felt too weak to stand. "If this is so, it is horrible."

"It is so," the girl insisted. "Mrs. MacIver told us more, just now. They had an hour's warning, and then the men came with the torches. The whole glen went up in the flames! Some ran in terror and hid in the hills, thinking they would be murdered, and some were so frightened they could only lie down and be sick. Niall Geddes, who was Mrs. MacIver's brother-in-law, shook his fist at the men and cursed them, and when they pushed him aside, his heart stopped and he dropped where he stood."

She gripped the back of a chair. "May I sit down, Mistress?"

"Yes, yes!" She kept thinking how peaceful the cottages had looked this afternoon while she sat on the ridge with Alick Gilchrist talking nonsense about a fairy hill, and all the time he had known what he was going to tell them down there.

"Alick asked if any wanted to come back here with him, but they said, 'Linnmore will be next.' "

"It will *not* be." Jennie pounded her fist on the table. "Is that what everyone's fearing? Can't you make them believe it won't happen here? Listen, Morag, the minister is going to help me start my school."

"Dr. *Macleod?*" The girl was aghast.

"Yes. He was very interested," she said emphatically. He could not have know the truth about the burning; a man of God would have had to speak of it. But she remembered some set or disturbed faces outside the church, and some tense, low voices. *Someone* had known. And if it was known in the village, how could Dr. Macleod have been ignorant?

"Dr. Macleod," Morag murmured, shaking her head. "He has not set a foot inside any cottage in Linnmore for a long time; he goes only to Linnmore House. Mistress, the ministers preach that the landlords' rights are the will of God."

That was a speech straight from Alick Gilchrist's mouth, Jennie was sure.

"Linnmore is quite safe. Do you think my husband would allow me to go on planning the school if such a terrible thing is to happen here?"

"Alick stopped at Linnmore House this afternoon to talk to the Laird, but he could not see him."

"Yes, I know. I met him." She thought: *I know now why he asked me if I had heard of the Year of the Sheep. He was trying to find out if I knew. What a babbling, inconsequential child he must have thought me. . . .* She was tired enough to lay her head on the table, but she knew she would not sleep now with all this seething in her.

"Morag, don't worry," she said. "And tell Aili. Poor Mrs. MacIver, she has sorrow enough, so don't disturb her tonight."

"Yes, Mistress."

The most terrible sentence a man can hear: *I shall evict you.* One hour's warning and then the torch. "Can you sleep after all this, Morag?"

"I am tired enough to die."

"Then sleep, and tomorrow you may have leave to tell them at home that Linnmore is safe."

The girl suddenly sobbed as if she could no longer hold back. "Oh, Mistress!" she choked, helpless and ashamed.

Jennie went to her and stroked her back. Her throat ached; she strained her eyes wide and stared up at the ceiling to hold back tears. Where were they now, those turned out of their home by their own countrymen with as little compunction as boys kick over an anthill and stamp on the hurrying victims? Her own homesickness for Pippin Grange now seemed an obscene self-pity.

In the four-poster Nigel slept as purely as a child. She wanted to wake him and tell him of the outrage and be comforted in his arms, but to break that innocent sleep would be mere self-indulgence. The only thing he could do tonight was to assure her that it could not happen here, and she already knew that.

She wished she could hand it all over to God, but as she'd told Aunt Higham, she sometimes questioned His motives. Surely He'd have a hard time explaining a good many things He allowed to happen and be piously explained away as His will.

Besides, one of His ministers had just lied to her. Or had he? She tried to remember the exact words. . . . *one of those unfortunate things, all too common.* Perhaps he hadn't lied, but he surely hadn't wanted to explain. She gave him credit for being unhappy about it, and at least he had promised to help with the school.

She slept at last, and it seemed as if she had just closed her eyes when she was awake again, with the light of a crimson dawn in the room. Red enough to be the reflection of fire, but a cold glare, like a winter sunrise foretelling a blizzard.

"What is it?" Nigel asked, up on one elbow, and she jumped. He put his arms around her. "I've been watching you sleep. You were frowning and twitching, and when you woke up—what an expression!" He laughed and cuddled her against his naked body, brushing his lips over her temple and brow. "What awful thing did you think of? A nightmare about spilling wine on your favorite gown?"

"The people at Kilallan," she said at once. "Where are they all? It's cold, it's going to rain, and they've been burned out of their homes. How far would they have to go to find shelter?"

His amused caresses stopped. He tightened as if holding his breath, then let it go in a long sigh edged with exasperation. "You did have a nightmare, didn't you?"

She put her hands against his chest and braced back against his restraining arms. "Are you trying to protect me from cold facts, my darling? Yesterday, when the smoke was all but choking us, you pretended it wasn't there. But Iain knew what it was; do you remember what he said? And Christabel claimed he was insolent."

"He is, you know," he said lazily, drawing her close again. "He takes advantage, just as I told you they do. When did you hear this nonsense about burnings at Kilallan?"

"Last night when the girls came back. You were asleep, and I went down to speak to them. Morag told me."

"Morag again!" he said angrily. "Why do you persist in believing every rumor, every fantasy—"

"My dearest, you *know* it's not a rumor or a fantasy; Mrs. MacIver's brother-in-law is dead because of it. Alick Gilchrist rode out to Kilallan yesterday to see for himself. It was hideous. He tried to bring some bewildered old people back with him, and they said, 'No, Linnmore will be next.' "

She burrowed closer to him, trying to entwine herself around his warmth. "Did you and Alick talk this over?" he asked.

"No!" she protested. "He never mentioned it. I told you what we talked about. But he must have been on his way back from there. He'd tried to see Archie, and now I know why. He wanted some assurance for the people. They're so frightened, Nigel. It's disgraceful that they should be so terrified of their own countrymen! These aren't the days of Cromwell or the Jacobite risings."

He stroked her flank, but the gesture seemed automatic. "Did he see Archie?"

"No, nor Christabel either."

"Doubtless Archie saw him coming and took precautions."

"Then it's up to you, isn't it, to tell them they're quite safe? That there'll never be clearing to make room for sheep? After all, there's room for both here, isn't there?"

His murmured answer was more a vibration in his chest than anything intelligible, but it was enough.

"I've told Morag already," she said, "but it will mean so much more coming from you. So—today—Nigel, will you?"

"Yes, yes, I will go." The promises were mumbled amorously into her hair.

Twenty-One

M ORAG WAS discreetly cheerful at breakfast, and Aili was almost her buoyant small self again. She gazed at Nigel as if he were a god, and he accepted this with magnificent unconcern. He was leaving after breakfast to ride around the estate on his errand of reassurance. "Patrick can divide the territory with me," he said. "I'll go there directly and tell him. I'd like to see everyone myself, but it's not humanly possible in one day."

"I love you more than ever," Jennie told him.

"You'd better."

The gamekeeper lived well out on the moors, off the road beyond the Pict's House. "May I ride partway with you?" she asked.

"No, you may not, my love. You would have to come home alone." He held her shoulder. "If you're absolutely sure of Dora, ride, but only on this side of the ridge. Will you promise?"

"Yes, love." Mock-meek, she held up her face to be kissed. When she had seen him off, she went into the kitchen and told the girls that as soon as Mrs. MacIver could spare them, they could go home long enough to take the promise that Linnmore wouldn't be cleared even if sheep were brought in.

Morag said demurely, "I have already been, Mistress. I woke early, and I was away home before even Mrs. MacIver knew it. My mother and Aunt Iseabal are here at the washhouse now to do the laundering, and they're singing like larks, except when they think of the poor souls of Kilallan." She glanced respectfully at a stony Mrs. MacIver. "Aili and I will go on with our work now, Mistress. Come, Aili."

When the door had shut behind them, Jennie formally offered her condolences. She tried to be as restrained as Mrs. MacIver was, but she couldn't help exclaiming, "It's criminal!"

"It is that, Mistress. My sister and her grandchildren walked from Kilallan and are with my father in the village. Her son is fighting in Portugal. His wife died when the last child was born. The English King wanted his strength and his courage, and may have his blood yet. The landlord, with all his land, wanted the wee bit Niall had, for sheep. No matter how little you have, someone who has more wants it and takes it, and the ministers tell us it is the will of God."

"I wonder how they know," said Jennie. "Perhaps they tell *Him* it's so."

"The children have been so terrified when they saw their dog killed for trying to defend the house, and their grandfather die, one of them has not spoken since, and he was always the bright, quick one. It is like a candle gone out." She had not raised her voice. "I asked Dr. Macleod what we were born for, if God willed such a life for us, and he only shook his head and could not look me in the eye. It will be a long time before I listen to the sermons of him or any other minister."

There was nothing that Jennie could say that wouldn't sound feeble and inane even to herself.

"If they clear at Linnmore,"—the low voice went on—"I will not stay in this house. This is not against you, Mistress Gilchrist."

"I understand that, Mrs. MacIver. But they won't clear at Linnmore."

Jennie went upstairs. The girls were just finishing the work, and when they'd gone down the back way she unlocked her keepsake chest and took out one of the sovereigns.

The girls had now gone out to the washhouse to help, and Mrs. MacIver stood at the table preparing the ingredients for a cock-a-leekie. She refused the sovereign at first until Jennie said, "You can't deny it to the children. It's for them."

For the first time the glacier poise was shaken, as if by a polar earthquake. "Thank you, Mistress Gilchrist," she said almost inaudibly. Jennie quickly left her. She knew she had to do something constructive to take her mind off the crimes at Killallan; if she went riding now, she'd still be preoccupied with last night's and this morning's scenes in the kitchen.

She put the small table by a bedroom window, opened the window so she could better hear the birds and the surflike rush of wind in the leaves, and worked on a list of needs for her school. The minister would be able to tell her where the materials could be got; he might have a friend at Inverness who would collect the lot. A pianoforte was out of the question for now, but might one find a guitar in Inverness? Hardly. She'd have to send to London for it.

Another letter to Aunt Higham, then, in the next post, and she would arrange to meet with Dr. Macleod sometime during the week. If Nigel rode to the village, she could ride with him. She'd enjoy that, and she could stop on the bridge, as she'd promised herself the first time they drove over it.

It was all very elevating to her spirits. When, without being asked, Mrs. MacIver brought her a pot of chocolate and some buttered scones, Jennie felt as if her morning had been extremely useful. She had Fergus saddle Dora, and she rode over to the home farm to look at newborn puppies and drink strong tea with Christy Elliot. The burning at Kilallan wasn't mentioned, and it was a release to talk knowledgeably about the care of young animals and the progress of the crops. Nigel was always in the back of her mind; she kept having a picture of him shedding luminous assurance in one dim cottage after another.

He came home in the late afternoon, as bad-tempered as she'd ever seen him. He'd been caught in one of those brief hard showers that blew over from the mountains, and was cold and wet. She had the girls prepare a hot bath for him at once. He was short with them, and he swore under his breath at his boots and threw them across the room. He drank down three glasses of wine in quick gulps like a nasty medicine. But once he was in the bath, and she offered to wash his back, he became the old Nigel.

"Surly beast, wasn't I? Inexcusable. But—forgive me?" He brought her wet hands to his lips. Bad temper washed away, blue eyes like the best of summer skies. "It's only that being a factor is damnably more complicated than being a soldier."

"Except that you can't get killed at it."

"I'm not so sure of that! Promise them the moon, but when we start the work, they'll be sure they're being cleared."

"But can you blame them, after Kilallan?" She sponged lather off his shoulders. "But you won't need to take down the existing cottages, so they can live in them while you're having the new ones built, and afterwards the old ones will do for byres. Once they realize their roofs won't be burned over their heads, it will be all right. It's that—that awful coming with torches, like Saxons and the Vikings!" She showed him the gooseflesh on her arms. "It's so horrible even to imagine, without experiencing it."

He was scowling at her, and she grinned at him. "Forgive me for telling you what you know. You must have already taken the old cottages into account. My duty isn't to instruct my husband in *his* duty, but to drink tea with Lamonts tomorrow. I have a strong suspicion Miss Lamont was Christabel's choice for you."

Nigel stood up, dripping. "Miss Lamont is what is known in some circles as a damn' fine woman. She weighs all of eleven stone, and in another ten years she'll reach twenty. The man who shares her bed is likely to be crushed to death in the night."

She laughed. "Shall I dry your back?"

"That sounds dangerously seductive. . . . Promise me you won't mention Kilallan tomorrow."

"I won't shout, 'Death to the landlords!' over the teacups, if that's what you're afraid of. Where will you be while I'm in durance vile?"

"Archie and I are riding into town to have a meeting with the joiners and masons. I insist that he must approve the final plans so Christabel can't accuse me of wasting her money. It will do old Archie a world of good to have some time away from her. He's been under the influence of the blue devils lately."

"I hadn't noticed that," said Jennie. "I thought he was in fine fettle yesterday."

"He's always quite the buck with *you*. But Archie's an eccentric, and growing more so. He broods, and drinks with it. Not good."

"What does he brood about?"

He shrugged. "Christabel perhaps. I know I would! Or having no sons, not even a bastard like Sandy. He likes to gamble at cards, but otherwise I don't think he ever sowed a wild oat in his life. He must regret that, don't you think?"

"I fancy that's one regret you'll never know."

He hugged her, damply. "Ah, Jennie, you're the light of my life."

She dressed in her willow green outfit and walked to Linnmore House through an open-and-shut afternoon, carrying a furled umbrella just in case. Before she reached the bridge, she put on her hat and fastened up her pelerine.

She crossed the little bridge with a fond glance for the primroses on the banks of the brook and walked briskly along the drive, anxious to get the afternoon begun and over with. Who knew, perhaps she might like the Lamonts; just because Christabel made a fuss over them shouldn't damn them for all eternity.

She could see between a bright-leafed beech and the sweeping dark boughs of a big spruce into the stableyard. No visiting equipage was there; no coachman lounged with his hat off and his jacket open, smoking a pipe with Iain and the grooms. But at the front of the house, a tall bay horse stood beside the steps, cropping grass. Perhaps the Lamonts had sent a messenger to say they couldn't come. She was dismayed at the prospect of a whole afternoon alone with Christabel and wished wildly that she did have needlework; at least she could keep her head bent and her fingers occupied while Christabel preached and advised.

The horse lifted his head and gazed mildly at her. She stroked his Roman nose and told him that with a nose like that he should be in Parliament. "In the House of Lords," she added. He seemed appreciative and interested in her reticule. "If I'd known you were here, I'd have brought you something," she told him.

The front door opened before she could lift the knocker. Armitage, who was always so impassive he could have been wearing a papier-mâché mask with extraordinary lifelike tinting and a small wart on one plump cheek, was slightly out of breath and, for him, effusive.

"Good afternoon, Mrs. Gilchrist. Would you care to wait in the library? Madam is detained at the moment." He was guiding her there as he spoke, like a sheepdog sent to herd a refractory ewe. "May I bring you something to refresh you after your long walk?"

The drawing-room doors were not quite closed, and there was a man's hat on the Tudor chest.

"It wasn't really long, and I don't need refreshment, thank you, Armitage." She smiled at him and got a smile back; he was definitely flustered. He must have been listening at the drawing-room doors and had almost been caught.

"I thought you'd gone to Inverness, Armitage," she said.

"Inverness?" He looked surprised. "Not until next week, Mrs. Gilchrist. If you do not require anything, I shall return to my work." He bowed and left her.

Nigel must not have heard correctly about the Inverness holiday, not that it mattered. She went to the library door and listened until the door to the kitchen wing closed; then she walked across the hall, pulling off her hat so her ears would be freed. Whatever Armitage had found so fascinating she'd be sure to find absolutely enthralling. And no need to be caught with her ear to the crack of the doors; the granite walls shut off outside sounds so well that she could stand by the console table straightening her neck frill before the mirror, watched by all the dead stags, and hear Christabel's high voice, clipped and arrogant.

"It is completely my husband's decision. He *is* Linnmore."

The answering voice was new to Jennie: deep, hoarse, but with the Highland cadence. "Mrs. Gilchrist, Linnmore would remember his responsibilities if you were not urging him to forget them."

"*Responsibilities!*" Christabel laughed theatrically. "To these parasites, these vermin? You forget where and who you are, Mr. Grant."

"On the contrary, I remember very well. When last I left this house, I swore I would never come back. But I broke my own vow to ask you again not to clear. There is plenty of room. The old folk, now—to drive them out is killing them as surely as if you fired a pistol into their hearts."

"How poetic, Mr. Grant. You may go now."

"As to who I am, I am no longer the factor here, but a man who can speak his mind on equal terms with any other man living. I will come back when Archie Gilchrist is at home."

"Mr. Gilchrist does not wish to discuss the matter further."

There was a silence during which Jennie's ear throbbed; she pulsed all over, as if she had been running hard in a bad dream. She saw her face in the mirror, staring, mouth open for an outcry that couldn't come. She saw also in the mirror the burly man leaving the drawing room. If he saw her across the hall, he gave no sign but walked rapidly out. The big front door slammed behind him. She swept up the hat from the chest and ran out, calling, "Mr. Grant! Please!"

One foot in the stirrup, he looked around, his thick features still suffused with rage, his eyes narrowed and inimical under bushy gingery brows. "You forgot your hat," she said apologetically.

He took his foot out of the stirrup and accepted the hat. "Thank you," he said brusquely.

"Mr. Grant, I'm Jennie Gilchrist. Mrs. Nigel. Will you please tell me what's going on?"

"Don't you *know?*" he asked incredulously.

She shook her head.

"Come away from those windows," he ordered her. Leading the horse, they walked along the drive toward the brook.

"I know they're going to have sheep," she said, "but they aren't going to make anyone leave. They're going to rebuild the cottages, make them more comfortable and modern, and—" Under the weight of his astonishment she faltered; the brave words trembled and died.

His voice came soft with pity, and his expression went from brutal to kind. "I do not like to tell you that today the writs of eviction are being prepared and that both Nigel and Archie Gilchrist are present."

"No, *no!*" she cried. "He told me—he *promised* me—that when everything was done, they would be better off!"

"Perhaps he meant better off dead. But their lives are as precious to them as ours are to us, poor as these lives are, and so short. Your husband was brought in to replace me, to do what I would not do and what Archie Gilchrist is too squeamish to do for himself."

Both her stomach and her head were spinning. She struggled for poise. "I wanted to know what was happening, and I thank you. But I believe that Nigel has been deceived."

"I hope that is the case," he said, but she knew he didn't believe it. He swung himself up into the saddle. "What's left in Scotland one day will be a generation of atheists. And who can blame them? Not God, unless He is in the exclusive employ of the landlords, as they seem to believe. I've said too much to you, lassie, but it's not likely I'll be seeing you again."

"Where will you be going?"

"To Canada. When all of the Highlands is turned into sheep walks, there's no place left for me. I've given Alick Gilchrist what I could spare, to help when the time comes. They could always live from the land and their few beasts, but when they are on the roads, gypsies will be rich compared to them."

She wanted to speak, but she couldn't. He said awkwardly, "I'm sorry, lassie. You have an honest face and a sweet one. Good luck to you." He touched his whip to his hat, and the horse trotted off. She had thought at first sight that he was an uncommonly ugly man, but now, as she watched him go, it was as if her only friend were riding away from her.

The hooves beat hollowly on the bridge, and under it the brook still cascaded toward Linn Mor, the primroses still glittered like spilled sunshine, the swallows still glided and swooped over the pond. The earth had moved for fewer than twenty minutes since she crossed over the bridge on foot, and in that twenty minutes her life had changed forever.

Nigel *couldn't* have known; he'd have never agreed! He had been deceived. Even now he was telling Archie so, and the lawyers, or the sheriff, or whoever was to write out the writs of eviction. Blanched with rage, he was stalking out of that meeting. He would come home and tell her they were leaving Tigh nam Fuaran, leaving Linnmore. If he could not save the tenants, he would not stay here to watch the dissolution.

It was so clear to her that she expected to hear the gray galloping along the beech avenue at any moment. She was frantic to get home. *Home!* It would be that no longer.

She looked back at the mansion. She visualized Christabel behind the red granite walls, going on imperturbably with her tapestry, like one of the more malignant Fates creating evil. She would not go back into that house for anything. She began to run, holding up her skirt and petticoats, and she didn't slow down until the band of trees hid her from any window on the western end of the house.

Twenty-Two

S HE WAS CLAMMY with sweat by the time she reached Tigh nam Fuarran. *I must look like a madwoman,* she thought. *What will I tell them? How can I even face them?* The thought of her glib promises and assurances made her sick enough to vomit, but she fought the compulsion. She crept into the house like a thief; there were merry voices and uninhibited laughter from beyond the door to the kitchen, and with the agility of desperation she ran up the stairs. At least no one would see her in this state.

She stripped off her damp clothes—everything clung perversely to her damp flesh—and standing naked, she poured tepid water from the ewer into the bowl and sponged herself. The first touch sent shivers over her body, and she was glad of the chill. It steadied her brain.

She let the air dry until she was really cold, but revived in both her mind and body. She put on the thin wool wrapper and rang for Morag.

Morag came at the run, her cap askew. "Och, what a start the bell gave us! We didn't know you were home! What is it, Mistress? Are you not well?"

It took an extreme effort of will to meet the girl's concerned eyes. "Not very well, Morag. I was walking around the grounds at Linnmore House when suddenly I felt so ill I wanted to get back to my own bed at once, and I came as I was, leaving my things behind." She began turning back the bedcovers, and Morag darted to help her. "Mrs. Gilchrist was busy with someone else, and there were no servants around, so I had better send a note by Fergus. Tell him to take Dora; she needs the exercise." She sat down wearily on the side of the bed. "He might keep her out an hour or so. . . . Will you bring me some tea, Morag, and I'll write the note for Mrs. Archie?"

"The kettle is on the boil now, Mistress. Will you be liking something with it?"

"Only the tea, Morag, thank you. And will you hand me my lap desk, please?"

Telling the lie the next time was much easier, especially on paper and especially because her dislike of Christabel had hardened into something very like hatred.

"Well, it *is* hatred," she muttered. "She's a wicked woman with a heart of stone."

Morag returned with the tea tray and more anxious inquiries. Would she like more covers? Was there enough air, or too much draft? Finally she left, taking the note. Jennie knew that her sudden illness would be accepted in the kitchen as a sign of pregnancy. She ached behind her nose and in her throat with wanting to weep, to *howl*; this called for more than a silent rain of tears.

Second by second she fought down the compulsion as she'd fought the nausea, and was relatively calm when she heard Nigel running up the stairs; he stopped outside the door and tried to open it quietly. She took her cup from the nightstand and sipped cold tea so as to be doing something ordinary. He came in on tiptoe, looking worried, and when he saw her smiling faintly at him, with the cup in her hands, he blew hard with relief. He dropped her hat, reticule, and umbrella and leaned over the bed to kiss her. Then he laid his hand on her forehead. "No fever, thank God."

"I'm all right," she said. "It's past now."

He sat on the edge of the bed, grinning like a boy. "I stopped off at the house and was shown your note. Christabel is *displeased*. You should have returned to the house even if it meant crawling on your hands and knees and vomiting all the way. Then you would have been taken home in the dogcart *or*"—he pointed one finger solemnly toward heaven—"been put to bed at Linnmore House."

"A fate worse than death." She groaned. "Were the Lamonts there?"

"No, and they displeased her, too. They sent word that some important connection was to arrive unexpectedly at Rowanlea, and they had to go there at once. Upon my word, Christabel was in a foul mood! I felt like a traitor leaving poor old Archie alone with her." He took her cup away and held her hands. "They're cold. How do you feel now? Should I send for the doctor? Where in the devil is Fergus? I had to unsaddle Adam myself."

"I'm sorry, dear. My fault. I said he was to exercise Dora after he left the note. And I don't need a doctor; I'm perfectly well."

"Archie was gleefully rubbing his hands and singing a song of a bonny wee bairn. Christabel insists that the abominable food you eat is responsible, and the way you rush about puts too much strain on your delicate female constitutions." He kissed her again, then kept his face close to hers. "Which is it, Jennie, my love?"

"I may be female but not delicate. I don't know about the other, so don't count your Gilchrists before they're hatched." She took his face in her hands; the dear familiarity of it under her palms and fingers, the warmth of flesh and hardness of bone, she would remember all the length of her days. "I'll tell you what made me sick. I met Mr. Grant this afternoon."

He jerked his head away from her hands. "The devil you did! Where? What did he say to put you in such a state? By God—I'll—" He pounded one fist into the other and jumped up.

"He said it first to Christabel, and I overheard. I ran out after him and asked him what was happening. He told me that the writs of eviction were being prepared this very afternoon and that you and Archie were there. You'd have to be, wouldn't you? Does Archie have to sign anything, or do you do that for him, too?"

He was staring at her as if the unimaginable worst had happened and destroyed both speech and thought. His fine color was muddied. The curves of his mouth, which she had always thought so pure and classic, seemed blurred, the lips pale and parched; he kept moistening them with his tongue.

"What else did he say to you?" he asked.

"That you were brought in to do the dirty work that Archie was too squeamish to do. Tell me that he was lying, Nigel," she commanded, reaching for him, and then, as he made no move to meet her but looked at her with the hard blue glaze over his eyes, panic took her by the scruff of the neck, and she begged, "Tell me, Nigel! Please!"

He slumped down on the edge of the bed, his elbows on his knees and his yellow head in his hands.

"It's true, damn it," he said in a muffled voice that sounded ready to break. "In spite of everything I've said, all my arguments, all my prayers, that harpy Christabel has the last word every time. You don't know how many hours I've spent with Archie trying to talk him out of it. He begins to see reason, and then I have to leave him to her, and the next day my work is all undone." He groaned. "I'm so devilish tired of it, and *him*. I've been deceived, and shamefully used—damn' degrading, makes me feel like a whore." He lifted his head and glared at her, red splashing his cheeks. "It's true Archie can't do his own dirty work; he's like Pilate, washing his hands of the whole business. He won't fish in the loch, or go to any other part of the estate, until it's all cleared out as if no one had ever lived there, and turned over to sheep. And *I* can't face them because of my conscience. Not if I can't promise them what they want to hear! I didn't go near any of them yesterday, Jennie. I lied to you."

"Oh, Nigel!" This time when she held out her arms, he came into them and lay against her with his head on her breast. She embraced it, stroking his hair and kissing it. "My darling, how hideous for you. Why didn't you tell me what you were going through?"

"I kept thinking I'd win out and you'd never have to know that clearing had even been contemplated."

"Don't ever make that mistake again. I'm not a delicate little strawberry blossom, to be blighted by the first frost! I could have helped, if only by listening." She kissed his forehead and his eyelids, and he kept his eyes shut and smiled under the caresses.

"When I'm with you, I want to forget it. The blue devils don't exist. I want only to shut ourselves into our own fortress and pull up the drawbridge." He opened her wrapper and fondled her breasts.

"But how could you have hidden it?" she protested. "As wretched as you've been?"

"Sh . . . sh . . ." He soothed her, and she lay back, giving herself up to his hands and mouth, luxuriating in her relief as well as her desire. She held him as if she had just found him again after a forced and terrifying absence.

But when the lovemaking was over, the facts were still there. Not only had the evictions been considered, but the process had begun. The writs were ready. The truth was going to erupt at Linnmore like a killing volcano. Her relief over Nigel's innocence and her loving compassion for him had obscured the view, but unless one turned and ran and never again looked back, there would be no escaping the molten lava flow and the poisonous shower of ash.

"Are you asleep, Nigel?" she murmured.

"No," he mumbled against her hair. "I'm in a blessed stupor. Absolutely delectable. Don't disturb it."

"I must."

"Call of nature?"

"I wish that was all it was. Nigel, what about the writs of eviction?"

"They aren't to be served yet. I've persuaded Archie to hold off a few days. At least I think I have, unless that b—unless Christabel gets another promise out of him while he's drunk tonight. And he is going to be very drunk, mark my words. . . . But first he will have our father's portrait down off the wall.

"Why?"

"Because he can't stand the eyes. When he has a guilty conscience, the eyes follow him, so he swears. The Old Laird would never clear. He would have improverished himself rather than evict, and he married both times for love, not a fortune. Like his younger son." He hugged her against him.

"If Archie has such a bad conscience about this, why does he do it? Does Christabel mesmerize him?"

"Perhaps it's a blow of defiance against our father. Remember the dogs."

"He doesn't seem to take much joy in his defiance, if he has to get drunk to help him bear thinking about it."

"Or to shut out Christabel," said Nigel, yawning. He brought his teeth together very lightly on her earlobe. "I have such a soft mouth I'd make a capital spaniel, don't you think?"

"Yes, and you have the long silky ears, too, and the soulful eyes. . . . Nigel, what are we going to *do*? You know you can't go through with this."

"The sheep are coming; we can't stop that. I can make weapons of all Archie's doubts, and they may be enough to defeat *her*. But I need him alone for a few days, absolutely separated from her."

"How can you manage that? Will you get yourselves lost on the moor, so everyone will think you've been stolen by the fairies? And when you come back, Archie'll be a changed man. . . . But wouldn't it be easier to arrange to have Christabel stolen by the fairies and never returned?"

"They wouldn't have her!" He squeezed Jennie and they both laughed. "This is how it will be done, if you will help."

"Anything!" she promised ardently.

"In the note Mrs. Lamont begs that both Mrs. Gilchrists drive to Rowanlea on Friday and make a long visit, at least until Sunday night or Monday morning, so that they can become acquainted with Mrs. Nigel and show her there is much life and gaiety in the Highlands even for someone lately come from London. I quote almost word for word."

She put her arms around his neck. "Away from you for two or even three nights? How can I stand it? We will live to be extremely ancient, and I shall sleep in your arms and you in mine every night of that long life." She sighed. "But if I must do this for Morag and Aili and the rest of them, then I must. How will you manage to convert Archie so Christabel can't undo your work?"

"It's devilish simple. When I have done convincing Archie, I shall simply renew the leases, and when Christabel returns, she can do nothing for another year. By then she will have no reason for swearing there is not room for both people and sheep."

Her principal joy, at this moment, was in knowing that she had never doubted Nigel.

Twenty-Three

I N THE EARLY MORNING of Friday they clung together, kissing greedily, murmuring in broken, passionate fragments, as if they were illicit lovers about to be torn apart by their warring and probably murderous families.

"It's too soon to be separated, too soon," she mourned. "Can't I send word that I have a chill? Or hint that the time of the month is wrong for me? I'll stay here in the room like an invalid, and you needn't come home all day—you'll have a free hand with Archie—Oh, Nigel, why not?"

"Because you're the reason for the visit, my darling, can't you see? The Lamonts are going to entertain for you. An all-female beanfeast. It's supposed to be a great lark. And speaking of larks, I hear one, and the sun is rising. It will be a fine day, a blessing on all our enterprises."

"I *hope* I'm not making this sacrifice in vain," she said grimly.

Morag and Aili packed for her. If she hadn't restrained them, she'd have gone with a trunkful of gowns and all her small supply of jewelry. "Heavens, I shan't be changing my clothes every hour," she protested. "But they're all so pretty, Mistress," Morag argued. "And the ladies will be wishing to see the latest London fashions."

But Jennie had no desire to be a clotheshorse for anyone. She included a riding habit and, hopefully, her walking shoes. There had to be some escape from three days of Christabel.

Nigel came up to tell her the chaise was there. The girls slipped away, and he took Jennie in his arms. "Oh, *Nigel*." A terrible thought was shaking her, and in a moment she would disintegrate. "What if you

169

have an accident? What if your horse throws you? What if this is—"
She couldn't say the words. *The last time I ever see you in this life.*

"My love, I am going to be spending most of the time safely in
Linnmore House beating some sense into my brother's head. And after
that I shall be *here*, renewing leases."

He hugged her roughly and kissed her all over her face, and then
walked her toward the stairs. "Dear God," he said fervently, "I hate to
see you go, but it's my only chance with Archie."

Christabel was unusually amiable, smiling roguishly at Nigel, compli-
menting Jennie on her appearance. "That fawn is most becoming to you,
Eugenia, and the scarf quite brings out your eyes. Really, you tan very
nicely. Such a warm, pretty tint."

Jennie kept a suitably modest expression and remarked with sincerity
that the day was lovely. As the chaise rolled away from the factor's
house, Christabel chatted dulcetly of the pleasures awaiting them at
Rowanlea. Her maid sat opposite, in the marble attitude of one expected
to be mute, deaf, and blind until spoken to.

Boxed in the chaise between Christabel's extraordinary behavior and
the maid's stony immobility, Jennie knew she was not going to enjoy
herself. But Christabel certainly intended to enjoy herself, and her woman
might even be a blithe soul among the other servants. Iain would be
comfortable around the stables, the best sort of men's club. . . . Or would
he? He'd barely looked at her this morning when he touched his hat,
and Dougal's freckled grin had been missing." She couldn't remember if
either had answered Nigel's hearty "*Good* morning, Iain and Dougal
Innes!"

But of course! They heard about the writs of eviction from Armitage,
and they had no way of knowing that she and Nigel were not part of
the plot. Perhaps she'd have the chance to say something to Iain today.

Christabel was promising treats as if Jennie were a favorite small niece
when suddenly she broke off and said in the usual manner, "*Lily!*" It
seemed to bounce off the ceiling and sides of the chaise and vibrate in
Jennie's ear. "Did you pack my sapphires?"

Lily's tongue flicked over her lips, and her eyes blinked rapidly behind
their light lashes. "You didn't mention the sapphires, Madam."

"I distinctly remember that I *did!* You *know* that I never wear my
blue satin without my sapphires. What could you have been *thinking* of?
This is very vexing! We must go back at *once*."

Lily, looking not too concerned, pulled on the checkcord. When the horses slowed, she opened the door, leaned nonchalantly out, and called, "Home again!"

Iain didn't answer, but in a few minutes they took the turn to the left, past the western end of Linn Mor, and drove around to the mansion. Lily moved to leave, but Christabel elbowed her way out first, still sputtering. "I shall have to see to them myself, to make sure."

The maid followed, barely flurried. She was paid excellent wages to keep her here, and knew she could make many a slip before Christabel would discharge her. Left alone in the chaise, Jennie took off her hat. She hoped that Nigel wasn't already at work inside the mansion delving for Archie's better nature. Christabel would soon put paid to that, unless Nigel did some expert lying. She couldn't endure sitting quietly and got out.

Iain and Dougal stood somberly at the horses' heads. Iain kept his head turned away toward Linn Mor, ignoring her approach, and the boy stared at his feet. She stroked a horse's face and said, "How long does it take to go to Rowanlea, Iain?"

"Five hours, it may be. With a stop." He faced her. "Mistress Gilchrist, it is not as we were led to believe," he said bluntly.

"We?"

"My brothers and their families live in Glen Bheithe. By tonight they will be homeless. I thank God my parents are not alive to see this day."

"Iain, what are you talking about?"

"You know, surely! That is why the mistress wants to be away just now. So when she comes back, there will be only the walls standing, and the smoke will have gone away."

"What are you talking about?" she repeated.

"The evictions. We all thought the Captain would not do it. There was talk of a school for the children. It was *believed.*"

His eyes did not judge; they were worse than that. It was as if he did not see her any more; it was the way he looked at Christabel.

"The Captain won't consent to the evictions!" she exclaimed.

"It will happen," he said, "before nightfall."

"No, *no!*" Her voice rose, and she cut it off and looked around; the front door remained closed. "The Captain came here believing one thing; then he found out another. He was very shocked. He has been trying to convince his brother that the clearing must not happen. He wants to renew the leases now, and then the writs of evictions cannot be legally served."

The familiar Iain returned, except that he was not merry. "Och, but it's glad I am that you didn't know! I said from the first the young Mistress has eyes as honest as these lads here." He nodded at the horses.

"Then you do believe me?" she insisted, trying to keep watch on the front door. "My husband wanted to be alone with his brother these few days so he could persuade him without outside influences." Was she a madwoman, talking thus to a servant? But Highlanders were different; they perceived you as a human being and expected the same perception from you. It had been the same at Pippin Grange, or else the Hawthornes simply weren't cut out to live on too exalted a plane.

He said gently, as if to a child, "I believe that *you* believe what you say. But I know the reek of burning thatch will lie over Linnmore this day."

She grew heated with indignation. "If you're sure of that, why are you still working for these people? Why aren't you with your brothers now, to help them?"

"Because my wages will help them more," he said stolidly. He moved to open the chaise door, ending the conversation.

She got back in her seat just in time before the front door opened and Armitage saw Christabel and Lily out. Christabel was unbecomingly flushed and short of breath, yapping at both servants. Lily, looking as remote as ever, followed her, carrying a jewel case. Iain assisted them to their seats and mounted the box; Armitage closed the front door, and to conquer the turmoil in herself, Jennie imagined him suddenly leaping into the air, clicking his heels, whooping like a drunken trooper, and commencing a manic and possibly indecent dance with the cook and parlormaid.

It was an enchanting vision, but it didn't work. She couldn't see anything but Iain's face; she heard nothing but his words. Christabel was talking, and it was a meaningless babble. The carriage rounded Linn Mor and turned onto the beech avenue. Jennie, trying to contain her inner trembling before it became external and visible, still hadn't the slightest idea of what the other woman was saying. Lily stared at that invisible point between Christabel's head and Jennie's.

The chaise rolled over the first bridge and now ran smoothly along between fields of growing crops and fertile pastures. The small flock of Cheviots were scattered like daisies across a green velvet slope.

"Ah, there's a splendid sight!" Christabel exclaimed with uncharacteristic enthusiasm, and it was as if she had run the point of a parasol into Jennie's stomach. She knew she could not possibly endure a five-hour drive to Rowanlea. She could not possibly endure a three-day visit there without knowing what was going on at home.

Nigel's warnings spun in her head; she *had* to go; she was the reason for the invitation and for Christabel's going. But she still had sense enough to know that Christabel, with all her gowns and jewels packed, wasn't going to give up three days of pleasure just because her young sister-in-law, the spoiled, giddy, capricious creature, balked.

"Eugenia, why is your hat *off?*" Christabel demanded all at once.

Jennie swallowed to moisten her throat and said loudly, "I have to stop at the farmhouse. Lily, will you signal Iain?"

Christabel exclaimed in annoyance. "Really, Eugenia, you could have done that at Linnmore House while I was getting my sapphires. Heaven knows what the accommodation is *here.*"

"It's not that," said Jennie. "I'd like my luggage set down, too. I am ill this morning and shouldn't be traveling. I'm not completely over whatever struck me a few days ago."

"Ill?" As disturbed as she was, Jennie couldn't help being amused at what Christabel suspected.

"Yes. I must get out, or disgrace myself and soil the carriage." Young Dougal opened the door and handed her out, then set her small trunk down on the side of the road.

Christabel said grudgingly, "We might wait a bit, until you feel like traveling on." Mrs. Elliot was coming out from the farmhouse.

"Please don't wait, Christabel. I shan't feel like going on."

"But will you be all right here, Madam?" Lily surprisingly asked.

"Yes, thank you, Lily. I'll be better now that I'm on my feet. It was the motion of the carriage."

"I know what you mean, Madam," Lily said fervently.

"How shall you get home from here, Eugenia?" Christabel called in a glass-cutting voice. "Oh, I forget. You're an accomplished walker. Whatever happens now is on your own head. So be it. Drive on, Innes."

Dougal returned to the saddle. Iain touched his hat again to Jennie, and the chaise moved away.

"There's not a soul here to drive you home, Mistress Gilchrist," Mrs. Elliot said. "Will you not come in and rest a wee bittie and have a good cup of tea?"

"I'm going to walk home from here, Mrs. Elliot. I'll come in and change my shoes, and then if I may leave my things here—"

"The lad will bring it all over later." Between them they carried the little trunk into the kitchen to keep it from the dogs' attentions. Warm new loaves graced the scrubbed trestle table, with a scent which under other circumstances would have made Jennie's mouth water. At Pippin Grange she'd have been begging for a thick brown heel spread with new butter. How long it had been, how far had she come. . . . Her head swam as she leaned over her trunk, looking for her walking shoes.

Mrs. Elliot walked out to the road with her. She was a sunny soul with no clouds in her universe; if she'd heard any dark rumors, they didn't affect her conduct. Besides, she doubtless had the average Lowlander's contempt for the people of the moors. Up until nearly a century ago the Highlanders had been regarded as savage tribes who occasionally descended from their mountains to steal cattle and anything else they could put their hands on. Before that, the Romans had tried to contain them behind fortified walls, but without much success.

It was true that nowadays the term *a Highland gentleman* possessed a certain burnished charm, and the Highland regiments were respected. But these with their poor gardens, their few animals, their hovels where the peat smoke escaped through a hole in the roof, what were they? Even people of their own name and remotely of the same blood despised them.

She said thanks and good-bye, and set off. Nigel expected to be with Archie all morning, perhaps all day. He needn't know until night that she had returned.

She crossed the bridge and turned left onto the bridle path that led away from the beech avenue and directly to Tigh nam Fuaran. She walked through a mist of bluebells, with birds calling overhead and fluttering through the underbrush. It was as if only songbirds and bluebells inhabited the world. How could there be anything wrong? She was shocked that she could even entertain the question. Iain Innes with his Celtic gloom was responsible; someday she'd tell Nigel, and they'd laugh, but not today; she didn't want to make trouble for the man. It would be a long time from now, perhaps when they lived at Linnmore House with their growing family about them. . . . *Nigel, do you want to know why I really came home that day?*

She left the woods opposite her house. Its gray stone was warmly washed with sunlight, windows were open here and there, and the curtains moved in the breeze. Crossing the driveway to the front door, she expected to hear the inevitable bursts of song or laughing, but she heard only the birds, as if they had truly taken over the world. The front door was unlocked, as usual; it was barred only at night.

The house was silent, and there was no one in the orderly kitchen. If the work was done, the girls could have run home for a bit. Why not? Mrs. MacIver might be up in her room, or she could have gone out for a walk, possibly over the ridge with the two maids.

Everything felt so good and so natural here that she was a little ashamed of her panic in the carriage. But the conversation with Iain sprang up in her mind again like a fire mistakenly thought to be dead; backing away from the deadly heat of it, she accused herself of having a shallow, easily terrified nature, with no faith whatever in Nigel, who should be the rock in her life. He was going to be exasperated with her, if not outright angry, and she deserved it.

At the same time she took pleasure in being alone in her own house for the first time in her life, and she wandered around, shifting a chair or an ornament; she looked at herself in the mirrors and sat on the sofa before one of the drawing-room fireplaces and tried to imagine herself being a hostess to a roomful of people.

She supposed it must come, even though nothing could enhance the life she and Nigel lived now. She sighed, not unhappily; the best thing about a party was talking it over afterward in bed.

She took a lump of sugar and went out to visit Dora, who came running the length of the paddock with her mane and tail streaming, pleased to see her and patently begging for a good chance to stretch her legs—or so Jennie was pleased to consider the vehement welcome. She went to the stable and called for Fergus. He appeared, looking sleepy as always.

She asked him to saddle Dora, and went up to her room and changed into her bronze-colored riding habit, leaving off the hat; who was there to see and disapprove? Christabel was a good distance away, and Nigel was going to disapprove of her for entirely different reasons, but in the meantime why waste a glorious day by worrying? She scooped up her skirt and ran downstairs.

Dora was ready for her outside the paddock, Fergus holding her head. Jennie was halfway across the lawn when a downdraft from the ridge swept low over the trees, carrying familiar pungence. She stopped; in the blue sky above the pines, gauzy specters like clouds were being born. She began to run. Fergus, too, was looking up, sniffing like an animal. The mare kept tossing her head nervously and blowing.

"What is that?" Jennie called.

"Burning," Fergus said.

Twenty-Four

"KEEP HER HERE," she said, and ran. When she reached the crest of the ridge, she could not believe what she was seeing, yet it was there before her, as hideous as one of the story paintings that had haunted her as a child, like "The Massacre of the Innocents." The wind carried not only the fresh gusts of smoke from flaming thatch but the indescribable din of terrified animals and children, men shouting, a woman screaming.

She saw one man trying to keep another from putting the torch to his roof; he was knocked out of the way, and as he went sprawling backward, a woman sprang at the arm of the torchbearer, and she too was swept aside. She scrambled to her hands and knees and then onto her feet, and ran into the cottage. The man with the torch kept shouting in at her, and when she didn't come, he set the fire anyway, and the thatch went up in a roar of black smoke and dirty flame. The woman came out, huddled over and holding herself together in a way that made Jennie's stomach crawl.

She heard herself shouting crazily, "Stop this! *Stop!*" She looked around wildly for someone, anyone, to go and help them. Then she saw the cluster of horses and ponies kept from harm's way over on the road near the peat. One of them, standing out among the others because of his height and color, was Adam.

So Nigel was down there somewhere. "He's trying to stop it," she said aloud. "Archie went ahead with it, but Nigel's trying to stop it." She went down the hill, trying to watch her footing but still see the scene below, and as her perspective shifted, she saw Nigel standing like a rock in the midst of chaos. He was looking at something in his hand. Near him Morag's father and mother were dragging a chest from their cottage, and Morag hurried out behind them with her arms full.

Surely Nigel would help them; that was why he was there. So why did he keep staring at what he held in his hands? All at once he lifted his other hand high, and brought it down fast, and a man darted into view with a torch and fired the thatch before Morag was ten feet away from it. Jennie could hear the roar.

Morag's mother stood as if turned to stone by the sight, and Hamish sagged over the chest. Morag ran to Nigel and spat in his face; the gesture was clear to Jennie. He swung his arm, and the backhanded blow nearly knocked the girl off her feet.

Jennie began to run, lost her balance, and tumbled down into the little valley. As she struggled up, she saw two small children running from the fires toward the brook, one dragging the other by the hand. They were nowhere near the stepping-stones when they plunged into the stream. Their heads strained above the deep fast flow, mouths wide in cries drowned out by the noise of the water. Clutching hands appeared and disappeared. Jennie threw herself headlong, fell into the brook, and regained her footing by a miracle. She waded waist-high in the rushing current and grabbed for the children with an insane strength, getting one by the shoulder and the other by the hair. She hauled them ashore before their frantic hands could drag her down with them.

She sat on the bank, hugging them to her, and they clung to her because she was an adult. Through their soaked scanty garments their bodies vibrated with shock. She didn't want to leave them, but she must, so she found them a warm hollow and tried to make it clear that they should cuddle there and wait. They knew a few words of English, and one of them understood her and mutely nodded.

Holding up the wet skirt that dragged down on her, she crossed by the stepping-stones and went on. A bedridden person was being carried out on a mattress, and now, closer to the scene, she realized that Nigel was holding his watch in his hand, timing another removal. If he had happened to look in her direction, he would have seen her for an instant before a swirl of smoke hid them from each other.

She wished he *had* seen her watching him.

Another roof went up, and there was a long scream as if a woman were dying in the fire. People kept trying to move their household goods out of reach of the blowing flames, and sparks. A dog yelped as if kicked, the crying of children mingled with the bleating of goats and sheep, and Jennie wished to be struck deaf. Hidden from Nigel's sight by a newly roofless cottage whose interior was smoldering, she saw Aili kneeling beside the old woman on the mattress; they didn't see Jennie.

She looked around for Morag. Over beyond Aili and the old woman, a safe distance from the smoke and sparks, Morag's wee cow seemed to have collected the goats, the dwarfish sheep, and the other cows about her, and in a hollow of the moor below them there was a little knot of women. Jennie recognized Morag's curly black head; that cow must have followed her.

Jennie walked timidly toward the hollow. She saw that the women were clustered protectively around another one, whose head Morag's mother held against her breast.

Jennie hadn't the courage to go farther. She was Nigel's wife, and if they spat in her face, as Morag had done to Nigel, she wouldn't be surprised. But Morag, lifting her head to look around toward the burning cottages, saw her. She jumped up and ran to her. To order her away? Jennie quivered but stood her ground.

"Mistress!" Through the anguish and the soot, the sweetness came. "You shouldn't be here! And look at you! Your clothes—"

"Morag, I didn't *know*—"

"I know that, Mistress." One side of her face was red from the blow. "Now go away, please. This is no place for you."

"There are two little children up there by the brook. They were running away in blind terror. They'd have drowned if I hadn't been there to drag them out. Someone should go to them."

Morag seized her hands and squeezed them. "It'll be Kirsty's boys! She's been frantic for thinking they were caught inside. She was fearing wee Colin ran in for his father's bonnet."

"Where is the father?"

"He died in the winter." She ran back to the others and bent over the woman on the ground, who struggled to sit up. Her face had been ugly in grief but was now transformed. Jennie had seen she was the older of the two pregnant women, and it was a wonder she hadn't gone into labor there on the ground.

In a little pause in the hubbub, Nigel's voice rang out clearly; the gamekeeper's shout answered, and then some command was relayed in

Gaelic. Unexpectedly Jennie became very calm. Now she understood; she was to have been taken out of the way.

"Whatever happens now is on your head," Christabel had said with that peculiar smile. She must be ecstatic now on her drive to Rowanlea, imagining what was going on behind her.

Morag turned to her, and they hurried to the brook. "I will not be going back to Tigh nam Fuaran, Mistress," Morag said.

"I know."

"I spat in his face."

"I know that, too. Did he hurt you badly?"

"Och, I was too furious to feel anything!" She laughed proudly.

"How long was I gone before it happened?"

"A half hour perhaps. Then the Captain told us the writs of eviction were being served all over the estate, and there would be one hour and then the torching would begin. He told us we could go home to help our families. But no one would believe it till the sheriff's men came. Donald John went at them with his fists and had his face laid open, and they arrested him and took him away." She said it as if she had no emotions left. "My father walked all the way to Linnmore House, but the Laird wouldn't see him. Then the hour was almost gone, and those others came on their horses—*he* came, and he stood with his watch in his hand and gave each ten minutes—"

Jennie couldn't bear to hear this. "Where was Alick Gilchrist?"

"He didn't come."

"Surely he knew what was going on, he could see across the loch—"

"And the smoke going up everywhere," Morag agreed. She turned and pointed north and west, and Jennie saw smoke rising from distant folds in the land.

"They are even burning the roof timbers," Morag said, "so we have nothing to start new with, if we found a place. They should have let us save the timbers."

Off to the far right of Alick Gilchrist's untouched cottage, smoke eddied from a hollow. "Lachy's hut." Morag's voice was dull. Lachy's hut, where they used to take the trout and fry them in oatmeal, Nigel and the sons and brothers of those he was driving out.

Jenny cried savagely, "Why isn't Alick Gilchrist over here risking his neck to help you? He had enough to *say!*"

"I don't know," said Morag softly. They crossed the stepping-stones and went along the bank to the children. Jennie was the alien now as Morag comforted and cajoled in the hushed, musical Gaelic. At last she could start back, holding a boy by each hand.

"I told them their mother was weeping for them," she explained.

"What about *her*? Is she going into labor? She'll need things—"

"We will take care of her, Mistress. And no one blames you." She went on with the children across the stepping-stones, and walked with her head up toward the smoking desolation. She didn't look back. For the first time in all this, Jennie's eyes filled with tears. Then she turned and blindly ran, stumbled, fell to her hands and knees, got up again, sobbing with a pain that wasn't physical. When she reached the top of the ridge, she looked back for Nigel. She didn't want to see him, but she couldn't keep from trying. Once before in her life, when her father had been carried home dead, she had insisted to herself that it was a dream and if only she could find a way to wake up, Papa would still be alive. Now she wished sickly for some fantasy to be truth; for that to be an evil, crazed, identical twin to Nigel, imprisoned until now, when he had escaped while her Nigel lay hidden from her, a bound, helpless prisoner. But while she was wishing it, she knew she was sane and wide-awake.

It had happened. Nothing could change it.

All the roofs had been fired now, and Nigel's people were walking away toward their horses. She leaned against one of the pines and watched the miniature figures in the distance. None of them looked back at what they had done. They reached the road and mounted; Nigel and two of them headed eastward toward the break in the ridge, and the others rode toward the west.

She went down to the coppice, skidding in her wet boots on damp places, snagging her skirt on bushes. But she was in control enough to be careful. To take a bad fall now would make her helpless among her enemies. She saw things around her with the obsessive attention to detail that accompanies such moments. When she passed the ferny spring, she noticed that the violets were drooped and faded; she heard the blackbird from one of the chimneys.

Dora and Fergus still waited by the paddock; the mare was grazing, and Fergus sat on the ground with his back against the wall. When Jennie came upon them, he got clumsily to his feet.

"You knew what they were doing, didn't you?" she said. After a long moment he nodded. His black eyes seemed bemused by her damp, disheveled clothing and scratched face.

"Where is your family, Fergus?" She tried to speak evenly. He answered something she couldn't understand, lifted his hands, and shrugged.

"No family?"

He nodded.

"Is there a short way from the top of the ridge"—she pointed—"across to the road? A way that will be safe for the mare? I must ride to Alick Gilchrist's house."

He took the reins and started off. Dora went agreeably along the track and through the coppice, but when the path turned steep, she was nervous. Skillfully he coaxed her along, repeating little sounds which Dora knew; sometimes she contributed a few of her own as if she and Fergus were holding a conversation. Again Jennie felt like an alien. She was needed by no one, not even her husband. With his brother and sister-in-law he had made her less than nothing.

It was Christabel who had proposed the visit to the Lamonts, not the other way around. When had they arranged it? The day when Nigel was supposed to reassure the tenants? When he'd claimed that his conscience had been too much for him? Of course! Christabel would suggest the visit to the Lamonts when they came the next day. How sympathetic they'd be about the problem with this delicate, sentimental girl Nigel had foolishly married. They'd be happy to help.

The Lamonts hadn't come because of the emergency at Rowanlea, and Davie Grant had appeared unexpectedly. But the note suggesting the visit must have gone back with the messenger who brought the Lamonts' regrets. Such a nuisance, having Jennie meet Grant! It put Nigel to the inconvenience of quieting his wife's hysterical fears. But he'd be able to talk her around, and he had done so, with consummate art.

Then Lily forgot to pack the sapphires, and Jennie had a word with Iain Innes.

Twenty-Five

D OWN BELOW, the people sat in stunned silence or moved slowly
about, aimlessly shifting their belongings among the ruined gardens
and the roofless double walls of fieldstone. Smoke curled up here and
there. Jennie kept her eyes on the mare's rump and tail. They went
diagonally southward toward the road along a track as clear to Fergus as
if he were a rabbit or a fox, but Jennie could not make it out for herself
in the heather.

When they reached the road, Fergus made a step of his hands to help
her mount, then waited for her to settle herself in the saddle. She
accomplished a weak smile with her thanks. He nodded and started back
at a shambling trot the way they had come.

Dora flung her head about, and Jennie murmured, "Gently, gently,"
stroking the arched neck. Then she let the mare out, and they fled
westward along the road. They passed the drying rows of peat and the
head of the loch, where the osprey was fishing as if nothing had happened.
Alick Gilchrist's cottage appeared and disappeared; light flashed off windows and was quenched by a brackened hillock. A gable showed, now
a whole roof, and a chimney. Then it all vanished behind a green fold.

She knew that Grant had given him money to help in the trouble
to come. Why wasn't he with them now? They needed him; someone
had to take charge. He could natter on like one of the three witches in
'Macbeth' about approaching disaster, but he had taken the man's money
and gone where he wouldn't have to see the dirty work done.

She was walking the mare now, looking for a clear track leading off
to her right, and found it, beaten hard with use. It wound up and down

around boulders and through heather and whin. She dismounted and led Dora, who was disinclined to be adventurous when she couldn't see what was beyond the next bend. Two crows suddenly erupted noisily from the heather and went sailing over their heads, and the mare almost ripped the reins from Jennie's hand. When the cottage appeared, more crows launched from the roof, all alarms and imprecations that had Dora in a ferment until she heard an equine signal of assurance; the brown garron trotted from behind the walled garden at the southern end of the cottage.

Except for the sociable pony, the crows flapping off across the loch toward the destruction on the other side, and the osprey suspended on beating wings above them all, there were no signs of life. Jennie fastened Dora to the garden gate and went in.

The cottage was stone like the others, and it had a thatched roof held down with weighted heather ropes. But it had windows and a central chimney, and there was no clutter about. The vegetables grew in well-weeded rows within the shelter of the wall. Clumps of daffodils bordered the flagged walk to the door; their self-confident gaiety was incongruous to her in the context of this place and the day's events, until she remembered that two women had lived here for their adult lifetimes, the one who had borne a son to Nigel's grandfather and the one who married that son. They would have also planted the unpruned rose bushes that sprawled in a healthy green tangle against the warm stone of the gable end.

The byre was attached to the northern end of the cottage, and its door stood open; a few chickens wandered in and out. Back at the gate Dora and the pony were nosing each other in friendly curiosity.

So the man had gone on foot somewhere and would be back tonight when it was all accomplished. "We'll have a reckoning, Mr. Alick Gilchrist," she promised him. "What did they pay you to be absent today? A share in what they'll make from leasing Linnmore to the sheep owners? If Archie didn't think of that, Christabel did; if they can't get rid of the agitator, they'll buy him."

The sound of her voice intensified the silence. She leaned against the cottage wall, all at once tired enough to die, or at least to cry, neither of which could accomplish anything for herself or those she wanted to help. She could not bear to ride back around the loch without doing *something*. She didn't want go back at all because sooner or later she would have to face Nigel, and the prospect sent shudders over her body in paroxysms, and her teeth chattered uncontrollably.

She rushed at the door and pounded on it with both fists, shouting, "Alick Gilchrist! *Alexander Gilchrist!* Open up!" Senseless, but it was a relief to shriek, except that it startled the animals and scared the hens, and she thought angrily that you couldn't even have the luxury of a good hard scream without having to consider someone or something.

A heavy, rhythmic thudding started up in her ears. Could she have a stroke? she wondered in alarm. Drop dead as Papa did? Trying not to give in to terror, she felt her pulse in her wrist and forced herself to breathe slowly and deeply.

Then she knew that her heartbeat hadn't gone wild. The sound came from inside the house. She lifted the heavy iron latch with no resistance, so the door wasn't barred on the inside. It swung open into a small hall dominated by a large press cupboard. On her right a door stood open to a sparsely furnished bedroom. Behind the closed door on her left the slow, laborious thumping went on, each blow accompanied by a loud clattering.

It didn't occur to her to be afraid. She opened the door and walked into a kitchen, where Alick Gilchrist lay on the floor by the cold fireplace. He was gagged, his hands tied behind him, his ankles bound. Lying on his side, he was driving his feet against the leg of a heavy oak table. At each impact the earthenware dishes on the table jiggled noisily.

"Oh, *my God!*" Jennie said. His wet and bloodshot eyes recognized her with utter disbelief; he shut them and sagged back to the floor and was so still she thought he had just died. His face was smeared with blood and sweat run together. When she saw that he was still breathing, she stepped around him and knelt behind him and began working at the hard knots of the gag, a man's handkerchief.

Be calm, Jennie, she admonished herself. *Easy does it.* . . . Strength flowed back into her fingers. Finally she got the gag untied, and when she lifted it away from his mouth, she saw it was bloody and threw it in disgust across the room. Then she put her arms around his sweat-drenched body and dragged him up and around to a sitting position and propped him against the side of the fireplace. He kept moving his jaw and trying to moisten his lips. They were bloody, and his nose had been bleeding, too. He couldn't speak.

"I'll get you a drink before I start on your wrists," she told him, using an impersonal businesslike manner to save his pride and control her own agitation. She stood up and looked around; there was a wooden bucket on a dresser under the western window. She took a cup from the table and dipped out cold peat-tinted water and held it to his mouth.

He drank in deep gulps, and said on an outgoing breath, "Thank you, Mrs. Gilchrist."

"You're welcome," she answered. "I'll do your wrists now." He hitched around sidewise, and she struggled with the rope, which was so tight that his hands were darkly swollen. The sight of them made her wince.

"You'd better get a knife from the cupboard," he said.

That was across the room against the south wall; dishes arranged on the shelves as the women must have kept them, drawers and doors below. "The wee drawer on your left," he directed her. She chose a knife from a jumble of cutlery, one that looked sharp enough to cut but small enough for her to manage without damaging him further.

Kneeling again, she sawed away at the rope between his wrists, afraid to use too much force for fear of slashing him. Suddenly the binding fell apart. He held his hands up to let the blood run back from them, pressing his bruised lips tightly together to stifle gasps of pain. Then he tried to use the knife to cut the ankle ropes, but he had no strength in his hands. In silence, she took the knife back and went to work.

When that was done, she moved away and sat on a stool across the hearth from him, beyond a basket of peats. The boots had kept the ropes from biting deeply into the flesh, but he had no feeling in his feet, and his hands were still too weak for him to help himself up. She gave him some privacy by looking around the room. For the first time she became aware of the loud ticking of the wag-on-the-wall clock above the chimneypiece. The place was barren of the things with which a woman would ornament it, except for those bright-flowered plates on the cupboard shelves; there was some masculine clutter, but it was clean.

She was resting involuntarily from the exertions and the emotional stress of the past hour; she was very tired, and her thoughts wandered. Hazily she wondered if Alick's grandfather had ever come to the cottage to see his son and if the baby's mother had been a contented woman or a bitter one.

Alick pulled himself up by the table, leaning over it, shifting from one foot to the other. Holding on, he hobbled painfully all around the table, grimacing at first. By the third time he was stepping faster and harder, and he walked away from the table to the window looking over the loch.

He stood there without moving or speaking for a few moments. At last he said in a low voice, "So. It is done."

"Yes, and I didn't *know*," she said vehemently. "I was supposed to go away on a visit with Christabel, but Iain said something—well, I stopped at the Elliots' and walked home. It had begun almost as soon as I left the house."

"They came here at first light to put me out of the way," Alick said, still looking out over the loch. "The gamekeeper's creatures. If you hadn't come, and the others thought I was away from home, and they were all driven away, leaving the place deserted, I'd have died. And a long, hard death it would be." He gave her a bright harsh stare. "Why *did* you come?"

"I wondered where you were, after the things you said." She was ashamed to say she'd thought he'd been bribed. "Why should they do this to you? What could you, one man, do to stop them?"

"I asked that, and they bloodied my nose for an answer. I *exist*, that is my crime. Was anyone hurt over there?"

"A man named Donald John was arrested and taken away."

He swore. It was Gaelic, but she knew. "They'll have him tried and transported before the week is out!" He went to the dresser and ladled water into a basin and splashed it over his head and face, washing away the blood and sweat. She took a towel off the back of the chair and handed it to him when he straightened up, groping. "Thank you," he said formally through the folds. He balled up the towel and hurled it away from him. "I must see about Donald John."

He went out into the hall and picked up a saddle from the floor beside the press cupboard. She followed him outdoors. By now she felt like a piece of fine porcelain that has been cracked but is still holding together. A tap, and it could shiver into fragments.

He stopped so suddenly on the walk that she almost ran into him. His head up like an animal's, he was looking northward to where a thread of smoke wavered skyward from the heather. He spoke under his breath, and dropped the saddle, and ran to the gate. He pushed by the animals and set off toward the tremulous filament of smoke. Jennie was behind him, half running to keep up.

Though the sun was warm, and heat beat up from the ground, drying her boots and tights and the skirt of her habit, she was cold. Miniature flowers, yellow and white, twinkled on the turf. It was as if she were seeing them for the first time in her existence, or anyone's, as if they had just now sprung up to celebrate the end of her world.

The roof of the little hut in the hollow had burned fast and fiercely. An old man lay dead before the doorway. His eyes were open in a wrinkled brown face framed with white whiskers. Alick knelt beside him and closed his eyes.

"How did he die?" she whispered.

"They killed him." He didn't look away from the dead face.

"I see no wound."

"It's bloodless. Straight into the heart. When you are eighty-nine year old, and you are dragged out of the place where you have lived out your life, and your forefathers before you, then the wound is clean and deadly. Look!" He touched the dirk in the old man's hand. "How did they miss that, I wonder? Och, they couldn't get it free of the dead hand, and they'd be afraid to, with him lying there looking at them. It's flattered Lachy would be, to think he frightened anybody. It would be the first time in his life." He stood up. "But he died fighting. There's a bit of blood on the blade . . . I will bury him later."

"I wish there were something to cover him with," Jennie said.

"He won't care." Without touching her, he steered her out of the hollow. The pony had followed them, and Dora, forsaken, whinnied back at the gate. "I am going to Linnmore House to give my cousin my opinion of this day's work. He will promise that no charges will be made against Donald John. And they will have all the time they need to collect themselves and their creatures and the use of farm wagons wherever those can be taken on the estate."

"Where will they go?"

"Onto the roads, that is all I can tell you."

She remembered the dispossessed on the road between Banff and Inverness, and the shame she felt. She could taste it now like the beginning of sickness, as if in another moment she must retch to get free of it.

"How can you be sure of seeing Archie?" she asked. "Of his seeing *you*?"

"*She* is gone, and his man won't be keeping me from him. Linnmore will hear me if I have to take him by the throat and knock his head against the wall to make him listen."

"But he will only gobble and go white and send you to the factor."
The word *factor* was just that, a noun, not a person she knew.

"I know how to be dealing with *that* man," he said with a cold smile.
"If it is needed."

At the cottage she thirstily drank a mug of the peaty water while he
saddled the garron. He led the way out, and Dora trustingly followed
her new friend. When they were back on the road and riding side by
side, Alick told Jennie that the tenants from the northern part of the
estate would doubtless trickle away through those hills out to the coast,
but many of those to the west and southwest would go through the
Roseholm lands.

"They will rest there before they move on. A few will stay. Roseholm
will never drive them."

"Is this what caused the bad feeling between the two houses?"

"Yes. The last time Sir Hector and his lady came here to dine, Madam
Christabel announced the great decision. Roseholm was arguing with
Linnmore that it should not be, but *she* was the greater talker. There
has been nothing between the two houses since."

"It seems that the London servants do talk," Jennie said.

"It came straight from the kitchen," he said with a wry grin.

"Then everyone has known and worried for a long time."

"Aye, but Davie Grant was holding back the Red Sea until Christabel
wore Archie out, and he discharged Davie."

"He gave you money—"

The response sprang at her. "Did you think I'd not give it to them?"

"*No!*" she lied. "*I* want to give you some to use for them."

They trotted along in silence for a few minutes. At least the mare
and the pony were serene in their companionship. Then he said very
quietly, "I beg your pardon. You can give the money to Fergus to bring
to me. He can be trusted. I will be away from home much of the time
now, but he will know when to find me."

"Agreed," she said.

When they came by the peat cutting to a clear view of the devasta-
tion, Alick said, "I am stopping here before I go on. Good-bye, Mrs.
Gilchrist. Thank you for what you have done today."

"I am going down there with you," she insisted. "There might be
something I could do, some needs I could fill from the house."

"It is better if you don't." He was adamant without raising his voice.
"Now is no time for them to have to think of manners."

He was right, of course. "But the girls have wages due them. Will you tell them I won't forget that?"

"Yes. Are you riding up across the moor or home by the long road?"

"Fergus led me along a shortcut from the ridge. I think I can find it," she said.

He nodded and turned the pony off down the slope. Jennie rode on, aching in her whole body, parched in spite of the long drink at the cottage. She was grateful for such physical sensations which were too strong to be ignored. But she knew that when she was out of these clothes, bathed, and physically rested, she would have no refuge left from the truth.

Twenty-Six

A LL THE WAY up to the ridge she kept her eyes averted as if from the sight of a mutilated body. When she'd gone over the crest and was leading Dora down the other side, she returned to that static, unreal world, a scene in a tapestry. The difference was that now she knew what existed over the ridge.

Fergus came out to take Dora. As usual he said nothing, but through the fog of exhaustion she thought that she perceived a change in him. She went in at the side door, recollecting how she had walked through the rooms a few hours ago, touching and admiring her possessions. In the hall she called Mrs. MacIver's name, but there was no answer, and the house felt empty. The woman must have already gone when Jennie first came back.

"I should have met her," she mumbled. "Why didn't I meet her?" Then she knew that Mrs. MacIver must have gone down with the girls, to help; she could have been one of those women vaguely seen through breaks in the smoke. She could have returned to Tigh nam Fuaran while Jennie was looking for Alick, packed her things, and left for the village.

"Well, she warned me," Jennie said loudly. "She was honest."

She went up to her room and stripped off all her clothes and flung them in a heap, boots and all. She would order them burned; she never wanted to see that bronze-colored riding habit again. It belonged not only to today but to the first time she had ridden with Nigel in the park, hardly believing in her own happiness. Today there were no such doubts of her rage and bereavement.

Standing in the tin bath in his dressing room, she poured tepid water

191

over her hair and her body and soaped and rinsed twice, but she still
felt soiled. With her hair done up on a towel, and drying herself with
another, she walked back into the bedroom.

Nigel was running up the stairs. Before she could move, not knowing
where she would go, he came into the room. He went perfectly still with
shock, and she too was motionless, stunned by his beauty as if she were
seeing it for the first time but not in adoration. *How art thou fallen from
heaven, O Lucifer, son of the morning!*

"What are you doing here?" he whispered.

"Should Dr. Macleod preach next Sunday on the whited sepulchre?"
she asked in a brittle voice she hardly recognized. "Or wouldn't he dare?
Of course he should be an authority on whited sepulchres; he's one
himself, along with most of his congregation."

"What on earth are you talking about?" He half laughed, like someone
who suspects the joke is on him and doesn't want to be caught out.
"Why aren't you with Christabel?" He came toward her. "Was there a
carriage accident? Are you all right? My God, you are so *lovely*! I could
go down on my knees to you. What a vision to greet and haunt a tired
man!"

She snatched up her wrapper and put it on. "Modest before me?" he
teased. "Or are you inviting me to take it off?"

"I saw you in action this morning," she said. "Captain Gilchrist
leading his troops in a gallant attack on savage hordes of lame men, old
men, pregnant women, young girls, and children. I missed the business
of Lachy, but I'm sure your men were magnificent. What I *did* see was
soul-stirring. I'll never forget it." This wasn't at all the trembling con-
frontation she imagined; she was both astounded and exhilarated by it,
knowing anything was better than crumpling abjectly in tears.

Nigel was white. "There *was* an accident, wasn't there? Did you
strike your head? Sit down, my darling, I'll ring for—"

"There's no one here to ring for, Nigel. And the accident was that
I could not be gotten safely out of the way as you three had arranged it."

"I don't understand!" He reached out for her, and she backed away
from him.

"Don't touch me, please."

"What went wrong?" he pleaded. She knew—oh, how clearly she
could see it—that he was keeping up this pretense to give him time to
think.

"There was so much wrong around this morning," she said, "that a dog would have been howling with the feel of it. But I walked out of here like a simpleminded child. However, I said good-bye to Lady Macbeth at the Elliots' and I walked back to Tigh nam Fuaran a little less innocent than before, but I still didn't believe—" She was going to break down, and if it happened, she was lost. So she would not. "Until I went up on the ridge and saw you with your watch in your hand and the men with their torches. I went down there, Nigel, but you never saw me. I was *there*!"

He collapsed into an armchair, putting his head in his hands as he had done when she first asked him about the clearance. "Dear Jesus," he said to the carpet, "it would have been all out of the way before you came back on Monday."

"And I would have taken it meekly as a *fait accompli*? Never asked questions, never made a protest, because out of sight means out of my empty little mind?"

He lifted a haggard face. "Jennie, Archie wouldn't listen to me! I could do nothing with him. She'd worked her damned evil spell before she left the house. So for us—for you—I had to do as I was told, don't you see?"

"You couldn't have argued with him for long. I was back within the hour. When was the time set for the clearing to begin? As soon as I had agreed to go away with Christabel?"

"I swear to you, it was none of my doing! I never wanted it!"

"Then why didn't you walk away from it, like Mr. Grant?"

"I—I—" He was scarlet now, trying to laugh. "What an inquisitor! You should be a barrister, my sweet! I simply did my duty, for you and for our children." He came to her again, and this time she was stopped by the wall; she stood passive while he tried to embrace her, kissed her blank face, attempted to draw her head against his breast. "In a little while you'll feel better," he murmured, "when everything is tidied up and the sheep come."

"You mean every*one*, don't you? It's too bad they all can't be buried decently out of sight, like Lachy."

"That's the second time you've mentioned his name!" He stood off from her. "What about him?"

"He's lying dead outside what was once his door."

"*Damn!*" He smashed his fist down on her bureau. "I'll have somebody's hide for that! I gave orders that nothing, nobody was to be harmed! Believe me, I wanted no brutality—"

"Brutality!" She laughed. "You killed Lachy when you allowed him to be evicted. Old Lachy, who let you fry trout over his fire at midnight. And what about Hamish, who taught you how to catch those trout? *Brutality?* Oh, Nigel you're both a knave and a fool if you believe what you're saying!" He backed away from her as if she'd attacked him physically. "What is it but brutality to turn people out of their homes at an hour's notice and even burn the timbers they'd need to start a new shelter if they ever find a place where they'll be allowed to stay? Bring on Napoleon! What worse could *he* do than you've done to your own?"

"Jennie—"

"Will you please go now so I can dress in privacy?"

"I have a right to be here," he said doggedly. "I am your husband and your lover. I can't believe this is happening, to us." His voice dropped to the secretive, amorous pitch she'd loved. "Nothing outside this house should affect us in this room." When she still kept her face turned away, he seized her by the shoulders. "You *shall* listen, and you *shall* understand. What's done is done. It's for us, and our children. The Cheviot is the Great Sheep, and it's our future. We'll make our fortune from the Cheviot, not from a pack of lazy peasants who'd rather poach deer and smuggle whisky than do an honest day's work. All the men are fit for, if you can catch them young enough, is cannon fodder, as you call it."

"You seem to have turned a few of them into efficient traitors and bullies."

"They had their work to do, and they did it. Call them what you will, our future depends more on men who can carry out orders than on the rabble we've just evicted."

"And transported?" she asked sardonically.

"I'll have Donald John released after he cools his heels overnight." He went out, slamming the door behind him and swearing. She wondered when he would realize the servants were gone, and then she was swamped in misery. She sank down on the bed, huddling herself together, knees almost to her chin. Nigel, saying cheerfully that he would do whatever a factor does, had known from the start why Mr. Grant had left and what the factor's work was to be. And she with her prattle about a school—no wonder the minister had been confused; he knew what was about to happen. Perhaps for a few minutes he'd believed otherwise and might even have been relieved; she'd give him that much credit. But she doubted that he'd ever argued with Christabel. The manse was too comfortable a nest for him to leave at his age.

No wonder the cottage people had been so happy; she and Nigel had come to them like angels of deliverance, and she had reinforced their hopes with her promises. She was a well-meaning little fool of the sort whose innocence is the most deadly.

She had curled up like this on her bed when her father died and Pippin Grange was no longer to be home. Almost everything gone from her in one great brain-splitting blast of thunder, but still there were her sisters sharing her grief.

Now it had happened again. Nigel had become her world, but he had been blasted away like the other one, and her sisters, even if they had been within reach, couldn't have shared this; they could not have reached her where she wandered alone, blinded and deafened, in the void.

And what about those others? She tried to think of them, but the meeting with Nigel had been too disastrous to allow for anything else.

She pulled the covers over her head and shivered until she fell asleep, though it was more like drowning; on the edge of it she saw her first image of Linn Mor as a black tarn, and it was waiting for her to sink into it without a splash.

When she awoke, the sun had clouded over, and the trees made the room dark. She felt drugged at first, and if she didn't move a finger or toe, hardly breathed, perhaps the pain wouldn't start up. But in a few moments her mind was achingly awake. *Poor Jennie Hawthorne,* she thought. *You fell in love with a glittering vision in the park, a marzipan soldier, and now, like many a woman—and you swore you'd never be one of those—your duties are to keep your mouth shut and your brain asleep, and bear children to a man you can never respect again, even if you ever stop despising him.*

"There are bears and wolves in the Highlands," Sophie had quavered, and Jennie promised her a Highland gentleman. *Darling Sophie,* she thought, *I'd rather take my chances with the bears and wolves than with any of the Highland gentlemen I've met at Linnmore.*

Twenty-Seven

S HE DIDN'T HEAR Nigel on the stairs this time. He came in quietly and stood by the bed, very tall, his hair pale in the gloom.

"Jennie?" he whispered. She could have stuffed the edge of the sheet into her mouth and howled at the anguish of hearing that whisper and knowing what she had lost. Or had never possessed. He leaned over her and saw that her eyes were open. He stroked the tangled damp hair back from her face.

"Have you had a good sleep? You needed it." He sat on the edge of the bed. "Put on a pretty frock, and we'll have dinner with Archie. He wants the company of a pretty woman tonight, the old dog. We can stay at Linnmore House until we have servants again. Your trunk has come from the farm, so you needn't even pack. . . . It needn't be long. Christabel's a dab hand at acquiring reliable servants."

"Christabel," she said from a scrapy throat, "is a dab hand at a number of things. But she is not staffing my house." Was he actually stupid? Or did he think *she* was, and that a nap had restored her good nature?

"Whatever you say, darling," he murmured, trailing his warm fingers down her throat in a way that, until this morning, had always bewitched her. When they wandered toward her breasts, she turned away from him, hunching up a shoulder as a barrier. His hand then capped the shoulder, the fingers gently kneading.

"It's time we picked out a puppy or two for you," he said. "Would you like that, sweet? Yes, you would."

She wrenched herself out from under his hand and sat up on the far side of the bed, pulling the covers tightly about her. "Nigel, I'm not a

196

child who's had a little temper tantrum and can be bribed into smiling again. I'm a woman who's seen something dreadful done, and it's still going on. It's only the beginning of the torment for those people out there."

"Archie's giving them all the time they need—"

"And I suppose he's congratulating himself on his generosity! I couldn't sit at the table with him tonight without wanting to hurl my plate into his face."

"Jennie, Jennie." He came around the bed and tried to take her into his arms, and she fought against him with elbows and fists. Laughing at first, he had to let her go. "What a spitfire! I never dreamed it!"

"Don't you understand, Nigel?" She was resolved to speak reasonably and give him no chance to turn her emotions against her. "You were— you *are* a part of the awfulness. I saw you doing those things, and there was no pity in you. You and your men were like soldiers sacking a captured village. Perhaps you didn't rape the women and kill the men, but it was a sort of rape and murder as far as they're concerned. And, Nigel, this happened all over the estate! Even if you were not actually at each spot with your watch in your hand, you were represented there. Do you think a few hours' sleep, or a month of sleep, will erase that from my mind?"

"They'll survive," he said sulkily. "They'll roost somewhere."

"If someone like Sir Hector Rose lets them. Or if they try to stay on some marshy bit that isn't even fit pasturage, or huddle on the coast somewhere, living on dulse and whelks. If they had the money to emigrate, some of them might survive that way." The epitaph at Elgin appeared before her mind's eye.

> If Lyfe were a thing
> That monie could
> Buy. The poor could
> Not live & the rich
> Would not die.

"Who's been poisoning your mind with all this? Davie Grant? Alick Gilchrist? The bitch Morag?"

She ignored that. "They're pulled up by the roots and thrown away. They're dispossessed, and so am I."

He looked wildly at her. "This is your home."

"You were my home, my whole universe, and then I found out how you've been lying to me almost since we met, and you've looked down on me for a silly, sentimental doll; you've discussed my silly, sentimental notions with Christabel." The name almost gagged her. "You've talked me over with her. How dare you? *How dare you?*"

His face contorted. "Be quiet!" he shouted at her. "I've had enough!" He seized her upper arms and savagely shook her. She made no resistance, she was as limp in his grasp as a dead hare, her head bobbing loosely as if her neck were broken. Suddenly he threw her back against the pillows and slammed out of the room.

She remained unmoving, forcing herself to take long, even breaths, until she heard hoofbeats going away along the drive. Then she dressed, brushed the snarls out of her hair and tied it back with a ribbon instead of doing it up, and went downstairs to find something to eat. She was so hungry it was a pain in her stomach, and to wonder how the dispossessed were eating their suppers tonight only increased her own desire. There was, of course, no fire in the kitchen, but she heated water over the spirit lamp for a pot of tea, and while this was steeping, she found bread, cheese, cold beef from yesterday's dinner, and a pot of the breakfast marmalade. She put everything on a small tray and carried it out the north door that looked toward the paddock. She could not bear the emptiness of the rooms with Morag and Aili gone; she missed Mrs. MacIver's reticent presence.

Though the evening was gray, it was mild here on the step. An advantage was that she could not see the ridge from here, she would have had to go out on the lawn for that. Dora grazed in the paddock, and the birds sang as they sang around battlefields and plague-killed towns.

When she had finished her supper, she took a lump of sugar to Dora. "At least I have you, you will never betray me," she murmured. Then she remembered both horses really belonged to Archie or perhaps even to Christabel. "I shall buy you, my darling," she promised.

So Archie wanted the company of a pretty woman tonight. And well he might, with his ancestral ghosts on the prowl; with enough wine in him he'd be seeing the eyes move in his father's portrait, and hear the lips saying words he'd never be able to shut out. What had he done with himself all day while the roofs went up in burnt offerings to the god of the landlords?

Had he paced the rooms, cracking his knuckles and yawning nerv-

ously, stopped frequently at the nearest decanter? Had he gabbled to
Armitage over a distracted game of billiards? Of course he wouldn't dare
poke his nose outdoors all day, for fear that a treacherous breeze should
waft a stink of fire down to him as he inspected the rhododendrons.

Then Alick Gilchrist appeared, like a murdered man arising from his
secret grave.

In all these imaginings, there was a large, staring blank for Nigel.
What will I tell my children about these days? she mused, fondling the mare's
ears. There would be children; that was her part in this, to earn her
food, clothing, and shelter. They wouldn't be born of lovemaking; Nigel
would beget them upon her.

But once a child was started, she wouldn't sleep with him again until
it was time to begin another. She put her face against the mare's neck,
grimacing and swallowing to keep from crying. What perfection it had
been, what absolute joy; she'd been continually dazzled by her good
fortune. In retrospect it had even been heaven aboard *Minerva*, the way
they had held each other's heads and tenderly washed each other's faces. . . .
Perhaps he didn't know then, and he was just what he seemed, she thought.
But he knew soon after we arrived, and then the lies began. The mare pulled
her head away to look at something, and Jennie lifted her own head,
rubbing her blurry eyes, and looked apprehensively around her. No, Nigel
wasn't back. Fergus was crossing the stableyard to the pump.

She took bedding from the chest and made up the bed for Nigel in the
room across the hall from theirs. Then she locked herself in and locked
the entrance from his dressing room into the bedroom. She read through
the long Highland twilight until she could see no more, hardly knowing
what the words said because she kept listening for his return. He hadn't
come when she put aside her book, and she lulled herself by trying to
remember psalms and long stanzas of poetry. Her father had made them
memorize "by the mile," they'd called it, telling them they'd be glad of
it in the times to come. She thought wryly that this was not the sort of
occasion he had in mind. But she was glad of it, as he'd promised; the
concentration helped, and she went to sleep trying to recover some lost
lines from Milton.

Nigel was not home when she went cautiously into the hall in the
morning, wrapped in her old wool robe and wearing the sheepskin slippers; they offered her more than mere warmth. She went down to the

cold kitchen and built a fire on the hearth and was starting one in the stove when Nigel came in the back door.

"What are you doing?" he exclaimed harshly. "That's slavey work! There's a girl coming up from the outer farm to do the cooking until we get a staff. Go upstairs, wash your hands, and change out of that disgraceful getup!"

A new tactic this morning; the masterful husband. The unshaven husband in rumpled clothes, cravat gone, shirt wine-spattered, who'd been drinking until all hours, slept badly in a strange bed at Linnmore House, and had probably been ill on arising; had jogged home fighting nausea, and was now about to show her he had no patience with her notions.

"I know how to build a fire," she said calmly. "If you want any breakfast, you had better clean yourself up first."

"Breakfast!" he said in disgust. He swayed, and she realized he was still slightly drunk. The stale fumes of wine made her own stomach queasy. She turned her back on him, not as calm as she looked after last night's shaking that had left bruises on her arm.

But he didn't touch her; he went out again the way he had come. A few minutes later she looked out a window and saw him stripped by the pump, pouring one bucket of cold water over his head, then another one, while Fergus stood mutely by. Nigel shouted at him, and Fergus came at a trot for the house. She ran up the back stairs to get towels and Nigel's dressing gown and slippers, and when she came down, Fergus was standing just inside the kitchen door. She handed him the things and said, "Just put his clothes in the washhouse. Someone will attend to them." Or not, she thought indifferently. "Fergus, have you food? There's no porridge, I'm afraid, but you could have a bowl of hot tea. Or some coffee?"

His mouth actually quirked up on one side at the word *coffee*. "Take the towels and the robe to the Captain, and then come back," she said.

He went and returned as rapidly as she had ever seen him move. He smelled of the stable, a comfortable pungence that reminded her of mornings with Nelson. She told him to sit down at the table, and she gave him buttered bread and some of the cheese and beef to go on while she made the coffee. He ate more decently than she had expected; evidently Mrs. MacIver and the girls had trained him. She made the coffee and heated water for Nigel's shaving. He came in wrapped in his

robe and with his hair in curling yellow ringlets, his high color back in
his cheeks. The blue dressing gown intensified the color of his eyes.

"Would you like your coffee before or after you shave?" she asked.

"Afterwards," he said bleakly. "Perhaps *that* will have been removed
by then." Fergus, cautiously but rapturously sipping his steaming coffee,
was oblivious of the slur.

"Here is your hot water." She handed Nigel the can, swathed in a
cloth.

He gave her a despairing look, as if to be forced to carry his own
shaving water were the nadir of his existence so far. He said in a low,
unsteady voice, "My God! How can you look at me like that? This is a
nightmare."

"Yes, it is," she agreed.

"Can't we wake up from it?" His mouth moved in a tentative, diffident
smile, his eyes wooed her. "Come upstairs with me," he whispered. "We'll
banish the nightmare together."

"I don't know how that can be," she said composedly. "You see, it
still goes on whether we sleep or not, and not only for us."

"*Them* again! Will you ever forget them?" It was a cry of outrage,
not a question.

"Never," she said. "Or what was done to me."

He stalked out of the kitchen. She poured coffee for herself and sat
down across from Fergus. Obviously he expected no conversation from
her but was not made uncomfortable by her. He cleaned up every crumb
of his food, drank every drop of the sweet, creamy coffee, then said,
"Thank you," in Gaelic and left.

Nigel returned, shaved and dressed for the day in fawn breeches, blue
coat, glossy top boots. He looked clean, fresh, glowing; for a moment
she experienced, like the flash of a knife and then the stab, the purely
physical desire she had known at first sight of him. He seemed maliciously
pleased, as if he had seen or sensed the quick wound and hoped to make
her suffer more. His motions were brisk, and his face was hardened with
purpose, giving a false impression of maturity. He was twenty-six, and
this is how he might possibly look at thirty-six. His smile was incandescent but automatic, as if she were a woman seen on the side of a
street as he rode by.

"I shall be away all day," he announced. "No coffee for me, thank
you. I'll breakfast at Linnmore House with my brother; we have a good

deal of business. The girl should be here this morning. She's a niece
come to visit from the Borders."

She nodded, watching him over her coffee cup, and his color increased. He said haughtily, "There's a pair of boots out near the pump.
You might see if your coffee-drinking friend could do a fairly decent job
of cleaning and polishing them. That is, if he hasn't been spoiled out
of all usefulness."

"Speak to him yourself," she suggested, "when he brings Adam."

He strode out, his heels striking hard. *Next time you'll do the begging,*
his attitude said. *I have other things to do besides crawl to you. . . .* He left
doors open behind him all the way, and she heard him shout for Fergus
as he stepped out of doors.

Twenty-Eight

S HE TURNED BACK the sleeves of her gown and washed the dishes from last night and this morning; then she went upstairs to dress. Her small trunk was in the passage where Nigel had brought it last night, and as she knelt to unstrap it, she could look directly into the room where she'd made up the bed for him, the huge affair she'd joked about to Morag. The door stood wide open, and she'd left it only partly so. Then he'd seen it when he came upstairs this morning, pushed it back, stood on the threshold thinking God only knew what thoughts. He had done well to speak to her at all after that.

They lie and lie, she thought drearily, *and they never expect the lies to turn back on them and drive deep.* She took no joy in knifing him, but she couldn't forgive him. Her pride made her fold up the bedding and return it to the chest before the new servant saw, though she'd know by nightfall that something was wrong. Perhaps she'd go back to the farm to sleep. Jennie hoped so.

She returned to the armoire the dresses Aili and Morag had packed with such pleasure. She could hear their voices now and resented the stranger who would come. She sat before the toilet table of which Morag had been so proud—was Lily the maid who had found it for her?—and brushed her hair up into a chignon. It was silky from the rainwater and felt alive as it slipped through her fingers and half curled about her wrist. In the oval mirror her face looked narrow and pointed, her healthy tan had lost its bloom, and her eyes looked as round and forlorn as a forsaken child's, with mauve circles under them. The hollows above her collarbones and at the base of her long throat seemed deeper.

Suddenly she was infuriated by all this heaviness; it was like being pressed to death. She jumped up from her chair and began to dress. There was nothing pleasant to anticipate, but she could be outside all day. She would climb Meall na Gobhar Mor if there was an approach invisible from Linnmore House. Morag would know— Morag was gone.

A murmur of voices came from below the side windows, and she ran to them eagerly, but she knew before she looked that she wouldn't see Morag and Aili. The Elliots' lad, Tom, was leading the pony past the dining room windows, his favorite shortcut to the kitchen. The panniers would be carrying the day's fresh cream, milk, butter, and anything else Mrs. MacIver had ordered. A girl or woman walked with the boy; Jennie could gaze down on her white cap and dark green shawl and the skirt of her print gown.

Jennie tied her walking shoes and picked up a knitted spencer, and went downstairs to the sound of laughter in the kitchen. The boy was leaning his crossed arms familiarly on a chair back, and the new servant was tying on a large white apron crackling with starch. She was unabashed by Jennie's entrance; the boy ducked his head at Jennie's greeting and left.

"Good morning, Mistress Gilchrist!" This was a freckle-faced young woman with reddish hair fluffing out under the frill of her cap. She had small, humorous eyes, and her large, firm arms were as freckled as her face. "I'm Leezie Lindsay, the same as in the song." She sang in a strong voice, harsh compared to Morag's sweet soprano, but true. " 'Will ye gang to the Hielands, Leezie Lindsay? Will ye gang to the Hielands wi' me? Will ye gang to the Hielands, Leezie Lindsay, My bride and my darling to be.' "

She ended in a whoop of laughter that shook her firm, high bust. "And here I am in the Hielands and I've had nae offer yet to be anyone's bride and darling!"

"It's early days yet," said Jennie. "First you must have coats of green satin, to kilt them up to your knee."

"Ye ken it then."

"It's one of the songs I grew up on."

"Och, it's a wee world," said Lizzie profoundly. It appeared that most Scottish servants, either Highland or Lowland, were unabashed by class distinction.

During the next hour Jennie showed Lizzie where everything was, beginning with the cellar. She told her how the shopping was done, and to keep a list of what was used so she wouldn't go short on anything. She thought ironically that she was making a good start on her metamorphosis into a simple housewife. In gentle, domestic tones she discussed her husband's favorite meals and her own, and the preferred hours for dinner and supper.

"I'm nae fancy cook like yon Englishman at Linnmore Hoose," Lizzie announced belligerently.

"Plain food properly cooked suits us," Jennie said. "I told Mrs. MacIver I would like to try Scottish dishes, and she did very well. You can do the same, I'm sure."

"Aye, I can. But havers! It was the dreadful thing these Hielanders did, to flit like that!" Her full mouth turned censorious. "But that's the nature o' the beast."

"They had good reason to go, Lizzie. Their families needed them; some very sad things have been happening around here." Lizzie opened her mouth, but Jennie moved smoothly on. "Our laundress won't be coming. I don't like to burden you with more beside the cooking and general housework, but you would be paid separately for washing if you could manage it until we find someone."

"Och, it'll be nae trouble!"

"Upstairs there's a damp riding habit and tights—"

"Did ye tumble frae your horse?"

"No, I lost my footing and tumbled into a brook." She could not bring herself to tell this earthy girl that she wanted the clothing destroyed; but she needn't wear it again. "Some of the Captain's clothing is in the washhouse. When you are ready to wash, Fergus will help you with the water."

" Tom was telling me about yon Fergus. He's a daftie, then?"

"Not at all! He's slow of speech, but a genius with the horses. He's to be fed in the kitchen, and fed well. He's especially fond of coffee for a treat. The others were patient with him, and I hope you will be, too."

"Dinna ye fash yerself, Mistress. I've as kind a heart as ye could find." Her lack of false modesty would have been refreshing if Jennie had been happier.

"I'll leave you then," she said. "I'm going for a walk." She carried the spencer over her arm; the uncertain sun was warm, but the shade was cold. Turning her back inexorably to the ridge, she walked to the front of the house and took the road to Linnmore House.

When she came to the pasture, she left the drive and crossed the meadow, ignored by the occupants. She ached for exercise that would work her body to the limits of its strength, and perhaps when she had reached that topknot of ancient rock she would have also reached some compromise or pattern for her future existence.

She walked along the edge of the woods, looking for the obvious start of a footpath. In the meantime Meall na Gobhar Mor disppeared; she could see only a gently rising slope of birch, beech, and fir. She waded in translucent green seas of wet young ferns and bracken, following first one way and then another, always trying to keep the open fields in sight through the trees to her right.

Suddenly she heard a man's voice very clearly and looked down through the trees and saw the roofs of the stable block of Linnmore House. She sat down abruptly at the foot of a huge oak, among violets and the fragile pink-striped blossoms of wood sorrel.

She sat there for some time, overcome by an almost frightening languor. She could hardly hold her head up without support. She settled herself more comfortably into the grass, leaning back against the massive trunk. *If I were a witch,* she thought drowsily, *I could be sitting here ill-wishing the Master and Mistress of Linnmore House. I really ought to try it; I might have hidden powers.* She smiled sadly at this, and fell asleep.

It was a heavier sleep than she'd had all night, as if she felt perfectly safe out here. From *what?* she wondered groggily as she tried to get her eyes open and move her leaden hands and feet.

She had no idea what time it was; she hadn't bothered to pin her watch to her dress. What did time matter anyway? She had all her life ahead of her. *Tomorrow, and tomorrow, and tomorrow, Creeps in this petty pace from day to day.* The very words dropped on her like iron weights. She got up quickly, hugging her spencer around her against a new chill in the air, and went back the way she had come. But slowly this time, yawning enough to blind her eyes with water and occasionally stumbling.

She had revived by the time she returned to the pasture. When she reached the road again, she looked back, and there was the Hill of the Great Goat in its familiar place against the dappled northeast sky.

"I'll find you yet," she threatened.

Now she was driven to the ridge; she had to go there and get it over with. It was like going to see the dead body of someone you had loved, or someone for whom there was no other mourner. It was the last duty you could do for him.

She scrabbled quickly up the track; no Narcissus reverie over the fern-fringed pool this time.

She half expected to see at least one sign of life there, even that of an animal, but the complete emptiness shocked her. There was nothing moving, not even a hen that'd escaped capture. Everything and everyone gone, gone, gone. The word tolled in her head like a bell. Not even wisps of fire still lived; showers in the night had taken care of smoldering thatch.

Yesterday morning the rooster had announced the sun; kids bleated after their mothers; children awoke; women arose and revived the peat fires that had been smalled for the night; men took buckets and went for water.

This morning the roofless cottages already looked like old ruins, not even of interest to the crows.

She turned away, beyond tears, feeling old herself. Abstractedly she patted one of the pines as if it were Dora. All morning at the back of her mind Lizzie Lindsay's tune had been just barely audible. Now she went on with the verse she had been trying to ignore ever since the girl first sang:

> To gang to the Hielands wi' you, sir?
> I dinna ken how that may be;
> For I ken no the land that ye live in,
> Nor ken I the lad I'm gaun wi'.

She went directly up to her room to avoid any conversation with Lizzie, though she would have liked a pot of tea. As she passed up the stairs, the silence of the house was that of bereavement. The ticking of the clocks had a sorrowful cadence.

Directly she entered the bedroom, she smelled Nigel's eau de cologne; then she saw him through the open door to his dressing room. He stood naked as Apollo, taking fresh smalls from the press. Without looking around, he said curtly, "We're expected for dinner. If you choose not to go, I'll say you're not well."

"If I'd gone, you and Archie would be dining alone. So—" She shrugged her shoulders.

"Christabel arrived home this afternoon."

"I suppose she cut her visit short because there was no need to go on with the charade," Jennie observed.

He didn't deny that it had been a charade. "It was only to save you pain," he said. "That's what we all wanted."

"No, it was to get a meddlesome nuisance out of the way," she said in a flat, tired voice. "Did you tell them about my school, and then did you all three have a jolly laugh at my innocence?"

"I have never mentioned your school! I have never laughed at you!" His whole body flushed. A less beautiful man would have been ridiculous standing there naked and angry. Not Nigel. This body had been her possession and could be again, every superb inch of it. He was excited now by an aphrodisiac combination of her indifference and his indignation.

"Jennie!" He came toward her. "To hell with dinner, let us sleep together again and make everything all right."

"Neither that nor a new puppy will make it all not have happened." She backed and turned away. "I'll go with you to dinner."

She shut the door on him and went downstairs to tell Lizzie they wouldn't be eating here, and she could go back to the farm for the night whenever she pleased.

"My but the Captain's a heartsome, strappin' man!" Lizzie told her with enthusiasm, and Jennie smiled. She returned to her room and looked over her gowns. Christabel would be decked out like a drum horse on parade; very well, so would Jennie be, but with considerably more taste.

She dressed in a velvet-spotted white gauze over a pink silk slip, and wore pink tourmalines with it. She touched her throat, earlobes, and the inner fold of her elbows with the subtle scent given her, surprisingly, by Lady Clarke. Her long sleep under the oak tree had rested her, and she had more natural color in her lips and face. She knew that by candlelight she would look about seventeen, which couldn't please Christabel.

It was unbelievable that she and Nigel should be dressing for dinner with a closed door between them and that it was her doing. But she had no temptation to open it.

Lizzie came bounding up the stairs to announce the dogcart, and Jennie wrapped herself in an India shawl she had never worn before. Lizzie admired it tremendously, also Nigel's forest green wedding coat. She saw them off, beaming like a proud nanny, and Nigel played up to Jennie before her and young Dougal. It came easily to him, as all his deceptions came, and she was forced to play a part to protect her pride.

Twenty-Nine

A T LEAST he didn't insist on making light conversation on the ride.
The sun had stayed out long enough to give them a golden evening
light, and Christabel and Archie stood out on the steps waiting for them.
Christabel *outside*, instead of guarding her complexion! Perhaps she had
thought it was safe to breathe the air, now that the vermin had been
removed. She was all ablaze with her jewels and a capucine crepe gown
much garnished with gold embroidery; the strong nasturtium color was
wrong for her, but it was extremely fashionable outside the Highland
wilderness.

"Well, here we are!" Nigel called before the pony stopped. He jumped
out, but before he could hand Jennie down, Archie was there. He set
her on her feet and took both her hands in his, his head tilted archly.

"Wee Jeannie! I've missed you!"

"We're so glad you've recovered, Eugenia." Christabel was civil in a
wintry way. "We were about to walk down to the pond and admire the
daffodils. They're very fine this year."

"Very fine." Archie pulled Jennie's hand through his arm and patted
it. Nigel offered his arm to Christabel.

"I had a new sweet-scented variety set out last year," she said. "They're
intended to be late, to follow the common kind that have always been
there."

"I believe my mother set many of those out," said Nigel, adopting
her drawing-room manner. "Very bright and jolly, what?"

"Delightful!" she said with a simper. "I'm certainly not criticizing
your mother's good taste. But it's charming to have them keep coming

209

along. I had these bulbs smuggled in from Holland. Yes, I confess it!"
she said playfully.

"Christabel, you're unpatriotic," said Nigel, and she tittered. A phenomenon. *Is this what Nigel's arm does to her?* Jennie wondered. *If she
had a fan, she'd be tapping him with it and saying, "La, sir!"*

"Ah, now!" Archie drew in a long, snorting breath. "There's a whiff
of it already. Breathe deeply now, Jeannie. Isn't that a bonny fragrance?"

"I'm afraid I can't smell anything," she said with the sweetest of
smiles. "There is such a scent of smoke in my nostrils; I can't seem to
escape it."

"You should have no peat fires at all in your house," said Christabel,
"not even in the kitchen. There is no getting rid of the reek of it."

"It's not peat," Jennie said. She felt Nigel's shift of stance as if bracing
himself. "It's the stench of burning thatch, and of roof timbers that
weren't saved, and feather mattresses and bedding that couldn't be gotten
out in time." She knelt gracefully and put her nose to one of the crisply
frilled creamy blossoms. "Even this near I can barely smell the flower. . . .
I wonder what they are all doing now, and where they were last night
when it was showering. If we have a long wet period before some shelter
can be found, it could be the death of some of the very old and the very
young. There's a new baby—if it's still alive. The mother went into labor
while her home was being burned down."

The elongated shadows of the other three fell across her and the
flowers and reached the water, but they were the shadows of statues.
Then Christabel said, "They will be wanting to serve dinner. My chef
has excelled himself today, he claims. We shall see."

So they were going to ignore it. Well, if the chef could excel himself
at dinner, so could she. She would make it truly memorable for them.
She rose and took Archie's arm again, and again he patted her hand,
but his haw-haw was nervous. They began their sedate stroll up the lawn
in the sunset light.

"The cuckoos have returned," said Nigel.

"Have they?" Christabel asked. "I hardly know one bird from another,
except for the blackbirds, of course. Tiresome things and so common.
They go on and on."

"Is there any special reason for the chef's great effort?" Jennie asked.
"Has there been another victory like Trafalgar? Has Sir Arthur Wellesley
captured Napoleon?"

Archie took the opportunity to squeeze her hand and whinnied happily. "We haven't heard the latest intelligences from Spain, Jeannie, dear, but there's no doubt Wellesley* will do it. And when he rids all Europe of Boney, he'll be given a dukedom."

Nigel seized on the subject so avidly that it was pitiful, if she'd been of a mind to pity. Almost contentedly she listened to the two men do the topic to death. Nigel was passionately patriotic for a man who'd gladly resigned his commission; Archie blazed with the fervor of a man who had no sons to lose. Tenants' sons who died or would die on European battlefields were no concern of his, especially since he no longer had any tenants except on the farms and in the village.

Christabel made approving sounds at intervals while they paced along as if to ceremonial music. When they reached the mansion and entered the gloomy hall, and the stags' eyes, Christabel said "Do you wish to retire for a few moments before dinner, Eugenia?"

"No, thank you, Christabel."

They proceeded into the dining room. Archie retained possession of Jennie's hand and would not allow Armitage to seat her. Nigel gallantly did the same for Christabel.

The food was excellent here, as it always was. Jennie was proud of the way she could enjoy it while she plotted against the other three.

"We shall have some music by and by," Archie said. "Now that Jennie's here to wake up the old pianoforte."

"If she feels quite well enough," said Christabel. "She's had several of these strange attacks lately. Really, they come at the most inconvenient times. I'm quite astonished to see you here tonight, Eugenia. I expected you'd be taken ill again."

"Perhaps you should see the doctor," Archie sounded concerned.

"No need," said Jennie blithely. "I know the reason for it, and I assure you that as the day goes on, I always feel very well."

Archie burst into a guffaw which he stifled with his napkin, but he couldn't hide his glee. Christabel said, "Is everyone finished with the soup?" She rang for Armitage.

The conversation was superficial. Jennie took no part in it, but Nigel assumed his London manner; it was almost inpossible to imagine this character standing in the midst of the smoke and cries, holding his watch

---

* Wellesley did not become the Duke of Wellington until the following summer.

in his hand and giving the signal to the torchbearers. Knocking Morag away with a sweep of his arm . . . When he gave Jennie a shrewd, humorless glance in the midst of a silly joke he was telling, she realized she must have been staring at him. She smiled and picked up her wine-glass.

"When do the sheep arrive?" she asked Archie, sounding merely curious. Nigel tried to introduce a new subject, but Archie took it that she was really interested, now that she'd gotten over her little upset about the evictions.

"Any day now they'll be leaving Northumberland. Your home, my dearie! But we don't know when they'll arrive. They'll not drive them too hard because of the lambs." He sprawled back expansively in his chair, rubbing his hands and flashing his teeth at her. "We have only to finish enclosing. Your husband's done fine work, hiring laborers from the village."

Probably he threatened them with eviction, too, Jennie thought. She kept a gently eager gaze on Archie's face, but she felt Nigel's apprehension and was pitiless.

"They were glad to earn sixpence a day," Archie went on. "But those other lazy devils were a different story. D'you know, in some parts of the estate they kept knocking down the stone dykes every night, after the laborers left?"

"Well, one can hardly blame them," she said mildly, "knowing what the arrival of the sheep meant for them. I wonder what they're eating tonight, and where."

"Don't let your heart bleed for them, Eugenia." Christabel's voice was acid. "They'll survive. That kind of people don't seem ever to die out."

In spite of your best efforts. Jennie just managed not to say it. Archie squirmed and tittered. "Come now, let's enjoy this grand meal!" He was ignored. Christabel's flush contrasted ill with her orange crepe.

"And where was that rabble-rouser Alick Gilchrist yesterday? Where was he, for all his cant about loyalty to the peasants? He wasn't to be found on the estate, I hear. Perhaps he was afraid he'd be expected to fight for them!"

Archie was sweating, running fingers around inside his cravat, twist-ing his head around, stretching his long neck. "He came here later to ask for extra time for them. I granted it."

"*After* the event. He's like the rainbow; he comes out when the storm is past."

"I understand," said Jennie, "that before the evictions began, he was visited in his house, stunned, tied hand and foot, and gagged. He could have suffocated if someone hadn't found him, or died slowly and horribly from thirst and hunger." She didn't raise her voice; she might have been describing a garden party.

Archie, sweating more profusely, said, "Superior duck," and forked in a mouthful that should have choked him.

"Where do you hear all this fustian?" Christabel asked Jennie.

Nigel answered for her. "My wife practices Gaelic with the servants and believes most of what they tell her, whether she understands it or not. She even has great conversations with Fergus, can you believe that?" He gave Jennie an amused and uxorious smile.

"Oh, Jeannie, Jeannie!" Archie laughed and shook his finger at her.

"He had a dramatic excuse for staying away," said Nigel, lifting his wineglass to Jennie. "Quite original and romantic."

"But it was I who found him," said Jennie. Nigel turned pale; she actually saw the red leave his cheeks. Archie's loaded fork stopped halfway to his mouth; his toothy grin was frozen.

Christabel asked with remarkable calm, "Whatever were you doing over there?"

"I watched the evictions at the cottages just below the ridge, and I too wondered where he was." Equanimity went just so far. She'd have loved to spew the facts into their faces, over the men's immaculate cravats and Christabel's powdered and gemmed bosom, but it would have left herself devastated.

"So I rode around the loch to see. If he hadn't had the strength to drive his feet against a table leg and make some sounds, I'd have gone away again. Didn't he mention it to you, Archie?"

"No, no!" Archie was huffing and puffing. *Lying too,* she thought.

"And he didn't tell you about Lachy dead, with a dirk in his hand, and the blood on the dirk not his own? It was a grand death for a Highlander, was it not? I hope he was piped into heaven. I'm sure he was, if there is any justice there. It certainly doesn't exist on earth."

"My dear girl." Nigel's voice was brittle as glass. "This whole experience has been devilish hard on you because you don't understand it. You've hardly eaten since yesterday, and now you're drinking too much wine."

"I agree," said Christabel. "What she needs is her bed and a good long sleep."

"Preferably forever," said Jennie. "So Nigel can find him a more comfortable bride." Nigel stood up, pushing his chair back so hard it fell over. "Would I sleep, do you think," Jennie asked softly of them all, "until the smell of burning's gone? It's not as strong as it was from the eight townships burned out last week, but if you could put together the reek from all the burning at Linnmore yesterday, it could compete." She nodded at them. "And by how many times would you multiply the scene I saw yesterday? You know, Archie. I don't. I can only imagine. And what I cannot understand—yes, Nigel is right, there's much I cannot understand—is how you can sit here, beautifully dressed, eating an elegant meal, discussing the wine and the sauces, when all this has happened, and you ordered it as you ordered the food."

Christabel tried to interrupt her. Across the table Nigel stood immobile. She looked at neither of them; she kept her eyes on Archie, driving the knife home and twisting it.

"Someday, when the bracken and the gorse have hidden everything but what's left of the walls, and the sheep are everywhere, you can stand on the ridge and look down and pretend there was never anything else on twenty thousand acres but sheep and their shepherds."

"*Jennie!*" Nigel shouted at her. "You forget yourself!"

"Never." She arose too. It wasn't wine she was drunk with, and the effect wouldn't last much longer. She left the room, leaving silence behind her. She picked up her shawl in the hall and went out.

She ran down the steps, past the rhododendrons, and over the bridge. She wanted to be well away from Linnmore House before Nigel caught up with her. But by the time she had reached the trees, he was still not in sight. She walked now in the twilight, feeling every pebble through the flimsy soles of her slippers, so she moved to the grassy verge. There could be no row with Nigel if she refused to answer; she had said all she was going to say. It had been enough to make sure that she'd never again be welcomed at Linnmore House, at least by Christabel, and she was the one who called the tunes to which Archie danced.

Nigel could go there alone as much as he pleased. He was not likely to be dismissed because of his difficult wife; he'd proved himself as factor, and he was still the heir, unless Christabel and Archie accomplished a biological miracle.

Obviously Nigel wasn't trying to catch up with her. Either he was so outraged he didn't trust himself with her, or he was receiving advice and commiseration from the other two. She pictured Archie, stuttering, fiery red from too much claret gulped down like water. "Fine little lass, my boy. Deserves the best. If there's a baby on the way, she'll soon forget all this nonsense; she'll think of nothing else but the wee bairn. We must have the old cradle down. Be patient with her. Women have strange notions at this time, they tell me." Sentimental tears in his eyes. "Dear wee Jeannie. Tender heart. Does her credit."

Christabel would not enjoy talk of wee bairns. "The sooner you have the whip hand, the better. She's been badly brought up, thoroughly spoiled. You'll do her and yourself no good if you allow these tantrums. She's a romantic little fool with dangerous radical notions, and it's up to you to curb her."

Jennie went up the steps and into the house, leaving the front door open behind her to the glimmer of twilight and the last sounds of birds. Lizzie had left a candle burning on the console table. The tall clock numbered the seconds of her life as she stood there, listening, and watching the small blossom of flame flutter and then steady itself. Then she sighed without knowing it and picked up a bedroom candle to light it from the other.

"Jennie," Nigel said quietly from the doorway, "when are you going to forgive me?" She went on holding the wick to the flame, her hand trembling a little. He shut the door and came up behind her and put his arms around her. She stood passively in the embrace.

"It's not a matter of simply forgiving." She kept her voice low. "You're a stranger to me, and I have to see if I can live with that stranger. It's too soon. All I know is that you have never been honest with me, so I don't know what to do now."

"I *honestly* love you, Jennie."

"But who *are* you?" She put down her candlestick, unclasped his hands, took the candle again, and went to the stairs.

He shouted after her, "If I weren't the man I am, I'd never forgive you for the way you humiliated me tonight!"

"Oh, don't talk to me about humiliation," she said wearily. "You've been doing that to me for too long! Don't follow me, please. I am so tired. I just want to be let alone."

Thirty

T HE HEAVY oaken front door slammed before she reached the head of the stairs. She set her candlestick on the floor of the hall, and by its flickering light she took the bedding out of the chest where she'd crammed it this morning. Her agitated shadow danced hugely over walls and ceiling while she made up the antique bed for him, listening all the time for his return; the finished chore would not have been approved by Lizzie Lindsay. Then she locked herself into their bedroom by both doors.

He hadn't come back by the time she had undressed, washed, and was in bed. The long-case clock chimed dimly and melodiously for the hours and half hours; she didn't know how many times she heard it before she fell asleep.

She woke at daybreak. The first thing she thought was that she hadn't given Fergus any money to take to Alick. She was deeply ashamed for having been so self-centered all day yesterday.

The second thing was that today was Sunday, but she was not going to church even if she was asked, as seemed unlikely. No one wanted her embarrassing questions or statements to disturb the genteel sociabilities around the church door, and she didn't ever want to lay eyes on Dr. Macleod again in her life.

He'll not christen my babies! she thought fiercely.

She got up and dressed in the blue riding habit; after she had given the money to Fergus, she would ride for hours. She unlocked her keepsake box and lined up her golden hoard on the bureau. The last time she'd done this had been on that morning in Brunswick Square when she'd sworn she'd be off to the north within twenty-four hours. *I had all my faculties then*, she thought. *I lost them in the park that afternoon. Now they're back, but it's too late.*

As a spinster she'd have been as free as the blackbird or the lark, in comparison with a woman who had perversely left a husband who hadn't married her for her money, who never abused her, who was not a drunkard, a gambler, or a womanizer; who adored her.

Jennie's sisters would understand her, but William, while deploring the reason for her flight, would remind her that the marriage bond was sacred, and her duty was to remain with her husband, to forgive him seventy times seven and be a high moral influence on him in the future.

The rest of the world (Aunt and Uncle Higham) would see that an immature girl had flung herself about in hysterical objections to sound business practice; strictly men's business too, and absolutely none of hers.

In Switzerland with Ianthe she'd be clear of the moralizing, but even if she used some of her sovereigns to go to the Continent, there she would be considered a light woman and fair game. If Nigel should divorce her, she would be ruined by the scandal wherever she was. Her sisters' love couldn't do much for her then.

There was a cannonade of knocks on the door from the dressing room, and she almost spilled the coins across the floor. "Jennie, open up at once!" Nigel shouted.

She was on her knees, scooping up the sovereigns, dropping them into the velvet bag. "What—what is it?" She tried to sound dazed, just wakened from deep sleep. She slipped the cord over her neck and thrust the bag into her bosom, where it nestled warm and heavy between her breasts.

"I'm sorry if I woke you, but I must talk to you before that damned woman gets here. I'm glad you could sleep," he said sarcastically. "I couldn't."

"I'm not ready to talk yet." She yawned on the last word. "I must have time to wake up and wash and dress."

"Why can't I come in now?" Soft and seductive words against the panels.

She didn't answer.

"Very well! I'll see you downstairs in fifteen minutes." In a few moments she heard him striding toward the stairs. She tied a narrow scarf of fine red and white checked wool around her neck with a loose bow that would droop and hid any hint of the bag under the snug-fitting jacket. She left the hat but took her gloves. Then she went out into the hall. A breeze blew up the stairs; he had gone out the front door, and she could see him standing at the head of the stone steps. She went along the passage to the back stairs.

I cannot listen to him now, she thought. *I have nothing to say to him that I haven't already said.*

She had to wrestle a bit with the heavy bar holding the outside door and began to sweat inside the wool riding tights. But finally the bolt slid back, and she escaped out into the cold shadow of the house and the morning chill.

She was uneasy about Fergus. Five sovereigns would represent a fortune to the boy, if he knew what money was. And even if he had never seen a gold coin before this, the gold in itself was beautiful, warm to both the touch and the sight.

"Fergus is to be trusted," she could hear Alick Gilchrist saying.

She opened the small side door into the stable, and the sun came in with her, heating her back while she called for Fergus. Motes danced in the sunbeams; emptiness answered her voice. Out in the paddock one of the horses whickered in response. She went across to the loose-box in which Fergus slept on a pallet of straw. He'd kept his belongings in a small, crudely made wooden chest. So few things to furnish his life, but such a vacancy when they and he were gone.

She took Dora's saddle out to the paddock. It was heavy, but she'd carried Bertie's saddle when she was a small girl, and then Nelson's. Bertie had stood like a rock when one child or another slung the saddle over his back, climbing up onto a wall to do it. He'd endured any amount of fixing and fussing, buckling and unbuckling, all the getting on and off to make inexpert adjustments. He would roll his eyes at them and sigh, but stood. Nelson was a different case, and Dora was as full of notions as he was.

Jennie heaved the saddle up onto the paddock wall and summoned the mare, who came willingly; after all, Jennie was the source of sugar lumps and turnip slices, and allowed herself to be nuzzled and blown upon during the search for delicacies. But Jennie had no strupach for her this morning, and Jennie had never saddled her. The menacing shape upon the wall could be a crouching beast whose one aim in life was to leap at the throat of an innocent mare.

Attracted by the small furor, the gray joined the group. He was not alarmed by the saddle on the wall, but he was intrigued by Dora's sidewise dancing. Jennie tried to croon like Fergus, gave up in favor of a few crisp commands, and when those didn't work, she decided she would have to walk, praying the whole time that Alick would be home to receive the money.

Nigel said from beyond the gate, "I'll saddle her for you. Hold her head." He came over the gate like a gymnast. His eyes were a hard, expressionless blue. "We were going to talk."

"There's nothing to talk about. It's all been said." Her voice trembled. How could she be speaking like this to her Nigel? (If he had ever been hers.) "If we're to go on, there must be no more trying to defend something that's indefensible. It's happened. We can't undo it. For now, I need time and space."

He didn't answer but set about saddling the mare, who stood cooperatively still. Jennie waited. The trembling had left her voice for her body. Nigel came around the mare's rump, his face flushed, and said, "I'll ride with you."

"I prefer to go alone."

"You're not going out there!"

"No," she said, meaning she was not going down to the ruins. "I have no wish to visit open graves."

His head jerked back as if she'd lashed him across the face but had infuriated rather than wounded him.

"Where are you going then?"

" 'Goosey, goosey gander, / Whither shall I wander?' Help me mount please."

He made a step for her and gave her a lift up. "I'm just going to ride, Nigel," she said calmly. "Why don't you use the time to write to your mother and tell her what's been happening here? I'm sure she'll be glad to know just how well you are doing."

He was more than flushed; he was scarlet to the temples and the rims of his ears. "She's another romantic idealist! And as for you, by God, if you hadn't been allowed to run free here, we'd still be happy."

"Because I'd be ignorant? You reason like a child, Nigel. Well, you are still a boy after all, aren't you? Don't you think I'd have heard of the evictions, even if I hadn't seen them carried out? You insisted that I visit Christabel, and that's where I met Mr. Grant."

"He had no right to say whatever he did to you!"

"Nigel, I'm a woman, not a toy! Even without Grant, don't you think

I could have put all the puzzling things into a whole? The girls and Mrs. MacIver would not have left this house without telling my why."

"I should never have had those sluts under my roof!"

He held Jennie's foot in the stirrup and rested his forehead against her thigh. Out of habit her hand moved toward the yellow hair, then arrested itself.

"My God, Jennie," he groaned. "What's happened to us?"

"Something we can't ever talk about again," she said, "if we're going to get through the years ahead of us." The words clogged her mouth like the thick dust of the desert in which her youth was to be used up.

He released her and stood back. "I've sent word to the sheriff there'll be no charges against Donald John. He should be free by now."

"Thank you. Let's hope he can find his family."

Biting his lower lip, Nigel opened the gate for her like a groom; she nodded to him and rode out around the house and across the driveway, to the woods where the bridle path began which led to the start of the road over the moor.

Thirty-One

FOLLOWING the wagon road down from the woods above the mill, she kept her head turned away from the sight of the dead hamlet in the hollow, her face toward the rock-studded hillocks that rose southward to the beginnings of the mountains. They were crowned with light while their sides were still blue or smoke-purple or black-forested in morning's deep shadows. In the clear air they and the heights to the west looked so unnaturally near it seemed as if she could ride to them in a half hour and vanish into their precipitous folds to realms as mysterious as the spaces among the stars or the bottom of the deepest ocean.

How silent the moor was, now that no one was there. The only sounds were the mare's hooves on the road, and the birds. When she was passing the loch, she thought it was safe to look down, and the water was lustrous as satin. Above its far shore the windows of Alick Gilchrist's cottage winked reflected sunlight. She couldn't see any smoke from the chimney, and it should be rising in this still air, unless he was sleeping late after some wearying days. But when she turned off the road onto the track among the rocks and the gorse, she had an emptiness in her stomach that wasn't all hunger; she wasn't surprised to find no one there, and the garron gone.

She didn't want to go back without leaving the money, and there was no reason why she couldn't leave it; who was there to steal it in this place? The door was unlocked, and she went into the kitchen. There were some oatcakes on the table, and a slice of cold bacon. Her mouth watered, and she ate one of the oatcakes, chewing each mouthful carefully and washing it down with water. She had a struggle to keep from taking another, and the bacon too.

221

She reached inside her jacket for the velvet bag, but she couldn't make up her mind to leave the money and go. There were things she had to know: where Morag was, and if the new baby had survived, and how the children were whom she'd pulled from the brook. She had no one at Tigh nam Fuaran to talk to, and she was in no hurry to ride back there to begin the rest of her life.

If she waited a little while, he might come; she left the sovereigns in the purse and rode back to the road, and continued westward around the curve, looking for the Pict's House. She traveled up a rise and passed between two high outcroppings of nearly bald gray rock, then descended into a sheltered bowl of moist heat rising from the dew-sequined heather, and a dry, strong heat falling from the sun. The road went through it, bisected by a brown brook bubbling along a pebbly bed. To her right, halfway up a shallow mound, there was a dark little doorway framed in stone.

The first sight of that black oblong amid the sunlit bracken stopped her like a threat. Dora was offended by the sudden restraint and tossed her head instantly. "It's all right, my darling," Jennie said. Now she saw that there was more than a doorway, but with the centuries the small hut of stones seemed to have been swallowed by the earth around it. And if that shadowy portal weren't the way into a fairy hill, it should be.

She would have been enchanted by it under happier circumstances. Now, absurdly, she felt like crying because she had been cheated of this simple joy.

Dora drank from the brook, and Jennie gazed up at the Pict's House, trying to imagine the builder and what his life had been. She was hot, and loosened the scarf, and opened her jacket at the throat.

Dora's head came up, and her ears pricked forward. She stared expectantly up at the road ahead where it disappeared behind the Pict's mound. Presently the big brown pony came into view. Alick was slumped in the saddle, his head drooping, his bonnet tilted forward over his eyes. He wore a folded plaid of a dark tartan over his left shoulder. He seemed to be asleep, letting the garron take him home. The garron seemed half-asleep himself, until he saw those in the hollow, and sped up.

Alick straightened in the saddle and rubbed a hand over his face.

"I'm sorry if we woke you," Jennie said.

"Good morning, Mrs. Gilchrist," he said with no great enthusiasm.

He took off his bonnet but drew his dark brows down as if his eyes were bothered by the light. He hadn't shaved, and the shadow of beard made him look very dark.

"I've brought the money myself," she said diffidently. "Fergus has disappeared."

"I'm not surprised."

"*I* am. We talked yesterday, as much as I could talk with him, and he seemed friendly and willing. But perhaps he didn't like the new servant. He wouldn't feel at home with someone who doesn't speak like a Highlander."

"Perhaps," he said absently. "Will you be stepping down?"

"Yes, I have questions to ask."

He dismounted, but she had slid off the mare's back before he could help her. The two animals moved off together, starting to graze. She pointed up at the stone doorway. "So that's the Pict's House."

"So it has always been called." They stood silent in the warm, buzzing hush as if neither could think of anything else to say. When he spoke again, she started.

"I buried Lachy that night, and I built a cairn over his grave. The only prayer I made was that he would be undisturbed until the call comes to rise. He believed in that."

"Do you?"

"If God is still on the side of the landlords when the call comes, who wants to rise up from the grave to have the whole bloody business begin again?"

"My view is that God isn't on anyone's side. He is as magnificently indifferent as those mountains."

"That is worth considering." Alick's voice dragged. "I have not been home since that night. I've slept wherever I happened to be when I couldn't hold my head up for a few hours. Last night it was in a barn at Roseholm." He knelt by the brook and scooped up water to drink and dashed some into his eyes.

She sat down on a small boulder. "I won't keep you if you'll let me ask my questions first."

"Ask," he said. He dried his face on a fold of the plaid and sat down in the heather with his knees drawn up and his arms folded across them.

"Where is Morag?" she asked. "Where did they go?"

"The minister was shamed into allowing them to shelter in a fir wood behind the manse. Out of sight of the kirk, you understand," he said softly, "so the ladies and gentlemen might not be offended when they go to worship."

"Where will they go from there?"

"They don't know yet whether it will be south or north or to the coast. It will be wherever they are allowed, and what difference does it make? They will be vagrants now. With the money from Davie Grant and you and myself, they can be buying meal to keep from starving for a while. They will have to sell their beasts because they have no way of keeping them, and they will be robbed in that business."

"What about the new baby?"

"She came too soon. She was buried yesterday morning in a corner of the churchyard."

Suddenly Tamsin was with her in the person of the dead baby, and she pressed her palms over her eyes and wished she could go on retreating into the darkness she made for herself.

He didn't move. She could hear the mare and the pony cropping grass, and the sound of the brook. She lifted her head and blinked her eyes to clear them. Alick was watching something high overhead. Her own eyes were too blurred and dazzled to make it out. "Were there any more deaths?" she asked.

"A man in Glen Bneithe fell like a tree and has not spoken since, and his face is twisted."

"I hope he isn't one of Iain Innes's brothers," Jennie said.

"He is not. . . . A woman at Coire na Broc had terrible pains in her heart and couldn't walk, but she was alive last night. Och, they are all living with hearts shattered from one thing or another."

"Tell me about Morag, please!"

"Morag is strong and good, like her mother and father. They help the rest with their courage."

"What about the people at Roseholm?" she asked. "How long can they stay there?"

"Some of the younger ones are going on to Fort William in the hopes of emigrating, if they can find work to pay their passage. But the others can stay. They will work for him, still grieving for their homes, but they can grow old and die in decency. Rose's factor is a good man, and Rose lives like a chief of old. He stands godfather to the children and gives away widows' daughters at their weddings. If he approves of the young men," he added dryly.

"This is what I expected to find in the Highlands," said Jennie. "I'm glad it exists somewhere, if not at Linnmore. What about the little boys I found?"

"When I last saw them yesterday, the minister's housekeeper was coming out to the wood bringing a strupach to all the children, and those two were not being shy."

She smiled, but sadly. "I hope they live to grow up. They felt like little birds in my arms."

"They will perhaps survive to be coal miners for short lives, or fishermen to be swept up by the English Navy. Or they will drown in the ocean on the way to America some day. I must apologize, Mrs. Gilchrist. I am not always being so gloomy. You may find this hard to believe."

"There's not much to sing about," said Jennie, "unless you're a lark." The desert dust was clogging her throat again. She knelt by the brook and cupped her hands in the icy water and drank from them. When she straightened up, he was watching her. He looked less haggard now.

"What will *you* do?" she asked.

"By my grandfather's will, my line is always to have a home here. I have twenty pounds each quarter, through a lawyer in Dornoch."

"But in your heart do you *want* to stay?" she asked. "To marry and raise your children here when it is all turned over to sheep, and knowing you have such enemies at Linnmore House? Not to mention Patrick MacSween and his men."

He seemed faintly amused by her intensity; there was a creasing around his eyes and a lift to one corner of his mouth, the embryo of a smile.

"Would *you* emigrate?" she persisted. "Many Scots do well in England, if they're not anxious to cross the ocean."

"I am not a Scot," he said evenly. "I am a descendant of Picts. Our blood was shed here to hold the land, and it was ours long before Kenneth MacAlpin of the Scots had himself crowned king of everything north of the Forth. If I am forced out, there is no other place for me in Scotland, and I will not live with Sassenachs. So I will have to cross the sea, but not until I know it is a life and death choice, because I am sure it will be my death."

She was impressed by a dignity that neither Archie nor Nigel had ever shown, and she was very relieved, too. "I'll be glad if you stay," she said fervently. "Will you tell me whenever you have news of Morag and her people? Perhaps I can send them a little money sometimes. A little is all I have. I never wished before that I was rich, but I do now."

"Whatever you ask, I will do."

"Thank you. Now I'll give you what I brought." She turned her back to him and took out the velvet bag. She did up her buttons again and went back and emptied the bag on the flat top of the stone where she'd been sitting. The gold coins caught the sun in a small blazing fire.

"Take what you think is best," she said.

He took five and put them in a pocket inside his coat. "Hamish will use it where it's needed. Thank you."

"My father died a poor man," she said as she scooped the sovereigns into the purse, "but he left my sisters and me each thirty sovereigns, not to be wasted on foolishness. I think he'd be pleased by this, but sad for the necessity." She walked up toward the small dark entrance to the Pict's House, tucked the purse back into her bosom, and knotted the scarf. Then she took her handkerchief from her sleeve and blew her nose. *No more tears.* Life was going to be difficult from now on, but at least she had a roof, and food, and the possibility of children whom she could love. Tears were a disgusting indulgence, the easy, self-pitying solace of cowards.

There was a loud snort and a jingle of harness, and Dora whickered excitedly. Jennie swung around and saw Nigel on the gray between the two jagged outcroppings through which she had come. He was bareheaded, and an errant scud of wind ruffled his yellow hair and the horse's mane.

Thirty-Two

J ENNIE'S first reaction was a jolt of purely sensual joy as her body remembered him in its most intimate places; almost instantly that was killed by the new response that had become hideously familiar in the last forty-eight hours. Her heart began to beat in a jumpy, irregular rhythm, causing nausea and breathlessness; the symptoms were stronger now than ever, and she wondered with a resigned acceptance if she were about to drop dead.

She did not. Nigel rode down the small slope, and Dora welcomed Adam again, while the garron watched with good-humored curiosity. Alick sat motionless. Coming to the burn, the gray wanted to drink, and Nigel allowed it. All the while he kept his eyes on Jennie. His face was very flushed again.

"You lied to me," he said loudly.

"I didn't lie." Her answer was quiet; considering the way she felt, it couldn't be otherwise. "I told you I was not going *there*, and I didn't."

"You will oblige me by returning home at once."

"I am not in the mood for obliging you, Nigel," she said equably. "When I am ready, I shall go back."

The flush darkened. "You will mount now and ride with me."

It was dreadful, a boy's pompous imitation of an autocrat. She felt an exasperated pity, which annoyed her as much as he did. "When I ride back to that house, I will ride alone. Don't command me, Nigel. I shall follow you in good time."

"Have you an assignation with this man?" he shouted, and stabbed his crop toward Alick like a sword. Alick observed him without moving.

227

"Oh, Nigel!" Jennie exclaimed. "That's too much, even from you!"

"Too much, after your shameless behavior the day before yesterday? Going to this man's *house?*" His voice climbed, and broke like an adolescent's. He made an effort to calm himself. "That episode can be overlooked; none of us have been quite ourselves for several days. But today there is no excuse for *this.*" Again the thrust with the crop.

"We have all been very much ourselves, I think. The last two days have knocked down all the pretty illusions."

"You natter on like a damned bluestocking, but I can put up with that." He forced a hearty laugh. "Come along now! We forget the past and go forward. We get on with life." He jerked his head sidewise toward Alick. "Bring the mare here."

Alick didn't get up. "Even if I were your ghillie, that tone would not put the leap on me," he said.

Nigel's mouth worked as if he were cursing in whispers; he dismounted, threw the reins over the gray's head, and walked through the heather toward the mare. She tossed her head coquettishly and stepped out of reach behind the garron, which didn't move but gave him a long, mild look. Nigel swore aloud and cut at the pony with his crop.

"If you please," Alick said courteously, standing up, "do not be striking my garron."

Nigel whirled to face him, the crop raised. "I'll strike you, then! There are ways of ridding this place of you. If one doesn't work, another will. Do you know what the penalty is for seduction?"

"Nigel," Jennie said, "go home before you disgrace yourself." Walking toward him, she smelled the wine; he must have begun to drink as soon as she'd left him.

"I'm already disgraced. *You've* disgraced me! I will swear to seduction if I have to. It's a gentleman's word over the rabble, every time."

"And will the lady's word be no good at all?" she asked. She felt as if she were taking part in a dream.

"*Lady!*" He spewed the word at her like vomit. "A slut who runs with the lowest of the low! Like calls to like. Secret meetings. Conspiring with this—this—"

"Cousin?" Alick suggested softly. "Though I have no great pride in the connection."

Nigel looked wounded and confused. Jennie said, "I'll ride with you, Nigel. We'll go now. Come, Dora, love."

She took a step to go past him to the mare, and he swung out a long arm and swept her out of the way and off her feet as he had struck Morag. He brought the crop down across Alick's face, threw it from him, and seized the smaller man by the throat with both hands and began to throttle him.

Jennie had fallen backward and sprawled full length. She scrambled up, tangling in her skirts, fought free of them, and grabbed Nigel's arm with both hands. She shook it with all her strength, but he was strong, his muscles iron-hard, and he was possessed with a lunatic fury. Alick's face was growing blue. She snatched up the crop and began beating Nigel around the head and shoulders.

"You'll hang, you fool!" she shouted at him. "Gentleman or not!"

With a sudden whooping intake of breath he released Alick and bent double, moaning, his arms folded over his lower belly. Alick staggered backward, his hands to his throat. As the pounding slowed in her head, she heard Nigel's groans. Then Alick dropped his right hand, and with a surge that seemed to come from his toes he struck Nigel on the jaw with an undercut, Nigel's head snapped up and back and he dropped.

"There," Alick said. His voice was strained, hardly more than a whisper. "He'll sleep for a bit and be all the better for it." He was rubbing his throat. The mark of the crop showed in a raised red welt across one cheek and the bridge of his nose.

"You can get yourself quickly home now. That was a dirty trick to do to a man, but he was killing me." He swallowed, and it was obviously painful. "He may have to walk it and be slow at that. But it will do him no harm. He will be quiet when he comes home, and clearer in the head, to be sure."

Nigel's face, tilted blindly to the light, was vacant. *Unlived -in* was the phrase that sprang to mind. And he had never looked so young to her before. He seemed as defenseless as a sleeping child, yet he had come within a breath of being a murderer.

"I brought this on you both," she said in a stammering rush. "I—I am truly sorry." It sounded inane enough to make her blush. "If he b-brings charges, I will testify that he attacked you."

"He will not bring charges." Alick kept looking at Nigel while still rubbing his throat. "No man likes to admit that this was done to him, what I did."

"But your life can be made miserable." She was more composed now, dealing with bleak truth.

Alick made a dismissive gesture and went after the mare. The disturbed animals had run off a little way. She watched him anxiously. Without going to court, without the matter's ever passing the borders of the estate, Nigel could harass Alick in every way possible; knowing what he and the gamekeeper and their men were capable of, she could visualize murder made to appear an accident or the work of tinkers or gypsies. They might even produce a man to hang for it.

It was her fault, and she would watch, and know, and be powerless. The garron had intercepted Alick and was affectionately bumping his forehead against the man's shoulder. Perhaps she could make a sort of peace with Nigel as a bribe for his leaving Alick alone. It would give her present life some useful purpose and assuage the guilt that was scalding her now.

She looked over at Nigel again, already planning to bathe his head with cold water from the burn, letting him wake up to her concern. And *remorse?* She set her teeth on that one, then thought: *I do feel remorse, but he needn't know for just what. I am truly sorry to see him hurt, but sorrier for the reasons.*

"Alick," she said. The sound of his first name from her mouth startled him into looking around. "Ride back to your house, and put compresses on your throat. I don't know if they should be hot or cold," she said. "Whatever feels best." Pain in her fingers told her she was wringing her hands; she stopped that. "I'll stay with him and see him home. Are you sure he'll be able to walk?"

"Och, yes," Alick said. "But I will wait a wee bit with you." He glanced down the slope at Nigel and, like Jennie earlier, seemed hardly able to look away. He took off his bonnet and wiped his forehead with his sleeve, still watching Nigel.

The defenseless, empty face. The arms flung wide, the hands lying loose, open, palms upward. Legs sprawling, booted feet oddly awkward, as if they had never walked or fitted in stirrups. The only moving thing about him was a lock of his hair, stirring slightly in a little breeze that came down into the hollow.

Sweat was pouring down her back. She blurted out, "He looks—" Sunlight burned her eyes, and blackness flickered and menaced around the arc of her vision. She blinked frantically, but still the dark came on, until she remembered to bend over double and let the blood go to her head. She straightened up, feeling sick, but the blackness was gone. She went and knelt beside Nigel and lifted one of the flaccid hands, but the only pulse she could feel was her own; her whole body beat with it.

A shadow moved across her, and she looked up. Alick was black against the blue and white sky like a burn mark on pastel silk. He knelt opposite her and put his fingers on the side of Nigel's throat. His hand was shaking; she saw his dark skin take on an ugly pallor, and the crop mark stood out like a bloody wound. He had to make several attempts to speak.

"I am a hanged man," he said. He stood up carefully and walked away down the slope toward the burn. She could not believe that Nigel was dead, but she could no longer look into his face. A bee lit on his nose and walked the length of it, between his fair eyebrows, across his forehead to his hair. Her held breath erupted in a harsh gasp; she sprang up and stumbled down to where Alick was. The water purled along at their feet, making its own sound.

Alick was shaking violently as if with chills. She spoke fast. "I will swear for you. You have the marks on your face and your throat. Surely the sheriff will see them if you go to him before they fade. I will go with you."

Gazing down at the bubbling brown water, he said tonelessly, "The sheriff is the landlords' man. I will go into jail to wait for the trial, and the marks will be gone by then. But there will be plenty to swear to the marks on *him*."

He turned to her. "Your husband came upon us in adultery, and I killed him. That is what they will be saying."

"Archie will believe me!" she cried.

"Archie is an amadan, a fool, and *she* will pay people to lie about what they have seen between us. We will both be gotten rid of. You in disgrace, and me to the gallows." He couldn't stop shaking. "My neck is already in the noose."

"*No!*"

He said with soft courtesy, "It is not your fault."

"It is, it *is*!"

The larks upwinging were birds singing in hell. She was half-wild with terror for them both, ready to sink down where she stood and will herself to a swift death.

Alick said suddenly, "Ride back. Say you found him like this, alone. Can you lie?"

"Yes." She was surprised by the strength of her voice. "To save a life." *If I can keep from feeling the truth is written on my forehead*, she thought. "I'll be distraught, beside myself. I'll need soothing drafts, laudanum to make me sleep. They can't keep at me then. And he could have been thrown! If I am to lie, I could say I saw it happen."

"No. You will be playing into their hands, you see." His painful throat made his voice husky. "There will be bruises on him from my knee and my fist, and they will think as they please, but you will not be a part of it if you say you *found* him like this. By the time they come for him with a cart I will be lost in the mountains." He felt inside his jacket and brought out his purse. "Here is your money, and Davie's. Iain will know how to get it to Hamish." They were walking toward the horses. "You must lead his horse back. The beast shouldn't be left alone out here."

In the dark entrance to the Pict's House, something moved. Alick leaped forward, Jennie's legs gave out this time, and she collapsed to the turf, wishing that the earlier blackness would return and shelter her.

A sibilant spate of Gaelic flowed down the rise. She lifted her head from her arms and saw Alick coming with a bent, frail, elderly man who hobbled along with the help of a staff.

"This is Parlan, from Coire na Broc," Alick said. "He says he will live like a rabbit on the moor rather than leave it, and I tell him it is like a rabbit they will snare him. . . . He was sleeping, and the loud voices woke him."

Parlan took off his bonnet. "Good day, Mistress," he said as if they had merely met upon the road. "The Captain looks as if his neck is broken. How could that be, with only one blow?"

"He saw it all!" Jennie exclaimed. "He can be our witness!"

"He is worse than no witness at all. He will be torn to pieces in the High Court like a hare by dogs." The picture, one of the horrors of her childhood, sickened her, but Parlan listened with bright interest, his bald head cocked, his watery blue eyes moving from one face to the other.

"On his own moor he is one man. Carry him away from here, and he will be old and confused and very frightened. They will be twisting his confusion to make the story they want. *He* has already told us what that will be." He jerked his head backward toward Nigel.

"What can we do then? Can you swear him never to tell anyone that he was here at all? If he could just erase it from his mind, hide it as if it were a whisky still. You would be safe in the mountains, and I—" The impetus ran out. How intolerable would it be to live in suspense, waking each morning to wonder if this was the day when Parlan rambled in his wits and forgot his oath? Among his own folk the story of the factor's death, and her presence at it, should be safe enough. But who could know what rumors might reach what ears?

She saw herself summoned to appear before the High Court to assist in an inquiry into the death of Nigel Gilchrist, questioned without mercy by clever men who had already condemned her as an adulteress and accessory to her husband's murder. *She* would be the animal thrown to the hounds: the exhausted fox, the hare paralyzed by terror.

Her chest constricted so she could hardly breathe; she gasped for air. An arm went strongly around her and kept her from falling. Life coursed powerfully through her, a rage that innocence should be violated.

"I'm not going to swoon," she said proudly. Alick released her. "Tell me this. You need not name names, but you have a place in mind, have you not? You are not simply going to live out the rest of your life as a fugitive in a mountain cave."

"I have a place, yes." He was wary. "I know where I am going."

"Could I reach England from there?"

"In time, yes."

"Then I am going with you. I have no other choice." A crowded rectory in Northumberland looked like very heaven. "I have a family who will believe me, no matter what Christabel says. Then I can go to the Continent and find employment and be safely out of reach of Linnmore House."

She watched the dark gray eyes change from wariness to obstinate refusal, then shift away from her, absently contemplating space, then return in dour acceptance. He had no more choice than she had.

He spoke to Parlan, whose answers came quickly back. She watched the expression on first one face and then the other, tried to guess what each intonation meant, vaguely understood gestures, nods, a fist softly thumped into a palm, and then the interlocked grip of four hands, tears standing in the old man's eyes as he spoke what was clearly an oath.

She felt as if she had been standing in this hot bright hollow for at least half her lifetime, and to look anywhere else but at the two men would mean seeing Nigel, and she couldn't do that. He dominated them all as it was, just by lying there dead.

Finally Alick came back to her. "He will do better with one simple lie than attempting to tell them a truth which they will not accept. And he will hold fast to this lie as if it is his life." Parlan nodded vehemently.

"The lie is that he has seen nobody. He has been walking across the moor from Coire na Broc since the evictions, lying up by day and traveling by night, to shelter in the Pict's House until he is driven out. He came upon the two horses and the garron, and the Captain lying so. He rides the garron to Linnmore House, leading the horses, and tells what he has found. A cart will be sent; men will search. I have gone; you do not come home. We will be deep in the mountains by then because Parlan will not go to them until the sun drops behind Ben Cheathaich. Are you still sure?"

She said with a bitter smile, "Yes."

"Then, if ever we are caught, remember I took you captive by force. You are my hostage."

"This is no time for chivalry. If ever we are caught, I will defend you. This is all my fault, and I'll crawl to my uncle if I must, to hire the finest lawyers, and I will sign over my inheritance to him to pay for them."

"If you don't say that you were taken, you will be damned for running away with me," he warned.

"I will say I was afraid you would be tried and hanged before you could be properly defended, and that I would be unjustly accused if I spoke for you. We were on our way to find someone who would believe the truth. *Someone* has to believe the truth!" she cried passionately at the two faces, and burst into tears.

She sat on the ground and wept into her hands. No one came near her. In the streaming red-shot darkness she saw Nigel lying dead a little way from her, she saw her whole life lying dead, and it had all happened so fast. *How could it have happened like that?* she cried piteously inside her head.

After a time she lifted her face and looked around her with bleary eyes. She expected to find herself alone except for the two horses and Nigel; the Highlanders would have taken the chance to slip away.

But they were up by the Pict's House. Alick was hanging a leather satchel over his shoulder by a strap. She went down to the burn and washed her face and drank. Alick came to her there.

"Parlan has given us what stores he has. He can take what he needs from my house, and he has the money to put in the hands of Iain Innes.

He will do it; he swore to it." He hesitated. "I kept out something. I will need it for what I intend to do."

"Give it all to him, Alick. Remember, I still have money, and they need all they can get." He nodded and went back to Parlan.

It was a relief to feel completely free of any emotion now. She knew that she was doing the only thing possible for her. When she got up from her knees, she felt surprisingly strong. She walked over to the horses and took Dora's head in her arms and kissed her nose; she reached out a hand and stroked Adam's neck. Alick whistled to the garron, who trotted to him.

"Why don't you take him?" she asked.

"Because I will not take him away from his home. It's enough that I have to go. Parlan will leave him with the Elliots. They grow a few kind hearts in Ayrshire."

When he held the pony's head between his hands, she looked away toward the mountains in the south. By sunset how deep would they be in the foothills? How far still from those mountains whose transitions from one pastel tint to another, as clouds passed over the sun, belied their brutality? She wanted only to be there, no matter what lay within those folds; anything to be away from the hollow.

"Are you still sure?" Alick asked behind her.

"Yes." Parlan was with him, and she surprised an expression of loving sadness on his toothless old face. She put out her hand, and he closed his gnarled fingers over it.

"Thank you, Parlan."

"It's a safe journey I wish you, Mistress, and peace at the end of it. You have a true heart. You could be one of ours." He put out his other hand to Alick. With wet eyes he spoke in Gaelic; then he and Alick embraced, and it was over.

Jennie and Alick crossed the brook and went up to the opposite rim of the hollow; the way south lay before them. Alick walked ahead of her through the whin and bracken, with a swift but easy stride, and she kept up without difficulty. She'd have gladly run if it had been possible.

They went out around a stony mound, and some distance before them a deep, forested crease appeared between two hills. She guessed that they were heading for it. Instinctively she looked back. Already a mile or so of uneven terrain had hidden the general location of the hollow, but now the loch had disappeared, though she thought she could still see the osprey hanging over it. Far away across the billows of moor that brightened and darkened under sun and cloud, there was the line of the great old pines against the sky.

She filled her eyes with them to imprint them for always on her memory. Then she turned and hurried to catch up with Alick.

Thirty-Three

S HE WALKED behind Alick in a trancelike state. When a grouse exploded out of the heather, she was brutally startled and cried out as if in pain; the cry echoed weirdly in the emptiness. The man didn't look around or hesitate, and she fell back into the mindless rhythm of their walking. She was impelled to turn her head often, only to see how the land flowed down behind them to wipe out what she had seen in the last five minutes. The sun-filled hollow might have been a hallucination; in fact, her whole life since she met Nigel was compressed into one massive hallucination of a man lying dead with a bee walking over his hair. By concentrating on the bee, she could ignore Nigel's face. She saw the bee with a pure and fiery clarity. It was a jeweled bee, a Cellini bee. It was the sort of vision that might haunt, or entertain, a madman.

Reality was the man walking ahead of her in coarse coat and breeches and scuffed boots. She had been watching those boots for years, it sometimes seemed; the dark pattern of the plaid folded over his shoulder had a ghastly familiarity, and the way the hair grew down his neck. The way the leather bag bounced softly on his hip.

She had no fear of him. It did not occur to her to wonder just with whom or what she was tramping off into the wilderness. She did not wonder where they were going. What mattered was the distance they put behind them before the sun dropped beyond Ben Cheathaich.

Not speaking, avoiding direct glances, they drank from streams that bubbled across their path or beside it. There were scurries in the bracken as small animals were taken by surprise. An auburn flash on a rise meant deer. Once, when she looked up, two golden eagles were circling the zenith. They could see everything, she thought dully: the fugitives here, the dead man there; the grazing horses and pony; the old man waiting, drowsing, for the sun to go down. But when would it set? The world seemed to hang motionless in space, no longer turning, their side of it condemned to eternal day.

In a small wood Alick cut two ash sticks and handed one to her. She was desperate to make some human contact, and her words gushed out on a shallow breath. "Thank you, it will be easier on the steep places. . . . How is your throat? Is it much bruised?"

He put his hand up to it. Above the inflamed marks of the crop his eyes conveyed nothing. She thought he hated her because she had brought this doom upon him.

She said valiantly, "I'd go alone if I could, and not be a responsibility. You could move faster alone."

"You could go back." There was more life in his voice than in his eyes. "I could return you to the sight of the road."

"No!" The violence made his lids flicker. "I'm sorry if that's what you want, but no, I cannot go back. Besides, it would put you at risk, to lose all this ground."

Alick sketched a movement, half bow, half shrug.

"We'd best be moving quickly on."

"All right. I'll keep up. I told you I wouldn't be a hindrance."

But she was afraid of that as the day wore by. She'd had only the oatcake, and she began to feel faint and struggled silently with her weakness. When he called a halt in a pine grove on the side of a hill, she dropped like a log onto the floor of warm dry spills and lay on her back. The tall tops swayed in circles in a wind barely felt down here; clouds blew over, great puffs undershadowed in amaranth smudged with soot. *It will rain and rain*, she thought. *Of course it has to rain. And there'll be no way to get dry, so the fugitives will die of congestion in the lungs, and that will be the end of a brief and terrible story. . . .*

In the meantime her feet burned and throbbed, and she sat up to take her boots off. He had been sitting on a log a little distance away, his elbows on his knees and his head in his hands, bonnet and plaid thrown off. Now he lifted his head and said sharply, "Don't take them off. You'll not be getting them on again."

He brought out the food Parlan had given him and used his dirk to cut off crusty bread and the hard, strong cheese. "We'll have a wee bit of the ham when we stop near water, for it'll be salty. A woman in the village gave this food to Parlan. His was burned up."

She chewed dutifully to start the saliva flowing to moisten the food. Night came late in the Highlands in warm weather. How many hours until it was too dark to see? She cautiously wriggled her hot toes, wondered how long the soles of her boots would hold out. *If I survive,* she thought ironically, *I may walk out of the mountains on bare soles tanned hard as iron.*

She tried deliberately to see Nigel's name cut in a polished granite gravestone, but she could not. Everything closed up in her from her stomach to her throat until she could not even breathe. She stared at Alick's ear and turned-away cheekbone in mute panic until suddenly he looked around, reached over, and gave her a hard shake. She gasped, and air rushed into her lungs. She twisted away from him, fighting tears. She heard him get up, and the soft susurrus of his boots on the slippery brown needles, going away.

He is leaving me, she thought with no surprise. *I was a disaster to him back there; I am a liability to him here.* . . . Then she saw the bonnet, plaid, the stick and the sack, still lying there.

She stood and limped off in another direction, going behind some gorse on the edge of the grove. Here she relieved herself, carried back to doing the same thing on a Northumbrian hillside.

When she went up the hill again, Alick had picked up his things and was ready to move.

"Will we walk all night?" she asked, trying to sound strong.

"Not tonight. Only until dark."

"Do you have a place in mind for stopping?"

"Yes, I have known it since I was a boy."

They went on in silence, up through the resinous ruddy shade of the pine grove to a world without trees where the sun still shone, and a wind blew hard at their backs, driving them across creased slopes of lead-gray rock; they descended into shadow like cold water, and eerie silence pulsed against her eardrums. She felt as lost as if they were alone on the moon.

Then, all at once, they came into a small glen where rowan and hawthorn were in blossom, and young-leaved birches gave an atmosphere of domesticity. The sheltered air was fragrant with spring scents, and musical with birds and the sound of a little stream.

She had been doggedly following him, watching his feet and her own footing, trying to shut out the desolation by ignoring it. Now she cried out in astonishment and relief, as if she had just awakened from a nightmare. They drank from the shallow stream, and no water so far today had tasted like this. She said eagerly, "Is this where we will stay?"

"No." He got up from his knees.

"Oh, why not?" she pleaded. "The grass is so soft. Look, primroses, violets! I didn't know there were such places among the mountains." *And I am so tired,* she went on in silence. *I could fall over now and sleep like a stone here.*

"No one could pay me enough to make me sleep in this glen," he said. "The place is up there."

In despair she looked where he pointed, and through a gap in the delicate foliage she saw another cruelly barren slope. The sunset was turning the rock to an angry red that was more threatening than the gray.

But it was evening at last; she supposed she should be grateful for that. She took her stick and followed him out of the glen, up through the thinning trees toward the cold glow. She could look back once in longing to the shadowy little sea of green and white, and then a bend in the track took her away from it forever.

They didn't go all the way up to the rock but stopped just outside the last pines. The place where they were to stay was a crude cave in the side of the hill, hardly more than an overhang of the ancient rock heaved up from the earth's boiling heart. The floor of it was earth, and there was one sign of human occupation, a rusty, battered pannikin.

Alick held the pannikin toward the western afterglow. "No holes," he said with grim satisfaction. "I was wondering was it still here. There's a spring below, just off the track. I'll be getting us some water."

He left her. She sat with her back against the wall, shut her eyes, and felt herself swooning toward sleep; no frightening images now, just black billows coming endlessly toward her, a night sea with neither stars nor whitecaps.

Reluctantly she awoke when he came back, lifting heavy lids. He set down the pannikin almost full of water, and took out their food. They had more off the loaf, more cheese, a slice of ham apiece, and drank water from the rusty vessel.

"Did you leave that here?" she asked him.

Busily eating, he nodded.

"How long ago?"

He shrugged one shoulder, swallowed what was in his mouth, and said, "Four years. A miracle it is to find it without holes eaten through it."

"Perhaps that is a good sign for us. For *you*," she said timidly.

"Perhaps."

"Who travels this track?"

"No one, now. It is safe for us."

"Where does it go?"

"For me, to Fort William and the immigrant ships." He settled against the wall, and tipped his head back, stretched out his legs, and crossed his ankles. In the fading light the whip mark was not so clear. He spoke with more ease, as if the soreness were going from his throat. "Once I am safely away, you will go to the authorities and say I dragged you away with me so you could not inform against me. Then you can go home. They will arrange it for you."

"Would I not be forced back for an inquiry?"

"Linnmore is rid of me. That is what they wanted. But if you should have to explain, make me out a villain so black-hearted they will weep with pity for you."

They were silent. The black billows were gathering up at the outer rim of her consciousness, a night tide beginning to return. Did she dare to take off her boots? Right now she felt nothing but the half-sickening, half-ecstatic slide toward the dark. From far off the soft Highland voice said, "When they know you are alive, they will surely send you the things you treasured."

But he will be under a stone, she thought she answered, but she couldn't be sure. What was she doing *here?* Falling asleep on bare earth in a mountain cave, after the nights with Nigel in the big tester bed?

All over. How could it *be* so suddenly, and not finished by his death but by him? . . . She roused herself to ask drunkenly, "What treasures did you leave behind? Beside the pony?"

"Mata, yes. And a few things." She knew it was a great deal for him to be saying. "A brooch my mother set great store by. A shawl of my grandmother's weaving, and the silver buckles from my father's shoes. And his Doune pistol is still there." Life stirred in his voice like rising wind among dead leaves. "A beauty she is. A pistol made by a gunsmith of Doune is a valuable thing these days. I am told that the English make presents of them to foreign kings. This was made for my grandfather Linnmore; she has gold inlaid, and his name inscribed. He gave her to my father. If I had her now, I could take her to America with me and sell her there, and I would begin my new life with gold in my pockets. But Archie will have her now," he said absently. "He always wanted her."

"Tell me more about your father," Jennie said.

"I never was knowing him. He went to America with Fraser's Highlanders when the colonies rebelled. I was born after he left, and he was killed there. My grandfather wept, my mother told me."

"And your mother?" she asked gently. "How long—" She didn't finish, sensing that he would not answer. "My mother died when my little sister was born." She went on. "I was six then. And my father's heart failed him when he was riding home from town one day last summer." She was surprised to speak the words with such composure, even knowing that if Papa's heart were still strongly beating, she would be safe at home in Pippin Grange.

"I am sorry for that," he said politely.

"There is no school on the estate," she said. "Who taught you?"

His abrupt laugh was harsh. "No one! My grandfather said I was to be educated, so I would have more of life than to be raised for a soldier. That was his wish, but it was not in his will."

"No schooling whatever then?"

"No, but I still wouldn't go as a soldier to free them of my presence. No man alive could make me do that. Take the English King's shilling and fight for *him*? What harm has this Bonaparte ever done *me*? What harm had the Americans ever done my father? He should have deserted, and stayed alive." He stood up. "We are needing to sleep."

She crawled out from the shelter, managing not to groan as her limbs were forced to move. In the clear blue-violet twilight Alick went down toward the pines, and she walked to some low shrubs a little distance from the cave. Something small scampered away, and she stamped her feet in warning before she squatted. Afterward she cleaned herself with a handful of bracken; she'd done this before, too. *Very useful knowledge now,* she thought ironically. *It's a pity I can't tell Alick how well prepared I am in wilderness ways.*

When they met again, he gave her the plaid, and she protested. "This habit is wool, and I have sufficient beneath it."

"Take it."

She took it. She planned to sleep sitting up, her back against the wall, rather than lay her head on the earth; she had a childish fear of things crawling into her ears. But the ache to lie down and stretch out was unbearable. She spread the plaid and lay from corner to corner of it, leaving two corners to bring up over her. She loosened her clothing as much as possible, wishing she could get rid of her boots and stays; then she lay with her arms folded under her head, watching him. He sat at the cave entrance, an immobile silhouette against the luminous night sky.

She hoped he was sleeping, and she felt guilty about having the plaid. But the black night tide was now murmuring hypnotically in her ears, and with a sigh of surrender she turned on her side, curled up, and drowned.

Thirty-Four

S HE DREAMED she was being chased by the deerhounds in the portrait at Linnmore House. They slavered with bloodlust, their eyes fiery red, their voices echoing and reechoing through her head. She was running, with her hands over her ears trying to shut out the sound, thinking she would die of terror in the next instant. She stumbled, pitched forward, and one had her by the foot. She would be tossed and torn like a rabbit; she *was* the rabbit, helpless in their great teeth—

The grip on her ankle tightened and shook her. "Wake up, wake up! It's only a dream you are having! *Wake up!*"

Sobbing and moaning, she fought clear of the nightmare into the gray half-light. "Where are the dogs? I heard them, I *heard* them!"

"You heard yourself." Alick was a shadowy figure kneeling beside her. He sat back on his heels. "And so did every bird and beast within ten miles."

"Did I wake you? I'm sorry." Her voice trembled with reaction to the death escaped if only in a dream.

"No harm done. I nap like a cat." He got up. "There'll be no dogs, not even ghosts of dogs, so you can drop them out of your night terrors. Get up now, we should be on our way."

There was a lake of mist below them, submerging all but the tops of the trees. He disappeared into it. When she was out among the low shrubs, the dew wet her boots and soaked the hem of her habit; there was plenty of moisture on the useful bracken, so she washed her face and hands with it, and dried on her scarf.

Their breakfast was more bread and cheese, and he had brought up another pan of water. The food tasted better this morning because she had rested in spite of the nightmare. Remembering that sent tremors over her, and he said sharply, "You'll not be taking a chill?"

"I don't take cold easily. I was remembering the dogs, the way they sounded and looked. No wonder Archie was afraid of them. And the poor deer!"

"The Old Laird never hunted with them. He was not a hunting man. Neither is Archie, but since herself became mistress, her Sassenach friends come in the summer and autumn, and great is the slaughter of anything that runs or flies."

"I'd hate that. Well, I won't have to see it, will I?"

He didn't answer but began packing the food and the pan. Again she had that sense of a door slammed shut between them and bolted, not ever to be opened again. Yesterday in the space of ten minutes he had become not only an exile but a fugitive, while she had been at Linnmore only a few weeks and would be returning to her own people and her own country.

She was ashamed of her flippant comment. How could he bring himself to be even civil to her? She stiffened her jaw to underline her determination to be as self-reliant and undependent as possible; he would never be able to say that she had held him back. If her boot soles wore through, he would never know. If her heels blistered, she would lean that much harder on her stick but never moan. And by an absolutely inhuman effort of will she might be able to stop having noisy nightmares.

Tramping behind him, she moved in the prison circle of her thought as he must be moving in his. The sunny hollow was always waiting like a punishment cell, and Nigel was still in it, even though he must have been taken away by now, and a letter would be on its way to his mother.

She searched for something immediate to obsess her, and found it, as one always could. There was nothing, she reflected grimly, like worrying about the body's inner workings to take one's mind off the larger issues. *They* became the larger issues. Her menses, for instance. How would she deal with something which up to now had been only a nuisance (she thought nature had evolved an abominable system for females) but never a serious problem, if it happened before she reached Fort William? She couldn't sort out dates in her mind; everything jumbled together.

She'd have to tear up her lawn chemise and borrow Alick's knife to cut up her scarf. In the meantime she hoped that short rations and nerves would keep the flow back.

The sun rose in a sky made of fire opals, and the earth steamed as the mists burned away. The trail went over the hillsides above the trees for the most of the morning. They surprised a ptarmigan, which thrashed around in the heather to divert them from her nest. A blue-gray mountain hare ran before them for a while and then plunged off the track and disappeared in the undergrowth. She envied him; in spite of winged and four-footed predators, the hare was at home.

The wind came up with the sun. They had to lean into it sometimes, and she felt as if she were pushing her head and shoulders with all her might against an invisible but overpowering force. But she kept her lips tightly shut so she couldn't gasp. The cold tore through her clothes, while the sun burned on her head.

They went down over a broad slope of scree, slipping and sliding, using their sticks to brake themselves. Once she almost went headlong and Alick thrust out his arm and it held her like an iron bar on a gate.

"Stay behind me," he commanded. It was the first thing he'd said since they started out at dawn.

On level ground at the foot, a stream ran among stones, and they ate and drank here, still with no conversation. Around them the mountains formed a threatening circle, as if they were biding their time in a monstrous cats-and-mice game.

She bathed her windburned face. Her nose and cheekbones felt afire, and on Alick the crop marks were almost masked by his burn. If her lips were sore, his must have been more so, after having been split by a blow and bruised by a gag.

But she was more concerned with the diminishing loaf and cheese. How long could they keep this up on so little? Already her clothes were feeling looser on her, and Alick's cheekbones were sharp enough already. The growing dark beard made his face look even thinner. If he were alone now, the food would last him twice as long.

Stop that! She rebuked herself. *No more ifs. All you can do is pretend you're not very hungry. A person can survive a long time on a few crusts if there's plenty of water to drink, and this land is overflowing.*

The afternoon walk was easier as they followed the shallow stream through a long valley. The wind was gentler down here, the sun's strength weakened by gauzy clouds. There were grassy stretches that were heavenly soft underfoot. The sound of the brooks and the calls of wheatears and plovers, all familiar to her, were company of a sort.

Yesterday's sense of continuing nightmare was gone, replaced by desolation. They seemed to be going deeper and deeper, farther and farther away *from* everything rather than *to* something. Yet the man knew where he was going; he certainly didn't intend to walk out his life in the wilderness; it was not wilderness to him.

How quickly one accepted, after the first frightening disbelief and rejection; one began to accommodate to the disaster, to try to live with it, sealing it off as oysters sealed off the intrusions into their shells. Except, of course, that there was no way of making a pearl out of what had happened yesterday.

She wished she could speak to Alick, but if he answered at all, it would have made her more lonely than before. *Someday I will be remembering all this in a different place, a safe place,* she comforted herself, *a long time from now, and I will be trying to recall details. I should pin my mind on them now to keep me from going mad.*

Melodramatic. Worthy of a Gothic heroine lost in one of Mrs. Radcliffe's castles. Jennie Hawthorne would not go mad. Beneath her grief, her guilt, and the still-smoldering outrage at being conspired against and lied to, she never doubted her instinct and capacity for survival.

So she looked around her as an act of faith, forcing herself to take in sounds, scents, colors. Almost instantly a stone rolled under her foot and she went down. Alick was well ahead and didn't notice, or was purposely ignoring her. She broke into a sweat, sure she had sprained her ankle; salt water ran in her mouth. But she'd only turned it, and after a few limping steps it was all right again. She watched where she stepped and used her stick more.

Hills were now closing the way ahead. The stream divided murmurously around boulders and rippled over pebbly bars and eventually flowed into a small loch in a deep, narrow glen. The loch lay like a shard of wet glass, streaked in dark and bright greens with the reflections from either side. Late sunshine stabbed into it, illuminating a group of deer drinking on the far side. Alick didn't go in their direction, but off to the left and up to rising ground. A pair of ospreys swept the sky in searching circles, sunlit birds whose calls took her back to that other loch.

Using their sticks, they climbed a track across an almost vertical grade. Their destination was another cave; this one was deeper, a natural chamber in the hillside, opening off a sort of terrace. The path went past the entrance and out around a jut of rock higher on the hill.

They pulled up masses of heather and bracken for their beds, hers well back in the cave and his near the entrance. He built a small fire of dry twigs just outside the mouth; Parlan had given him his tinderbox as well as his food. He broiled slices of ham in the pan, and they wiped up the fat with bread. No hot food had ever tasted so good before, and Jennie had a hard time remembering she'd intended to have a delicate appetite. Afterward he fetched their drinking water from one of the inevitable springs. This one bubbled out of the ground on the other side of the path, just below the lip of the terrace.

They sat for a little while on either side of the dying fire, cherishing it while any sparks of life remained. They were still silent with each other, but relaxed with the food and the prospects of a night's rest. At least Jennie was, and she hoped he was. Sitting only these few feet from her, he was as distant as those southern mountains that now glowed carnelian in the last sunlight as if they were burning from within. If *he* was burning within, his self-control was as inhuman as the mountains. Sooner or later he must flame out against her, and she wished it would happen and be over with.

The peaks dulled to a dead russet and retreated into the oncoming dusk. "Do we go that way?" she asked diffidently.

"We do."

"From here they look completely impassable."

"They are not."

She took a sip of water. "Have you walked to Fort William by this route many times before?" She felt an idiotic desire to laugh at herself. *And do you visit London often, Mrs. Gilchrist?*

He surprised her by answering freely. "Aye, and to other spots in between. You could go to Fort Augustus if you wanted, and there is a road even to Mallaig. That is hard to find, but it is there."

"But you said no one uses this trail now. Why is that?"

"There are other ways, better ones. It was an old way for the whisky smugglers. They gave it up when the excisemen discovered it."

"So it's known," she said, with a prickle of alarm. "Mightn't someone think of you using it?"

"No, they would not," he said, "and if they did, still no one would come after us."

"Why?"

He shrugged. She knew he was being evasive, and she would not pry, but she had no intention of letting him escape into silence again as long as there was a chance of getting words out of him, any words.

"Aren't you afraid they might expect you to go to Fort William?"

He moved uneasily. "I think they will be looking for me at Mallaig. My mother came from there, and I have people on Skye."

But they could still be watching at Fort William. She locked her cold fingers together.

Alick said unexpectedly, "My grandmother forbade her son to marry on the estate, for fear it might be his own sister. My grandfather was a man of great appetites, you see, so they could never be quite sure."

"How did your parents meet then? Mallaig is a long way from Linnmore."

"They met at Fort William." No details.

Her next question surprised even her. "Alick, were you ever married? Or are you leaving anyone behind?" He was mute and motionless in the near dark. She was appalled by herself, then thought defiantly: *If it angers him enough so he'll break out against me, so much the better.*

"Whar has that to do with anything?" he asked flatly.

"Nothing, and it's no business of mine. It was inexcusable of me to ask. I apologize." She went outside and walked a short distance along the upward path. She was still squeezing her chilly hands together. So she had separated him from more than his home; like a great natural disaster or an enemy ravaging the countryside, she had blown his world to bits. Never mind what had happened to *her*; she had merely repeated the crime, innocently or not.

She wanted to run back to the cave and accuse herself to him before he could say anything, even if so doing she'd go to pieces and thoroughly disgrace herself. But at least there would be no more concealment between them.

Of course one couldn't do it. If only for good manners alone, one would carry on as Alick chose. He wanted to get to Fort William and free himself as quickly as possible, with no frenzied scenes on the way; she was burden enough as she was.

She forced herself to breathe deeply and concentrate on externals. The scents of the hillside as it dampened with dew, the call of night birds, and over all a silence so entire that she could hear fish jump in the invisible loch below.

When she had control of herself, she returned to the cave. He was not there. In the half-dark that passed for night in the Highland summer she saw that he had dropped his plaid across her bed of heather and bracken. She put it on his. When he came back, she was curled up with her back to him. She heard him sigh as he lay down.

She awoke to footsteps. At first she thought Alick was outside and just coming back to the cave, but then she realized she was hearing hooves as well, the muffled leisurely tread of an animal on the path. Coming up. Coming nearer, with a faint creak of leather, a jingling; a horse blew softly.

She sat up, hugging herself together; she wanted to whisper to Alick but couldn't unglue her lips. She forced her hands loose and crawled over to him, for the shelter of his granite composure.

Before she reached him, she knew he was shaking in long, convulsive crescendos like a man with the ague. She felt the vibrations and heard the fast, shallow breathing through his nose, as if his mouth were clamped shut to keep his teeth from chattering, and he couldn't get enough air. Then and there she knew herself to be disintegrating, teetering dizzily on the brink of the abyss. Involuntarily she resisted the lethal impulse to go over.

She pressed herself against Alick's back, her cheek against the rough wool, the scent of it and him in her nostrils. She put her arm around him, not knowing whether it was for himself or for her, only that she was terrified and if *he* was, they could only huddle together and wait.

The tremors that shook his thin, hard body were so strong that they shook her also, and she hung on all the tighter. She heard muted footsteps now; the man must be leading his horse up the incline. Either he was an innocent traveler, or he was someone who knew where Alick must be and was coming straight to him like a bee to the hive. And Alick was afraid; he was seeing the gallows, and the noose hanging, and himself being dragged to it.

The steps came nearer. The horse blew again; the creak and jingle were louder. There was the faint scrape of a boot sole on rock.

The steps slowed as they approached the cave mouth and stopped. She saw nothing against the night sky, but she heard the animal shake its head the way Dora did.

Alick had stopped breathing, under her hand she felt his rib cage swell with the held breath. She held her own.

Shadows passed the opening, filled it up, blotted out the stars; she smelled horse, and tobacco scent exuded from wool clothing. Then the stars returned a few at a time as the shadows moved on. The footsteps died away on the upper path.

She released her breath and her arm at the same time. She was still afraid; if the man had come for Alick, he would not chance entering the cave in the dark, but could be waiting somewhere around the side of the hill to ambush them by day.

"Alick, I am so frightened," she whispered abjectly. He turned his head so fast that his cheek brushed against her face, and it was cold and wet.

"It was *him*."

"Who?"

"The exciseman they killed." He was still shaking. "He is always on the watch for the murderers. That is why no one travels this track now, for fear of meeting him."

"Are you saying that was a *ghost*?" Her s's were hissing like his. "Two ghosts, man and pony?"

"They brought the pony back with them. But if the poor beast has died since, he could have joined his master. Mata would seek *me*, if we were both dead."

"Alick, are you serious?" But she knew he was. "Who killed this man? Linnmore men?"

"Och, no. They used to come from the north of us and ride across the moor in the night. . . . I am ashamed of myself, but I cannot help this."

His fear permeated the cave and clouded out the image of the hunter waiting in ambush. She wanted to tell him that no ghosts smelled of tobacco and pony sweat, but she knew he would not even hear her. The horror he had heard about was real, it had passed within ten feet of him, and who knew how many times they would meet it again? For him to have taken this way had demanded more courage than she could have dreamed. She was responsible, and she couldn't protect him any more than she could against the sheriff's men.

"Could we move our beds together," she asked humbly, "and sleep beside one another, and share the plaid? I am so frightened, and I'm ashamed, too."

Anger stopped the shaking. "You are a woman. It is not dishonorable for you."

"Honor, dishonor—what do they matter now, any more than being a man or woman matters? We are two human beings, and something is out there." She went back to her bed and bundled up the heather and bracken and dumped it down by his. Then she lay down on it, but he stood in the cave entrance.

"It's just for companionship," she said crossly. "I am not going to seduce you, and I don't think you have any intentions of seducing me." She saw and heard Nigel shouting the ridiculous accusation in a breaking voice.

But she had broken through to Alick. "In any case," he said ironically, "I would be in no condition to do so at this moment." He came and lay down beside her. She covered herself with half the plaid, and he took the other half.

"There," she said. "It's not likely to be back tonight." *It's waiting for us in the next glen or on the next hill,* she finished silently. But the closeness, even without touching, was a sedative for them both. Then Alick, almost falling asleep, jerked awake, exclaimed unintelligibly and sat up, staring toward the entrance. She put her hand on his arm.

"It's all right, there's nothing there," she said.

"You need to sleep," he muttered. "We've a long way to go. Sleep, and I will watch."

"Neither you nor I murdered him," she said patiently, "so what have we to fear? . . . How did it happen?"

He lay back again. "He was one of them, you see, but he had secretly become an exciseman. His wife wanted him to be *respectable,* she called it. He was to turn them all over to the authorities when they came down from the mountains. There was one who suspected him, his own cousin, and in Glen Socach they got the truth out of him and cut his throat with his own dirk and buried him. That is why I said no man could pay me enough to sleep there last night. . . . But they met him the next time, you see, and the one who killed him was brought home half-mad. Since then no one goes this way."

But someone else does, Jennie thought. "What is the nearest town to where we are now?" she asked him.

"Why do you ask that? Do you want to go there?"

"No! I want to go with you to Fort William, as we planned. I was just wondering how far we had come in two days. It seems like a hundred miles."

"Thirty is more like it. Strathpeffer and Dingwall are twenty miles away and more."

Less than a month ago she had ridden through those places in a happy daze. Now she was concerned only with the man who had probably ridden out from one of those towns. If a big enough reward were offered and he wanted it all for himself, he would have a pistol in his belt and the confidence that he could take his prisoner without a struggle. But there *would* be a struggle; Alick would not go back to be humiliated and then hanged.

He fell asleep again, and this time he wasn't awakened by any horrors; his even breathing should have lulled her, but she was trying to think how she could save them both from the man lying in wait.

Thirty-Five

S HE AWOKE to find herself curled against Alick's side, and her two
hands were clasped around his upper arm. Stupefied by heavy sleep,
disoriented, she had barely realized where she was, and why, when the
arm was gently removed; he rolled away from her and left the cave. She
could see out; it was morning, and in the south the mountains that had
burned like embers last night were fair against a sky that might have
been as blue all the way to Spain. The ospreys were already fishing the
loch, and their calls pierced the upper air like arrows.

She was so saturated with sleep she could hardly move a limb. She
flexed fingers and toes, and stretched cautiously. She thought with anguished greed of a hot bath, fresh clothing against clean skin, a hot
breakfast; of waking up at last in some safe place with everything awful
wiped off her slate; of being Jennie Hawthorne whose worst ill was
homesickness.

What you want, my stupid lass, is the impossible, she said to herself.
*There's no going back in time unless you lose a good part of your wits. This
is the here, this is the now. . . . And Alick's been gone too long. How long
have I been lying here? Did I drop off again?*

Nothing but her mind wanted to move fast; she groaned in protest
while she got herself up. She'd heard no other sounds in the primitive
silence except birds, but if the man had attacked him from behind and
knocked him senseless, he would be bound and thrown over the pony's
back before he knew it.

She saw it all in such ruthless detail that when someone stooped to
come in, black and anonymous against the light, she put both fists up
to her mouth and backed away.

Without a glance at her Alick picked up the satchel. She slipped out and went to the shrubby place she had found last night for privacy. Just beyond this the eruption of rock pushed up and out like the prow of a petrified ship, and the path went around it and out of sight. She walked under the projection until she could see what lay behind it. Nothing but empty green hillsides and stands of trees, opalescent with the vapors rising from them. But she almost stepped in pony manure.

When she came back, Alick had built a fire and was holding the pannikin over it. As the water began to steam, he dropped a handful of dry leaves into it.

"What are you making?" she asked.

"A tea for us, with hawthorn and whortleberry leaves. I gathered them up in Glen Socach. They should be dried in the sun, but this will be better than nothing." He set the pan off the fire. "It is strengthening to the blood; it will put heart in us." He began cutting off bread and cheese.

"Is it also useful for keeping ghosts away?" she asked.

"Are you finding me a joke?" He didn't raise his voice or look up from what he was doing.

"No," she said, "but this morning I am convinced that was not a ghost last night."

"I have no doubt whatever of your opinion of me," he said stiffly.

Her dignity was equal to his. "My opinion of you is that you are a human being for whom I have caused much trouble, and you are behaving much better than I deserve."

"No one is blaming you for anything." He laid a slice of cheese on a slice of bread.

"*I* am," she said briskly, "but I'm not going to belabor the point. What I want to say is that I almost walked in pony droppings this morning. Somebody was out here last night, who must have heard our movements in the cave and smelled traces of our fire."

"Then I have made a fool of myself for nothing."

"I'm not saying the ghost of the exciseman doesn't exist!" she said angrily. "I'd rather it was a ghost out there than someone who's followed us or come out from Fort Augustus to hunt us down!"

"It is nothing like that."

"How do you know?" she said belligerently.

"I am just sure." He was imperturbable.

"Just sure the way you were just sure it was a ghost last night?"

"The tea has steeped long enough. Here." He produced a deep-bowled wooden spoon from Parlan's supplies. "Sup with this."

It was bitter, but it felt good in her stomach, and it made the hard bread and cheese easier to eat. They took turns with the spoon. It was a point of honor not to be squeamish about small things. Besides, the one time she had seen him laugh, his teeth had looked healthy, and when their faces had been close together last night while they listened to the footsteps, his breath was clean. It was probably both weak and overnice of her to consider such things, but she couldn't help it. There were so-called gentlefolk with whom she wouldn't have shared a spoon. "I hope he isn't waiting for us farther on," she said. "When you were gone this morning, I thought he had seized you."

"He will not be waiting. He is an innocent traveler. He doesn't know about the exciseman, or he is not afraid of meeting him."

She said irritably, "Do you have second sight? How can you be so positive? You were positive we'd meet no one, but someone else *is* here. You have no weapon but your knife, and he could be armed to the teeth."

He didn't answer that. "Here. It has cooled a wee bit." He held out the pannikin. "Drink the rest of it."

She obeyed. Then she took the pan across the path and down to the spring and rinsed it and wiped it out with moss. The day that had begun in such beauty was changing. Scarves of mist were floating over the loch. They would walk in cold fog, possibly rain, straight to their doom. The food she had eaten was surging around in her like a wherry tossed on the waves. She climbed back up to the cave, where he was stamping out and grinding out any last sparks of their fire.

"All you care about is knowing he wasn't supernatural!" she said. "You'd rather have a dangerous man out here somewhere than a poor homeless spirit. That makes everything all right, doesn't it? Perfectly safe. Oh, you are so smug standing there!"

"Smug?" he repeated quizzically. "What is that?"

"It's what you are," she retorted. "It was not a ghost, so you can tell me *my* fears mean nothing. Nothing else can do us any harm. Not a flesh-and-blood man with a pistol in his hand, and the promise of a good reward. No, *he* can lie in wait for us, just so long as he's not a ghost!"

"If he is lying in wait, he is being well entertained."

It was like a hard hand clapped across her mouth. Her own voice echoed in her ears, bouncing across the loch from the opposite slopes.

She was ashamed, embarrassed, and infuriated. But he had driven her into this behavior, and her anxiety about the stranger remained. She could not be or even sound contrite.

"I am sorry for shouting," she said in a low voice. "But I am as afraid of that man as you are of the exciseman."

"There is another way we could travel from here. They were sometimes driven down to it by snow on the heights. But they didn't like it."

"Why?" She kept her voice down. "What's wrong about it? Surely there are no villages out here?"

"No, but some glens are too narrow and too dark, and sometimes there are others traveling through them for reasons that have nothing to do with whisky. They wish to be unseen, to have the place to themselves, you understand."

"What you're saying is that you would rather take your chances with one man up here, who might be perfectly innocent, than with God knows what down below."

Alick nodded.

"You could have told me that earlier," said Jennie, "and not let me go on and on."

"Och, I would never interrupt a lady when she is speaking her mind," he said.

The fog, carried on no perceptible wind, silently surrounded them. The loch and the opposite hills disappeared; the path was blotted out ahead and behind them. Cold moisture dampened their skin and silvered their clothes. They walked in an eerie stillness broken only by their footsteps. The ospreys had long since gone in search of visible fishing grounds. All other life on earth could have died during the haunted night.

When the track dipped down below the tree line, they passed through a fir wood, but there was no sense of shelter here, only entrapment. It was dark under the trees; the mist writhed among them in strange shapes; there seemed to be a supernatural wind stirring the tips, though they'd felt nothing on the high slopes. They came to a little glade around a spring, and the man and pony had undoubtedly spent the night here. So he'd gone on instead of lying in wait; Jennie felt a little better, but not much.

She wanted to break the spell, but she couldn't think of anything to say. Alick was not a man who encouraged unnecessary words; he was too busy trying to save his own life, encumbered by her for weal or woe. She was terribly afraid it was going to be woe.

There was a sudden scrabble and scamper right over their heads, and she cried out in shock, straining to see up into the fir boughs. For what? She couldn't imagine, but her whole chest cavity seemed to reverberate like a drum.

Alick said something in Gaelic, then translated. "A pine marten. A harmless wee beast." For Jennie the fright had been cathartic. The unseen animal restored the world to her, and she felt lighter and easier both in her limbs and in her mind.

They surprised a group of deer on a ridge just above them; one moment they were there, coats dark with wet, and the next moment they were gone. There was a thinning and brightening of the mist, and a north-west wind arose and drove the fog before it. In a little while the sun shone, and Jennie felt like singing a hymn of thanksgiving. *I'm a sun worshipper,* she thought. *May my lord make his face to shine upon me and give me heat and light and hope.*

She might be a little delirious, she thought cheerfully, but it was a pleasant delirium, to appreciate the comfort of her clothes drying on her; the sight of eagles soaring in the limitless sky, the white threads of waterfalls down mountainsides, the dark pelts of forested slopes, the porcelain blue sheen of the lochs.

It was all very near Eden after the bad night and the raw, blind morning. There was no place up here for the stranger to be hiding; everything was clear and bare. They stopped at noon on a rock shelf overlooking a broad green valley through which small streams meandered in a glittering tracery. The call of a curlew rose at irregular intervals to Jennie and Alick where they sat with their backs against warm stone. From the height of land above them water ran down and filled a hollow in the rock, from which they drank; the overflow trickled down to the valley to join one of those sparkling threads.

Their strupach was another surprise from the sack, the roots of a plant called cormeille. He had gathered them this morning, while she'd been wondering if he'd been taken prisoner. She honored her vow not to be squeamish, and took his word for it that a small quantity would keep her going almost as well as the bread and cheese did.

When she didn't hesitate, he showed his approval by opening a conversation. He showed her a track that led down to the valley beside the narrow wandering channel of the overflow from the rock pool. "There are fresh hoofprints in the damp moss," he said. "He will be far away by now, through the pass there." He pointed to a notch in the western wall of the hills.

"Where is he going, do you suppose?"

"Out to the coast, I'm thinking."

"I wonder why," Jennie said.

"All who travel this way are not fugitives," he said.

They set off again, southwest along one of those upheavals of gneiss like frozen surf, rearing above the green strath with its curlews and meandering streams. It was not difficult; after all, it had been a track for laden ponies, not for mountain goats. But the slight euphoria caused by the appearance of the sun and the disappearance of the stranger was wearing off. The day seemed to go on forever, and so did the way ahead, each twist in the track opening out to a different but equally endless vista.

The illusion that the mountains were continuously rearranging themselves was emphasized by the constant shifts in the light and shadow as the immense clouds boiled up over the northwestern peaks and blew across the sun.

The cormeille root had done what Alick had promised. They were not hungry again until late afternoon, when they stopped and had a bit of bread and cheese and drank some water. Alick said only one thing.

"I will be needing to snare our food now. The ham will be gone tonight, and the bread soon after."

"Can you tickle trout?" she asked.

"Guddle them, you mean? I have done it, but I would not like my life to depend upon it."

There was nothing to say to that. If he had no luck with his snares, they could live for a time on water and perhaps cormeille root if he found more of it. But they'd hardly be able to travel fifteen miles a day; it was unlikely they'd ever walk into Fort William; their ghosts would join the exciseman.

They started on again, with the long Highland evening ahead of them. Her thoughts moved independently of her body. This was the third day from the hollow by the Pict's House. Three mornings ago Nigel had saddled Dora for her and said, "I will come with you," and she had said, "No." But he came anyway, and now he was dead.

He is dead and gone, lady,
He is dead and gone,
At his head a grass-green turf,
At his heels a stone.

The old ballad sang itself in her head, and she would never be free of it.

"Stop this!" she hissed. Alick stood still and waited without looking around. "I'm talking to myself!" she said loudly.

He nodded as if it were nothing strange, and went on. Now she was back in the immediate world again, and it was no better, no worse, than when she had left it.

Up ahead of them a new rock formation towered against a backdrop of roiling purple and pewter clouds. "What is that?" she called to Alick. "Is it man-made? A shrine? An *idol*? Is this a place where savage tribes used to worship? Did they hurl human sacrifices over the cliff?" She laughed wildly. "I shouldn't be putting ideas into your head."

Alick ignored this. "It's called the Cailleach, the Old Woman. There are many stories about her. One is that she is watching for her husband and eleven sons to come back from battle. They never come because they are dead in some far country, and turned to stone, like her."

"Isn't there a kinder story? That she protects travelers, for instance?"

"Aye, there might be one; there are tales enough. You could make one to please yourself, as the rest have done."

"Do *you* have one?"

He almost smiled. "There are enough lies told without me adding to them."

The clouds were moving off to the southeast, and as the wind dropped, the new ones came more slowly, so when they went down into pine woods again, the showers of sunlight dropping through the green roof warmed and illuminated the shade below. Unseen life fluttered and sang in the treetops. She kept looking up in hopes of seeing a pine marten.

They left the golden rain for the shade of a deep small glen like the one in which the exciseman was buried; hawthorn foamed with blossom; birches and oaks stood in a green sea of ferns and bracken. They startled a fox mousing, and he was gone like a streak of fire.

"Pass your stick through the bracken like this," said Alick, demonstrating. "It will warn an adder away."

"Adders!" She stood rigid on the spot. She knew about them at home, but in her present state of mind she had never given them a thought here. "Are there a great many?"

"I have seen an adder only once in my life," he said, "but I do not wish to be surprised that way again."

She followed him into the waist-high green tide, fearfully swishing her stick back and forth before her. When they came out onto a stretch of turf, her forehead and nape were wet.

Shallow water flowed down through the glen over a pebbly and sandy bed, splashing up in miniature surf whenever it met a boulder of any size. The short grass beside it was spattered with the little yellow flowers of tormentil and the white ones of wild strawberry plants, and there were patches of whortleberry with blossoms like tiny waxen bells. It was warm here even though the sun had long since left it, as if it still stored some of the day's heat.

Alick dropped his plaid and the bag. "We will sleep here tonight. We were late starting, and it would be dark before we reached the place I had in mind."

"Was it my fault?" she asked with false meekness.

"We will not be blaming anyone," he said tranquilly. "You might be gathering some dry wood while I am gone." He disappeared abruptly past an elder thicket. She heard him for a little while, then nothing except a fine, thin, little birdsong. The eagles were absent from the zenith, but at a lower level some sort of hawk, not like the buzzards of the moor, was hunting. She wondered how long the small singing bird would live.

Thirty-Six

N ERVOUSLY sweeping her stick back and forth ahead of her, she went into the high bracken again toward the biggest birches. These looked scarred with the years and showed where limbs had broken off. She found old dead branches under them; she also found a well-trodden path through the bracken, evidently used by animals coming to drink. There were a few deer droppings on it and some smaller ones. She loaded one arm with as much of the light dry wood as she could manage and went back by the animal path, still sweeping her stick before her but with slightly less trepidation. Earlier she'd felt like someone wading through murky waters over an unknown bottom.

She came out to the brook downstream from Alick's plaid and sack, at a spot where the earth was trampled and broken at the water's edge by a confusion of hoof and paw prints. More droppings, none of them fresh today. She was proud that she was clearheaded enough to search for the sign of a man's foot. There was none. She recognized the fox's dainty step, and she was more intrigued than alarmed by a large, round, catlike print. Lynx or wildcat? It was only a two-legged predator that she feared.

She followed the edge of the stream to their belongings, dropped her wood, and went back for more, this time taking the plaid. She spread it on the ground, and by going from one thick old birch to another, she collected a good amount of fuel. She drew up the four corners and tied her scarf tightly around them, then hoisted the bundle over her shoulder. She allowed herself to think of nothing but the immediate present, not last night, not tomorrow's journey. Not Nigel, not what lay after Fort

William. For now she had no past and no future; she wanted something hot in her stomach and then a long sleep with neither ghosts nor nightmares.

When she came back to the campsite, Alick was just bringing a load of fir boughs. An eyebrow went up at the sight of her with the huge bundle on her back, and she couldn't resist a small grin of triumph as she untied the scarf and tipped out the contents.

"You've wrought well," he said.

She bobbed. "Thank you, sir!" No smile from him; this was not a situation for amusement. He went away again. *Ah, well,* she thought, *I should be glad that he speaks to me at all.* She looked longingly at the sack; she was sure she could use the tinderbox to get their fire started, but she wouldn't be so presumptuous. She sat on the ground and tried to concentrate on sorting out the natural sounds around her so as to keep her thoughts in the narrow channel of the *now.* She no longer feared his absences as desertion, but he was gone a long time, and the glen began to lose its stored warmth.

He brought more fir boughs and carried his bonnet full of cold, dripping watercress. "My head is clean," he said, straight-faced. "There'll be no wee beasties straying among the cresses."

"I'm sure of it," she said just as solemnly.

"Now if you'll be pulling bracken for our beds, I'll be cooking our supper."

"Shall we put them together again tonight and share the plaid?" she asked. "There may be frost. I can feel the chill."

There was no nonsense about him. "Aye, it could be," he agreed. Vigorously she pulled bracken and spread it thickly over the mattress of fir. She wondered if he'd been embarrassed or alarmed this morning to wake with her hands clasping his arm and her forehead against his shoulder. Likely as not he'd been grateful for the human contact while he suspected the murdered exciseman to be roaming around outside. Well, she'd been grateful, too; it was probably that contact which had helped her sleep.

He fried the rest of the ham, and they ate slowly, making the most of every mouthful, alternating ham with watercress and the bread with which they'd wiped up the melted fat.

"We'll have more meat for tomorrow, I'm thinking," he said, and she knew he had made and set some snares. She and her sisters had destroyed them wherever they found them, but then their lives hadn't depended on snares.

When they settled for the night on their comparatively soft bed, with Alick silently refusing the plaid, they saw for the first time the crescent moon. The sky was the color of her Wedgwood jasperware, with the moon delicately embossed in white upon it. *Forbidden comparison,* she sternly rebuked herself. *No past, remember?*

"It's so deep, this glen," she said, "after the hilltops. I feel as if we're seeing the moon from the bottom of a well. Well, at least we're not seeing it through glass, or over a left shoulder." Her body was relaxing, but she was too keyed up to sleep, much as she had longed for it.

"How many miles did we go today?" she asked. "Fifteen? *More?*" she added hopefully.

"Far enough," he conceded. "We will do better tomorrow; we can be on our way at first light. Sleep now."

She turned on her side and looked at him from under her lids. His eyes were shut, and he lay on his back with his ankles crossed like a Crusader on his tomb. His beard was recognizable as a beard now. His nose had a mild, aquiline sweep to it. The crop marks across it and his cheekbone were still there but faint.

She could not sleep on order, though her limbs sank with a delicious heaviness into the bracken and fir, and the rippling of water so close to them was sedative. She tried to let herself go with it, but she was horribly aware of what clamored at the doors of her consciousness, and she didn't know how long she could hold out.

Beside her Alick was motionless. She couldn't hear his breathing and knew he was awake. *I must sleep,* she thought. *Please let me sleep. How can I walk fifteen miles tomorrow if I don't sleep? It will be daylight before I know it.* It was better in a cave, to curl up and sleep like a badger in his sett. Old Brock, fearing nothing.

Coire na Broc. She tried it aloud, timidly. "Does that mean 'corrie of the badger'?"

"Yes."

"I wanted to learn Gaelic," she said. "I love the sound of it."

He said suddenly, "You mind that you asked me this morning if I had the second sight? I do not, but there are whole families with it in the Western Isles, my mother said, and she could tell strange tales. But it was not in her family."

She wondered what he was coming to, but she was glad he was talking.

"There is a wee touch of it in Fergus. His grandfather, now, they tell stories about him. I am thinking that perhaps Fergus saw Tigh nam Fuaran without you in it, and it frightened him away."

"Now *I* am frightened." She tried to make light of it, but the goose-flesh was tightening along her arms and legs.

"I am just supposing, you understand," he said gently.

The theory of second sight had always fascinated her when her father used to talk about it, but when it touched her existence, she was repelled. If someone like Fergus could see what was to happen, it was as if everything had been laid out for her and she had mindlessly followed the plan. Still, if one could believe that hard enough, it should take away guilt; but Jennie Hawthorne did not wish to believe that she was anyone's or any *thing's* puppet, and if guilt was the price you had to pay for such insolence, so be it.

Fergus had gone away simply because he missed Mrs. MacIver and the girls; they had been his only family for so long. Lizzie Lindsay's accent had been harsh and upsetting to him, and the way she'd looked at him the first time he ventured into the kitchen, even if she'd meant no harm.

"What will you do in America?" she asked.

"I am willing and able to do anything with my hands. They must be building roads and making cities. My back and my legs are strong. It will have to be hard labor because I am a man of no learning whatever."

"How much is 'no learning'?" she asked. "If you mean you are not a scholar, neither is Archie, nor my Uncle Higham. Nor—" She almost said "Nigel."

"I am a man who cannot write his own name."

That silenced her, and he added with a bleak smile, "An ignorant peasant."

"No, no!" she protested. "The way you speak, the way you use the language, I would say you had a good store of learning."

"Och, that's the Gael of it. Words we love, and we all have the great memories on us, because everything must be passed on by word of mouth. I could give you stories and odes by the hour, with not one word changed from the way I learned them, but that would be in the Gaelic, and no good to you whatsoever except to put you to sleep."

"Did you ever wish to write and read, or were you contented as you were?"

"In my grandfather's will he desired me to be educated. I didn't know that until my uncle Linnmore, Archie's father, him they call the Old Laird, died. I was around ten, and upset and worrying about what was to become of us with him gone; he had always a kind word for me. I thought, *Shall we be driven away?* So my mother told me about the grandfather's will. The roof was safe over our heads. Then I wanted to know when I was to go to school, and she hushed me as if I'd asked how to call up the One we don't name. I was not to ask questions of *anyone*."

"The Old Laird had ignored his father's wishes then," she said. "You should have been learning long before ten."

"Och, he was a bit careless," he said tolerantly. "But an honest man. Who is to know what he'd have done if he had lived? He must have thought there was time enough. *He* is not the one I blame."

"Who then?"

"My mother died of a lung fever when I was thirteen. I was fair wrung out at the graveside, and the Reverend Doctor Macleod"—he pronounced it with sardonic precision—"was kind enough to pat my shoulder. So I asked him, through my snuffles and my hiccups, if he would teach me to read and write."

"That one!" said Jennie scornfully. "What did he say?"

"He put me off with his poor excuses. I know now that he feared the ill opinion of Linnmore House, Archie and his mother's kin who had caused Nigel's mother to go away. But then I would have cursed the reverend gentleman if I'd had the mind and the strength after the days and nights of weeping. I think that he saw it in my eyes."

There was no drama in his voice, which made the story all the more chilling. "Who took care of you after that?"

"The woman who tended my mother in her sickness was a widow with her sons away in the Army, so she stayed with me until I was seventeen. One son came home alive, and he was done with this country and England, so he took her to America. They asked me to go, but I said I would never leave Linnmore."

And now you're running from it, she thought. *Because of me.*

"What about Mr. Grant?" she asked. "Would he have taught you?"

"He had serious troubles. A wife slowly dying, and him worrying about clearing ever since Bliadhna nan Corach."

"Everyone kept saying the Old Laird would never clear."

"He wouldn't, but when he was dead, then Archie's mother's people came in and the possibilities began."

"What sort of woman was Archie's mother?"

"Och, if she'd had the strength, she'd have been another Christabel, but she was forever losing a child, the poor woman. Only Archie survived, and he was a prince to her." His short dry laugh could have meant anything. "My mother did the fine laundry at the house, and the smoothing, the goffering, the mending of lace and silks. She had the delicate hands on her, and they could be light as a moth's wing. When I was small, I went with her, and played about the stables. All the servants were Highland then, and the cook would give me a strupach, and the men gave me a rag to polish a bit of harness. And they'd set me on a horse's back. Man!" Laughter leaped into his voice. "High up, I was, with my hands in the mane and my knees clenched tight, thinking I was holding the great beast in, when he could have shaken me off like a leaf."

She knew what it had felt like when she'd been lifted to the back of a huge shire horse, but she didn't speak for fear of interrupting the flow. He might have nothing else to say for the rest of the journey.

"One day I wandered around the house and followed the brook down to Linn Mor. I had heard the maids talking about wild swans that lighted there. Archie was a great gowk of a lad then, and myself this tall." He lifted one arm and measured from the ground. "He saw me and tried to set his father's dogs on me, but they knew their playmate from the stables and bounded to me with laughter . . . and dogs *can* laugh, or so I knew in those days."

"Yes," she murmured.

"Archie kicked a stone bench in his rage and nearly broke his foot. After that his mother forbade me the place. You'd think I had smote the lad hip and thigh. My mother left me at the cottages the next time, but I soon followed her, thinking of the strupachs and my friends the horses and dogs. But I stayed out of sight of the mistress and Archie. The Laird was often out at the stables and gave me many a penny in those days. Indeed, he was often at the cottages, riding his horse everywhere on the estate, the deerhounds with him but foridden to harry a goat or a hen."

"Archie was afraid of those deerhounds, Nigel said—" Her voice shut off; her heart gave a great flurry of beats that frightened her, and she pressed her hand against her breast. He turned his head to look at her. Compassion or curiosity? She licked her lips and said resolutely, "Did you know the second Mrs. Gilchrist at all?"

"She was a fine woman. Like you, she loved the moors and wanted to know every inch of the estate, and everyone on it. She would have been good for Archie; he was fond of her. A great pity it was that the master died before his time, and Archie's mother's kin came in like carrion crows. She was crowded out and took her young lad back to the Sassenach country."

"Did you know *him* then?" It took courage.

"I was eight when he was born, and I mind the celebration. There was feasting for everyone on the estate. And with all those who came for the christening, there has never been that many people at Linnmore House since. A new prince was born."

Again she couldn't be sure if he was being ironic. "His nurse was aunt to Morag, sister to Hamish. She brought him often to Loch na Mada, and it was everyone's darling he was, with the pink cheeks and the eyes blue as gentians, the yellow hair, and the grand smile on him. The cailleachs, the old women, called him Grian, for the little flower that comes so early in the spring. It means 'sun' in the Gaelic. . . . After his mother took him away, and he'd gotten some years on him, he came back for his school holidays. Archie cares for him as much as he could care for anyone, I think." After a little silence he said thoughtfully, "For years he was still the darling about the cottages."

"I gathered that." The words scraped her throat. "By the way they wanted to welcome him. But he wouldn't go near." She squeezed her eyes shut and her hands into fists, as if so doing would squeeze him out of her brain.

Suddenly the man said roughly, "I've been running on like a drunken bodach."

"I wanted to hear it. I appreciated it."

"It's as I told you. The Gael is full of words, pressed down and running over. It's a wealth that's no good to us, and it's a curse to be able to put words to the sorrow and rage that's in you. They only drive the blade deeper into your heart."

"I know," she said. "How well I know." It was almost too much to admit. She struggled for a solid handhold like someone caught in the breakers. *Don't give in, don't go under.* . . . "You can learn to read and write in America," she said over the tumult. "You can hire someone to teach you."

"I'm too old," he protested.

"You are not. Let me tell you about the Ettrick Shepherd, James Hogg. He didn't know how to read and write until he was twenty-six, and now he's a famous poet. 'Kilmeny' was one of our favorite poems; it's about a girl who was stolen by the fairies. I loved it long before I ever dreamed I'd see Scotland. Listen.

> 'For Kilmeny had been she knew not where,
> And Kilmeny had seen what she could not declare;
> Kilmeny had been where the cock never crew,
> Where the rain never fell and the wind never blew.
>
> But it seem'd as the harp of the sky had rung,
> And the airs of heaven play'd round her tongue,
> When she spake of the lovely forms she had seen,
> And a land where sin had never been.' "

"Aye, that would have to be the land of the Fair Folk, wouldn't it?" he said gruffly. " 'Where sin had never been . . .' Twenty-six, you say. But he was no common man. He had the great gift waiting to be born." She started to speak, and he said, "Go to sleep now."

His manner was cold and forbidding. She knew he was regretting his weakness in talking too much; he was ashamed of his ignorance and of admitting it to her, of all people. There'd be no more talk tonight, and perhaps no more all the way to Fort William. He possessed the fatal pride that would forgive neither himself nor her.

She shut her eyes and tried to breathe into sleep, or make him think she was sleeping. In a few moments she felt him stir, half raise up, and then the plaid fell lightly over her.

Later something woke her. She heard it in her sleep and was left with the fading echo of it in her consciousness: the cough of a deer, or a fox barking. The air had grown much colder. Alick was curled on his side away from her. She moved as close to his back as she could without touching him and spread half the plaid over him. He sighed in his sleep, and she held her breath, but he didn't stir. She lay back. Lulled by the voice of the stream and the warmth generated by the closeness of their bodies, she slipped under the surface of sleep.

Thirty-Seven

S NATCHING at the blanket and pulling it off her was no way to wake her up. "Nigel, stop!" she tried to protest, but her throat felt thick and dry. What a joker! With her lids still fastened shut, she seized the thick wool to hold on, and it was yanked even harder. He exclaimed in Gaelic (how very odd of him!), and she forced her eyes open and looked into a long piebald face topped with horns; the yellow eyes that returned her stare with equanimity had horizontal pupils. They belong to a goat, which gave the plaid another peremptory twitch.

"Leave that alone!" Jennie said angrily, hanging on. Her voice started up a chorus of infant bleatings, and two kids peered around their mother's flank as she strongly opposed Jennie's possession of the plaid. Jennie bundled the plaid to her breast. "Are they wild?" she asked, not wanting to take her eyes away from the goat's.

Alick sat up. "She's that tame, she's one of the family!" He sprang up, scattering bracken. The spotted kids cried "Mama" again and ran to the far side of their mother. She herself didn't move; she was too enamored of the plaid.

The plaid, everything, was white with frost. In the east the sky was clear as spring water; the morning star was a dazzling white light. Shivering, and slightly sick from her sudden waking, Jennie wrapped herself in the plaid, making sure of the dry side, and looked from the obdurate goat to Alick. She saw his consternation, and she was afraid.

"What does it mean, tame goats out here?"

"That someone's living near." He swore in Gaelic, so low he could be barely heard over the brook's voice.

"Dia! We should have been on our way an hour ago. It is my fault. I slept too long." He seized his damp bonnet before the goat could and jammed it onto his head. "I'll see to my snares first. Don't let her at the bag." He took his stick and went off through the silvered bracken. Taking the plaid and the bag with her, she backed off a little way and relieved herself, watched with unblinking interest by three pairs of golden eyes.

She had barely straightened up and adjusted her clothes when the three children materialized.

They had come from downstream, probably by the animal path. There were three of them; it would be hard to guess their ages as they were probably undersized, but the girl was clearly the middle child. The boys wore ragged kilts of two different and dirt-dulled tartans, loose homespun shirts. The girl wore a sort of coarse-woven shift that came a little below her knees, and an old tartan shawl was pinned around her. All three were barefoot in the frost. They were grimed with peat smoke, and the pungence of them and the animals moved with them in an all but visible aura.

They confronted Jennie in shocked silence; the goat had all the aplomb. For Jennie it was like being face-to-face with creatures wilder than the goats, and she wondered what they thought of her. That she was a ghost, or some evil spirit from the brook?

Forcing a smile, she said, "Good morning." There was a flicker of expression like a leaf shadow, a sense of pricked ears. She tried it in Gaelic and got no more response. The goat made a halfhearted snatch at the plaid, then went to grazing on whortleberries, and the kids tried to nurse.

"She is a very nice goat," Jennie said lamely, pointing. Their eyes followed her finger. "Maith," she tried. "Boidheach." Apparently it didn't sound like "good" and "pretty" to them. The combined gaze returned to her face. The older boy's eyes were opaquely dark like a gypsy's, but the younger two were gentian-eyed, the color amazingly vivid in their smudged faces, and red-headed.

Alick emerged from the elder thicket, a dead hare dangling from his hand. If he was dismayed by the children, he didn't show it, but spoke to them softly. The older boy answered, pointing southward down the glen. He volunteered something in a swift rush of words which either angered or alarmed Alick. Jennie couldn't tell which, and she could hardly bear the suspense.

The children's meager faces grew even smaller with anxiety. The smaller boy knuckled his eyes, and the girl hugged her shawl tighter around her skinny shoulders and wiped her eyes with an edge of it. The older boy pressed his lips together until they whitened. All three never looked away from Alick. He shook his head in irritation and spoke across at Jennie.

"They live near the way we'll be traveling. They came out from Fort Augustus; they don't know how long ago. The father was doubtless in trouble of some kind, like me. Now he has left them, and they don't know whether he is dead or not. The mother is sick. They are afraid. Do we pass by on the other side?"

The children's eyes turned toward her. "I suppose we can stop and see," she said, damning the goats that had led the children to them. She couldn't read his expression. "Would *you*, if you were alone?" she asked defiantly. "Or would you run? I'll do what you say."

"I would stop and see," he said with resignation. He put the hare away and slung the bag over his shoulder. She folded the plaid and gave it to him. They picked up their sticks. The children and the goats led the way, then Alick, and she came behind. Oh, God, if they'd only waked earlier! What if the woman was bearing a child? What if she had some deadly sickness they could contract? What if she was *dying*? The new worries charged around and around like panicked sheep that will soon begin throwing themselves over a cliff.

Suddenly she had a picture of herself with Alick, children and goats, all trailing into Fort William as a poverty-stricken, evicted Highland family. But the wife and mother would be wearing a blue riding habit with velvet collar and cuffs, which would dangerously mar the picture. She could wrap up in the plaid, but the skirt, even though frayed and soiled, would show, and the remains of the elegant boots. Maybe the dead woman had clothes that she could wear, and something different for her feet; and so that no one in Fort William could guess that neither she nor her children could speak each other's language, she could pretend to be a deaf-mute. *Or a harmless lunatic, Jennie*, she suggested. *You could do that with no trouble whatever.*

The children ran splashing across the brook in their bare feet, the goat picked her way from rock to rock, and the kids hopped delicately behind her. Jennie and Alick took the goats' way. On the other side they climbed among alders, rowans, and birches into sunlight and fast-melting frost. The children and the goats scampering through the dapple of sun and shade under the trees belonged to another land and time; the grove should have been olive trees, and the children about to encounter a god in disguise.

The trees thinned out on leveling ground, and the children broke into a run, but the goat turned aside to eat some plant that had caught her tawny eye; the kids pushed their little black muzzles close to hers. The children were running across a broad shelf of open land littered with boulders and random slabs like prehistoric ruins. The site was sheltered from the north and east by a high bulwark of rock; ranged along its spine three more goats stood out against the sky, turned into horned statues as they watched the children and sensed the strangers.

They drew and held the eye at first, until there was an agitated eruption of crows from below. The birds went up into the sky shrieking and came down among the sentinel goats. Then Jennie saw the hut. It was half-masked by the two rowans before it and their broken shadows falling over the heather thatch and the windowless walls of rough stones.

The children were clustering beside the open doorway, with hens squabbling and picking around their feet. Then the children were swept apart by an arm; a man sat on a bench against the wall.

"Father is home," Jennie murmured. Father, laughing in his beard, was bestowing rough caresses and playful taps on his young, and a woman came stooping out of the low door. She wasn't dead then, or even close to it; she'd gotten over whatever attack had frightened the children. Jennie stood where she was, waiting for Alick to say, "We will be going on now."

But the man was calling to them in a strong voice made more resonant by the wall behind him, and Alick answered him.

"We must accept his thanks," he said to Jennie.

A child handed a crutch to the man. He put his hand on the nearest shoulder and stood up, tucking the crutch under his left arm. He was fast, even nimble, in spite of an obviously deformed left foot. He wore a faded kilt and homespun shirt, knit hose to the knee, and the tough homemade brogues she had seen at Linnmore.

Out in the full sunlight his curly hair and beard were a splendid flaming red. The gentian-eyed children got their color from him, but not their fey shyness. He swung himself toward them smiling, speaking in Gaelic. He was smaller than Alick, and the hand he put out was large for the rest of him. While they shook hands, he kept on talking, Alick sometimes spoke, and Jennie waited for it to be over with so they could go on, and stop somewhere to eat.

Unexpectedly he shifted from Gaelic to English and spoke directly to Jennie. How did he *know*? Had she looked *that* blank? Or was it the riding habit?

"It's a fearsome story they've been giving you, and the shame is at me for the great inconvenience. But Jock Dallas thanks you for your kind heart." His accent was even stronger than Alick's, and his voice had an unhurried and almost amused quality about it.

"There's been no harm done," Alick said. "We'll be going on."

"I was off stravaiging and took a fall, you see, already having the bad leg on me, and I had to lay up a wee while on it before I could come home. And the wife had a complaint of her inner parts," he said delicately, "and when I didn't come, the fear made it worse. Och, it's a great lament she makes when things go wrong. She had the children in a rare burach." He lifted his shoulders and spread both hands in a mock-helpless gesture, and smiled directly into Jennie's eyes. *My, how he fancies himself*, she thought. "Now surely you'll be letting me give you a good breakfast for your trouble," he said. "The oatcakes are still warm from the girdle, and I have trouts that were leaping in their glory not an hour ago."

Jennie tried to get a clue from Alick. "I'll not be taking no for an answer!" Jock Dallas warned them. "A hot meal now, before you go," he coaxed Jennie. "And the sight of another woman will rejoice the heart of my Kirsty."

Something about the tall, gaunt, motionless figure, waiting by the hut as if she hardly dared hope they'd stop, touched Jennie, along with her own poignant desire for hot food. *Any* food.

Apparently it was as much of an obligation to accept Highland hospitality as it was to offer it. Alick nodded. Jock laughed and brandished his crutch like a claymore. "Come along then!"

When they were almost to the cottage, he stopped them. "Sit ye in the sun there," he said, waving them toward a slab as if offering fauteuils in a drawing room, "and I'll see what else the woman of the house has in her cupboards. She'll be wanting time to set a bounteous table, you might say." He limped rapidly toward the hut. The children were sitting on the ground under the rowans, and he called to them as he approached, and they got up and ran out around the end of the hut, and out of sight; the hens scattered, clucking, before them. The woman went back inside, and her husband behind her.

"If she has extra clothing laid away," Jennie said to Alick, "perhaps I could buy something and be rid of this."

"Don't show her money!" Alick exclaimed. "Offer to exchange, but don't let them know about the gold. Come with me." He stood up, and when she hesitated, surprised, he reached for her hand and pulled her up. "Quickly!" He put his arm around her waist and walked her toward a thick tangle of wild rose bushes east of where they'd come from the trees. The mother goat was there, eating tender tips, and she rolled her eyes at them as they went by. Alick pushed Jennie ahead of him around behind the thicket.

"Give me your money, quickly," he ordered her. She fumbled nervously with her scarf, and he untied it impatiently. She pulled out the velvet bag and ripped it off over her head. He put it over his own head and tucked the bag down inside his shirt. She had a chill at the stomach that took away hunger.

"Why don't we go then?" she whispered.

"If we refused his food, it would look strange to him. We'll make good use of it. Eat well; it's your duty to us both." Suddenly he cocked his head, listened and made a "wait" signal with his hand, and left her, calling back, "You'll be fine now, mo ghaoil." From farther away he was explaining suavely, "My wife needed to retire, and she is afraid of meeting an adder."

"It's too busy around here for those fellows!" Great laughter. Jennie waited a discreet interval while Gaelic conversation went on outisde the bushes. She could hear the goat eating.

She counted ten more seconds by crocodiles, then made her appearance, her eyes modestly downcast as was proper for a lady who has just relieved herself and heard it publicly announced instead of ignored.

"Come along, come along!" Jock Dallas shouted merrily.

The only light came in at the door and from the peat fire on a large flat stone in the middle of the floor; the girdle hung down over it by a heavy chain from a beam, and the trout rolled in oatmeal were cooking upon it. Beyond the fire the woman of the house awaited them, smiling diffidently and adjusting a neck handkerchief she must have just put on. She was lacking a front tooth, and the straggling black hair looked like a particularly untidy bird's nest; the draggled hemlines of a dark short gown revealed a dirty striped petticoat and bare feet. But she had the long throat, the cheekbones, nose, and jawline a Christabel would have envied. The frowsty hair grew back from a widow's peak; the dark eyes were heavily lashed; the eyebrows could have been drawn on by an artist's brush.

Jock Dallas was joyfully expansive in his lilting broken English, but Jennie hardly heard him. *His Kirsty was a beauty once,* she thought in amazement, *and this little red bantam rooster possesses her all to himself out in the wilderness.*

She smiled and walked around the hearth with her hand out. "This is very kind of you," she said.

"It's you who has been kind." The woman's hand was shy like her smile. "We will be eating now. If you please."

The byre end was crudely partitioned off, and the smell of cooking and peat subdued that of goat.

They sat on benches at the roughly built table, and Jennie thought dryly that it was just as well the only light came in at the door so she couldn't look too closely at the dishes. She and Alick each had a heavy earthenware plate for their food, and one three-tined black fork between them; otherwise there were wooden spoons, bowls, and mugs of different sizes. The goat's milk was in a pottery jug. It was cool and creamy to drink, and the warm oatcakes were crisp. They had goat's milk cheese, and heather honey in the comb, a total surprise. "Oh, I'm famished for something sweet!" Jennie exclaimed happily. She was having no trouble doing what Alick had called her duty to them both. Neither was he.

The grilled trout was ready. The wife apologized for having no potatoes, and there had been no time to gather and boil greens. "But would you be liking some eggs?" she asked anxiously.

"Oh, no, thank you, this is perfect," said Jennie. She'd have liked to eat the trout with her fingers, but Alick had given her the fork, so she supposed they all expected her to use it.

The hens wandered in and out, and Jock talked on and on, intoxicated with a new audience besides a submissive wife. He took credit for the honey, though allowing wild bees some part of it. He had his own peat bog. "Mind you, it's some great distance from the house here, but the little ones are sturdy, and I have made then creels to fit." The willow-woven creels were stacked in a corner, and bedding was rolled up against the walls. Besides the table and benches, there were two large chests and a few blackened pots sitting on another bench. Tools leaned in a corner; she recognized a spade and a rake and the implement she'd seen the Linnmore women using to cut peat.

"It's our own wee kingdom out here," Jock bragged. "I envy no laird; I'm a laird myself!" He thumped his chest. "I have everything, and no one can drive me away from it."

"You are the monarch of all you survey," Jennie suggested.

"That is it exactly, Mistress! The town hated me. Och, I hate the town! I never go near. I never will again." He nodded his red head toward his wife. "Kirsty goes."

"To market sometimes in Fort Augustus," she explained in her very soft voice. Her English was easier than Jock's. She never looked directly at Alick, only from the side of her eyes. "I have goats or a kid now and then to sell. A few eggs, honey. I have no wool nor flax to spin, and no loom, but I barter for our clothes. The women who weave need certain plants for their dyes. I gather those, and herbs for medicine. Sometimes I take in exchange something not because I need it, but so there will always be something in the chest I can take to market."

"Don't be forgetting the brogues I make," said Jock. "And these." He held up one of the bowls. "Smooth as your finest china, they are, and the spoons are better than silver, for they never tarnish." He clapped his hands on his bare knees. "Ah, Mistress," he said to Jennie with a mischievous grin, "and what is a Sassenach lady doing here?"

Alick's knee touched hers under the table, and he laid his hand over hers beside her plate and squeezed it, at the same time giving her such a sweet and open smile that she was astonished again. She lowered her eyes, and had no trouble blushing, because the whole hideous story was suddenly burning her up.

"We are eloping," Alick said. "And she is not a Sassenach, but she had the misfortune to be educated in England. I am her father's ghillie. I *was*," he corrected himself. "Three days ago I took a groom's place to ride out with her, and we had a handfast marriage in a cottage on the moor." He pressed Jennie's hand again, and she kept her eyes on her wedding ring. "She is wearing her own mother's wedding ring," he said, "until I can buy one for her."

"But to take a young lady like this through the mountains!" Jock sounded shocked. "It is hard for her, surely."

"When we went to her father with the truth, he became violent," Alick explained. "We fled. We are hoping by the time we get to the coast, the Laird will be seeing reason. If not, we cross the seas, and he will never be seeing his daughter again."

Kirsty sighed. "It is like one of the old songs we used to sing."

"I have heard," said Jock, "that in America it is not important who is a gentleman or a lady." Jennie knew he was watching her; he was a rooster, right enough, with only one hen to tread. He must hate his exile for more than one reason, in spite of his bragging about his kingdom.

"But I am no common ghillie," Alick said haughtily. "My father was a gentleman, and the Laird knows it. If I had my true name now, there would be many a surprised face. Aye, and in London, too."

"Och, I am sure of it," Jock agreed. "It's the gracious guests we have, Kirsty. A lady and half a gentleman." He laughed and again smacked his big hands down on his knees.

Jennie's stomach crawled with her anxiety to be gone, but not without leaving the riding habit behind. She lifted her head and spoke to Kirsty. "Would you have anything in your chest you would exchange for this riding dress? I am thinking of a gown and petticoat like your own, and some stockings and brogues." She glanced over at Jock with a smile; in for a penny, in for a pound. He responded with such unabashed carnal pleasure that she could only wonder at the blindness of the other two, or the powers of her own imagination.

"Yes, yes," Kirsty said, touching a velvet cuff with a timid finger.

Keeping his eyes on Jennie's as if promising a rendezvous, Jock rose from the bench. "We should let the ladies get on with their bargaining," he said. Alick nodded somberly and stood up. Kirsty put the leftover fish on a trencher with a stack of cold oatcakes, and Jock took that and the jug of milk out to the children.

Thirty-Eight

K IRSTY WENT at once to one of the chests. She brought out a short gown of dark blue, a wool and linen weave, and a tartan petticoat, both quite clean, knitted stockings, and a tartan shawl like a small plaid, called a guilechan.

She held up a linen cap with dangling tapes. "You'll not look a proper Highland wife without a mutch."

Looking like a proper Highland wife while clawing one's way through the mountains and sleeping in caves? However, Kirsty was well into the spirit of the occasion and was now digging for ribbons to garter the stockings. "You should save those for your little girl," Jennie protested, but Kirsty said she could get more.

"My habit is in a sorry way, I'm afraid," Jennie apologized. "But the wool is good."

"And the *velvet!*" Kirsty's eyes glistened. She had never seen anything like the riding tights; she was enraptured with the lawn chemise and drawers with their lace insertions. Jennie hadn't intended to give them up, but when Kirsty excitedly burrowed into the chest and came up with coarse linen drawers and a shift, she didn't protest.

She put the underwear away quickly as if Jennie might change her mind. She couldn't hide her greed for the stays.

"Take them with my blessing," said Jennie. "I hate them. I only wish everything was freshly laundered. I am ashamed to exchange soiled clothing for clean."

"A lady as dainty as yourself—how long would it take you to be dirty?" The stays went into the chest.

"I *feel* dirty. And I haven't had a brush or a comb to my hair since—since—" Her tongue stumbled and stuttered.

"What beautiful hair it is." Kirsty flattered her.

"So is yours, that lovely raven black."

"But no *curl*. It's my Jock who has the curls."

And a cloven hoof besides, I wouldn't be surprised, Jennie thought. Kirsty produced a battered metal comb; perhaps she washed and combed her own hair before she went to market. When it was too late, Jennie remembered lice, but beggars couldn't be choosers any more than they could ride horseback on wishes. She'd rinse her hair somewhere before the day was out.

The linen felt harsh against her skin, but she'd grow used to that, and she was rid of the stays, rid of the habit and its hateful association with the sunny hollow. She was fastened into the gown and petticoat, the guilechan folded around her shoulders and pinned with a cheap circular brooch. The married woman's mutch was tied under her chin, and she was wearing Kirsty's own market-day brogues.

There was no doubting Jock's talents here. The brogues were calf hide, and toughly tanned with alder bark, reinforced over the toes with extra leather. They were held firmly to the foot by crisscross lacing of leather thongs across the open instep, and the ends tied securely around the ankle.

"Look at you!" Kirsty marveled. She caressed the thin, soft leather of the boots, calculating what she could get for them. "Will you be needing the scarf now?" Greedily she fingered it.

"Yes," said Jennie. "I'll need that for a towel, if my flow comes," she added, and Kirsty drew her mouth down and nodded shrewdly.

"What will you do if you have to go over the ocean? Does it not take money?"

"We will have to find work first. My husband is strong and capable. As for me, I was not raised to be useless." This at least was the truth. "Now I must go out and show my husband that he has got himself a proper Highland wife."

It seemed a long time since the men had gone out, and she'd heard no sounds but that of the hens beyond the open door; what if Alick's throat had been cut the instant he was out of her sight? And where were the children? She'd have even welcomed the goats.

She tried to walk decorously to the door. The sky was dulling with clouds, an ordinary event but ominous to her now. When she saw the men sitting on the slab where she and Alick had waited before the meal, she felt light-headed with relief.

"Now if only I had the Gaelic, I would be perfect, would I not?" she asked them.

Jock hopped up. Balancing on his crutch, he still could give her a deep, courtly bow. "You are perfect now, Mistress."

"Do you see why it's I who goes to market?" asked Kirsty. "So beulach he is, I might not see him come home again." She let off a surprising hoot of laughter. Manners made Jennie force her own laugh; she did not care to be undressed by the eyes of a stranger.

"You look well enough," Alick said offhandedly to Jennie. He nodded at Kirsty. "Thank you for your help, Mistress Dallas, and the good food. Now we must be moving on. A worry is at me for staying so long in one place."

"The children would tell us if there was a soul within a mile of us," Jock protested. "They range far and wide like wee foxes. It's darkening, too. You will be caught in a storm before night."

"I'd sooner chance that than armed men riding out from Fort Augustus. The word could very well be there by now, and if they sought us here, it would bring harm to you, too. No, we must go." He was setting the plaid over his shoulder as he spoke; then he put out his hand to Jock. "We thank you for your hospitality."

Jock waved away the hand. "Stay, man!" he pleaded. "We could hide you if need be so there'd be no trace. The wee ones would never tell! Tonight we'll feast on venison; it's hanging in a bothy now. We have no uisge-baugh, * but the cailleach makes a rare wine from rowan berries. It's as fine a drink as the best claret." The gentian eyes shamelessly wooed Jennie. "Let the storm come, and keep safe and warm by our bonny fire. Tomorrow you'll go all the faster for the rest."

"I thank you again," Alick said. He handed Jennie her stick. "But if you've ever known in your heart that the black beast is at your heels, you will know how I feel now."

"Och, do I not know? Jock retorted. "Then I will show you a shorter way to the track you'll be following."

"Good-bye," Jennie said to Kirsty, "and thank you. I wish you well."

* Gaelic for whisky

"And I am wishing you the same," said Kirsty. Jennie saw the children crowding at the byre end of the hut and waved to them. The only response came from the boldest goat, she that had desired the plaid. She bleated.

Jock led them into the woods past the rose bushes where Jennie had given Alick her gold. He swung along so rapidly before them that the deformed foot hardly seemed to touch the ground. He was talking the whole time, whistling at birds, looking around at them to address Alick in Gaelic and laugh. Alick was wooden, and Jock winked at Jennie.

"He hasn't always the face on him like a minister, eh, lass? Not when you two are alone in the heather!"

She gave him a tight little smile and tucked her hand inside Alick's elbow. Jock's grin broadened.

"Och, I keep forgetting you're man and wife, and a handfast marriage is as good as any!" He turned back again and began to whistle a jig.

Behind them everything had vanished off the earth: clearing, hut, goats, children, Kirsty. Even the mountains could not be seen through the thickly interwoven ceiling of boughs and leaves. With no warning they came to the edge of a deep corrie full of rocks and bracken. On the far side of it the land rose to a pine wood that reached almost to the spine of the watershed.

Balancing with a hand against an oak trunk, Jock pointed across the corrie with his crutch. "When you're up there, you'll see the way. If you traveled the road you know, following the stream, you'd have more hard climbing in the end. I'll just go a wee bit with you." He swung himself forward. "Follow me, Mistress! It's an easy path I'll choose for you!"

She took a step, but without a change of expression Alick held her back and himself walked directly behind Jock. "If she stumbles," he said pleasantly, "I'll break her fall."

Agile as a goat, Jock led them down a serpentine course that looped around protruding fangs of rock, but didn't avoid smaller ones. Jennie didn't look ahead; she concentrated on placing her feet, so she almost caromed into Alick when he stopped suddenly because Jock unexpectedly bent down to adjust a lacing.

When he straightened up, he whipped around, swinging the crutch in a wide arc, and she had just time to see the savagely joyous grin in his red beard when Alick jumped free of the crutch meant to entangle his legs, and had Jock bent backward over a slab and gasping. Alick's knee was on Jock's chest, and his dirk was at the throat under the red beard.

"Run, Jennie!" he was shouting. "*Run.*"

She ran, plunging headlong like an animal in terror, keeping on her feet by a marvel; she didn't think what was before her or behind her; she knew just enough to run and run until she could move no more and had to drop where she stood.

She did so when she could not inhale without pain, and her mouth and throat felt seared. She had gone into the corrie and a little way up the other side; she had not tripped and been thrown by rocks hidden in the ferns. She was alive, but for how long? Her heart was going to explode in the next instant. She lay quaking against the earth. As the pounding died away in her ears, she heard someone coming, and she heaved herself onto her hands and knees and crawled deeper into the tall bracken. There was that place on a man where, if she hit hard, she could make him helpless long enough perhaps for her to get away. If Alick was dead and she had to wander alone, she would die alone too. So be it.

"*Jennie.*" Alick was there, and she began to cry. He sat beside her in the bracken and held her in his arms, smoothing her head and murmuring Gaelic comforts as if she were a child. Finally he said in English, "It is all right now. He won't follow, I swear it. Are you able to stand now?"

"Yes, yes," she sobbed. "Now that you're alive."

Thirty-Nine

T HEY WENT on up through the pines at a good stiff pace. They had lost their sticks, but hardly felt the need of them, they were in such a hurry. At first Jennie kept looking back with the regularity of a nervous tic, but Alick caught her at it and said curtly, "It's the way ahead you should be watching. He'll not be following us."

"Are you *positive?*"

"That I am. But we will be meeting bad weather up above. So don't be spending yourself in backward looks."

"I can stand anything!" she exulted, rather breathlessly. "Rain, hail, snow, a tempest, now that we're free of him! I've some sturdy clothes, and Kirsty's brogues helped me to run from him, and we had a good meal, and you still have the hare for our supper. Alick, you cheated Old Nick at his own game!"

"You'll not be singing hosannas," Alick said grimly, "if we are caught in wind and snow. You will be praying not to be blown off the mountain."

The earlier dull silvery light had changed now. Back in Northumberland she'd seen late snows, perilous for the new lambs, those cold blue-black clouds rushing from the northeast and the trees creaking and swaying over their heads as the wind rushed through the tops with the long roar of surf. But in the euphoria of escape she was unafraid of anything nature sent against them.

She had lost the wifely cap somewhere, and she tied her scarf around her head and knotted it under her chin. The thick wool gown and petticoat over the substantial undergarments, the small plaid and the heavy stockings were all more protection than the riding habit had been;

she was free of her stays, and the brogues felt light yet substantial on her feet. Her body was heated inwardly by the hearty meal. So even with the air wintry on her face and hands she felt snug, though she saw the irony of that cozy, homely word when they left the shelter of the wood for the windswept ridge of the watershed.

There was a brief lull, and they stopped for a few moments to get their breath. Tarnished sunlight with no warmth to it broke through a ragged hole ripped in a great swatch of bruise-dark cloud. Below them, the wood hid the corrie, and the thick boscage on the other side seemed utterly foreign to her, as if they'd never followed a whistling Jock Dallas through it.

"Is this really a shortcut to our road?" she asked, and he laughed. He sounded genuinely amused, and she said defensively, "I thought he might be telling the truth about *one* thing. Some people do, to salve their consciences."

"And what would be making you think he had a conscience?"

"*Had?*"

"No, I didn't kill him, though it was in my mind and in my hand too, when I had my knife at his throat. When he stopped and bent down that time, he pulled a sgian dubh from his stocking, and that would have sliced *my* throat soon enough. He's still alive, but with all he can do to crawl home on his hands and knees. I broke his crutch and threw the pieces in two directions and his dirk in another."

"But why would he want to kill you if he didn't know we had money? She'd have seen the bag when I changed clothes, but I didn't have it then."

"He would kill me and ransom you back to your family. Even if we'd told him no story at all, there was still those clothes of yours and the Sassenach voice, and myself as I am, wild and common as gorse!" He said it all without emotion. "He knew he'd get your name from you soon enough, once you'd seen me murdered and you were left with them, afraid to close your eyes for fear he'd be at you when he was drunk enough. I think he has no sense whatever when he's in drink, and to call him a beast dishonors decent and innocent beings."

The memory of Jock Dallas's grin and eyes and his soft, laughing voice sickenend her so she could not say what she was thinking: *He would not need to be drunk.*

"I saw," Alick said, as if he read her mind. "And so did she."

"Do you think *she*—"

He shrugged. "She is his creature. Who knows? We'd best be moving on. I have a shelter in mind, but we are a long way from it on Jock Dallas's short road."

She looked into the saturnine bearded face and said painfully, "And if he had molested me, then he couldn't return me, could he? Even to set me along on the road to Fort Augustus? For fear they'd be combing the mountains for him when they knew what he'd done."

"Aye. You'd die, too. He'd lose the fortune in ransom, but he'd still have the gold he'd found around my neck."

The first flakes spun past their faces. Alick took her by the arm and started her moving. The wind whirled about them, the snow blew stinging into their faces, and it was an invisible world. Jennie knew that if this storm had caught them before they met Jock Dallas, she'd have been much more terrified. She was uncomfortable, the wind sometimes took her breath, and the snow whipped blindingly into her face; but they'd just escaped murder and rape, and she had no intention of collapsing and dying in a May snowstorm.

When the track became too narrow, he put her behind him and shouted for her to hang onto his plaid. "It won't last! How is your courage?"

"Stupendous!" she shouted back at him.

It didn't last. The storm went whirling and writhing and ghosting out into space, and the sun shone; white peaks dazzled against a blue sky. On every twig of whin and heather snow crystals flashed all colors of the spectrum and died in glory. Jennie's hair hung wet where the scarf had slid back; their clothes began to steam like the terrain about them. Their faces were red from the wind and stinging snow.

They walked all day on what they had eaten that morning, across stony water courses, sliding scree and through corries, and along the lower sides of mountains. The cries of upland birds echoed in the great silences; deer appeared below or above them or across a glen. Eagles rode the wind above it all.

Alick cut them new sticks in a grove where they rested and drank. Late in the afternoon they picked their way across a spongy bog where pools mirrored the sky, and frogs croaked. Small flies rose up in tormenting clouds and made Jennie frantic with annoyance until they climbed up to a heathery ridge into a fresh breeze, and here they walked through a ruby sunset light.

"We're all alone on a red planet," she said. "This must be like walking on Mars." Alick didn't answer. The light changed to a brassy afterglow, and the thin white moon moved with them through the long twilight, seeming to give off cold as the sun gave off heat.

At dusk they were up on a hill again, with a glen full of night below them. Suddenly the hill broke in two, and they went into a narrow defile where she stumbled drunkenly among boulders. Alick came back and took her hand and led her into a cave.

The narrow approach to it cut off almost any light from the sky except just at the entrance. She knelt down, felt around for a flat place, and stretched out on it without a word. Alick set about his chores as surefootedly as if it were broad daylight. He collected dead wood and dry twigs, started a fire, skinned and dressed the hare by its light, and cooked it.

She crawled groggily on her hands and knees to the fire. The meal was all in silence until he offered her another portion on the tip of his knife and said solemnly, "It's sorry I am that it's not venison and wine we're dining on, with a song from Jock Dallas. It's the grand ceilidh we'd be having, wouldn't we now?"

Jennie laughed, and wanted to, which was surprising. "Do you think he's home yet?"

"Not by himself," he said thoughtfully. "I may have broken his other leg. They would have to come and drag him home."

"I think the deformed foot is really a cloven hoof," said Jennie. "I have no pity for him, only for the children. I don't know about Kirsty. She could simply *not* return from Fort Augustus someday, or take the children and go when he is off stravaiging, as he calls it. Alick, were they all lying this morning, do you think?"

"I think he was away from home," he said, "but the woman was neither sick nor fearful, because he is often away from home. I think we are not the first travelers to meet three pathetic bairns who can fill their eyes with tears and put the tremble in their voices."

"They can't be such little horrors!" she protested. "Surely their mother made them believe she was sick, and worried about their father. Remember how glad they were to see him!"

"To know what he'd brought home this time. Where did they all run to? 'Go and see what I have brought,' he said to them, 'and be quiet about it.' Och, that was slipped quickly in, like a hot knife through butter. . . . Beulach, she called him, and she was right. I distrusted him from the start."

"What does *beulach* mean?"

He searched for words. "You might say he was too charming altogether."

"I thought that was just Highland courtesy."

"But one Highlander can always tell when another is a liar."

" 'When Greeks joined Greeks, then was the tug of war!' " said Jennie. He looked up quickly, and she said, "I can't take credit for that. What was it he brought home beside the trout, I wonder?"

"I think he came home riding on it. I left him for a minute of privacy—you understand—and I slipped away from where he thought I was, just to look around without him. There was a black pony grazing below the bothy."

"Couldn't it have been his own?"

"The saddle is in the bothy with the venison. Too good a saddle, too well taken care of. And that is a pony that has been cherished on oats."

She lost appetite for the hunk of roasted meat in her hands. "What are you trying to say?"

"I wonder how far the mysterious traveler is now, he who passed our way two nights ago. Something tells me he is food for the ravens and the foxes, and his clothes and saddlebags are in one of those chests."

"She told me," Jennie said, "that she could always find something in her chest to take to market."

"And that's no wonder, as long as there's a traveler to pass by within a few miles."

"Alick, you tell me all this and expect me to sleep tonight!" she cried fiercely.

"What's done is done," he said. "We can't bring the dead back to life, and we're safe for the night. Think only of that, and of good food in your stomach."

"And what if we meet another outlaw, or a pair of them? You never expected to meet a murderer when we stopped in that lovely glen."

"No," he agreed gravely, "and no one can tell about tomorrow, unless we had poor Fergus here. So we sleep safe while we can."

There was now no discussion about sharing the plaid. They lay side by side on the sandy floor and Alick seemed to fall asleep at once, but she stayed awake, staring out at the narrow wedge of pale moonlit sky and dim stars. It was much quieter here than down in the glen; the silence was unearthly. *Still, I shouldn't like to hear something stirring in the depths of this cave,* she thought. Her body was fatigued, but her mind wouldn't rest; she went over and over the incredible events of the morning. Faces circled in procession before her; eyes, beginning with the black and gold stare of the goat twitching at the plaid, and then the children's eyes, one pair bottomless black, the others purple-blue as gentians. Lovely eyes to cast the spell of death.

Then the man himself. If she believed she'd ever met evil before, it was nothing compared to this. In the weakness of exhaustion, with the loneliness of the hour emphasized by the sleeping man beside her, she wondered if the Devil did indeed exist in spite of Papa's explanation of Satan as merely the name of a symbol for evil. Why could he not have sons on earth, as Jesus was God's son, and she had just met one of them?

"Jennie Hawthorne, you are a fool," she whispered. "A *disgusting* one." Alick stirred, and she went on excoriating herself in silence. *You're alive; so is Alick. None of the things took place that could have happened. So don't be an utter ass. Perhaps Alick is wrong about the traveler, perhaps he's right, but forget him. We can't bring the dead back to life. . . .* And she thought about Nigel.

His death had been an accident which he brought upon himself, but from a distance, and not only that of geographical miles, she saw him now clearly as a mere boy driven wild with bewilderment at his wife's inexplicable behavior. He'd seen nothing wrong with his own—he wasn't ordering a wholesale massacre! These people, such as they were, would exist somehow, and when they were out of sight, nobody needed think about them again. Turning the land into sheep walks could only enrich his wife's existence. How could he have expected she'd be in such a taking, she who had melted into his embrace from the first? How could she speak to him with such rage and contempt? He loved her as much as ever, didn't he? What happened with other people, and peasants at that, had nothing to do with Nigel and Jennie, the lovers.

He simply couldn't see what he had done. Yet he must have known that those others whom he had betrayed had loved him from the time he was born. For weeks he had known what he was about to do to them, and he was perfectly carefree, except that he would not face them until the day when he came with men and torches. And in his perverted and deadly innocence he couldn't understand what this had destroyed in his wife.

She wanted to turn over, but she was afraid of disturbing Alick's sleep; she envied the way he could drop off so suddenly. She had taken off the brogues, and now she lay wriggling her toes, flexing her ankles. *I'm rid of those damned stays,* she thought, *and those boots I didn't dare take off. And we must have walked for twelve hours today. So why can't I sleep?*

Suddenly Alick shot upright, shouting hoarsely in Gaelic, so hard his voice cracked.

"Alick! Wake up!" she called, trying to shake him by the shoulder. He knocked her away from him with a backhand blow that sent her against the wall of the cave. She crouched there, hoping it was a nightmare and not the onset of insanity. He kept protesting and arguing with his invisible persecutors, and then all at once, shockingly, he wept.

She had never in her life heard a man weep, though she'd seen traces of it on her father's face after her mother died. She'd never heard these sounds of complete despair wrenched up from the gut. She was awed almost to paralysis, huddling against the cave wall with her hands over her ears until she could bear it no longer. Then she crept across to him and put her arms around him, pulled his head against her shoulder, and held it there, rocking back and forth as he had rocked her in the bracken.

"It was only a dream, Alick," she murmured. "Only a dream. You're safe from whatever it was. It's gone. Only a dream, Alick. There . . . there . . ." She pressed her cheek hard against his hair, holding him so tightly her arms were aching.

She thought the paroxysms would never stop, but they slowly quieted. She kept expecting him to shake her off with a savage humiliation that would make the rest of the journey very difficult. But as the convulsions decreased, he slumped heavier in her arms as if he were totally unconscious. She was relieved and hoped he'd remember nothing of this in the morning. His nightmares must have been more exhausting to him than the day's march. *And I'm still wide awake,* she thought wryly.

She managed to lay herself down and him with her. He moaned in his sleep, and she froze, ready to tell him she had clutched at him in her own night terrors, but he didn't wake.

Lying on her side with his head against her breast and her arms around him, she found her own head wasn't comfortable; she missed the guilechan which she'd folded up for a pillow. She shifted slightly until she could lean her head against his and timed her breathing with his.

The next thing she knew she was waking up, and they had changed positions; he was holding her. She sighed, and his light embrace broke open, and she rolled away. She felt the plaid being tucked in behind her, and he left the cave.

When she heard him coming back, she sat up and stretched. "Good morning," she said through a manufactured yawn. "Is it a good one?"

"Fair enough," he said tersely. "What it will be half a day from now there's no telling." She wrapped the big plaid around her shoulders and reached for her brogues, tying the laces with cold fingers. Then she went out through the stony passage. She found her spot for privacy among the furze on the upper side of the track, behind a thick sheet of lichened gneiss coming out of the ground like a tilted gravestone.

"All the comforts and conveniences of home," she said aloud, remembering the flowered ironstone chamber that lived so complacently in the satinwood nightstand bedside her bed in Brunswick Square, and the tall china slop jar in her and Sophie's room at Pippin Grange and how they'd squealed at the touch of the cold rim on winter mornings. Consciously she was pretending that Tigh nam Fuaran had never existed; at least during her waking hours she had some control over this.

She washed with wet heather, very scratchy but better than nothing, and dried herself on her scarf. The morning was mild and smelled of rain. Everything stood out with the razor-sharp delicacy of a Japanese print. The mountaintops were inked in blues and purples and blacks, some decorated like Fujiyama with fresh snow, and draped with the lace of waterfalls.

They breakfasted on the rest of the hare, and tea steeped from more of the hawthorn and whortleberry leaves, saving the heel of the loaf and the last of the cheese for their midday stop. He had found some cormeille root, and that would help out.

The rain began as light blowing showers at first, coming and going. Wavering veils of mist obscured a distant peak; then it would reappear. Gleams of sunshine brought out the rich spring greens as emerald and peridot, and turned running water to gold and silver. It was warm in these intervals, and even during the showers one sensed the presence of the sun. But soon the storm shut down on them, the rain pelting so fast that the track was running with water. Water beat into their faces, into their mouths and eyes. Water seemed to gush from every crack and crevice.

Jennie's clothes were soaking through, her feet squelched in wet stockings and brogues, but she was not cold yet; exertion kept her warm. They stopped for breath whenever possible, once under an overhang with a curtain of water dripping before them. "We're moving down all the time," he told her. "We'll go through a wood, and that will help. Then we have only to cross a corrie, and the cave is not far beyond that."

She nodded, sniffling. Her nose was running, and she wiped it on the end of her sodden scarf. "Are you all right?" he asked her.

"We're alive, aren't we?"

"Aye, you can say that." His mouth lifted slightly at one corner. "You're a stiff-necked one, I'll give you that."

They ducked out through the screen of water.

They rested next time in the fir wood, where the rain couldn't reach them in its full strength, and the storm seethed high over their heads instead of around their ears. After they'd sat on a dead tree for a few minutes, a raw cold crept into Jennie's bones. Alick, imperturbably wringing out his bonnet and smoothing it on his knee before he put it on again, looked as if he'd never felt chilly in his life. Jennie did not take off her scarf and wring it out; her head wasn't too cold as long as she didn't disturb it.

"We have only to cross a corrie," he said. When they reached it, the harmless trickle of a hillside brook had become a torrent. White water stormed down the rocky bed, flinging up spray wherever it met opposition, and poured thundering into the loch below.

They climbed up beside it through drowned vegetation, skidding on wet moss, looking for a narrowing, and finally they saw stones appearing at fairly regular intervals across to a low place on the opposite bank. The water slid swiftly around them but rarely over them.

Alick turned to her. Rain was running down his face and off his beard. "Across there!" he shouted above the roar, pointing. With rain beating into her eyes she could see nothing but a blur of shapes like green monsters of waves, and the towering shadow of very high land through blowing draperies of water and mist.

"Can you do it?" he shouted again, gesturing at the stones in the freshet. She nodded. She and her sisters had often hopped over flooded burns, but never in such a tempest and never across anything this wide. However, there was only one way to go, and that was forward.

An eagle glided low through the corrie, riding the wind on a level with their faces, seeing them with an eye of fearsome predatory intelligence; they saw the great wingspan, the strong beak almost as long as the head, and the glint of gold on the neck. He went on out over the booming falls and across the loch, powerful and free, and they stood looking after him, forgetting for the moment where they were and what they were about.

"All right now," Alick said. "You'll be using your stick for balance. Set it firm each time." He stepped out onto the first stone, turned, and held out his hand to her, and as she took it and put her foot forward, he went on to the next one. She teetered, but they gripped hands hard, and she drove her stick down with all her strength. At once the water attacked it with a giant's force, but it held.

And so on to the next stone, and two more. Occasionally water splashed over her feet, but they were soaked already. The unrelenting clamor of the flood and the sight of it sliding by so fast would have made her dizzy if she hadn't had to concentrate on placing her stick and reaching for Alick's hand. They came to a stone that was rounder, harder to balance on. Alick had no trouble, but when she stepped onto it, one foot slipped; trying to keep her balance, she involuntarily loosened her weight on her stick, and it was instantly swept off the bottom and out of her grasp. She fell headlong into the current.

Alick jumped in after her, but she was carried swiftly beyond his reach like one of the dead branches being swept along with her. It was not deep, but it was so strong there was no standing up against it. She struggled to get to the bank, but the force of tons of water in spate was too great for her to cross, and when she caught hold of a rock, her chilled hands slid weakly off. She was turned, tossed against boulders, and washed away from them before she could even try to hang on. She hit an elbow, an ankle, her head, and all the time she was thinking, in a deadly quiet spot in her brain: *When the waterfall hurls me into the loch, I will be too cold and too exhausted to swim, and so this is the end of Eugenia Hawthorne. I'm glad he still has the money. It will give him a good start in America.*

She was being dragged not by water but by hands that gripped wherever they could get a firm hold—one in her hair, one under her shoulder. She was scraped and bumped and finally heaved up a muddy slope from which clods of turf kept breaking away and taking her back down again, but by now she was clawing away for dear life.

Lifted and slung along by any means possible, she found herself on land which, if not dry, was firm, and below her the flood raced on toward the smoking falls. And Jennie Hawthorne was not going over them.

She sat up rejoicing, and shook her head to first one side and then the other, to get the water out of her ears. Her hair had come down, but her scarf hung loosely around her neck, and the little plaid hadn't become unpinned. She still had her brogues. Alick sat a little way from her, tipping water from his boots. He was drenched from his feet to his middle. She was completely soaked to the skin, but in the joy of not drowning she was hardly conscious of the cold, and the rain beating down had no impact now.

Alick looked as if nothing had happened except that somehow he'd stepped into water over his boot tops. *If there ever was a true gentleman,* she thought, *he is it.*

His stockinged feet were in very bad repair, toes and heels almost worn away. Calmly he held up one foot. "It's moggans they'll be before long," he observed. "Hose without any feet whatever. Barefoot they'd fight in the old days but with moggans on. I could never see the sense in it."

"Thank you for saving me," she said composedly, not to be outdone by him.

"It's welcome you are, entirely. Did I hurt your head? Your hair was all I could reach at first."

"I didn't feel a thing," she assured him. Wet tendrils dripped over her forehead, but with nothing to wipe on she let the water run. "It may interest you to know that when I thought I would drown I was glad you still carried the money."

"I am returning it to you now." He reached inside his shirt.

"No, please keep it. It's enough to carry these sodden clothes without adding to it. The money is safe with you, and if I have another such accident and you can't save me, then use it with my blessing."

"At Fort William I will be returning it then."

"We will be *dividing* it then. I owe you your passage money at the very least." Suddenly she burst out laughing. She felt a little drunk and enjoyed it. "Listen to us! What a ridiculous conversation! We ran away from murder this morning and nearly drowned this afternoon, and we sit here in the rain, drenched to the hide, talking as if we're in a drawing room."

He actually grinned. Encouraged, she said, "And in one way my tumble was a blessing. It's sure to have drowned any fleas or worse I picked up in Castle Dallas."

This time he laughed outright. "I would not be too sure of it! Highlanders are a hardy breed, fleas and all." He pulled on his wet boots, still smiling. "We'll be going on now. It's not far."

She was hugging her knees, unwilling to unfold and lose the deceptive warmth. "How will we ever dry? Wait for the sun to come out again?"

"That's often the way it must be." He reached down a hand and pulled her up, and she was immediately aware of all the places that ached or stung, and she was unsteady. She looked down at the cataract crashing into the loch in clouds of spume and then turned quickly away, swallowing.

"It's over," Alick said austerely, "and you didn't drown."

"I shall probably freeze to death instead," she said. "You could have let me go, Alick. It would have been quicker."

He didn't dignify that with an answer.

Forty

THEY REACHED the new cave in about a half hour of tortuous walking. The rain was moving off, and the pauses in the wind were now longer than the gusts, but the traveling was the most tiring yet for Jennie, because she was lame from her pummeling in the flood, and her drenched clothes dragged at her legs. The track was washed out in spots. She was concentrating so hard on not being a burden that she'd have refused Alick's help at these places if he hadn't firmly taken hold of her by the arm or around the waist. He shook his head when she tried to make a token protest, and propelled her on.

They had to climb over and through a jumble of big boulders on a spongy and streaming slope, and she thought it was an alternative way for one that completely disappeared, until she saw the cave opening behind it.

This was the deepest one yet, and he told her there was another chamber beyond, and a story of a passage through the mountain to the other side. "But I never was having the desire to find out for myself. I was always thinking it would be like being put alive into my coffin."

"Don't!" she exclaimed, seized by a violent chill that seemed to have nothing to do with being wet. She tried to see fearfully into the depths of the cave. The southern and western skies were brightening as the storm moved off; a shaft of sunlight shot down past the large screen of boulders, across Jennie into the cave, and aimed at a large, untidy pile of dry, broken boughs. Alick laughed aloud in spontaneous pleasure.

"Beannachd leat mo coraid!" he exclaimed.

"What is it?" she questioned eagerly. "What did you say?"

" 'Blessings on you, my friend,' for the man who left us that. And a bed, too." The bracken and heather piled over fir boughs was not yet all brown and dead. "Now you must get out of those clothes before you are taking a bad chill!" He took an armful of the dry wood to the mouth of the cave, and some of the driest heather for kindling.

"And what will I be wearing besides my skin?" she asked.

"My plaid, to be sure. Will you be keeping the fire going while I set my snares?"

"I am not entirely stupid. Doesn't it worry you that someone has been here and may be back? That he left the dry wood for himself?"

"Och, he is in Fort William by now, or perhaps away on a ship. No, he left the wood for the next ones to come." He was on his knees getting the fire started. By the first leap of red-orange light his face showed up deeply absorbed but not drawn with apprehension. Whatever terrors had assaulted him in his sleep last night, he must have completely forgotten them. "We will leave wood for the next traveler." He stood up. "There now. Feed it a little now and then." He dropped the plaid on the bed and went out.

She was alone with the tiny snapping of the fire and the company of the small flames and the eternal sounds of running water outside. She stripped off her wet clothes and allowed herself the licentious luxury of kneeling naked beside the fire while she skeptically examined the plaid. It was damp on the lower edges from his plunge into the stream, and so were the folds that had been outermost over his shoulder all day, but the inside was quite dry.

"Remarkable," she said. With some experimenting she turned it into a garment; she belted in the voluminous folds by her scarf tied tightly around her waist, and brought the upper part of it up over her head and shoulders like a particularly roomy shawl. She fastened it under her chin with Kirsty's brooch. Spacious folds fell down over her breasts, but her arms were free under the loose covering.

She sat by the fire and held her drawers to it. The warmth was delicious; even her feet, tucked in under the plaid, were warm. She didn't know how long before her clothes could be dried, she might have to put them on again while they were still damp, and the way she felt now she could have lived as cozily in the plaid as a snail in its shell; but they would have to use it as a blanket tonight. The small plaid, or guilechan, was too saturated to be of any use to her.

But we're safe, she thought, *and that's the important thing. At least I've had a bath. At least this wood was here for us. Supposing it hadn't been? At least the weather is clearing again. Tomorrow the sun will finish drying our clothes as we walk. And we must be close to Fort William, or at least close as a Highlander reckons it, which could be a mere fifty miles or so.*

Jennie Hawthorne of Pippin Grange and Brunswick Square was crouched before a fire in a mountain cave, naked except for a wild Gael's plaid, and the wild Gael himself out foraging for food. She had to laugh out loud at the unqualified fantasy of it, which was better than shrieking like the old lady in the nursery rhyme, "This be none of I!" Or being struck dead by horrified amazement.

The drawers were a little less damp, so she substituted her shift, turning it over and over in her hands. Now and then she gave the fire another small stick.

Alick brought water and a handful of small limp plants he began to steep in the pannikin. The cavewoman was enough a creature of her past life to hide the underwear she was trying to dry.

"What is that?" she asked.

He gave her the Gaelic name and handed a plant over to her. She recognized the delicately striped pink and lavender petals of wood sorrel. "For a fever if you have one, or to keep it away," he explained.

"What about your wet clothes?" she asked, alarmed by the prospect of his falling ill; his mother had died of lung fever.

"They'll be drying on my back; it won't be the first time. You will keep the plaid tonight, and I'll be burrowing under the bracken there." He stirred the sorrel broth with the horn spoon. "We won't be traveling on tomorrow. It will be a fair day, and we will lay up here, and your gown can be drying in the sun."

You're sure it will be safe to stay? she almost asked but stopped herself in time. She had to believe he knew what he was talking about, she wanted so much that day of rest and sun.

"That will be very nice," she said primly. "Is this one of the caves that Prince Charlie slept in while he was escaping after Culloden?"

"It is said so, but it is said about many caves in the Highlands."

"Like all the houses where Queen Elizabeth is supposed to have slept. Of course, she was a lady who did travel a good deal. I have never forgiven her for beheading Queen Mary Stuart. They say she didn't want to, but nonetheless she signed the death warrant."

"Och, queens!" He waved them away with the spoon as if they'd been midges. "Sup this. But with care. It is very hot."

The sorrel tea and the last bit of the bread made their supper. She heaped most of the loose dry stuff to one side for Alick to crawl into, and laid her shift and drawers on her portion. They were partly dried, and her body warmth through the plaid should finish the job by morning.

It took her some time to get comfortable because of all her sore places, but finally she settled down on her side facing the fire. Alick sat cross-legged beside it, his face faintly lighted by the small, flickering flames. Whenever he added a bit more fuel, the light sprang up and illumined his face against the darkness outside. The whip marks had almost gone, and his mouth was healed. The tremulous light seemed to give him a play of expressions around his mouth and eyes, but she knew it was an illusion as candleshine gives life to a painting or a statue's features. He was as remote from her as if he were dead. Gone as far from her as Nigel had gone, all at once, five days ago in the hollow.

It occurred to her then that last night he might have been dreaming of the gallows. She took that horror to herself and almost called out to him, just to break the spell, but restrained herself. She half shut her eyes and watched the little flames shimmer and dance through her lashes until she mesmerized herself into sleep.

When she woke up, she was stiff from lying curled in one position all night long, like a baby folded up in the womb. No wonder it hated being forced out of that warm, comfortable, dreaming darkness into the abyss of light, she thought as she tenderly moved each limb. The fire was out, and she was alone in the cave. The scent of the day came in, that of a fine morning after rain. Above the screening boulders small puffs of fair-weather clouds wandered like grazing sheep across an azure field.

She thought Alick had just left the cave and would be back in a few moments; then she would gather herself and the plaid together and go outside. She lay there waiting, warm in the nest, refreshed by sleep, optimistic even though she was hungry and they might not have anything to eat today. The calls of eagles and a kestrel's whistle were now as familiar to her as the blackbird's song. She saw herself as a minute figure in an animated miniature painting, perfect in every bijou detail, kneeling by a window in Brunswick Square and listening to the blackbird on a chimney pot.

Well, I didn't run away with the gypsies, she thought, *but this is a fair approximation of it.*

Alick didn't come, and after a while she couldn't wait any longer. She put on her dry drawers and shift. Her stockings were still wet, but the brogues had dried, and she worked them in her hands to get some of the stiffness out before she laced them onto her bare feet. Her hair fell in snarls and tangles down her back. She belted the plaid around her middle again, but she couldn't find the brooch. She remembered taking it off last night because it pressed into her breastbone when she curled up. It would be somewhere in the crumbling dry heather, but she couldn't stop to look for it now.

Holding the plaid around her shoulders, she went outside. Gorse grew beside and above the cave, and she picked the driest approach to a protective clump, amused at her instinct for privacy when there was not another human soul in sight. Where *was* Alick, anyway? Below her, the leaves of a stand of mixed hardwoods rippled under the wind like a celadon sea streaked with bronze and silver. Beyond that, a shimmer of water must be the loch into which the flood poured from the corrie. The other side of the glen was a mountain that began in deceptively gentle stages apparently carpeted in pastel velvets; the summit of sheer rock raked the clouds.

The entire setting was magnificent and, except for her and the winged predators, empty. Alick had gone. So that's what he had been planning while she lay watching him last night, respecting his preoccupation. He had the gold, and she was too much of a care and a liability; had she not brought him to the foot of the gallows? Fort William was close enough now, and he couldn't wait.

She crumpled on the ground, hunched over her knees, and moaned, "I knew it, I *knew* it!"

Something in her maintained a rigorous control and leashed her in before she could reach hysteria. She sat up and breathed deeply a few times to steady herself, then went back to the cave. She had no intention of waiting passively in one place to starve to death, but she had every intention of walking until she dropped. The track had been very clear in places. When it was not clear— She refused to consider that. First things first . . . At least he had left her the plaid. He couldn't have taken it from her without waking her, and he intended to be leagues away before she ever stirred. He would be at Fort William very quickly;

he could walk twenty hours of every twenty-four if he chose. No wonder he'd told her last night that they would lie up today; she would sleep all that more soundly.

She felt the potent temptation to go to pieces, and she said aloud belligerently, "I will *not*, and you can't make me!" She collected her damp clothing and took it outside. "Well, I have no reason to hurry now," she went on, for the company of her own voice. "I can take time." She spread the gown, petticoat, the small plaid, and the stockings over gorse bushes to finish drying. The sun was hot enough now so that the plaid was too much, and she took it off.

In the shift and drawers she climbed up on the biggest boulder screening the cave entrance and examined her bruises and scrapes as if it really mattered if anything became infected. So far the raw spots looked clean. Now for water. The slopes were no longer running with it, but there should be a spring or a stream nearby. There had been one at every stopping place, and he couldn't have carried the pannikin of water all the way up from the loch and had much left by the time he reached the cave. The pannikin! She slid off her perch and ducked into the cave. Ah, he had left her that, too.

The cave was hateful to her now, and she hurriedly left it and perched on the rock again. Supposing she could find cormeille on the way, how long would that and water sustain her? She would admit neither the hope nor the possibility of meeting anyone who could aid her, and dying alone in the wilderness was preferable to encountering another Jock Dallas. What about adders? She had no means of cutting a stick, so she would simply walk where she could always see her footing.

On the slope below her, Alick came out from the trees and walked up the stone-studded incline. She was incredulous at first; she thought she was deluding herself in the first stage of delirium caused by fear and hunger.

But it *was* Alick, moving at the steady purposeful gait which had set their pace for five days. He carried a slender pole in his right hand, and something swung shining from his left hand. He disappeared in the general blur as her eyes ran with tears the way the hill had run with water. She wiped her cheeks with the backs of her hands, but the tears kept dripping down. Blindly she felt for the plaid and mopped her face with it. She was deeply ashamed for having doubted him, and he was not to know about it.

Then she realized that she was dressed only in her undergarments, which might shock him. Laughing weakly and still sniffling, she tied herself into the plaid again. She went into the cave and began rooting through the bedding for her brooch, not hurrying, so she'd be busy when he came.

"Good morning!" she called when she heard his step. She didn't turn around.

"I thought you would still be sleeping."

"I'm looking for my brooch," she said. "Where can it be?" She wasn't acting now, but truly mystified. "You don't suppose Kirsty's really a witch and cast a spell to get her brooch back, do you? If so, I'm glad she didn't claim her clothes, too."

"I took the brooch," he said. "I was needing it to make a hook." He held up a string of trout, smiling at them the way he had smiled at her when he was pretending to be her husband.

"Oh, *Alick.*" She had barely enough breath for it, after what she'd gone through in the last hour.

"There was nothing in my snares this morning, so I fished."

She giggled foolishly. "Is this a fine trout that I see before me? Or is it but a fine trout of the mind? Come, let me clutch thee! . . . I know I sound drunk, but it's better than bursting into tears."

"Aye." He agreed with obvious relief. "Here is the pretty part of the brooch, but it will be doing you no good now."

"The brooch is feeding us," she said. "And Kirsty expected to have it back in her chest long before now."

"Och, we should have asked for more. She'd have given us anything, so sure she was of her man."

"Will you keep it for me?" Jennie asked. "Until we reach Fort William? I'd like it to remember these days by."

"I would not think you'd be having the hard time remembering any of it," he said. He put the brooch in the bag, which had been there against the cave wall in clear view all the while.

"My things must be nearly dry by now," she murmured, and went outside, holding the plaid around her shoulders. Everything was still a little damp, but she was much too warm in the plaid. Her clothes could finish drying while she wore them. But she didn't put on the stockings.

He broiled the trout on a hot flat stone, and they had two apiece. He was so pleased with himself that he was talkative and described how he had cut the slender ash sapling for a pole, cut a bit of rag from his shirttail for a lure, and raveled threads from the same place, tying them together to make a line.

"And we'll not need to save for tonight," he said. "I'll be catching more."

"May I go down to the loch with you?" she asked meekly. "Or will I spoil your luck?" The instant she said it she thought: *I've already spoiled his luck. His life.*

But he didn't hesitate. "You are welcome to go. It is quite pretty down there."

"Will your knife cut hair?"

This time he was surprised. "Why?"

"Look at mine! It's worse than ten birds' nests. I've no comb, and even if I could unsnarl it, I've lost my pins. If you could cut it off here"— she touched the nape of her neck—"the worst tangles will be gone, and I can comb the rest of it with my fingers."

"I will try," he said soberly, "but it will be more sawing it off than cutting."

"I don't care, as long as I'm rid of it. It will only get worse and worse until it's impossible to clear."

"Come out here then."

She sat on a rock with her head tilted forward, and gazed at her clasped hands in her lap while he lifted the heavy mass off her nape. He was surprisingly delicate about it; his knuckles brushed her neck only once.

"Don't be moving now," he warned her. "I will be pulling a little."

"I shan't move."

"It's curling around my hand like a live thing. It's not wishing to die. Is it sure you are?"

"Yes, I am sure. Please, Alick."

Holding the thick swatch tautly away from her with one hand, he cut across it in small, cautious motions. She felt one release after another, until her nape was completely out to the air. He blew on it and brushed away some short loose hairs. "There," he said. "After this I can be setting up as a lady's maid."

"You have a better touch than most of them," she said. She ran her hands over her head. "Thank you! My head hasn't been this comfortable since the first day they made me put it up. What can I do for you? Can I wash your shirt in the loch this afternoon?"

He laughed. "I have nothing to wear in its place. And if I am needing to make a new line, clean threads might frighten the fish."

Forty-One

S HE SAT on the warm sand, burrowing her bare toes in it, sifting it
through her fingers. She was watching Alick dress the trout he'd
caught from the outer end of a long natural jetty of rock that projected
a good way into the loch. While he was fishing, she had woven a small
mat of coarse grasses, on which he laid each cleaned and washed trout.

Unconsciously she traced her name in the sand, suddenly saw it, and
inspiration sprang up full-blown. She didn't give herself time to think
twice.

"Alick, there's something I can do that will help you in America."

"What would that be?" he asked skeptically. He straightened up and
carried the handfuls of entrails up to the edge of the trees and laid them
on the turf beside a log. "A wildcat and her kittens were sunning there
this morning," he said. "She will be back to see what we were doing
here." He returned to the water and knelt down to wash his hands.

"I wish I could see her," she said enviously. "Do you think she robbed
your snares?"

He shrugged. "Herself or a fox. They are welcome, as long as I can
be fishing." He folded an end of the mat over the trout and set it in the
shade of the rocks. Then he sat down to clean his knife.

"This is what I was thinking I could do for you," she said. "I could
teach you to read and write. In a few days you could learn a good deal.
You already have the words, you told me so yourself."

He began scouring his knife clean with sand, as intent on it as if he
were all alone. She pushed on. "You will be able to sign your name and
not make just a mark. And once you know the letters and their sounds,
you can read almost anything."

"I will not be Alick Gilchrist in Fort William," he said bluntly, keeping at his work.

"If you have to write a name there, you can write anything you choose. But we'll start with Alick Gilchrist." She smoothed a place, and wrote his name. She thought he was obstinately refusing to watch until she glanced up quickly and caught him looking from the corner of his eye. She grinned.

"Come along, Alick. You do it now."

There was a suspenseful interval when she was afraid she'd gone too far, a woman condescending to his ignorance; irreversible blow to his male, and Highland, pride. Then he wiped the knife on his breeches and returned it to the sheath on his belt. He knelt by his name and drew out the letter A below the one she'd made. "That is A," he said with dignity. "I am knowing that much."

"Then we're off to a flying start," she said briskly. She named each letter as he drew it. They repeated the process three times, until he spoke every letter without prompting and was writing his name with some ease. She commenced on the rest of the alphabet, and by the end of an hour he was almost letter-perfect; she began putting words together, and then simple sentences. He was so quick that she ventured into the inconsistencies of the English language. This could not be memorized in one session, even if she could think of everything at once. But the moment of triumph for them both came at the end of the engrossing afternoon when he wrote, "I have caught five trouts," and signed his name.

He stood back to gaze at it, his head cocked, and then looked at her, not quite smiling but with a fresh lustre in his eyes. She was immensely proud that she had been able to get through to him. Wisely she didn't say anything about what they would do tomorrow.

They had stopped at the spring on the way down; it gurgled out of the earth above the hardwoods and fed a little brook that ran down through the grove to the loch. They left the pannikin there, and on the way back Jennie filled it, and Alick gathered a bonnetful of young nettle plants to boil as greens for their supper. After they had eaten their trout and drunk the last of the water in which the nettles had been cooked, Jennie took the pot back to the spring to rinse it out and refill it. She washed her face and cleaned her teeth with a twig of bog myrtle.

Walking back up to the cave, she felt a rare peace. She had a stomach full of good hot food; yesterday she'd had a bath even if by accident; she wore no stays; her skirts were comfortably short, her bare feet delightfully free in brogues, and her head delightfully free to the breeze. She ran her fingers through her hair again and again, enjoying the looseness and lightness. It was curling around her neck and ears, and she remembered what Alick had said about the rest of it curling around his hand like a living thing that did not want to die.

What had he done with the hair? she wondered. Thrown it deep into the cave, perhaps, where it might be discovered by some later traveler and mystify him till the end of his days. And where would she be by then? And Alick?

The evanescent peace had been purely physical. Nothing could quiet the mind but the narcotic of exhausted sleep, and then one sometimes dreamed.

They sat outside the cave in the long late sunset and afterglow. The moon appeared, and the sun went down red behind the mountains, which he named aloud; the recitation sounded like a litany or a prayer. The loch was, appropriately, the Loch of the Speckled Trout.

"A man knows he will always be eating here if he can fish."

"I take it this isn't the territory of the dead exciseman."

"Not for anyone who is not knowing about him. I think myself he does not travel here. It is too far from where he was murdered."

"How long will he walk, do you think?" she asked. "Until he is avenged?"

He shrugged. "I have heard it said that such souls are not knowing they are dead until someone makes it clear to them, but who will be doing that?"

"In the"—she was going to say "English"—"in my church they have rites of exorcism." She didn't add that her father had told her it was all foolishness. "How long will it take us to reach Fort William from here?" she asked.

"We will be walking for a day, sleep one more night, and go into Fort William the next day. We are staying here two more days, over the Sabbath. On the Sabbath no one stirs. On Market Day, the crowds will help hide us."

"I can't believe that we're almost there." She was tight with dread, and England seemed farther away than ever. Alick's lips were thinned and pale in his beard, and his eyes were fixed on space, unseeing, she was sure.

"Yes, we are almost there," he said. "And then it is over. However it will be going with me, you will be on your way to your sisters."

"No! I *told* you that if they take you, I speak for you. If I don't, they will think you murdered me on the way."

"And how will you be explaining that you ran away with me if you don't tell them that I stole you?"

"That," she said haughtily, "is a story for the costly advocates to invent." It was a brave but senseless flourish, and she knew it, and he smiled at her statement as if at a child, as if he had gone beyond fear. But when—*if*—they walked him white and alone to the gallows, how would it be then? Only a saint could go up those steps in his chains as if he had already passed into another world. Even Jesus had cried out on the cross.

It was one thing to play the fiddle on the gallows like the legendary MacPherson, quite another to be resigned to death when you were innocent, because you believed there was no justice for you.

No. No! I won't have it! Nigel is dead, Archie is cowering in Linnmore House, wallowing in wine and self-pity, and Christabel is rejoicing at having got rid of three of us at one blow. She's seen Nigel into his grave, and she'll make a pilgrimage to see the hanging so she can be sure Alick's well and truly gone. If she can't see me dead as well, she can be sure I'll never come back over the border.

Jennie's belly caved in when she thought of those contemptuous hands laid on her books, her family keepsakes, her few jewels, the miniatures, the old robe and slippers—darling Ebony—how that woman would sneer.

Alick said urgently, "You are not to be afraid."

"I'm not afraid; I'm furious. I wonder if Christabel has already gone through my belongings. She would leap at the chance to pry."

"I am sorry."

"Why? It's not your fault!"

"You will be sending for them surely."

"Who is to force her to have them packed and sent?"

"Are you grieving for *things* when your life is safe?"

It was a gentle reproof, and she was furiously ashamed. But the outburst of hatred for Christabel had been like a cold sea wind blowing away a plague-carrying miasma. She said strongly, "There will be a ship for you, I know it."

"It is almost midnight. I am ready to sleep."

The next two days moved slowly on one plane and sped on another level. They were two more days without traveling, and with plenty to eat, but at the end Alick and Jennie would set out to keep a tryst from which there could be no turning back.

They lived on fish, greens, meat, and Alick's herb teas. The snares yielded a cock grouse and a hare before the wildcat could get them, or the fox that Jennie heard barking at dawn; the high sharp sound rang with echoes from slope to slope. They saw eagles, one of which could have been the bird that rode the wind past them in the flooded corrie; a pair of ospreys appeared to fish the loch. They were like familiar spirits to Jennie, and she tried to see them as an omen of good luck. Deer drifted across the pastel slopes beyond the loch.

One could see the fair weather as another omen. It meant that they could stay out of the cave all day, and they spent hours at the loch, writing in the sand. She showed him the difference between script and print, small letters and capitals.

"Now I will be able to read my name on the advertisements in Fort William," he said.

"Would they be printed and posted so soon?" She tried to sound hardheaded. "Especially if they look first at Mallaig? Besides, you are not going to be Alick Gilchrist in Fort William, you told me. You had better be thinking of a new name.

"Tomorrow," he said, unwilling to part with himself yet.

When he was not fishing or working at his lessons, they gathered all the broken wood they could find and carried it up to the cave, both for their own use and to leave for the next comer, Alick cut new ash sticks for them.

They talked in the evenings, or rather she did; he asked her questions about her growing up and her sisters, and she suspected he was keeping her going so she wouldn't question him. He was free to be sunk in his own thinking while she diverted herself with spoken memories. But often he surprised her by an observation, or even laughter, which showed that he had been listening after all. It was no hardship for her to run on about Pippin Grange. It lessened the distance between her and her family and kept her from dwelling on the interim perils.

She expected to sleep badly on the last night, but she had got used to the comfort and safety of the cave, and during the evening she had told him how she would like to go to Switzerland, where Ianthe was. "So you will be thinking of me there when I am thinking of you in America," she said, defying him. She *had* to be right about a ship for him; she went to sleep convinced of it, and never knew if Alick lay awake or not. As usual he was gone when she woke up, and the plaid was tucked around her.

It was a cold and foggy dawnbreak, and she was hard put to maintain her convictions. Oh, why couldn't it have been an exquisite dawn, full of diamonds and birdsong?

"There will be a ship," she chanted, bundled in the plaid, arms crossed over her midriff, icy hands squeezing her lean flesh above her elbows. *"There will be a ship."*

She wished there were a God of whom one could ask favors, or a pantheon separate from the impersonal indifferent Creator. She wished she were a Roman Catholic and could pray to a particular saint. The belief that you were heard by some dear soul sitting on a footstool by God's throne, who then passed on your message, must have been as comforting as a hot bath or a cup of steaming chocolate.

Both of which awaited her, and many more comforts, material and otherwise. *There will be a ship.* She got up and found her stockings.

Forty-Two

AFTER THE BREAKFAST of cold broiled trout and potentilla tea, Jennie had a clawing in her belly that hurried her off into the bushes. "Oh, *no!*" she groaned. "What a way to start out! If this is an omen, it's a frightful one."

She didn't feel nauseated or light-headed; it had to be caused by a bad state of nerves, and why not? There was enough to have nerves about.

There was a mute farewell to the cave, and they set off into the fog. They had been on their way about a half hour when the clawing began again and would not be ignored.

"I have to drop back," she called to Alick.

"Are you ailing? Should we be waiting another day?"

"It's only from too much food, I'm sure. I don't feel ill."

The path had been going gradually downward, and they had come to a giant thrusting fist of rock, knuckles and all. "I will be just beyond this," he said. "Be careful. Use your stick."

She crouched in the bracken and cleaned herself up afterward with handfuls of the wet green fronds, and washed her hands with more of it. Going back to the track, she had no fear of not finding Alick; he had had too many opportunities to leave her. Still, when she approached the great gneissian fist, the sense of complete solitude was strong enough to make her scalp prickle.

The fog lay in opaque layers around her. She leaned in against the lower part of the fist to pass it, feeling as if a step off the wrong side of the track would be a step off the world into infinite space.

She didn't see Alick, but to her right something enormous moved on the slope, towering in the fog. It walked in air or, more horribly, on a fall of rock too sheer even for a goat. She couldn't hear its footsteps, but she was sure she felt them shaking the ground.

There's nothing, but I'm seeing it, she thought. *I'm losing my mind. This is how it happens.*

With all her strength she forced a sound from her throat. It was like trying to cry out in dreams when only a strangled croak comes. But it was heard. Alick came out of the fog and took her hands and rubbed them hard between his.

"What is it then? What's at you?" She couldn't speak, and he shook her. "Jennie, answer me!"

"I'm losing my mind," she wheezed. "I saw a spectre." She couldn't take her eyes away from the spot. "Up there. Huge. Hulking. Like the fog shaping into a monster to devour us."

"There's nothing there but fog now, and it's thinning. No monsters." He pulled her down into the shelter of the fist.

"I *saw* it, Alick." She kept wriggling around to see. "If I didn't, I'm going mad!"

"Och, it's only Am Fear Liath Mor, the Great Gray Man of Ben Tee. There's many a Great Gray Man in the Highlands."

"He was *there*? He *exists*?" She shook, and he hugged her against his chest.

"It comes with the fog. Who knows what it is? It always has been, and it always will be, long after we are gone." He even tried to make her smile. "You might have been seeing a *wee* man and he would be leading you into a fairy hill like the lass Kilmeny. And you would never be seeing Fort William, and I would be missing that ship you are so sure about, because I would be growing old searching for you."

He stood her up and put her stick into her hand. "Then there would be another Great Gray Man out here then to be putting terror on wanderers." She was weak-kneed, but his efforts deserved something from her.

"Alick, if I should be lured off to fairyland, I forbid you to look for me. After all we've been through, it would be a crime for you to lose your ship because I ran off with a wee man in a green suit."

He gave her shoulder a rough little shake. They went on, stopping after a few hours for a strupach of cold trout and a drink of water. Evidently the Great Gray Man had cured her of the disorder in her belly. The fog was going fast, but there was no sunshine; it was a quiet world of white sky and white water, subtle grays, dark smoky blues, vaporous greens, sooty black.

"Where will we be sleeping tonight?" she asked him in late afternoon.

"On this side of Mile Dorcha."

"What does that mean? What is it?"

"It is the Dark Mile."

"I hate the sound of that," she exclaimed. "It's like some long avenue of terror one must travel, full of fire pits and dragons, and at the end there's no safety, only more terrors."

"It is only a bit of forest between Loch Lochy and Loch Arkaig. It would not be surprising to be feeling terrors there; the earth has been soaked with too much blood. But that was all long ago. It is not phantoms I fear now."

They slept, if you could call it sleeping, in a hollow scooped out by nature from the side of an almost vertical rise. They reached it by using their hands as much as their feet. To lose your grip and footing simultaneously could mean a fast, bouncing, bruising roll down the steep and the chance of a fall into the boiling river at the bottom.

They built no fire, and their water came from a trickle running over a rock; it took nearly an hour for the pannikin balanced beneath the drip to catch enough for each of them to drink. Jennie thirsted greedily for Alick's pungent brews as she had earlier lusted after large bowls of steaming coffee or pots of scalding hot tea.

There were only a few hours of darkness, and that wasn't really dark but a long gloaming. Ironically, now that they were so close to Fort William, she felt a homesickness for the cave where they had spent the last three nights. She didn't love the stars now; they told her how quickly the earth was turning inexorably toward day, and she was still getting no more sleep than quick catnaps, from which she'd be suddenly aroused either by a bird or animal sound or by herself. And there were times when the noise of the water inexplicably increased.

Alick lay motionless as a log, too quiet. She knew he wasn't sleeping, and she wished she could speak to him. There was a great deal she wanted to say; perhaps she'd be able to tell him a little of it before they separated for good. A few fumbling, inadequate phrases weren't going to make up for what he was losing, but half her soverigns would ensure that he didn't arrive a pauper in America. If he would accept them, she'd give them all to him, except for what she needed to carry her from Fort William to Sylvia and William.

Apart from this, what could she say? That she wished she could know how he did in America? It was as unthinkable that, after the enforced intimacy of the last week, they should never know anything more about each other, as it was that her lover was lying under a stone behind the yews in Linnmore churchyard.

Alick was up and out of the hollow when the half-light was coldly whitening. When he came back, she went. She had to perch precariously in the heather behind a wind-worn thorny little shrub, and wondered at the instinct for privacy that could dictate behavior out here where the only other living soul was out of sight.

There was no dew-wet bracken handy for washing her face and hands. There was no morning fire. But she shivered less from the raw damp chill than from anticipation. Alick, without speaking, insisted on her wrapping up in the plaid while they ate the last of the cold meat. She'd have liked the relief of mentioning her state of nerves, but considering the probable state of his own he wouldn't appreciate hearing about it.

Silently they began the downhill walk, braking themselves with their sticks. At the foot they turned left and followed the stream southward until they came to the Dark Mile.

The wood lived up to its name in the hours before sunrise. The two moved in a twilight as bitingly and deadly cold as if the sun had never reached through the branches since the forest's birth. They walked in a hush where the dripping of heavy dew and their own soft footsteps and heartbeats were the only sounds.

Yet she knew that it was really only a wood, and on a hot noon it would be a place of pleasant coolness and shade. But she was relieved when they began to hear birds, and once, looking down, she saw hare droppings. Then Alick, who had been ominously wordless since they started out, cleared his throat and said, "We will be coming soon to Loch Lochy."

"You mean we're all the way through Mile Dorcha?" Already she was warmer and lighter, down to her soaked brogues. He didn't answer, but in a short time the southern end of Loch Lochy lay below them to their left, silvery past the trees. The day was warming rapidly as the sun diffused its heat through an opaline film of cloud.

The river Lochy ran from the loch of that name to Fort William, to Loch Eil and the great arm of the sea, Loch Linnhe, down which the immigrant ships sailed to the ocean. Alick and Jennie crossed the river by an old stone bridge below the falls, and here they began to meet other people on their way to Fort William, either for the market or to board a vessel.

Jennie had put the guilechan over her head and fastened it under her chin with a pin Alick had made from the fishhook when they needed it no longer. The other women either glanced at her without interest, being too involved in their own worries, or nodded and gave her a soft "Madainn mhath." She was afraid to return the "Good morning" for fear her poor Gaelic would give her away, but she smiled and put two fingers to her lips as if to sign that she was mute. For that she received looks of sympathy, and she felt not a bit guilty of deception, but rather pleased with herself.

More traffic filled the road, human and animal. Little black cows, some with calves, a few black-faced sheep and lambs, goats and kids—all were going to market. Hens clucked in baskets; children rode on shaggy ponies carrying loaded panniers. Those people without four-footed goods or poultry to barter carried their merchandise—or their belongings—on their backs, done up in their plaids.

Alick fell into conversation with two men, one young and one a bearded elder, walking beside a cart in which three excited small children perched on two substantial chests among sacks and bundles. The younger man led the pony; the older sometimes gently cautioned the children about their noise. The young man talked freely with Alick, often smiling; Jennie didn't have to understand Gaelic to know that this group was emigrating and that one of them, at least, was eager to go.

Two women and a young girl followed the cart; one woman carried an infant wrapped in a plaid, and kept glancing down into the little face and then licking her dry lips. Drying from fear, Jennie knew. The older woman gazed straight ahead from a mask of anguish carved in stone. The girl, about thirteen, with a creel on her back, was quietly weeping, wiping her eyes with a corner of her shawl; then they would fill and run over again.

Jennie turned away; it was not decent to look at them. A month from now would the baby still be alive? Or those little ones who were now so ecstatic in their innocent excitement?

Fort William was dwarfed into a toy village by its surroundings; Ben Nevis, off to its southeast, was the highest mountain in Scotland. The procession went along the road past a collection of thatched stone hovels and desultory onlookers, and streamed into the one crude street of the town.

Forty-Three

S HE WAS UNPREPARED for the relentless volume of the noise that surged down the narrow street. She had gone to town on market days at home; she had been on the streets of London at their busiest. But after the primordial silence of the wilderness, when the loudest sounds besides their own voices were those of water, wind, and birds, the uproar here assaulted her ears like an artillery barrage.

She was no longer afraid of any human predator's pouncing on them; she feared only being swamped and drowned. She hung onto Alick's arm, and he charged unswervingly on, his bonnet pulled low over his eyes. She felt like a mere appendage as he swung her around groups or through them; no offense was taken at this, it was considered a part of the good-humored jostling. Once she crashed into a sergeant's iron-hard midriff, and he steadied her with a grip on her elbow and a few jovial words in a broad Devon accent. Alick never looked around, but his arm cramped her hand hard against his side, and she was dragged on.

It was a mild day of light wind, with the sun burning through a low ceiling of cloud that pressed down and held in the stench as well as the noise. She felt manure squash under her brogues, and once she looked down just in time to avoid splashing through a puddle of urine where some cattle had just gone by. An insidious pungence of rotting fish united all the other stenches into a stirring, nose-prickling authoritative alliance. Jennie needed a deep breath but hated to draw one. She supposed that Alick was heading directly for the shipping, and she hungered and thirsted for a clean air off the water.

Suddenly he stopped short, and the opposing streams divided around him and Jennie. He was watching a lad posting advertisements on the walls of a building. The youth had an untidy head of thick straw-yellow hair and wore a long apron over his shirt and breeches. His stockings slid in folds halfway to his heels. When he finished his chore, he looked around, saw them watching him, and gave them a friendly grin. When he went back inside, the scent of roasting meat and potatoes came out past him.

Alick stood staring up at the broadsheets, and she shared his suspense and anxiety as he searched them all for his own name, afraid that it was there but that he couldn't find it. She scanned them quickly. They were shipowners' advertisements in English. She put her mouth close to his ear and said, "You're not there. It's all about ships."

"And that's what I'm needing." He wiped his forehead.

"They make everything sound very fine. And *dear*. How many of these people today can afford a passage?" She read one aloud. "But that ship won't be here for another ten days. Another one goes in a fortnight and will stop at Fort William only if enough passengers will be embarking here."

He gave her a look of utter despair, and she knew he was thinking the words he had said to her when he looked up from Nigel's body. *I am a hanged man.*

"But there are ships here already," she argued. "Those people we walked with—they must be sure of something; they can't be simply hoping against hope."

"No, they have paid their passage already. They sail today."

"Then let us go and see for ourselves. Someone might lose heart and decide not to go, and you'd be there—"

"We'll just be stepping in here first." He breasted the stream, towing her behind him and in through the door where the straw-headed lad had gone. When it had shut them off from the street, he said, "A friend of mine who is in the Army is married to the Sassenach woman who owns this place. He is away in Spain."

They stood in a square entry with steep stairs going up directly ahead, a closed door on either side. A confusion of voices and the pervasive scents of food, ale, and tobacco seeped out around the one to the left.

"Wait here," Alick ordered. He went into the noisy room. By the light from the window on the stair landing she saw that the steps were passably clean, though the floor wasn't, what with all the coming in off the street. She sat on the third one up, averted her eyes from the condition of her brogues and ankles, and leaned her head against the wall. When she shut her eyes, she began to swoop back and forth in dizzying downward swings, like a courting woodcock. Only *he'd* have known exactly where he was going.

It seemed to her that she had not been this tired all the time in the hills, except for that first scarifying day.

Someone came in, talking, from the street. Through her lashes she saw a youngish couple with a child, and at sight of her drooping there they instantly subdued their voices and quieted the child, with the instinctive good manners of the Gael. She closed her eyes and began the woodcock descent again.

"She looks 'alf-dead," said a strident Cockney voice so close that she jumped.

"I am *not*!" she said at once, opening her eyes and sitting up.

"Alick, you scoundrel, what 'ave you been up to?" The woman with him was taller than he, and stout, wearing a serviceable figured cotton dress and a white fichu. Her sleeves were rolled up above her elbows, and her bare muscular arms were folded across her considerable bust. Her pale hair was done up in a little bun on top of her head, and she looked down at Jennie from small yellowish eyes under almost nonexistent eyebrows. Her nose was ludicrously tiny for the rest of her, but the surprise was the long humorous mouth that was twitching now with both amusement and dismay.

"Up you go, love!" she said vigorously.

"Where?" Jennie asked.

"We are having a room here," Alick said politely.

"You're coming up, too?"

"Of course 'e is, love," the woman said. "You don't think 'e's deserting you now, do you?"

She switched around Jennie and ran up the stairs. Jennie pulled herself up, gazing at Alick, and he nodded. "It will be all right."

The woman waited by an open door to the right of the landing. "'Ere you are, love, my finest!" She waved them in. "Kept special for the gentry and me man's kinfolk and his old whisky-smuggling comrades." She winked outrageously at Alick. "No nahsty little animules in the bedding, and my own bedroom right below, so it's quiet as the grive. Do you tell me 'er nime, laddie, or is she Lady X?"

"Jeannie," said Alick reluctantly. "Nancy MacNichol."

Jennie put out her hand. "How do you do, Nancy?"

"Nancy's always flourishing, but she'll do better when 'er man comes back." She looked cannily into Jennie's eyes. "Whatever made you choose this one to run away with, dearie?" She threw back her head and laughed boisterously at Jennie's confusion.

"Never mind Nancy! She's only teasing you. Now then, Alick—"

Jennie didn't listen. She was looking about her as if she had been transported in her dreams like a maiden in a fairy tale from one country to another, and was still dazed. Moving like a sleepwalker, she leaned against the doorway and untied the brogue laces without seeing what she was doing. She stepped out of them and then walked onto the scrubbed floor.

The room smelled clean and was well lighted by two windows with white curtains. The bed was made up with a blue and white woven coverlet, a plain nightstand beside it. A scarred armoire had a wall to itself. The washing stand held a white earthenware basin and ewer, and there were clean towels on the rack. A small square table stood between the windows, with two straight chairs drawn up to it. There were three candlesticks on the narrow mantelpiece, holding candles of varying lengths; a fire was laid but unlit in the little grate.

Nancy was chaffing Alick in her loud, roistering way, but he didn't speak. Jennie went to the windows. The misty white heat of the sun burned through the glass. She looked out over a clutter of roofs toward the pale sheen of Loch Linnhe and the ships riding at anchor; the fort stood on a promontory off to the right, its flag hanging limp.

She was actually *here*; the room was real, Nancy MacNichol indubitably existed, and Alick was still there, though as silent and dark as a shadow. So why did everything out there except the sea gulls have no more substance for her than a series of very pale watercolors?

"Niall always told me you were the deep one, Alick, you sly dog," Nancy was saying. "Now I believe it! Eloping with an English lidy! Now, young miss, what'll it be first, 'ot water or 'ot tea, or both together?"

Laboriously Jennie turned her attention back to the room. "Both," she said gratefully.

Nancy slapped Alick familiarly on the shoulder and went out. They heard her heels on the bare stairs and her lusty welcome to a newcomer off the street.

"She's heard nothing," Alick said to Jennie. "I am knowing by the way she *is*, you see. She is not one who can be hiding things; she has only the one face." He reached into his shirt and brought out the little velvet sack. "Here is your money."

She tipped the sovereigns out onto the table. There were twenty-four left now. She counted off fifteen and pushed them toward him. His gaunt cheeks were dark red under the beard, and he pushed the money away. "I have a little. I will be taking just enough to finish paying for my passage, no more."

"You will need something when you get there."

"And you will be having to pay for your journey back to England."

"Take half then." He was still obdurate, and she flared at him. "Alick, *take* it! This is no time for a duel of wills! We were comrades out there on the moors; why should it change when we're inside four walls at the end?"

He turned his head sharply away, and the tilt of his bonnet half hid his face, but she could see his free hand knot into a fist, open, and clench again.

"I know I try your patience, Alick," she said humbly. "But I have done so much damage to your life, at least I can see that you don't arrive penniless in America."

Without meeting her eyes, he picked up twelve coins and put them in his purse. "Thank you. I will be off to the ships now. If I find a place, I will be staying on the vessel till she is sailing." His voice was strained as if something pulled too tightly around his throat.

"But how will I *know*?" she demanded. "I have to know if you are safely away." She felt inexplicably close to tears.

"All you are needing to know is that I am gone, and you will be going home," he said flatly on his way to the door.

She followed him, speaking to the back which she had followed for so many miles. "Alick, if they—*if* the other thing happens, you must tell them *at once* where I am, so they'll know you didn't do away with me. And I'll tell them that you didn't force me to go with you. I came because I was terrified of my husband. He struck me, you defended me, and we were running away from him, not knowing he was dead but *because* I was afraid of him."

He stood with his hand on the latch, and she couldn't tell whether he heard her or had simply shut her off. "I can swear he almost killed you," she said unsteadily. "And I really was afraid of what he had become."

"If I find passage, I'll be somehow letting you know," he said over his shoulder and looking past her. "You will be giving the ship a day's start, if you please, and then Nancy will tell you when the coaches come and go."

His thumb pressed down on the latch, and the door clicked open. She could not believe it was over like this. She wanted to make some gesture, but what? They had suddenly become completely alien to each other. Her hand moved on its own and just brushed the folds of the plaid. He swung the door open wide and walked out of the room.

She listened to him going away down the stairs and then fell face down across the bed. In the darkness the room spun about her, and she sat up dizzily, in time to see three gulls flying on translucent wings between her and the sun, calling to each other in the harsh skirling cries remembered from Pippin Grange. She was rocked with the violence of sudden endings: Papa's death in Ember Lane; Tamsin dying like a little bird; Nigel struck down in the hollow by the Pict's House; and Alick gone like this.

There was a rap at the door, and Nancy came in with a tray which she set on the table. The boy followed with a heavy iron teakettle from which he filled the ewer, grinning self-consciously and very scarlet around the ears.

"Angus, take those brogues back with you," Nancy said, "and give them a good brush."

"Thank you!" she called after him. She walked in her stockinged feet to the table and lifted the padded cozy off the teapot. Fragrant steam rose from the spout; the substantial slices of bread and butter looked as exquisite as rose petals. Nancy poured the tea. She had brought two cups, and Jennie speculated wryly that this astringent company was as good as anything to fetch her back to the realities of the situation.

Nancy put two lumps of sugar in Jennie's cup without asking. "You need it, love. God knows what that wild man of yours 'as drug you through. Though I can guess, being married to one of 'em myself." She looked affectionately into her teacup, as if seeing her Highlander's face there. "Och, aye, as this lot says. Lord, I laugh sometimes! What a lingo! And their English is as queer as the Gaelic. But I like 'em, you know. Would you think a London bird like me could endure it?"

"No," said Jennie truthfully. "How do you happen to be here?"

"My first man—'e was from Portsmouth—and me started this little business when we was posted 'ere. Giles was going to be the great landlord be'ind the bar when 'is time was up. Well, it was the 'eart that took him off before 'is time. Big 'andsome man in the prime going down like a great oak." She stirred her tea rapidly.

Jennie said, "That was how my father died."

"Then you know what it's like. The suddenness, and not believing it's so. But I 'ad friends 'ere, and this place was filling a demand. That's what business is, supply and demand. A family can come in and get a decent meal; I never 'ad no goings-on and never will. And Niall MacNichol's a good man. But 'e better come 'ome to me," she said calmly. "I'm not losing two of 'em."

Suddenly her hand shot across the table and took Jennie's left one, turned it over palm upward. "Yes, it's a wedding ring, right enough, not one with the stone turned round." She chuckled. "I said to Alick when he asked for a room, 'Where's your marriage lines then?' and he never quivered an eyelid. " 'We 'ad a handfast wedding,' 'e says, 'and she's wearing 'er mother's ring.' "

Jennie smiled. Her head kept wanting to turn to the windows. The farther shore was half-veiled in haze, its heights almost invisible. Loch Linnhe was white and still, the ships lying above motionless reflections. Little boats scuttled back and forth between the anchored vessels and the Fort William shore.

Nancy rose briskly. "You're anxious, and no wonder. You'd best be washing yourself while the water's still 'ot. I brought you some soap, rose-scented it is, too. And eat your bread and butter, love! You're so puny 'e'll 'ave to shake the sheets to find you!"

"I'll do my best, Nancy." She took a sovereign from the velvet bag she'd left on the table. "I'd like to pay you for the room now and for all this help."

"Alick's already paid for the room. When 'e comes back, I'll expect you downstairs for a good dinner. Is there anything more you need? A change of underwear? I'll wager it'll be better than whatever you're wearing under that outfit."

"It would be nice," Jennie admitted. "And a dentifrice and a toothbrush. I've been cleaning my teeth with twigs."

"Aye, I can find you something." She shook a finger in Jennie's face. "And don't *worry!*"

The tea had quieted Jennie's stomach, and she ate bread and butter as she undressed, trying not to wolf it. She wished she could enjoy fully the sensuous pleasure of the hot water and the perfumed soap, and genuine towels to stand on and for drying herself. But she couldn't even prolong the experience; she had to hurry back to the windows, wrapped in the coverlet from the bed.

Now a breeze was ruffling and darkening the loch, and small craft were raising their brown sails to catch the wind. The tide looked to be full. There was a good deal of activity aboard two of the ships. The decks were crowded; men climbed the rigging, and the great mainsails went slowly up, the topsails were unfurled, the huge anchors rose dripping from the loch. The rowing boats pulled away and waited at a little distance; she could see handkerchiefs and scarves waving from the ships, and in the small boats the men and boys swung their bonnets over their heads.

Then the sails began to fill, and with massive and leisurely grace, one slightly ahead of the other, the two ships moved down the loch, their stained canvas nearly black against the hills that now became a sunlit green as the freshening north wind dispersed the haze.

At this moment Alick Gilchrist was leaving Scotland forever.

The soft voice was in her ears. *You will be giving the ship a day's start, if you please. . . .* Obediently she calculated. Tomorrow at high tide the two vessels would be twenty-four hours on their way, well out to sea past Mull if they didn't make a stop at Oban or Tobermory to take on more passengers. She had better wait another day to be sure.

The ships were going away down Loch Linnhe, gliding steadily and sweetly before the wind like a pair of dark swans. Why did she feel so bereft? She and Alick were not brother and sister, not old friends, not lovers.

But they had been something closer than any of these. The successful parting at the end was the consummation of their hopes: safety in exile for him, home for her. Now she should be breathing as easily as the two ships moved. Appalling visions could be exchanged for that of Sylvia serenely plump with child in the rectory, and William saying, "My dear, *dear* Jennie!" A blissful visit to Pippin Grange, Sophie's strangling hugs, and Nelson rolling his eye at her as if to say, "But didn't you bring me anything?"

This was what should be, except that she could not find it. She had been too long and too intensely somewhere and something else.

I never even wished you a safe voyage, Alick, she thought. "Beannachd leat mo coraid," she said aloud. "Blessings on you, my friend. I shan't watch you out of sight."

She went and lay down on the bed, shut her eyes, and tried to call the other faces. They came but only unsubstantially, like ghosts. Only Alick was solidly there, simultaneously dominating the room and standing on the deck of the immigrant ship in his old coat and breeches and scuffed boots, the plaid over his shoulder and his bonnet over his eyes. Between that and the beard, and with so much weeping going on all around him, nobody else would see or care if he looked his last on Scotland through tears.

Forty-Four

A PEREMPTORY RAP at the door startled her so that her hands flew up and the coverlet slid off her shoulders. The message had come, then.

"It's me, love!" Nancy came in. She carried the fresh undergarments, a pair of clean cotton stockings, and the brogues.

"So you're starting for America, the two of you, in just the clothes you're standing in. They'll rot off you before you get there. *If* you get there without going to the bottom or dying of the cholera. The only way I'd be on one of those ships, I'd be dragged aboard in chains as a convict. 'Owever, everyone to 'er taste, said the old woman as she kissed the cow. But, Jennie, m'dear, you need something else to wear."

"I know," said Jennie. So the message hadn't come yet; meanwhile she must go on pretending. "Does anyone ever sell clothes at the market? I wouldn't care what they were, so long as they were clean. Alick should have a change, too."

"You two should 'ave planned your elopement better. 'Ere's your toothpowder and brush, and you can take that soap. It's 'ard-milled; it'll last if you don't use it every day but make do with a good scrub in seawater. I've brought you a comb, too."

"Thank you," said Jennie meekly. "I'll go out and see if I can find some clothes for us. And perhaps a carpetbag."

"Old clothes—yes. Maybe. But the folk around 'ere don't know such things as carpetbags. They tie up everything in a plaid, and Alick's got one, besides that satchel of his."

"Then I'll look only for clothes."

"Yes," said Nancy contemptuously, "and if just one of our brave

324

English lads just 'appens to pass by and 'ears a lidy speaking from that fancy dress of yours, not to mention offering a gold sovereign—which none of these folk would be able to change—" She made saucers of her eyes and lifted her hands in eloquent resignation.

Jennie looked forlorn, but not for Nancy's reasons. Until Nancy knew for a certainty that Jennie had been left behind, she had to believe that the two hoped to be embarking by nightfall. But once the message came, Jennie could take to her bed in apparent shock and grief at her betrayal, and not be well enough to stir for two days. Then some officer's wife would doubtless lend her a decent outfit to travel in, and a nightgown for the inns, while despising her for eloping with a peasant who'd ruined and deserted her.

Let her, Jennie thought. *If I'm a fallen woman, it's no skin off anybody's nose but my own. My family will believe me anyway.*

"Give me one of those gold coins," Nancy ordered. "I'll change it out of my money and do what I can for you." She sighed ostentatiously. "I don't know why I put myself out like this, I'm sure. But Niall would want me to. Thick as thieves, these 'ighlanders."

"I don't know how we can ever thank you," Jennie said.

Nancy snorted. "You're young, but 'e should know better! Off on a ship just like that! When you're out there in the middle of the ocean, with the sails ripping and the masts splintering, you'll be thinking that whatever you ran away from is a deal better than the way you're dying!" She went out and slammed the door.

Her visit had been as reviving as a cold plunge into a mountain stream, accidental or otherwise, and this time Jennie had struggled out by herself. There was still a faint soreness of her scalp from Alick's grip on her hair when he'd saved her, and her bruises had now gone from purple and blue-green to pale chartreuse.

"Well, Jennie, love," she said, sounding as much like Nancy as possible, "get on with it!"

The underclothes were too large, but Nancy had provided pins. After the homespun linens, the cambric felt like gossamer against her skin. The white cotton stockings wouldn't have lasted or warmed in the wilds like the woolen ones, which now lay crumpled and forsaken on the floor, and she picked them up and rolled them neatly together. They needed only to be washed; she wouldn't desert them after the way they'd befriended her.

Angus had done a masterly job of cleaning the brogues. She was of half a mind to keep them to show the family. Besides, she felt a genuine affection for these sturdy and reliable companions of the journey. She'd find some way to carry them; she could even giggle, though feebly, at the thought of doing up her souvenirs in the guilechan and arriving at the rectory with a small tartan bundle on her back.

She cleaned her teeth and combed her hair. Then she sat down at the table to stare out and wait for the message, but it was a mistake to go to the windows. She poured more tea and made herself sip very slowly, all the while looking everywhere but out at the place where she had last seen the two ships.

Somebody ran up the stairs and came in without knocking. It was Alick.

She was as dumbstruck as if she were seeing his fetch, his *Doppelgänger*. And he, after one miserable look at her from his gray eyes, turned his head away. He poured Nancy's cup full and drank the tea without milk or sugar.

She said quietly, "What happened?"

He picked up the bread and butter she hadn't eaten, folded it, and ate it in two bites, washed down with more tea. Then he sat down across from her and spoke just as quietly, as if he were holding in shouts and curses.

"There were two ships sailing on this tide, and they had no room! Nobody lost heart so he couldn't be making his feet leave Scottish soil. How could this *be*? Just because *I* must go or hang?" His eyes were glistening. "Hundreds, between the two ships, and not one give up or drop dead on the shore with the great grief and the excitement? All I am hearing of the immigrant ships is about the great wailing and moaning and taking on, so you could stand on Ben Nevis and hear the keening as the ships go down the loch. Dia, there was weeping enough, between those going and those staying, and some were as wild-eyed as cattle with the great fear on them, but"—he threw up his hands—"no one stayed back."

He finished the rest of the tea and drank the milk from the jug. "I was waiting even after the anchors came up, thinking some soul might be desperate enough to jump overboard and swim for one of the little boats. But, man, if there was, his friends were laying strong hands on him and dragging him back."

"What would you have done if someone had come ashore?"

"Hired the wee boat to row me out. The captain would be taking me when he knew I could pay. Why not? He would be getting two fares for one passenger. They were sister ships, too. Six crossings they have made already. Lucky they'd be, I was thinking. I was watching them as long as I could see them, and I could still hear the pipes playing 'We Shall Return No More.' "

And all the time I was wishing you safe voyage and blessings, Jennie thought. *Well, at least now I can say it to your face.*

"What do we do now?" she asked. "There's one ship still out there, and I see masts above the roofs. Are any of them immigrant ships?"

"I was about to be asking questions around the shore when the soldiers came. Search parties boarding everything, even the wee craft where a man could never be hiding. They rowed out to that one." He nodded. "American, she is." He sat back and folded his arms across his chest. His fingers pressed hard enough into his biceps to turn white at the tips. "For me, I was thinking. They'd come just too late to search the sister ships, and if I'd been a lucky man, they'd have been too late to catch me."

"Where could you hide?"

"I was not running off to call attention to myself. So I was standing there with my bonnet over my eyes, leaning my arms on a hogshead of herrings like a lazy Highlander sleeping on his feet, while they passed not this far from me." He unlocked his arms and stretched one of them out. "I could have touched them." A glimmer of pride lightened his voice.

"I'd have dissolved on the spot," said Jennie.

"Och, well, I was glad of the hogshead to hold me up." He gave her a twisted grin. "And it was so busy there, too, they would not even be noticing me."

"What do we do now?" she asked. Her doubled fists went up to press her mouth in her old childish gesture.

"But it wasn't me they were seeking. I saw them bringing him off a boat from Lewis, a poor devil of a deserter. My heart, for all its mad jigging, went out to him. But perhaps they'll be giving him his chance yet, to volunteer to be killed in Europe instead of hanged in Fort William. But I'm shaking yet." He held up his hand to show her. "And I was thinking before that I was ready if they took me. Dia, who is ever ready to be hanged?"

She reached over and took his hand between hers, as much for her own comfort as his. "Remember, I said there would be a ship for you. Now let us go downstairs and eat a good dinner and look like any Highland husband and wife in the crowd."

"We will be looking like that as long as you are keeping your Sassenach accent to yourself."

"I shall be mute." She put the small plaid over her head and gave him a demure smile.

When he opened the door to the taproom, Jennie almost lost her already weak courage. The place was packed and smokey from cooking and tobacco, but she had an awful expectation that at least one pair of eyes resting upon them was about to light up with a fearsome intelligence. Then Angus whistled through the shifting blue haze and the noise, and beckoned them to seats on a bench at the end of one of the long tables. He brought them plates heaped with well-done mutton with plenty of gravy, potatoes, and mashed turnip. Jennie couldn't eat much of hers, but Alick cleaned both plates. She wished they could be back in one of the boxes along the walls, where high-back settles gave an illusion of privacy, but these were all occupied. However, she and Alick were mercifully ignored, except when someone asked for the salt or the mustard. With her shawl over her head and her eyes kept down, she looked like a shy wife frightened by the crowds, and Alick was so obviously keeping himself to himself that it was only manners for the rest to leave him so.

Nancy was behind the bar; her strident voice whooped in laughter, clanged out orders to Angus and greetings to newcomers. Occasionally she called something in Gaelic which, with a Cockney accent, sounded like no other language on earth. This was always received as if she were the great wit of the world.

Alick told Angus he would settle with Nancy later, and they went out into the hall. He said at once, "I'm off to the shore now."

"Let me go with you."

"It's no place for a woman."

"That's ridiculous, after all we've been through!"

"So I am being ridiculous," he said stiffly.

"Are we *quarreling*?" She was aghast. "Alick, I meant only—" She broke off as two men came out, burly in their serviceable thick homespun, plaids over their shoulders. They touched their bonnets and went into the street. She recognized them as two who had been eating in one of the boxes. She said rapidly, "I meant only that I'm no longer a delicate, protected, garden flower. I'm as tough and prickly as gorse. So if we are not advertised as fugitives, let me go. I promise I won't speak a Sassenach word."

He sighed. "You are determined. What can I be doing against it?"

"Not a thing, and I might bring you luck."

"*Luck!*" He laughed. "The only luck for me is bad luck."

They went out into the street, where the fresh wind had dispersed most of the pungence. Another man and woman had stopped just short of the two stone steps. The woman was wrapped in a full cloak which dragged on the ground as she bent over, and she was sobbing. The man looked up when he felt the presence of strangers, and his face was ugly with strain. His eyes met Jennie's in a naked appeal for help.

Alick was trying to steer her past, but she wouldn't move. "What is it?" she asked the man. "Can I help? Alick, ask him in the Gaelic."

But there was no need. The woman's hand came from under the cloak groping for Jennie, who took and tightly held it. The man said in a rush, "The fear is at her. You are another woman, you could tell her."

"Tell her what?"

With a gasping cry the woman bent lower. Jennie put her arms around her and realized that she was pregnant; she kept her head down, her face turned as if in shame, and couldn't seem to stop crying. "Elspeth," her husband begged.

Alick said grimly, "I am just going, Jeannie."

"Not without me." Her eyes dared him to defy her, and he was the first to look away. "Let us take a few minutes to help these people, Alick." It was too late now to worry about her English accent, and anyway, all she meant to these two was womanly compassion. She guided Elspeth inside. Instead of escaping while her back was turned, Alick followed along with the husband. He was not pleased about it, but he was there.

Nancy was busy drawing ale, and Angus was distributing laden plates at the far end of the room. The box was still empty. Jennie hurried the woman toward it, and once they were all four shut in between the high backs of the settles, they were in a little oasis of quiet. Elspeth took out a handkerchief and wiped her dark eyes. She was older than Jennie but still young, with a comely face wide across the cheekbones and a full mouth, bitten now, and still trembling. The man beside her was less ugly than he'd first appeared; he was plain and bony, but he had a good mouth and intelligent eyes, and he showed a genuine tenderness for his wife. He kept an arm around her shoulders, smiling with anxious encouragement whenever he could catch her eye.

"We are Andrew and Elspeth Glenroy," he said to Jennie. "And much obliged for your kindness."

Alick sat beside Jennie, tapping his fingers on the table and watching their nervous dance. *Who are we?* Jennie asked Alick in silence but, receiving no inspiration, changed the subject.

"Have you eaten?"

"I couldn't eat!" Elspeth Glenroy said. Her tears brimmed again.

"Some tea then." Jennie watched to get Angus's eye. "Is it near your time?" she asked.

"It's three months yet. But it could come early, with the rough seas and if there was sickness." Angus appeared, his grin blazing.

"Could we have a pot of tea, Angus?"

"I'll be asking herself!" He waded off through the crowd, ignoring any other calls on his attention.

"We went down to look out at the ship, the American one," Andrew Glenroy said. "Our gear was being taken out on the high tide. And suddenly this fear was at her that the wee one would be born on the voyage, and die, and be buried in the sea. She is healthy; it is a healthy child we would have! And she was ready until now. 'He will be born in America,' she was saying. 'He will be no one's tenant.' " He appealed to Alick. "There's land promised us. We will be our own landlords. And now," he said despairingly, "she is afraid."

"If you don't go now, can't you go later?" Jennie asked. "When the baby is born and grown a bit?"

Elspeth nodded eagerly. "Och, it's happy I'd be to go then!"

"If you are not sailing now, how would you live from now until then?" Alick asked Glenroy.

"I am a carpenter and a stonemason. We will live. The trouble is—" He became voluble in his distress, as if sympathy had breached a dam. "I have paid our passage, you see, and for a cabin. The money was hard come by. We've kin we can be staying with; her sister was weeping like a waterfall to see her go. But we can ill afford to lose what I have paid out, and nothing to show for it."

"Why can't you be going to the captain and ask for it like a man?" Alick said impatiently.

"Och, he has a hard eye on him and likely a hard heart to go with it! It's not only that. I'd be having to face the minister for leaving them without an English speaker. There's not a soul of them, not even him, to make things clear between them and the Yankee captain."

"A *minister?*" Jennie asked. "On the side of the people?" Alick stopped drumming his fingers.

"Why, it's a whole congregation from Strathbuie going to America. I was mending a hearth at the castle when I was first hearing of it. The minister and the men came to tell the Laird that they were all going before his people could burn them out. They were selling their beasts and their furniture, and the Laird was so happy to clear them without any trouble he said he'd be putting something toward the purse, and he gave every man a dram and was shaking his hand and wishing him luck." He smiled. "One man had come home from the Army with an arm gone, and finding his wife and his parents under eviction orders. So he thanks the Laird for his courtesy, drinks to *him*, mind you, and says, 'If the ship sinks on the way to America, we will all be coming back to haunt you and your issue forever. There will be such a crowd of us in this old castle not one of ye'll ever be having a sound night's sleep again!' The Laird took it for a curse and turned white. He tried to laugh, and it was like a skull grinning."

He took a melancholy pleasure in this. Nancy came to the table with a huge teapot on a tray and four cups. "This is no tearoom," she announced ringingly, "and I wouldn't want anyone to get ideas."

"It's a special case, Nancy," Jennie said, "and we thank you from the bottom of our hearts."

"'*E's* a special case." Nancy flicked Alick on the shoulder and went away again.

Jennie poured the tea, and the Glenroys both drank thirstily. "Tell me about the American ship," Jennie said.

"It's owned by a man who was born a Scot and went to America as a wee lad—och, in an immigrant ship, too—and rose up to become one of George Washington's generals. He is having this great property, you see, and businessess, and he ships timber to Lewis and such places with no forests. He has been advertising for people to come and settle. To be their own men, not the landlord's."

His sigh of longing was almost a groan. "I want to go so bad it fairly makes my teeths water." Elspeth went on calmly sipping her second cup of tea.

"He'll be advertising again, surely," said Jennie.

"Aye, but will I be getting my money back now? And it will be just as hard to face the minister. He is depending on me, you see. We wanted to go, and I offered myself, knowing he needed me because he has no English. He is a good man, a true man of God. He was born with the gift, and he was not needing the schools and the universities to teach him. But—he has no English."

"Then who arranged all the business?" Jennie asked. "Who wrote the letters? How do you know this general exists?"

"Och, wasn't he himself born on the estate, and his father a cotter? And now he's a gentleman; in America a man is not having to be born to it. He wrote to the factor. He knows how it fares with us here; he knows about the sheep coming."

"And you believe the factor?" Alick said contemptuously. "He could be spinning it all out of cobwebs and moonshine just to be rid of you."

"I believe him!" Glenroy said fervently. "Have we not heard of the General all our lives? He sent for his parents after the colonies won the war. Besides, the factor is not an evil man; he has no stomach for violence. He is wanting a clean conscience."

"He can never have one," Alick said. "Those people are all being driven, no matter how they go. There is no room for them in their own country."

"Let the landlords have it," said Glenroy. "We will be free men in America. The ship is waiting; a brig, they call her, the *Paul Revere*, for some American hero. She is new and clean, they say. And"—he leaned forward and tapped Alick's chest—"we pay much less than what the law is saying, because the General himself owns the ship. It's couples he wants, and families, no single men above sixteen unless they are old grandfathers who can't be left behind. If they stay and work hard, he will be giving back the passage money after the first year."

"We've been looking for a ship," Jennie said. "If we paid you what you've paid for your passage, and you took Alick to the minister now and introduced him as your cousin—" Alick's head snapped up, and she hadn't the bravado to look around at him. If anything stopped her momentum now, she wouldn't know how to get started again. "Your cousin, Alick Glenroy," she went on smoothly, "who will take your place, with his wife. They both speak English. All that needs to be changed on the passenger list are the first names, you see."

The Glenroys were gazing at her as if mesmerized. "We are running away," Jennie said; if she sounded composed, it was because she hadn't the strength to sound otherwise. "My people will never accept our marriage. They will be offering rewards for me soon. But I am over twenty-one, I am old enough to know my own mind, and I do not accept their choice for me. They are not above bringing my husband to trial"—Alick's arm jumped against hers—"for seduction." She lifted her chin proudly. "If there was any seduction, it was on my part. I will not have his life destroyed, and mine with it. Now you know about us, and we are at your mercy."

"It's safe you are with us." Elspeth spoke up while Andrew was still fascinated beyond speech.

"Could we buy your chests and some of your clothes?" Jennie asked. "We came away with nothing. I traded my riding habit for these with a woman we met."

"Andrew," said Elspeth, "take your cousin to Mr. MacArthur now. He is staying at the manse here until the ship sails," she explained to Jennie. "Then you will be going to the ship and getting your tools, and take from the chests the things for the baby and our Sabbath clothes and my wee box, and the rest you may buy, Jeannie Glenroy. There's blankets, sheets, too, and enough pots to set up housekeeping with."

"Well, then," said Jennie, feeling as if she were walking the orchard wall at Pippin Grange with a parasol in a high wind, "shall you and I go upstairs and transact the business while the men are about theirs?"

"I must be speaking with you," Alick said blackly to Jennie.

"When you come back."

The two men went out, rather like sleepwalkers, she thought with an instant impulse to giggle. She took Elspeth up to the room, where Elspeth lay down gratefully on the bed. Relieved of her fright, she was pretty again, though it was a prettiness that would grow heavy with the years. Still, there would always be an open, honest kindliness there, if not the same touching vulnerability.

"I can't be thanking you as it should be," she said.

"You *have* thanked me. One good deed repays another."

"We will go to America," Elspeth said strongly. "It is only for the baby I am afraid, not for myself." She smiled. "It will be very nice to have cousins already there."

"And for us to welcome cousins," Jennie agreed. She felt dishonest, as she had not felt downstairs. "Tell me about your sister," she said.

"Och, when she sees us back at her gate!" And to the accompaniment of Elspeth's happy anticipation, Jennie gazed out over the roofs at the American brig in Loch Linnhe and wondered just what she had done.

Forty-Five

E LSPETH'S VOICE ran down, and she fell asleep suddenly, like a child. Jennie considered her situation. She had been seasick all the way up the eastern coast to Banff; how long would it take to cross the Atlantic on the brig *Paul Revere*, even with fair winds for the entire distance, which was not likely? She turned her wedding ring around and around on her finger. It was loose now, she had grown so thin. What a paradox if, in the years to come, one affectionate memory of Nigel should survive: not of their lovemaking, but of the way they had tended each other during their seasickness.

Six weeks of it at the shortest. Could she survive? Would there be daily deaths and burials at sea for those who couldn't? A tempest could bury them all at sea. Lost, lost, lost. No markers, nothing. Gone from the face of the earth.

She had been in mortal fear so many times lately that now she recognized the onset with a dull ache of resignation. *Here it comes again, and I am so tired. All I want from life now is to be safe for the rest of it.*

Jennie, Jennie! she could hear Papa say. *You're always asking for the impossible. No one is safe, ever. To be in constant danger is the human condition. Never pray for safety, but for courage. And pray to yourself; you are the only one who can answer.*

Ah, Papa, she told him, *neither you nor I ever expected that I would be running away from a man lying dead in the heather, with a bee walking over his yellow hair.*

Now she slipped away in escape to her sisters: to Sylvia with her young in the rectory; to Sophie running down the oak staircase at Pippin

335

Grange, out the gate and across the sands, her hair streaming in the wind off the North Sea, dogs and young cousins behind her; and to Ianthe walking her charges by Lucerne. All of them were positive in their own lives and thinking she was positive in hers. After all, she was married to a beautiful man with whom she'd fallen in love at first sight, and had gone with him to live in the land which inspired Walter Scott.

The happy views of the sisters went up in fire like the thatch when she realized that by now they were in mourning for her, believing she'd been dragged off and probably murdered by the man who had killed her husband. She put her fists to her mouth to cram back the inarticulate sounds that tried to force their way out. Her whole body shrieked and strove for action; if she could have jumped up and run to them now without stopping, she would have done so. She felt wild enough, strong enough. Was this the strength of a madwoman? she wondered, trying to hold herself in the chair.

The seizure slowly loosened its grip on her, and she slumped over the table with her head on her arms. She felt as weak as if she'd actually been running for leagues, but lucid. She laid out her deeds and her prospects in the unsparing Arctic light of reason.

She didn't return to the Pict's House, or to any earlier time, and castigate herself for what she should or shouldn't have done. That was over and done with; nothing could change it. She went back to the last hour. In a two-minute speech which seemed to have been made by someone else inside her skin, she had exchanged the certain embraces of her family (a week away from her at the most) for six weeks or more of ghastly uncertainty. (Except that she could be sure of being seasick.) An epidemic might break out on board ship, and she would die that way, or Alick would, and her attempts to atone would thus have killed him as surely as if he'd been hanged. Or they both could die along with everyone else if the ship was destroyed.

But if it works—if it works. Hope was like the slow push of the blood back into frostbitten fingers and toes. Agony and life in one. If it worked, Alick would be safe beyond a doubt. If he didn't want to be one of the General's settlers, he could go anywhere he chose. She could keep herself by teaching, or work as a servant if she had to, until she had accumulated enough money and bravery to put her on a ship to England.

So all she had to fear was the first voyage; she'd worry about the second when the time came; she'd already survived Jock Dallas and the flooded corrie. She'd promised Alick a ship, and there lay the brig *Paul Revere*. Why not take all this as a sign that they would actually step foot on American soil?

And see Red Indians, Derwent. She wished she could hug him now and kiss his pugnacious little face.

No more sentiment. The essential thing now was to put an end to her sisters' anguish at once; she could let them know she was alive without pointing at Alick. Elspeth slept quietly on, and she let herself out of the room as quietly as a professional thief.

The room downstairs sounded as busy as before. Jennie opened the door and peered gingerly around it. Nancy wasn't in sight, and a skinny man with a big Adam's apple was behind the bar.

"Mistress?" Angus came to her, his radiance undimmed by the odorous murk.

"I was looking for Nancy."

He pointed past her at the door across the hall. "She will be just resting her feets now, Mistress."

"Then I won't disturb her—"

Angus darted across the hall and knocked neither loudly nor tentatively, but with a nice blend of good manners and self-assurance.

Nancy responded promptly. "*Now* what?" she snarled.

"The lady is here, Mistress MacNichol." He winked at Jennie as if they were of the same age and station, and went back across the hall.

Nancy opened the door and said graciously, "Well, Lidy X, please to step in."

Her parlor was cluttered and gaudy, but immaculate. All glass and metal surfaces winked and shimmered, and a little coal fire made it very hot. "I'm sorry to disturb your rest," Jennie said, "but I wanted to tell you we have engaged our passage. We sail tonight."

"I surmised something was up! Those 'eads together over the teacups. I was just 'aving a bit of read and a laydown, and then I was coming up to see you, with this."

She reached behind a violently magenta sofa and brought out an elderly carpetbag. "It's me own," she said. "*What am I keeping it for? I* says to meself. I'm going nowhere. So I might as well let it go for a few shillings. And I bought you both a change of clothes, such as they are. I looked in all the seams, and I couldn't find any animules. But shoes I couldn't find for those narrow feet of yours."

"The brogues will do on the ship, and I'll find a shoemaker as soon as we land."

"If it's not in the wilderness, and *if* you land," said Nancy gloomily. "I've put in two towels, too, and you'll 'ave that scented soap. Now 'ave you thought of your other needs?"

"Other?" Jennie was blank.

"Your monthly flow! Of course, if you and 'im been 'oneymooning from there to 'ere, you might not 'ave the problem for the next nine months. Be a good thing aboard ship, I should think. 'Ard to manage in close quarters." She slapped her thigh. "Oh, what a blush!"

Jennie touched a very warm cheek with very clammy fingers. "But we—I mean—we have been too tired and too apprehensive—"

"Well, then!" Nancy was triumphant. "I packed away something in the bottom of the bag for you."

"I can't tell you how much I appreciate all this," said Jennie. "Do I owe you any more money?"

Nancy emphatically waved that away. "So you've found you a ship as soon as this."

"Yes, the people you saw us with decided not to go at the last moment, and we are buying their tickets."

"That's a bit of luck, if you fancy a long voyage in an immigrant ship," Nancy said caustically.

"This is the American vessel. It's new and clean, better than most, they say. Nancy, if I write a note to my sister, would you mail it after we're gone? I'll give you the money to have it franked, and for the paper and ink."

"I'm a pauper if I can't supply that. Besides, if you leave tonight, I can let the room again and make double on it." She drew out a chair from the table by the window. "Everything's there. Trimmed those pens myself just yesterday. Paper in the drawer. I like a good, thick, elegant paper," she said carelessly. "Sealing wax and candle *there*. When you're finished, just leave it under me rock from Brighton, and I'll see it on its way tomorrow." She went toward a door opening into another room. "I'll go back to my book. I don't 'alf fancy this Mrs. Radcliffe."

You and Charlotte, Jennie thought. She imagined Charlotte weak and ill from weeping, and she couldn't bear it. She sat down at the table, and in the next room a bed creaked as Nancy settled onto it with a sigh of pleasure.

"Dear Sylvia and William," Jennie wrote. "I am alive, and I am well, and I am going to America. I have done no wrong, but other persons have. Believe me. Please let the Highams know I am safe. Kiss Sophie for me and send Ianthe my dearest love. I embrace you in my heart and will come back from America to do it with my arms. Tell the babies their aunt Jennie adores them. Good-bye, but only for now. Your loving sister Jennie."

She folded the letter and addressed it to the rectory and sealed it. She placed the polished stone on it and would have called to Nancy, but she heard a strongly melodious snoring from the bedroom, so she tiptoed out with the carpetbag.

Elspeth was still asleep; she must not have really rested for days. Jennie went to the window and looked out at the brig *Paul Revere* again. *I am going to America!* she thought incredulously. *It's as if I were going to the moon.*

There were feet on the stair and a rumble of men's voices, a tap at the door, and Alick and Andrew came in. Andrew carried his plaid like a sack over his back. Elspeth stirred and turned sleepily toward him, and he smiled as if she were the only other person in the room. "My tool chest is just there on the landing." He lowered his tartan bundle to the floor. "Everything else is here."

She sat up and put out her hand to him. "I thank you, Andrew. And we will be sailing to America when *he* is ready." She patted her swelling front. "What was Mr. MacArthur saying?"

"He was disappointed, but he bore up well, when I told him the other Mistress Glenroy could be teaching English words on the voyage. He is very anxious himself to be learning them. You are not offended, Mistress?" he asked Jennie.

"Not in the least! I wish I'd thought of it myself!" She sounded too jovial, and she was not eager to face Alick yet, but she was very aware of him.

"Elspeth, lass," Glenroy said, "there is a cart going away now. They were seeing their kin off at noon. We can be traveling with them halfway to your sister's if you are ready."

"Dia, I am ready!" She almost sprang off the bed, blooming like a peony.

"We haven't settled with you yet," Jennie said.

"Imagine forgetting that!" Elspeth said merrily.

The cabin fare, the clothes, blankets, and household goods took most of their combined shares of sovereigns, but it left them enough so they wouldn't step onto American soil with empty purses. Elspeth hugged and kissed Jennie, and cried again. They all went downstairs, the men carrying the heavy tool chest. When they came out onto the step, a cart drawn by a dapple gray garron was coming slowly up the street through the human traffic; an elderly pair, white-haired under mutch and bonnet, sat on the seat. The man stopped the pony by the step and gave Andrew a ponderous nod. His wife had been crying, but she brightened when she saw Elspeth, and called her "mo ghaoil" as if she'd always known her. Alick and Andrew lifted the chest into the cart, the tartan bundle went in, and Elspeth was heaved up to sit on the chest. Andrew took up his position beside the garron.

The men shook hands without speaking, and Elspeth wiped her eyes and called promises to Jennie. "We will be meeting in America! It's the fine ceilidh we'll be having!"

"Yes, we will," Jennie answered. "A whole week of them!"

The old man, having had enough of all this, spoke to the pony. Elspeth would have kept waving and calling back all the way up the street, but the old woman engaged her attention. Andrew, walking beside the pony, looked back once, lifted his bonnet, and then faced forward again.

"Is it mad you are?" Alick said ferociously. "Do you know what you are *doing*?" If gray eyes could be said to blaze, his did.

"Yes, but this is no place to discuss it." Jennie went inside and up the stairs, and he followed her. The instant they confronted each other behind a closed door she seized the advantage before he could open his mouth.

"You need a wife for this venture," she said. "In name only; I don't propose to embarrass you. When you are well established and your wife through her *own* efforts has saved enough for her ticket, she will go home to see her family. If something keeps her from coming back, I am sure the General won't evict you, poor man, because you have lost your wife."

He ripped off his bonnet and slammed it against the wall. "You are so ignorant! A lady like you to travel in those conditions! Not only dangerous but dirty! Aye, the ship looks clean enough now, she has been just carrying timber, but when they begin to get sick—at both ends, you understand—"

"A lady like me!" She mocked him. "Why Alick, I'm no more than a gypsy right now, but I can pass as a good wife long enough to help you. And as for dirty—there'll be plenty of saltwater to wash in. We have a cabin, remember, we can keep it clean ourselves, and we'll have a change of clothing from the chests, besides what Nancy bought for us." She nodded at the carpetbag. "You might start by having a wash now under the pump out there in the yard, so we'll go aboard *Paul Revere* like the respectable Glenroys that we are. That beard makes you look like a pirate, but I'm sure Mr. MacArthur will vouch for you."

She held out a towel from the rack. "You won't want this scented soap, I suppose. Why don't you ask for some in the kitchen?"

He yanked the towel from her hand and walked out.

Nancy brought them coffee, rolls, and cold meat. She drank a cup with them and wished them Godspeed, dubiously. "I 'ope you 'ave plenty to eat, that's all."

"I was hearing that the captain has put enough oatmeal aboard for an army," Alick said. "Orders of the General."

Nancy blew the General away like a feather. "Oh, 'im! And what about water? Oh, the tales they tell about water stored in indigo casks and going poison, if it's not bad to begin with!"

"The water casks are new wood," Alick said. "Everything about the ship is new. This is her—her—"

He glanced at Jennie, who said, "Her maiden voyage."

"And is the captain new, too? Is it 'is maiden voyage?"

Jennie, exacerbated by nerves and knowing Alick was the same, kept expecting him to fly apart in one way or another, but surprisingly he laughed.

"He is not looking very new, Nancy. And he has been here before, in another ship."

Belligerently Nancy came up with more objections. "Think about the cholera, and the dysentery, and the typhoid! One ship arrived in Nova Scotia with everybody, passengers and crew, sick with typhoid, and they'd been dying like flies on the way. I feel it's my duty to warn you, you two being babes in the wood, so to speak."

"And you have warned us," said Alick. "You have done your duty, Nancy, and I am thanking you. Jennie, we can be going aboard now."

It would take them perhaps ten minutes to reach the shore, but

Jennie had faced with less trepidation the walk from Linnmore to Fort William. All the fears that surrounded the voyage were as nothing compared to the anticipation of being seized before they boarded the ship, or afterward, before the ship sailed; she remembered those search parties, and she knew that Alick was remembering, too. He had a deathly pallor, and she sensed that the hands which laid the plaid over his shoulder were not steady.

Suddenly Nancy seized him by both shoulders and gave him a great loud kiss. "You take care of 'er and yourself, you 'ear me?" Her little eyes were wet. She hugged Jennie. "When I see the what's-'er-name back 'ere, I'll know *she* reached America anyway."

"I'll get word to you, Nancy, I promise," Jennie said. "You'll mail my letter, won't you?"

"It will go out on the coach tomorrow."

She wouldn't watch them out the door, but Angus did, insisting on shaking their hands and talking all the time in Gaelic. Alick smiled and slapped him lightly on the arm. When they had left him behind, Jennie said, "What was all that about?"

"He is going to America; he swears it on his mother's grave."

The sunshine of a cloudless evening flooded Loch Linnhe with a hot topaz light. They had to wait on the shore for a place in the ship's boats, and this was a fresh torture. The one advantage was the great crowd made up of those who were actually going, those who always gathered to see off a shipload of emigrants, and those who were living precariously from hand to mouth while waiting for a chance to go. There was a great deal of weeping, both quiet and stormy, but at least no families were being wrenched apart; the group for *Paul Revere* was leaving no one behind.

Jennie saw two women farther along than Elspeth, and as many elderly people as there were children. The majority of the couples were sturdily in their prime, and there was a good sprinkling of young men who evidently preferred emigration to the Army. Now, with the Great Sheep coming, too many soldiers would return from the war to find their homes burned like those at Kilallan, and their families scattered, if not dead. This way a man and his wife and children would all live or die together.

She was especially moved by the very youthful couples; she guessed that many a marriage had been arranged to take in the lads over sixteen, and some of them must have just reached that age, they were so downy. These youngsters and the children weren't weeping; they were as touchingly eager and innocent in their wide-eyed view of the world as any young animals.

She was so taken with watching and listening that her and Alick's turn came as a surprise, and for that little while she had actually forgotten to be afraid.

They were the last to leave the boat and climb the ladder. She had wondered why the minister hadn't been on the shore to be a comforting shepherd to his flock, but she found him here, a beaming little wisp of a man, standing at the head of the ladder beside a ship's officer with a passenger list. He called each arrival by name and shook hands, then pointed out the name on the officer's list so he could tick it off. The minister might not speak English, but that wasn't necessary here. He gave Jennie an especially cordial greeting.

"Alexander Glenroy?" the officer said. "Yes, I remember. We met this morning." He was young and had hard blue eyes in a tanned face with a long, sharp jaw. "And wife, Jean?"

"Yes, I am Jean," Jennie said, holding Alick's arm.

"Thank God for English speakers!" the officer exclaimed. "The old man will include you every night in his prayers." His grin took years off him. "The General will appreciate you, too, I reckon. Been a good many years since he spoke this whatever you call it."

"Gaelic," said Jennie. "It's the speech of the Gaels." *I am talking with an American*, she thought in awe.

"It's new to me. This is my first landing in Scotland."

A crewman came and said a few cryptic words to him, and pointed. A small boat rowed by one man, but with three others aboard, was approaching the ladder.

"Here they come looking for stowaways again!" the mate exclaimed in annoyance. "Excuse me, ma'am." He touched his cap. The minister, not understanding but alarmed by the tone, looked worriedly from one to the other.

Alick pulled Jennie away from the ladder but stopped short of the crowded bow deck. The minister followed them, questioning Alick in Gaelic. He got a terse answer, but apparently it relieved him; he and his congregation had nothing to do with stowaways.

The three men came nimbly up the ladder. No one was in a uniform, and the Highland voices were mild, but officialdom was an all but visible aura.

"We will just be looking for stowaways, you understand."

344   Elisabeth Ogilvie

"There are no stowaways aboard this vessel, sir." The mate was civil. "You may inspect the passenger list. Everyone is accounted for; there are a few more to come aboard, and they are all listed here." He held out the list, and one man took it. The other was smilingly insistent; how could one be sure there were no stowaways? A man could have been smuggled aboard in a chest, for instance.

"We have no stowaways," the mate repeated.

"We will be seeing your captain, if you please."

Narrow-eyed, the mate beckoned to the crewman, who led the three off past Jennie and Alick. The mate looked over at Jennie and humorously shook his head, and she forced a smile. The minister went back to the ladder to welcome the next boatload of emigrants, and Jennie and Alick walked slowly forward until they could find a clear place at the rail in the bows. There was so much confusion around them that they could have spoken to each other without being overheard, but neither could find a word. Sweat ran down Jennie's back, and Alick's face was bedewed with it.

They were not stowaways, they had paid, but they were still fugitives, and who knew what the port officials might be discussing with the captain?

In a very short while the officials returned, bade the mate a courteous farewell, and went down the ladder to their boat. Obviously they had not been allowed to search the ship, but they were not greatly disturbed.

The last emigrants came aboard, the ship's boats were taken in, and the square sails were unfurled. Jennie and Alick stood transfixed, watching the men raising the anchor; an almost stunned silence settled briefly over the crowd as it realized the ship was moving. Shouts and cheers sounded over the water from the watchers onshore, and were raggedly returned from the brig; everyone crowded to that side to wave or to weep, or to gaze in a granite silence like Alick.

Then through all the bustle attending a ship's departure, there came the first long, piercing, warning wail of the pipes, and the Lament began. Jennie's scalp tightened; the gooseflesh rose on her arms under her clothes. The piper was aft, unseen by her, but she didn't need to see; she was *hearing* it, the anguished notes of a wild grief and a heartbroken promise; *We shall return no more.*

She could hardly see the wet faces and streaming eyes around her. To keep her own from overflowing, she looked up at the American ensign fluttering from the masthead, above the sails filling with red-gold light as well as wind. The slow measures of the farewell drove into her heart, but they were not killing blows; not for her.

She took Alick's hand and warmed it in both hers. "I promised you a ship," she said, "and this is it. Now I promise you we are not going to drown. I will see you safe in America, with your own land under your feet."

He didn't speak, but he didn't turn his face away. Taking her hand, he put it through his arm, and together they walked away from the crowd to the deserted starboard rail. In this hour of heartbreak and weeping all around her, with the pipers crying *We shall return no more*, she looked up at him and she realized that this was a man she could trust.

Silent together, they watched the Ardgour hills darken against the western sky as *Paul Revere* moved down Loch Linnhe toward the Firth of Lorne and the Sound of Mull, thence to stand out to the open sea.

Catalog

If you are interested in a list of fine Paperback
books, covering a wide range of subjects
and interests, send your name and address,
requesting your free catalog, to:

McGraw-Hill Paperbacks
1221 Avenue of Americas
New York, N.Y. 10020